where
echoes
die

Also by Courtney Gould

The Dead and the Dark

where
echoes
die

a novel

courtney gould

WEDNESDAY BOOKS
NEW YORK

First published in the United States by Wednesday Books, an imprint of St. Martin's Publishing Group

WHERE ECHOES DIE. Copyright © 2023 by Courtney Gould. All rights reserved. Printed in the United States of America. For information, address St. Martin's Publishing Group, 120 Broadway, New York, NY 10271.

www.wednesdaybooks.com

Designed by Omar Chapa

Library of Congress Cataloging-in-Publication Data

Names: Gould, Courtney, author.
Title: Where echoes die / Courtney Gould.
Description: First edition. | New York : Wednesday Books, 2023.
Identifiers: LCCN 2023004289 | ISBN 9781250825797 (hardcover) | ISBN 9781250825711 (ebook)
Subjects: CYAC: Sisters—Fiction. | Grief—Fiction. | Supernatural—Fiction. | Mothers and daughters—Fiction. | Cities and towns—Fiction. | Lesbians—Fiction. | Horror stories. | LCGFT: Horror fiction. | Novels.
Classification: LCC PZ7.1.G68634 Wh 2023 | DDC [Fic]—dc23
LC record available at https://lccn.loc.gov/2023004289

ISBN 978-1-250-82579-7 (hardcover)
ISBN 978-1-250-82571-1 (ebook)

Our books may be purchased in bulk for promotional, educational, or business use. Please contact your local bookseller or the Macmillan Corporate and Premium Sales Department at 1-800-221-7945, extension 5442, or by email at MacmillanSpecialMarkets@macmillan.com.

First Edition: 2023

10 9 8 7 6 5 4 3 2 1

To Grandma, Grandpa, Daisy, Jan, and Warren. The world is smaller without you, but I feel you at my side, always.

Much of the thematic material in *Where Echoes Die* involves grief, loss of a family member, and emotional abuse at the hands of family. This book also involves intense descriptions of mental illness, PTSD, and memory loss. For a more detailed description of sensitive content, please visit gouldbooks.com/wed.

In the town of broken dreams,
the streets are filled with regret.
Maybe down in Lonesome Town
I can learn to forget.

—RICKY NELSON, "LONESOME TOWN"

where
echoes
die

1

In Arizona, on the road between nowhere and somewhere, there is a moment where sunrise and sunset look the same.

Or maybe Beck's been driving too long. She's got that twitch in her calves, the kind that scuttles through her legs and begs her to get moving beyond the shift of her foot from the gas pedal to the brakes. She holds a hand up to block the light from her eyes, palm facing the sun, and she feels the last heat of the day die behind the jagged horizon.

Roads in the Southwest aren't like the roads back in Washington, all tunneled with trees so thick you can't see the sky. There's no deer crossing signs, no falling rock warnings—actually, Beck can't think of the last sign she saw on this highway. Deep in the desert, the road is like a weathered conveyor belt, rolling the car through an unchanging backdrop of red dirt and sky. They crossed the California border in Yuma three hours ago, but parked on the sloped shoulder of the highway, it feels like it's been days since she saw another car. The world is all one long horizon, unchanging even as dusk washes the sky pink.

She shouldn't have pulled over, not when they're almost there. The goal was to soar down the coast, tear past LA, and get to Arizona without stopping. But there's something about the sky just now that eats at Beck. The pink's not quite right, too light, watery as a washed wound.

Beck unearths her mother's notes from her backpack and sighs, wipes away the sweat beaded on her nose. She leafs through the loose papers until she finds a plain piece of printer paper with a sketch of a desert sunset. She traces her finger along a shaky pencil line that points at the sharp cliffs. Next to it, her mother has written, *Not here.*

"What does that mean, Mom?" Beck asks under her breath.

If it was her mother here, she would probably take a thousand pictures. She'd snap this horizon from every angle and pin the photos to her office wall. She would stare at them until they untangled for her. Ellery Birsching's greatest talent was looking at a thing until it let her understand it. The sheer force of her will was usually enough to get what she wanted. She'd done it to story subjects, to broken sinks and stuck garage doors, to morning crosswords and jigsaw puzzles littered around their little green house. To Ellery Birsching, everything had an undercurrent of *real* truth; the raw kind most people tried to hide. Every person had a story she could extract like honey from the comb if she just waited long enough.

If her mother was here, Beck imagines she could explain the strangeness of this sunset in minutes. After all, this desert was her favorite subject.

Ellery's old Honda crackles, hot and exhausted, at the side of the highway. Beck pats the car once, gently, on its baking silver hood. This is the first breather she's given the car since they left Sacramento in the morning and it's a miracle it's still chugging along. Beck props a foot on the hood of the car and stretches her taut hamstring. Her audiobook grumbles from the stereo and Beck realizes she hasn't been paying any attention to any of it since they turned onto this highway. The windshield is smattered with bits of gravel and dirt, a battlefield of bug corpses splattered across the glass. Through the glass, Beck watches Riley.

Riley, Beck's little sister, whose head is lolled back against the headrest, blond bob splayed at her shoulders. Riley, who promised she'd stay awake the whole drive because she knows Beck doesn't like to drive in the quiet. Riley, who's been asleep for the last five hours, who's only fifteen and *can't* drive yet, so she has the luxury of sleeping the whole way down. To Riley, this drive is as simple as closing her eyes outside of LA and waking up in Backravel, Arizona.

Nowhere, then suddenly, somewhere.

Not like Beck, seventeen and the oldest Birsching left. She gets the honor of feeling every miserable moment of this drive. Her eyes are dry from staring out the windshield, watching the horizon, begging civilization to finally appear.

But maybe that's karma. After all, coming to Backravel was Beck's idea. And maybe it's only fair that the person who suggested a twenty-five-hour drive in three days, cooped up in an old Honda almost guaranteed to perish before arrival, be the one to do all the hard work. Beck props her wire-frame glasses at her hairline and presses fingertips into the swollen bulge of her eyelids. She sucks in a deep breath. It's fifteen more miles to Backravel. Fifteen miles until the end of all this in-between. In Backravel, she might be able to turn some of her questions into answers.

She climbs back into the driver's seat as her GPS reminds her, *"Continue on AZ-85 for ten miles, then take the right exit onto Backravel Access Road."*

"Hey." Beck shoves Riley's shoulder. "Did you hear that?"

Riley groans and turns over in her seat. Her eyes open a sliver, irises too glassy to be fully awake. "We're there?"

"Fifteen more minutes."

Riley blinks once, twice, and then she's asleep again. She looks like a fawn when she sleeps like this, too-long limbs all folded into each other, chin tucked against her chest. The thrill of arrival doesn't electrify Riley like it does Beck. But whatever fears Beck might have about this trip into the unknown—about what they'll find in Backravel—it's too late to turn back now. She grips the Honda's steering wheel, swallows the last of her lukewarm energy drink, and she drives.

She doesn't think about the letter in the glove box, hidden tenderly under the car's registration and an expired can of pepper spray. She doesn't think about the loopy, disjointed handwriting on the envelope, unmistakably written by Ellery Birsching's shaking hand. She doesn't think about how her mother wrote a letter from beyond the grave.

Beck Birsching doesn't think, she just drives.

•　•　•

The place they pull up to is a squat little house in a cluttered row of squat little houses. SYCAMORE LANE, the sign at the start of the street reads despite the lack of sycamores—or trees in general—in sight. The house is all faded white siding, capped with a slate gray roof missing a handful of tiles. A paint-chipped trellis stands woven with white flowers and scraggly green leaves that seem out of place among the red rock. A bike is tilted against the front porch, red dust caked into the underbelly of its tires. The sky behind the house is like pool water at dusk, cool and fluid and shimmering in the near-dark.

The whole neighborhood looks like any other neighborhood back in Everett. Beck's not sure what she expected. Something more sinister, maybe. Something clearly diabolical enough to explain her mother's fascination with this town. But this—an entirely ordinary street in a maze of other perfectly ordinary streets—makes too much sense. Ellery Birsching was never interested in the obvious thing.

There's virtually no information on Backravel online. A quick search will tell you that it's an unincorporated community in southwest Arizona, but there isn't a picture in sight. In Ellery Birsching's notes, though, Backravel is documented in aching detail. Essays, sketches, anecdotes describing rusting military infrastructures and great desert mountains, a lonely mansion on a deep red plateau. Maybe Beck expected to see the whole of it the moment she crossed into Backravel, but there's none of that on Sycamore Lane. It's just a handful of houses and the quiet.

Wind tunnels down the black road, gently rocking the Honda. The car hums and hums and then, with an unceremonious yank on the keys, it falls silent. The engine gurgles softly in the quiet, finally allowed to rest, and Beck closes her eyes. She shakes Riley's knee until her sister stirs, pale face washed in tangerine light.

"Okay," Beck says. "We have to call Dad."

Riley presses the heels of her hands against her eyes. Through a yawn, she asks, "Tonight?"

"Tonight."

"*Now?*"

Beck eyes the front door of the house. "Before we go in, probably. Just in case we're too busy later."

"Ugh." Riley pops her neck. "You want me to do it?"

This isn't just a phone call; it's a diversion. In two weeks, they're supposed to be arriving in Texas for their permanent stay. They're supposed to dive headfirst into their father's world of suburban barbecues and family movie nights and total, complete normalcy. It'll be an entirely new world, and the idea of it leaves a bitter taste in Beck's mouth. This was why he left them, after all. Just like everyone else that fluttered in and out of their world, their father got tired of Ellery Birsching's Backravel obsession. He wanted things to be *normal*. And while, as their new sole guardian, he might be okay with a two-week, supervised trip to Palm Springs before the permanent move, he certainly wouldn't be okay with a two-week trip to the town that caused all their troubles. If he knew where they were parked right now, he would be on the next flight to Arizona.

They have to get this call just right, have to place this first lie delicately, or this trip will be over before it's even started.

Beck chews the inside of her cheek. Riley's offer is kind, but they both know it'll be Beck making the call. As long as they've been alive, it's been Beck doing the dirty work while Riley provides the emotional support. Riley is straightforward, logical, direct and cool and bright as a Washington morning in the fall. And Beck is the slippery one who knows the right words to say and when to stay quiet. She's the one who smooths things out like a palm over wet clay. She can explain away parking tickets and detention notes and calls from school about cigarettes in her locker.

Riley offers to help because she's a good sister who doesn't want to seem useless, but there's no question about who will cast the first lie in their big charade.

"I got it," Beck says. She pulls her phone from the cupholder by the charging cable, catching a bit of sunlight in the cracks of her screen. She taps out her father's phone number from memory. She should have it saved by now. She turns to Riley. "Just talk when I tell you."

The phone rings for only a second, then static crackles on the other end of the line.

"Touchdown?"

Their father's voice is too light, like he's on the brink of laughter. This is how he's always been, like everything amuses him. Their mother's funeral was the most somber Beck ever saw him, and even then, he was the most content person in the room. Beck swallows and tries her best not to resent him for it.

"Just landed a few minutes ago," Beck says. "LAX is crazy. We can't talk much. Gabby's grandma will be here to pick us up in a second."

"Nice, nice, nice . . ." Their father clears his throat. *"Well, I won't keep you. Put your sister on the phone."*

Riley looks at Beck with the kind of eyes a deer makes seconds before it's roadkill. Beck slides the phone onto Riley's palm and mouths, *Just be cool.*

"Hey, Dad," Riley says, and Beck thanks whatever higher power exists that they aren't on a video call. Riley's put-on smile is skewed so happy she looks manic. Lying to their father might be part of the assignment, but it's clear how deeply Riley hates it. "How's Julie?"

A pause.

"She's just watching the new Bachelor *episode. She uh . . . okay, yeah. She wants to know if you already saw it."*

"Not yet," Beck cuts in before Riley can fumble her way through another answer. Riley sinks back in her seat, relieved. "We'll catch up when we get to the house. Tell Julie no spoilers."

"Sounds like a plan."

"Oh, Dad, that's Gabby's grandma pulling up," Beck says. She waits a moment, then says, "We gotta go, but we'll call you later."

"Alright. Love you girls."

"Love you, too," Beck says while Riley gives a half-hearted, "Bye."

When the call ends, they're left in the quiet. Beck stares at Riley and Riley stares back. They're in it, now. They've committed to this trip and this lie and there's no worming their way out of it. It's just Beck and Riley alone in the middle of the desert. After all their years of treading water to stay afloat, this is what they've got left.

Beck reaches into her back pocket and slides her thumbnail over the rubber-banded bills there. Seven hundred dollars, minus the cost of gas in Southern California. Even less once they pay for their room. She tries to swallow the lump of panic in her throat because it's not just about the money. Now they need pictures of their trip, phone calls to their father, stories from a trip to Palm Springs they never took. Now, Beck has to untangle the massive knot that was Ellery Birsching before this fever dream ends.

Someone knocks on the driver's side window.

Beck scrambles back in her seat, nearly crushing Riley in the process. A man stands outside the window, stooped low with his hand cupped at his brow so he can see inside. His blue-checkered shirt is tucked into the waist of khaki slacks, fastened in place by a thick brown belt. He looks like he's stepped directly out of a cubicle, not the middle of an empty highway in an even emptier desert. Beck isn't sure if she's more shocked by what he looks like or the fact that he's the first non-Riley face she's seen in hours. She adjusts her glasses, forcing her tired eyes to focus.

The man motions for Beck to roll down her window. She does, just a crack, and a stream of dry wind slips through. The man straightens. He pulls his phone from his pocket, checks the screen, and smiles.

"Rebecca Birsching?" he asks.

Beck stares a moment too long. Her full name sounds crooked coming from anyone but family, like the vaguely familiar name of a stranger. The last time she heard it was at the funeral, echoing off white walls punctuated with golden flower-shaped sconces, rickety folding chairs in neat rows, the urn at the end of a too-long aisle. *Rebecca Birsching,* the pastor said tenderly, *would like to speak.*

She bites the inside of her cheek, dragging herself back to the present. She can't think about the funeral, can't go back there yet. Not right now.

Beck exhales. "That's me. And this is Riley, my sister."

Riley waves.

"Perfect. I'm Greg Sterling." The man takes a step back and motions to the little white house. "This is our humble abode. I believe you're staying with us."

Beck smiles. "Right."

"Nice to meet you," Riley chimes. She crawls out of the passenger seat and peels a candy wrapper from the bottom of her pale thigh, flicking it to the floor of the car, which is already layered with fast-food wrappers and trash from the grueling drive. Mr. Sterling notices the mess immediately, scrunching his slightly upturned nose. He quickly stifles his distaste.

Outside the car, the quiet buzzes like bug wings and the air on the blacktop bakes, shimmering in the fading heat. Beck steps out of the Honda and locks it. She rocks forward on the balls of her feet, tries to gauge if she's been driving too long or if she can really *feel* the road under her sneakers more than usual.

"You girls are right on time for check-in," Mr. Sterling says. "I'll walk you through your space, then the night's all yours. I'm sure you're exhausted."

"It's so cute," Riley says. "I can't wait to see it."

Mr. Sterling eyes the house, then offers Riley an apologetic smile. "Oh. Well, you girls are welcome to visit with us in the house, but let me show you where you'll be staying."

Riley shoots Beck a concerned look, but says nothing.

Beck opens the trunk of the car and hoists their damp cooler to freedom. It's lighter than she hoped it would be at this point—they have less food for their actual stay than she planned for. She'll have to buy more food. The wad of cash in her pocket burns.

They follow Mr. Sterling around the back of the house, which opens to a lush backyard. Like the front of the house, red dirt is neatly packed to the edge of the yard, bordered with clean stepping stones that lead to a sliding glass door. Neat lines form a garden along the wood fence, filled with bursts of green herbs and white wildflowers. Lavender as tall as Beck shifts in the cool breeze, tips curled like fingers. A net of round-bulb string lights connect the house to another building—a trailer, silver and dim in the low light. The wheels are gone, replaced with wood blocks, but the rest of it is intact. Between the trailer and the house is a fire pit so clean Beck is positive it's never been used.

Riley shoulders past Beck, clutching her backpack tight at her shoulders. Mr. Sterling laughs a little at her eagerness, but he waits for Beck to move before following them to the trailer door. Behind him, the windows of the main house are empty, blinds shut. It's so quiet here Beck wonders if Mr. Sterling lives alone. She wonders if he's the only person living in this whole neighborhood, since she's yet to see any real signs of life.

"We put the trailer on blocks just as a safety measure," Mr. Sterling says. "We used to travel all over in this guy, but since we've turned it into a rental, we decided to keep it grounded. Didn't want any guests making off with it in the night."

"You guys get a lot of guests out here?" Riley asks.

Mr. Sterling shrugs. "A fair few, I'd say. It helps being the only rental in town."

He fumbles with his keys a moment, then pries open the trailer door. Riley wedges inside and Beck follows. Like a shadow, only half-there, she follows.

The trailer is nicer than she expects. A modern kitchenette with all-black appliances, a chrome-lined red table with cushioned booth seats, a pullout sofa facing a perfectly square TV. At the back of the trailer, there's a bed lofted above a set of cupboards, so close to the ceiling it looks like a coffin. A thought pricks at Beck, quiet and stinging. Mr. Sterling wasn't lying—when she looked for a place to stay in Backravel, this was the only option within an hour of town. With how many times their mother came to Backravel, it's likely she stayed in this exact trailer. It's likely she slept in this casket bed, nose almost touching the ceiling while her thoughts churned. Beck wonders, when she tucks herself under the purple and orange hand-stitched quilt tonight, if she'll still smell her mother's favorite perfume in the fabric.

She drops the cooler in the middle of the room and sucks in a breath.

Mr. Sterling's voice comes into focus.

"I don't know what you two have planned for your vacation, but I hope you'll spend some time in town. We've got tons of neat shops, and there's a great bike trail around the big plateau." He turns on the sink, then turns it off again. "My oldest, Daniel, is about your age. He can take you girls into town tomorrow, if you want."

"Sure," Riley says without hesitation. "That sounds great."

Mr. Sterling offers a curt, slightly awkward smile. When the silence settles, he pats the tiny slab of counter space and turns to leave. It's too quick, and they're missing the most crucial step of this exchange. Beck has half a mind to just let Mr. Sterling forget the payment. She feels for the cash in her pocket and sighs. She motions for Riley to wait and quietly follows Mr. Sterling outside.

At the sound of Beck on the trailer steps, Mr. Sterling pauses. Beck offers a cautious smile. She pinches the zipper of her jacket, tries to gather up what she's going to say before she blurts it out.

"Can I talk to you for a second, Mr. Sterling?"

Mr. Sterling nods. His brow scrunches with concern. "Of course. Is something wrong?"

"My dad was supposed to call you." Beck laughs, uneasy. Her cheeks burn. "It's about the payment. I know your listing said the payment has to be made by someone over eighteen with a card. But . . . my dad was kind of hoping we could do something different?"

"Different how?"

"I was hoping you'd let us pay with cash."

"Cash?"

"I can pay every night," Beck says, "or I can pay the whole thing now. Either way. I just . . . can't pay with a card."

"Cash . . ." Mr. Sterling repeats. He scratches the back of his head. "I don't know. Our setup is already unusual. I'm not even sure it's legal for you two to stay here without a parent or guardian. I had to get special approval from Ricky. I'd rather keep everything else above the table, you know?"

"Ricky?"

Mr. Sterling waves a dismissive hand. "Your dad can't pay with a check? Maybe he could mail it?"

"No," Beck says, too quick. "I'm sorry. It just . . . can't go on his account."

"Okay, okay . . ." Mr. Sterling relents. He considers a moment, lips pressed into a thin line. "You two have never visited before?"

"We haven't."

"Hmm." Mr. Sterling rubs his jaw. "You look so familiar."

"My mom visited a few times," Beck says, casting the understatement of the century. "Maybe you met her?"

"Maybe. Your mom knows you're here?" Mr. Sterling's expression softens. "I'm not trying to extort you girls, but maybe your mom can spot the bill for now? And then you can work out the details later. I'm just trying to brainstorm what would be easiest."

It shouldn't hit Beck the way it does. The mention of her mother shouldn't send her plummeting. Beck closes her eyes, steels herself, fights off the obnoxious wave of ache that swells in her. Immediately, Mr. Sterling seems to understand. His skepticism falters and he unfolds his arms.

"I'm sorry. I didn't realize."

"It's okay," Beck says. "She, um. We used to live with her in Washington, but she . . . yeah. She loved Backravel. So we're here now."

"I'm very sorry for your loss," Mr. Sterling says. "This might sound strange, but I'm glad that it brought you here. I think you'll find you've come to exactly the right place."

Beck blinks at that.

"You know, I'm sure we can figure out the payment," Mr. Sterling continues. "Let me figure out the nightly breakdown and we can do a cash payment. It sounds like you girls have been through enough already."

It's a victory, even if it doesn't feel like one.

"Thank you," Beck says, but she's gone.

She's standing in a hospital room, eyes tracing the neat lines where sterile white walls meet, matching her pulse to chirping machinery. She's listening to a doctor explain why no treatment will fix this. His voice is muffled like the rumbling of thunder from miles away. She's slipping her fingers between Riley's, but her gaze is fixed on the oaks outside the hospital window as they sway and crash. She's looking anywhere but her mother's face, skin pale and eyes empty, a streak of gray hair resting soft against the bridge of her nose.

She's Beck, but she's gone. She's been gone for three months now, an insect flitting uselessly in a hospital room–shaped trap. She's nothing but wires and chemical cleaner and the doctor saying, quietly, *I'm sorry.*

• • •

When Beck steps back into the trailer, Riley sits at the booth table. Her backpack is on the seat next to her, and her suitcase is open at her feet, clothes spilling out on all sides. A leather-bound book is open on the table in front of her. Tenderly, Riley flips to the next page, eyes narrowed, mouth sloped in a cautious frown. Without looking up, she says, "Can you come here?"

Beck pulls off her glasses and cleans them with the hem of her T-shirt. Her chest is still tight the way it's always tight when she starts to slip into the bad memories. But she takes a deep breath, then another, and she makes her way to the table.

The book is a guest log. Names are written one after the other in sloppy handwriting. Names, dates, messages. Riley traces each line with her pointer finger, then stops halfway down the page. *Delia Horton. January 2012.*

Beck goes still.

"That name sounds familiar."

"Huh" Beck breathes.

Riley shoots her a questioning look. She turns the guest book to face Beck. In the middle of the page, Beck finds Delia's guest book comment written in neat, tiny handwriting. *Such an interesting town. Will be back soon.*

"Okay?"

Riley holds up a finger. She flips to the next page. Halfway down, another entry with the same name. This one is from March 2013. Beck's breath catches when she reads the comment. *Such an interesting town.* Beck exhales. *Will be back soon.*

"Isn't that weird?" Riley says. "I was looking to see if I could find Mom and I found this lady. I swear I've heard that name before. Maybe in the notes?"

Beck flips to the next page. Delia Horton's name rears its head again, this time in December 2013. *Such an interesting town,* her message reads. *It feels so familiar and welcoming, like I lived here as a kid.*

"How many times is she in here?" Beck asks.

She slides into the booth next to Riley and fishes through her own backpack, shuffling past the opened envelope to grab a pad of sticky notes. She flips through the guest book, sweat beading at her brow, making a tally of each time Delia Horton wrote her name in the guest book. Because Delia Horton isn't just a name. Maybe it's just a coincidence that a name she specifically came here to look for has presented itself to her this quickly. Each time Delia Horton writes her name, it's like she's arriving in Backravel for the first time. Like she's never seen this trailer. On the tenth time, in August 2016, her message changes slightly. *Such a welcoming town. It feels like home.* An entry in June 2018 reads, *Such a gorgeous little town. I'll bring my girls here soon!*

"She sounds like Mom," Riley says. "Talking about bringing her kids here."

"She does," Beck agrees.

The last entry from Delia Horton, dated April 2019, reads, *Such a strange little town. I think I'll be here again soon.*

"Twenty-three times," Beck whispers. "She came to Backravel twenty-three times."

"Wow." Riley flips back through the pages, counting again. "That might be more than Mom. I wonder why she stopped coming."

"Me, too."

Riley eyes Beck and her expression sobers. The last light of sunset is gone now, and only the pale lightbulb on the trailer awning outside illuminates the kitchen table. A low groan of wind soars over the trailer, but Beck can't move. The inside of her mouth is tangy like iron.

"Hey," Riley says. "Breathe. It's just a weird coincidence, but we don't need to go detective mode. This is a vacation. Just leave it."

"Okay," Beck whispers. "I'll leave it."

It's a lie. Beck stares at the page a little longer. How many times did Ellery stumble back to this town? Was the thing that kept Delia Horton coming back the same thing that drew in their mother? After all her years of wondering what it was about Backravel that drew Ellery Birsching back over and over like a toy train on a track, she's finally in the heart of it. After years of looking at the name Delia Horton in her mother's notes, she's seeing it here in the flesh. All the pieces of Ellery's greatest story are here in Backravel, waiting for someone to connect the final dots. And maybe Riley doesn't want to finish their mother's investigation, but Beck will. Their mother wanted them to finish her legacy.

One way or another, here in Backravel, Ellery Birsching wants to be found.

2

BEFORE

"Oh, *this* is good."

Ellery Birsching sits at her computer, pen between her teeth, soft rock mumbling from her laptop. Her blond hair falls in wisps from the knot gathered at the back of her skull. It's a Saturday morning. Beck is eight years old and Riley is six. Riley sits in the living room with their father watching cartoons, but Beck couldn't care less about what a group of cartoon superheroes accomplish. Saturday mornings in the Birsching household are quiet, which gives Ellery Birsching the mental peace to work on her craft. And there is nothing in the world Beck loves more than watching her mother work.

This Saturday morning is special, though, because her mother isn't just working, she's *discovering*. This is her mother's favorite part of the writing process. She's just turned in a vulnerable piece about a local power company scamming customers while simultaneously underpaying their employees, and now, before that story has even printed, she sets her hungry gaze on something new. With one story out of her hands, she starts over again, feeling around the internet like a hand reaching for the light switch, just looking for something to catch.

She swivels in her desk chair and levels Beck with a mischievous grin. "Listen to this. *My buddy was driving from Dallas to LA to visit me and fell asleep at the wheel. He told me he distinctly remembers running the car into a ditch. He stopped for help in a little town in southern Arizona to get the car fixed and ended up staying there for over a week. When he finally made it to LA, he told me he didn't remember anything about the week in Arizona. But when he checked his bank account, he'd spent thousands of dollars in this town with no memory of what he'd bought.*'"

"Woah . . ." Beck trails.

"That's not even the best part," Ellery says. "When he crashed, apparently this guy had a leg injury. He took pictures of it on his phone." She clicks her mouse a couple times, then the printer hums to life. A single page slides out like a tongue hanging limp over the mouth of the printer. "When he got to his friend's place, he had no injuries. He was totally healed. No scars or anything. Like he never even got hurt."

Beck nods. She's not entirely sure what that means, but the electric joy in her mother's eyes tells her it's something good. This is how it always begins—a little spark that catches her mother's attention. A single note pinned to her whiteboard, like a seed planted in an empty flower bed. With time, the notes will grow to cover the whole whiteboard like they always do, a lovely wallpaper of anecdotes and potential leads, arranged in a way only her mother can possibly follow. Beck dreams of tracing her fingers over the collected pages, soaking them in until she sees the story the way her mother does.

Beck mashes her knees close to her chest and rocks back on the carpet. Outside the door, the floorboards creak. Beck leans back and spots her father in the doorway, hands on his hips. His eyes find the paper in the printer.

"What do we have going on in here?" Beck's father asks, rounding the corner. He leans against the doorframe with a half-smile.

"Picture this," her mother says. She sweeps her arms through the air like she's clearing the scene, setting the stage for a great presentation. "An isolated town in the desert. A tight-knit community more than eager to help a lost traveler. But in the process of helping, they're also doing something heinous."

"Like what?"

"Shh," Ellery hisses. "I don't know yet. Something *bad*. Probably. Anyway, these people, they take you in, treat your wounds, set you free with nothing in your bank account and all your memories gone. How is that possible?"

"Drugs?"

"Maybe. But that only explains the memories, not the wounds. And what's the point of pumping people for cash?"

"What reason does anyone have for robbing someone else?" her father muses.

"Could be nothing." Ellery's expression crinkles in thought. "But it doesn't feel like nothing."

"Maybe it's magic," Beck says.

Her mother smiles at her, reaches out, and pinches her cheek once. She straightens Beck's glasses and turns back to the doorway. The light through the office window just catches the soft round of Ellery's cheek, bathing her face in white light. "You heard her," Ellery says. "Maybe it's magic."

"Sounds like a real story," her father says.

"A *potential* story."

Riley appears behind their father in the doorway, making this a family meeting. She links her fingers in front of her, rolling back on her heels. Riley's never liked the office much; it's overcrowded with paper and stuffy when all four of them are inside. Beck prefers the office less crowded, too. Riley and their father have their cartoons. They have football games on Sundays and fried cheese balls and prank videos on YouTube. If Riley inherited a part of their father's soul, Beck inherited their mother's. Her intense focus, her comfort in the quiet, her love of story. Her nagging, unending need to understand a picture for all its details.

"I see a piece of paper in the printer," her father says. "Are we getting serious already?"

"No, no . . ." Ellery shakes her head. But she pauses, eyes the little flap of paper in the printer. "No, I'm just getting a feel for it."

"Put it up," Beck says.

Her eyes find the empty whiteboard and her fingers tangle in the carpet. She's hungry, too. She's starving for her mother's next story, the next fascination that will fill their empty hours. Her parents lock eyes and Ellery smiles. With a pinch of mischief glowing in the dark green of her eyes, she plucks the paper from the printer—the post describing the traveler—and she tapes it to the whiteboard.

For a moment, all four Birschings stand in silence, staring at the first piece of paper, imagining how it will grow. Beck imagines the thrill of watching the story expand and she smiles. She doesn't understand yet that this story isn't a gift, it's a poison. She doesn't understand the way her mother's digging will blacken her nails forever, will twist her mind and wring it out like an old sponge. Beck doesn't understand yet that this first piece of paper won't blossom, it will grow into a noose.

She doesn't understand yet, but she feels it under her skin. Something big is coming.

3

When Beck opens her eyes, for a moment, she's back.

She's back in her mother's office before it was consumed by Backravel. Before the stale caramel walls were impossible to see under all the notes. Paper pinned one page over another, corners overlapped like new wallpaper, fragments of thoughts and leads tiled like mosaic. Before Ellery Birsching lost her job at the local paper, before their father left, before the center of the dining table became a mountain of overdue bills and notices. Before the walls ran out of space and the notes were taped over the windows, choking out the light. Beck breathes deep, lets herself live in the memory like the last decade was only a long nightmare.

But she isn't back. She's not sitting in the center of the office floor, picking at loose staples in the carpet, watching her mother tap furiously at her keyboard as a new story bloomed. She can't smell the last dregs of a clearance linen-scented candle burning on the windowsill. The walls here aren't brown, they're gray, punctuated with metal siding that gleams in the early morning light. The flashing blue button on the TV blinks, slowly luring Beck back to reality. She's not home, she's *here*.

Backravel. The center of all her trouble.

Beck curls her fingers around the hem of her quilt and pulls it over her face. Cool morning light filters in through the window slot beside her mattress, leaving her shoulder warmer than the rest of her. It's too quiet in the trailer, which means Riley's already awake. If not, she'd hear her sister's snoring. Usually it's Beck who doesn't sleep, up later and awake earlier, perpetually exhausted.

"Did you even sleep?" Beck groans.

She shifts farther under the blanket, lets the warmth roll over the bare skin of her legs. The thick scent of burnt *something* stings the air. From the floor of the trailer, meeker than Beck expects, Riley says, "I don't know how to make coffee."

Beck peers over the edge of her bed and her grip on the mattress tightens. The floor is covered in stacks of paper. Beck's backpack sits on the kitchen counter, open like a yawn. The bursting manila folder inside is gone, clearly emptied on the trailer floor. Beck's stomach drops.

"What are you doing?"

"You said you packed all of this."

"Why were you going through my bag?" Beck asks. But she can't even summon up the energy to sound angry. Looking at the notes on the floor only makes her feel numb.

For a long moment, Riley doesn't say anything. Her quiet is anxious, fingertips brushing over the notes, shoulders slumped. If she's angry, it's quiet anger. Maybe the notes conjure up that same feeling of cool hopelessness in Riley that Beck always feels when she looks at them. No doubt Riley also pictures the dim light through the papered windows, the scent of dust collecting in dark corners.

Beck sighs and swings her legs over the edge of the bed, tilting her head to avoid the ceiling. She should've known that Riley would find the notes within seconds of settling in. She's like their mother in that way—in fact, it's the *only* way the two of them were ever similar. If she's suspicious at all, she can't leave things be. There's a signature Ellery Birsching determination that glitters in Riley's eyes, even now as she sits dejected on the trailer floor. Beck's looked in the mirror a thousand times and there's nothing glittering there. Just a blank green stare, sallow and empty.

"Is this *all* of it?" Riley asks finally.

She picks at a sticky note stuck to one of their mother's drawings. She doesn't look up, but Beck sees the subtle twitch of her nose, almost quick enough to miss. Like a rabbit's nose. She's trying to hide her frustration, but she can't completely bury it.

"Yeah," Beck admits. "Yeah. It's all of it."

Every note from Ellery Birsching's office back in Everett, lovingly and tenderly peeled from the walls and windows, hoisted from overburdened file cabinets and uncrumpled from an overflowing recycle bin. Packing the notes was supposed to be their compromise; Riley wanted to shred the notes completely, but Beck was the one who insisted they keep them. She knows, she *knows* it was wrong to bring the notes here, but she can't imagine standing here in Backravel, Arizona, without a decade of Ellery Birsching's meticulous notes. She can't let them yellow in a box in Texas while the town that spawned them is right here, alive and ripe with answers.

"I'm sorry," Beck says, gathering up a fistful of her blanket. "I shouldn't have brought them. I just felt like . . . I mean, if we're going to be here, shouldn't we take her thoughts with us?"

"Except we're not here to research Mom's story," Riley snaps. "We're here on vacation. We're honoring Mom, right? This . . . these are the worst thing about her."

Beck traces her fingertips across the afghan on her bed and she hopes that Riley believes this is the greatest lie Beck has told about this trip. She can't tell Riley about the letter, can't tell Riley that this *isn't* just a vacation. It's the last chance she's got to finish Ellery Birsching's great, incomplete magnum opus. There would be no trip without the notes. Here in Backravel, the notes are her bible.

Riley pulls a sticky note free and flattens it gently under her fingertips. The words on it, written in fat black Sharpie, are too smudged to read. "There's so much of it. Looking at all of it gives me so much anxiety."

"I know," Beck says. "Me, too."

She slides off her bed and crouches next to Riley, running a hand lightly over her sister's back. With the notes splayed out before them, it's easy to see the way Ellery's focus faded over the years. The notes might've been coherent at first—story beats she planned to use, diagrams of buildings, partial maps of Backravel as she saw it—but in the final years of her life, the notes became nothing but a mess. Beck knows because she's read them a thousand times. Some pages are almost entirely blank save for a drawing of a bike tire or a loosely sketched sunrise or a ladder leaning against a wall. Some are stream-of-conscious narratives. *You can drive toward the same sunset for hours,* one note says, *but you're not any closer to the sun.*

On a sketch of a sheep, Beck traces a note in her mother's handwriting: *What would you do if you found it?*

Her breath catches and she stands again. Carefully, she and Riley sort the notes back into their folder, tucking the last remains of Ellery Birsching away from the harsh Arizona light that streams in through the trailer blinds. Every little page of her, flaked away over years and recorded in panicked detail, safe in Beck's backpack. The quiet is uneasy, hot even in the white morning.

The sun is high overhead, granting them a sliver of coolness in the trailer, when someone knocks at the door.

Today, it's not Mr. Sterling visiting them. A slender woman in a soft purple crewneck and matching cloth headband stands on the other side of their narrow door. Her sandy-brown hair is paper thin and falls in a single sheet over her shoulders. Lingering awkwardly behind her is a boy who looks too tall for his own liking. He looks determinedly away from the trailer, hands stuffed in his pockets, a swoop of black hair nearly obscuring his eyes.

"Good morning. I'm Ruthie. You met my husband last night," the woman says. When she smiles, the subtle wrinkles at her eyes smile with her. There's something soft about her that makes Beck relax, even if it's just slightly. "Did you girls get some good rest?"

"We're still adjusting to the time change a little," Riley says, skirting around her self-imposed all-nighter. "I tried to make coffee earlier. Sorry about the smell."

Mrs. Sterling peers around the trailer door. "Oh. That thing. Greg should've warned you that it barely works. Anyway, since you're both up, I thought you might want to head into town. Daniel can show you the way. He's about to leave for work, so you can all go together."

"Oh," Riley chirps. She eyes Beck, then nods. "Yeah. We would love that. If that's not too inconvenient."

"I can drive us," Beck chimes in. "Then me and Riley can look around."

Both Mrs. Sterling's and Daniel's eyes snap to Beck at that. They eye each other and don matching frowns. "We have extra bikes, actually. All three of you can ride in together. Are you both sixteen? We have helmets."

"I'm not," Riley says.

Beck's eyes narrow. "We can drive."

Mrs. Sterling's smile doesn't relent. "We'd prefer you didn't."

Now, Riley turns. There's a quirk to her brow, questioning but cautious. Before she can protest, Mrs. Sterling softens and tries again.

"We try to be conscious of our effect on the environment here. Not to mention Greg told me how you girls drove all the way from Washington," she says. "It might be nice to give the car a break."

Before Beck can speak, Riley says, "We'd love to bike."

They get dressed, pressed to opposite corners of the trailer to keep from knocking elbows. Finally, they spill into the Sterlings' backyard. The late morning is quiet and bright blue, cooler than Beck expects. There's a bite missing in the air that Beck's used to in Washington. The wind here is warm and sweet and dry. Beck stretches her arms and tries not to think about how far she is from home. How there's no home left if she were to drive back the way she came. How she's not sure what home is waiting for her driving forward, either. She stands here in Backravel with her roots bundled in her arms and nowhere to plant them.

The Sterlings stand by the fire pit with two bikes, one pink and one black. A helmet is buckled to the pink bike, which they've apparently picked for Riley. Daniel waits for them at the gate leading to the main road, one foot propped on his pedal. He's ready to go with or without them. Beck and Riley nod to each other once, then mount their bikes and take off into the great wide morning.

• • •

Daniel isn't much of a tour guide.

He doesn't say a word on the way into town, pedaling silently with his lanky limbs scrunched up, too small for his children's bike. He reminds Beck of the kind of misfits she used to cling to back in Everett, hair a block of box-dyed black, cheeks sallow, and eyes sunken like he hasn't slept in a week. There's something odd to the structure of his pale face. A child with a face that looks much older than him.

The highway is a straight track, horizon on either side of them a crooked rim of red rock. Riding down the center of the valley, it's hard not to feel like they're in a bowl. Beck looks over her shoulder, eyes the shrinking houses of Sycamore Lane, and she wonders how often people actually *leave* this town.

On the highway shoulder, fifteen minutes past the Sterlings' house, a sign juts up from the red dirt.

WELCOME TO BACKRAVEL, ARIZONA

EVERY DAY IS A GIFT

"There's the sign," Daniel says, wheezing a little. He doesn't slow or even look at it. He only throws a vague gesture at the sign and keeps pedaling until patches of squat buildings begin to appear in the hazy heat. "And here's town."

Town is certainly a word for it. If Beck thought the houses on Sycamore Lane were just like the houses back home, Backravel proper is the opposite. The main highway transforms into a precise, well-maintained street. Ellery's notes described downtown Backravel as a mishmash of new infrastructure and old, abandoned buildings. Just like she said, half of the buildings that open up as they enter town look brand-new, assembled from dark glass and

metal beams. The other half looks like it's from an entirely different world—dilapidated, rusting military structures tucked between
brand-new construction like one town has been laid on top of another. The sidewalks are bright and beautifully groomed. Squares
carved into the sidewalk every few yards house thin, white-barked
trees with bright green foliage. It's an oasis in a sea of red. Beck has
to blink over and over to convince herself a real place can be this
vibrant.

"Wow," Riley says, pedaling to keep up with Daniel. "It's beautiful."

They pull up to a square building a few blocks into town. A sheet
metal sign bolted to the front of the store reads LEMONDROP: FRO-
ZEN YOGURT AND GOOD COMPANY. The store itself is another oddity,
encased between a collapsing control tower and what looks like an
abandoned barracks in shambles. Beck leans onto one leg, keeping
her bike balanced as she surveys the rest of the town around them.
It's like a dream, seeing it in person just the way Ellery described it.
Beck pictures her mother standing in this exact spot, shaking her
head at the insanity of this place, and her heart flutters.

"It's just how she said it was," Beck says.

Riley eyes her but says nothing.

Daniel unlocks the doors and motions Beck and Riley inside.
He gathers his hair into a knot and secures it over the band of a
lime-green visor. White sunlight tilts through the floor-to-ceiling
windows and Beck studies the reclaimed wood countertops, the industrial barstools, the faux fireplace fixed between two leather sofas.
It's dizzying to look at, modern in a way that implies there's more
money in Backravel than Beck thought. Through the skylights, she
can just make out the corner of the abandoned control tower's slate
roof.

"Anyway, time to open up," Daniel says, fastening his lime-green apron. "My friends are coming over in a few. You guys can stay or go look around. I'm only working four hours today."

"We should stay," Riley says. She eyes Beck and her smile softens with concern. "Unless you're not up for people today."

Beck blinks. It's not fair when she puts it like that. Like the two of them are from two different planets when it comes to people. After the funeral, this is how it was all the time. When your mom dies, the whole world turns into a parade of strangers saying how sorry they are, how much they loved her, how much dimmer the world will be without her. Mobs of people Beck didn't recognize arriving unannounced at their door in Everett with baked dishes she had to clean and mourning cards she had to pack. Navigating new waters was so much easier for Riley because *people* are easier for Riley. She's never had this fear of presenting herself to strangers with a genuine smile and niceties she actually means. So Riley was the one who faced the world for both of them, ushering the mobs inside, seating them on the worn-down sofa, accepting their gifts and cards. And Beck laid quiet in their mother's bed, staring at the curtained window for hours, watching the wind move the trees softly outside. Riley was too ready and Beck was too raw, ribs split open too wide, guts exposed to anyone who looked at her too long.

"You don't want to see more of town?" Beck asks. She fiddles with the zipper of her backpack and tries to stay grounded here, in Backravel, in *now*. "Then we can meet back here in a few hours."

"Or we could meet people first," Riley says. "We're here for two weeks. Maybe Daniel's friends can recommend stuff?"

"There's an official tour." This is Daniel, cutting in as he emerges from the back room. He cranks the lever of an espresso machine, unbothered. "Avery'll take you around the whole thing. If you wanted to wait."

"Avery?" Beck asks.

"Yeah."

Daniel offers no further explanation.

"Who's Avery?"

"Ricky's kid," Daniel says as if that covers it.

Before Beck can press on, a bell jingles at the front door. A group of teens file into LemonDrop, four in total. They're less awkward-looking than Daniel, but all together, they make a strange assortment. If this was a group of kids back in Everett, Beck would never peg them as friends. A girl at the front of the pack wears a loose white blouse and tight jeans, black hair flattened and yanked into a ponytail. Another girl wears a T-shirt for a band Beck's never heard of, a chunky lip ring, and eyeliner so thick it's like it was applied with a paintbrush. One of the boys with them is tall—even taller than Daniel—with basketball shorts and a baggy black T-shirt. The other boy wears a plaid button-up tucked into his straight-legged jeans. Riley seems to spot the oddness of the group, too, pausing for only a moment before flashing a signature Riley Birsching smile. Daniel looks up at his friends, but he makes no introductions. There's a silent moment that crawls by before Riley steps forward.

"Hi," Riley says. "I'm Riley. This is my sister, Beck."

At the front of the group, the girl with the black ponytail smiles. "You're the ones in the trailer."

Riley nods.

The girl motions to herself. "I'm Katie. This is Jack, Andy, and Megan."

Down the line, the other three kids wave. Beck waves, too, though she's sure her smile is less convincing than Riley's. Back home, Beck lived comfortably in her small band of acquaintances—a cluster of near-dropouts that met behind the track to smoke and skip class. She's never been like Riley, who fits seamlessly into any crowd like a missing puzzle piece.

"Should we head out?" Beck says, quietly, to Riley.

"I think we should stay?" Riley says. "Can we relax? Just for a little?"

"You guys can totally hang out with us today," Katie butts in. "It's probably better if you wait until Avery's tour to look around, anyway."

Avery. It's the second time someone has mentioned the name and the tour. The vagueness of it starts to grate.

"I'd rather go look now," Beck says.

Riley says nothing. An uncomfortable quiet settles between them. Riley looks at Daniel and Katie and the others and Beck knows what she's thinking. She looks at Beck with the same face she wore back home, lingering in the doorway after visitors, quietly asking if Beck was well enough to talk to people yet. She isn't angry; she's sad. Beck's face is hot, but she doesn't relent.

"Are you coming?" she asks.

Riley purses her lips. "I'll stay."

Beck scowls.

Before Riley can ask Beck to stay, too, she moves. The others watch them in silence and she knows they can feel tension here, hot and uncomfortable in the empty yogurt shop. Riley is welcome to stay and chat with the other kids, though. She's welcome to make friends and relax, but Beck has a job to do. She has a story to piece together and she doesn't have time to waste.

She shrugs. "Cool. See you later."

"Beck—"

Beck shoulders her bag and makes her way back out of the shop, chest tight and head spinning. She knows she's the unreasonable one—the one making problems for Riley and everyone else—but it doesn't stop her from leaving. The sun is high and the air is dry and she's alone the way she's always alone. Alone surrounded by people, swirling in a toxic cocktail of her own thoughts. She doesn't want to meet Daniel and his friends because she didn't come to Backravel for them. She came here because the ghost of Ellery Birsching lingers at her back, even now, asking her to dig deeper. To finish what she started a decade ago.

Beck Birsching came to Backravel to unbury the truth.

4

It takes Beck fifteen minutes to ride the trail that circles Backravel's miniature downtown. There's a gas station sitting on the road into town, but only the one. Like Mrs. Sterling said, there's only a handful of cars in the whole town, each of them still in their driveway, veiled by red-dusted car covers. As far as she can tell, the cars are unused. Beck wonders if any of them still function. Instead, outside every house, there's a cluster of bikes with red dirt caked into the tread of their tires.

Other than the gas station, there's a convenience store, a dentist, a gift shop, a gym, a grocery store, and other standard small-town fixtures. Like LemonDrop, each functional building is pristinely constructed with matching wood siding, black pavement, and bright steel beams. Lush green shrubs claw their way through tasteful gravel patches. The white sun glints from every glossy surface in town all at once, casting the world in an unearthly glow.

Beck doesn't care about the new buildings, though. She cares about what's between them.

At first, she thought the control tower and the barracks outside

LemonDrop were the bulk of it, but the farther she glides through town, the more abandoned military structures crop up. It's just like she read in her mother's notes: a rusty old mess hall, a radio antenna, a crumbled shooting range beyond the rows of houses. All untouched and ignored. For a town apparently deeply interested in appearances, it seems strange to leave the ruins out in plain sight.

Out of sight of LemonDrop, Beck gets to work. Most of her mother's notes skip the big picture, focusing on the little details of Backravel—names that interested her, observations about the town's layout, little facts about Backravel's history—but very little of it addresses a bigger picture. It's not the way Beck's brain works and it never has been. Back in Everett, Beck saw the world in a blur. It was easiest that way. She existed one day to the next, noticing absolutely nothing if she could help it.

She can't help picturing what her morning would look like today in a world where Ellery Birsching never died. On a summer morning in Everett, she'd be waking up at noon, eating a bowl of oatmeal before fixing eggs for Riley and her mother. She'd do the laundry on autopilot, check her mother's bank account for red flags, then slip into the cool quiet of her bedroom to watch Netflix until it was time to sleep again. Until her eyes felt like they were sinking through their sockets. She existed without stopping, because letting her mind rest was dangerous. Friends, school, and all the rest of it were just watery details she lost the minute they were out of sight. She didn't like details then because details made time slow down. Lingering in the same day over and over, it was like time itself slipped by, quick and easy as a summer breeze through the window. There's a piece of her even now that wishes she was still in her bed, cycling through that same mirthless loop.

Beck feels for the letter folded up in the pocket of her windbreaker.

It's the same letter she found slipped into the mail slot of the house back in Everett, the letter she stashed in the glove box of her mother's Honda for the fifteen-hundred-mile trek to Arizona, the letter she's read a thousand times by now. Beck unfolds it and traces the tender loops of Ellery Birsching's unmistakable handwriting: *Come and find me.*

The guilt racks her all over again. She shouldn't be lying to Riley about the letter or her real reasons for coming to Backravel. But if Riley knew she was here chasing the ghost of their mother's unfinished story, she never would've agreed to come.

Beck shoves the note back in her pocket. *This* is what matters. She can't look at Backravel the way the old Beck Birsching would, letting all the details slide by. She needs to look at it like the award-winning, relentless journalist Ellery Birsching. At least, she needs to try. Beck musters up her mother's sharp eye, her obsessive mind, her hunger for the specific. There are details here that she knows Ellery Birsching devoured.

She makes another loop around Backravel's downtown on her bike, then stops, fumbling for her notebook. On a blank page, she scrawls out: *There are no churches in Backravel. There are no cemeteries in Backravel.*

Beck pulls her phone from her pocket and starts a recording. "Rebecca Birsching," she says, "June sixteenth. I don't know how many people live here. Less than a thousand, I think. There should be some kind of church, but there isn't. Check Mom's notes for anything about religion. And, uh, check Mom's notes for cemeteries, too."

Beck pedals back into town proper and squeezes her brakes in front of Quick Stop, the succinctly named convenience store. She parks her bike in the middle of the sidewalk since there's nowhere to lock it up.

Inside, Quick Stop looks like any other convenience store from back home. A bell jingles, signaling her arrival, but the store is empty. The air conditioner buzzes quietly. A handful of refrigerators line the back wall, stocked full of Gatorades and iced coffees and bottled waters. Beck touches the wad of cash in her back pocket. Her throat is drier than sandpaper, but there's only so much of Ellery's cash left and they have to make it last the full two weeks. It's too early to start spending, but a couple water bottles can't hurt. She plucks two from the refrigerator and makes her way to the register.

Before she can ring the bell, a man steps from the back room. For a moment, when he eyes Beck, he looks afraid. He blinks, shakes his head, then smiles. The rhythm of it sends a chill up Beck's spine; it was nearly robotic, like he reset himself before speaking.

"Found everything?" he asks.

"Yeah." Beck plants the water bottles on the counter and throws a pack of gum into the mix. "Yeah. I think that's everything."

The man scans her meager pile. Beck angles to read his name tag: FLOYD. Without looking up, Floyd says, "What brings you to town?"

"Oh. Just visiting and, um . . . sightseeing."

Floyd nods. "Any specific sights you're seeing? We don't usually get many tourists here in town. Maybe I can give you some suggestions."

Beck pushes a loose strand of hair behind her ear. "That's very . . . nice. Me and my sister are staying with the Sterlings. Today's our first day in town, so I'm trying to kind of get my footing."

She lingers in the quiet a little too long. The part of her that naturally swerves to avoid conversation butts heads with the part of her that's here to ask questions. Beck cracks her knuckles against the linoleum-lined counter. She rakes over the highlights of her mother's notes, fishing for anything she can ask Floyd about.

Floyd beats her to it.

"You already had your tour?" he asks.

"No. Not yet."

"Huh," he says. He glances out the window, almost quick enough to miss. "Well, you'll have an easier time looking around once you get the tour. There's some good town history in it, too."

"Is this, like, an official tour?" Beck asks.

Floyd arches a brow.

"Is it required?"

"I guess not," Floyd says. "You . . . don't want the tour?"

"No, no, I want it," Beck says. "I've just never been to a town with an orientation. That's all."

"It's not required," Floyd says, "but it's a good idea. Backravel isn't like most other little towns. It's more helpful to get the basics down before you dig deeper, in my opinion."

"Yeah, I guess," Beck says. "It really is an interesting town. The person who gives the tour . . . they're in charge of town? Or have some authority?"

"Avery," Floyd says. "I wouldn't say she's in charge, really. That would be more Ricky's role."

"Ricky," Beck repeats.

Daniel had mentioned a Ricky at the shop. Beck makes a mental note of it, though she's not sure what it means. If she remembers right, there was a Ricky that frequented her mother's notes, but it's all blurry now. In all the years she spent visiting Backravel, her mother must have met him.

"How long are you girls staying?" Floyd asks.

"Two weeks."

Floyd pauses, placing his price scanner on the counter. A gush of cool air wafts from the AC. He mulls the answer over longer than Beck expects. Finally, he says, "That's quite a long vacation. You're not visiting anyone specific?"

"No. We—"

"'Cause I swear I've seen you before," Floyd continues. "You're not related to the Isaacs? Wait, you said you were staying with the Sterlings."

"I've never been here before," Beck says. "I'm sure."

Floyd, apparently unsatisfied, shrugs.

Beck glances outside and her eyes catch on a light from the top of a nearby plateau. The light transforms, softening from blinding to a mild glare. The light is coming from a set of windows, she realizes, square and black and angled directly at the sun. There's a building on the tallest plateau, massive and entirely alone. Just like her mother's notes described. She should be used to seeing the strange places from Ellery's notes in the flesh by now, but each time, the wonder feels brand-new.

"What's that?" Beck asks.

"The treatment center?" Floyd asks. "Oh, you should definitely visit while you're here, if they let you. People come from all over to see it."

"What kind of treatment center?"

"It's hard to explain," Floyd says. He nervously looks out the window. "It's best if you let Avery talk about it on the tour."

Beck rolls her eyes. Of course he wants her to wait for the tour. Everyone in Backravel seems to be allergic to answering any questions outside of the tour. It better be one incredible tour, Beck thinks, or she'll be asking for a refund. She shakes her head. "You've been inside, though?"

Floyd scoffs. "'Course I have. We all have."

He watches her now, waiting for her to leave, but she lingers a little longer. There's something ominous about the way he says it. *We all have.* A treatment center that everyone attends but won't describe? She sees why her mother couldn't leave this alone—every word of it begs you to dig a little deeper.

"How long have you lived here?" Beck asks.

Floyd narrows his eyes, but he doesn't answer. The air feels cooler suddenly, though Beck suspects that's because it's just occurred to her that there is absolutely no one outside. Not one person walking the sidewalks or sitting in the park. There's no idle chatter to fill the empty quiet. She wonders what Floyd was doing in the back room before he greeted her. There's too much dead air in Backravel.

"Never mind," Beck manages. She gathers up her things and steps back into the dry heat. The treatment center continues to glare in the brilliant white light. Beck traces the thin black road leading up the plateau with her eyes, waiting for any traffic, but the road is empty.

Just like the rest of Backravel, it's beautiful and empty.

• • •

By the time Beck makes it back to LemonDrop, the store is closed.

Beck pedals up to the front door, but there's no point. It can't be right. She tries to work it out in her head. She left LemonDrop just after it opened at ten. She biked the perimeter of town, stopped at the store, and talked with Floyd. It hasn't been four hours, she's *sure* of it. But when she checks her phone, it's just past three in the afternoon. It's been five hours since they arrived in Backravel proper.

It wouldn't be the first time she's lost hours like this. But this isn't like before—she didn't *choose* to zone out. This time, it feels like her hours have been stolen.

She whips around and inspects the center of town, but it's empty, just like before. The sun is off-center, just beginning to tilt down toward the plateaus on the horizon. Three in the afternoon, it seems, is correct. All the other bikes are already gone, and any trace that Riley was ever here with the others is erased. They're gone. Her chest feels tight. She never should've left Riley alone with them.

Beck unlocks her phone and there's a single text from Riley waiting for her with a time stamp from half an hour ago. *sorry,* it reads, *we're heading back to the trailer. lmk when you're on the way.*

Beck types: *thanks for leaving me lol*

She erases it and tries again.

k leaving now

Beck doesn't usually mind being alone. Biking along the strip of highway back to Sycamore Lane, she starts to wake up. She tunes in to the labored rhythm of her own breathing, the whirring of her bike chain, the way her thoughts start to slip by. She focuses on the details she came here to investigate—the main players in her mother's notes that she's actually found so far. There's the mysterious building on the plateau, shiny and all alone. The *treatment center,* as Floyd described it. Then there's Delia Horton, the name that popped up more and more frequently in her mother's notes as time passed. What began as a question—*who is Delia Horton?*—transformed into pages of notes describing a woman just like Beck's mother, inexplicably drawn to Backravel over and over through the years. A woman with a family and an impossible sadness.

But the most confusing part of the notes, and the part that tugs at Beck's imagination the hardest, is the thing her mother only referred to as the "source."

She doesn't know what it is, what it does, or even *where* it is. But as the years crawled by, it's the thing Ellery was the most interested in. Countless pages in the unruly stacks of Ellery's notes are dedicated to her search for the mysterious object—if it's even an object—and its location. Old maps of the desert basin, academic essays on the history of the Southwest, interviews with people living in Backravel about noises they've heard in the desert. It's the thing Ellery wanted to find the most, and it's the thing she never could. It's the thing Beck *has* to find before she resigns herself to Texas and a normal life.

Beck slows to a stop along the highway and tilts onto one leg, wiping away the sweat at her brow. The desert is strange here, too quiet and too open. Ellery was positive the source, whatever it is, was out here in the unexplored desert. Tufts of gray grass spurt from the rock and the sky feels too low against the horizon. Beck closes her eyes and, faintly, she hears something roar in the distance. A mechanical whirr sounding under her feet. The tread of her sneakers feels thinner here, almost like she's barefoot on the road. She tastes iron on her tongue. A sensation like cold water pools in the pit of her stomach.

When she opens her eyes, she sees a spot of color in the dusky haze of the roadside.

To the right of the highway, maybe a hundred feet from the concrete, is a little campsite. A single red tent discolored by dirt. A meek campfire with a vein of smoke stretching for the sky. An old pickup truck is tilted onto its front fender where it's missing a tire. In the center of the campsite, a woman sits alone and stokes the fire. Her black hair is in a tangle over her shoulder; a massive denim jacket obscures most of her legs. There's something wrong about this; this is the same road Beck took into town with Daniel and Riley earlier, but this woman and her campsite weren't here when she rode past before. She's sure of it.

When Beck pauses, the woman looks up. She goes still, staring at Beck with wide, frantic eyes. Beck's blood goes cold.

The woman stands. Before she can take a step toward the road, Beck kicks her leg up and starts pedaling again. She shouldn't run away from the strangeness; if she was Ellery Birsching, she'd stop and learn more about the woman in the desert. She'd learn why she's out here in the empty, scorched land beyond town because Beck's mother never cared if she was facing danger head-on if there was the chance of a story on the other side. But Beck isn't her mother.

She's afraid.

By the time Beck soars back to Sycamore Lane, the sun has dipped below the horizon and the Sterlings' house is quiet. It's too early for sundown, especially in the summer and especially in the desert. The clouds are slate gray, splotched like a paint spill above the bluffs and outlined in gold. The sky behind them is empty and the cool wind smells like woodsmoke from someone's grill. Beck's feet hurt from walking and pedaling all day, even if it didn't feel like all day. She catches her breath.

Daniel's bike is leaned against the front porch again, joined by Riley's pink bike and helmet. Beck pedals beyond the porch, opens the garden gate, and wheels her bike to the trailer. She pauses beside the door and unslings her backpack from her shoulder, leaning against the trailer. The cold of the metal seeps through the fabric of her windbreaker and T-shirt until it tingles up her spine. She closes her eyes.

The back door of the Sterlings' house opens and someone steps into the backyard. Beck assumes it's Mr. Sterling given the light jingle of keys in the stranger's pocket. He probably wants to invite her in for dinner—the scent of roast meat drifts into the dry summer air and Beck's stomach growls. She wonders if Riley's already inside. She's probably already nestled herself comfortably into their family like she did with Daniel and his friends in the morning. It only takes a day for Riley to find her footing; Beck doubts she's *ever* felt her feet on solid ground.

"Hey," Beck says without looking up. "Is Riley already in there?"

"I'm sorry," Mr. Sterling says. "Can I help you?"

Beck looks up. Mr. Sterling stands with his hands on his hips. His posture is defensive. *Nervous.* He smiles, but his eyes are fearful. Beck adjusts her glasses, blinking slowly like it'll make anything clearer. It takes a second too long for his question to register.

"Me?"

"Yes. You."

"I'm Beck," she says. "I'm . . . we're staying here?"

"Beck . . ." Mr. Sterling scratches the back of his head. "Oh, wait. Like Rebecca? Rebecca Birsching?"

Beck swallows. "Yes?"

Mr. Sterling extracts his bulky cell phone from his back pocket, studying the screen. Just like yesterday. After a moment, he shakes his head. "I didn't recognize you from the profile. You're here right on time. I wish you'd come to the front door. You *really* scared me."

"What?" Beck manages.

"I was told you'd be checking in with a sister?"

Beck doesn't move. The trailer door opens behind her and Riley stands behind the screen in a T-shirt and gym shorts. She stretches like she's just woken up. When Mr. Sterling sees her, his eyes widen. He takes a step back, eyes darting between the two of them like they're armed and dangerous.

"What's happening?" Riley asks.

"I don't know," Beck says softly.

The back door of the Sterling house opens and Mrs. Sterling stumbles into the backyard. She rushes to her husband's side and touches the crook of his elbow. This seems to help, even if just slightly. She smiles at her husband and says, quietly, "This is Beck and Riley. They checked in *last* night. You remember that."

She's reminding him, not asking a question.

Mr. Sterling studies them now, the breeze between them all only a whisper. He's angry and afraid all at once, an expression Beck recognizes too well. He looks at his wife, then, stiffly, he nods.

"From last night. Obviously."

Beck's heart races. She studies Mr. Sterling and it's clear he isn't lying. He doesn't remember them.

"I'm sorry," he starts, clearly unsettled. "I think I'm going to . . ."

"We're going to have some dinner and then Greg is going to lay down," Mrs. Sterling says. Her smile is wide and frantic. She ushers Mr. Sterling toward the back door but keeps her eyes on the trailer. "I don't know what you girls brought for food, but how about I bring you some leftovers? And then we can all have breakfast tomorrow morning. I'm . . . very sorry about this."

"What's—" Beck starts.

Mrs. Sterling cuts her short. "Sleep tight, girls."

With that, the Sterlings disappear back into their house and Beck and Riley are left in the endless, swallowing quiet. The curtains at the back of the house rustle, then tear shut. Beck turns to Riley and watches her through the screen door.

Slowly, she says, "What . . . the fuck?"

5

BEFORE

Two months before her mother's death, Beck Birsching spends her Tuesday evening like any other. She leaves school in the early afternoon without saying goodbye to anyone, walks to the corner store while Riley finishes orchestra rehearsal, buys a frozen pizza for the three of them to share. The cashier at 7-Eleven knows her too well by now, grabbing a carton of french fries from the warming tray before she's even made it to the counter. She pays with a handful of cash she took from her mother's dresser and slips outside to wait in the cool Washington afternoon.

She is a simple machine with a single purpose: to keep the Birsching family afloat.

While she waits for Riley to emerge from the orchestra room, she checks her mother's bank account. Another chunk of money gone for a plane ticket, and Beck doesn't need to guess the destination. She sighs, slinks down against the wall of the school, and she closes her eyes. Ellery's last piece for that online magazine only raked in a few hundred dollars, and it took months to clear edits. The money coming in is less and less, and the empty space between checks stretches longer and longer. Even if she's done her best to truck through this without stopping, she can't deny it's getting worse. Every day, things are getting worse.

Beck doesn't think about it. She doesn't think because thinking will kill her. It'll kill all three of them.

When Riley emerges, they walk home.

Riley talks about her day, about how unfair Mrs. Fox's grading is, about how the baseball team got caught with spiked seltzer on campus and won't get to go to prom, how her friend Toni's parents are going to buy her a car for her sixteenth birthday. Beck listens the way she always does, eyes glued to the pavement, fixed on the grass that juts through cracks in the cement. She listens and she thinks about how their phone company informed them the bill would increase this month. She thinks about how she didn't do laundry last night, so now they've got a pileup next to the washing machine she can't ignore anymore. She made the mistake of going to school with unwashed clothes once and the snake wasn't worth a night off. She thinks about how she'll ask her mother about the plane ticket—*Do you think you could wait until April to go?*—but there's no point to that. If Backravel is calling, her mother is going to answer. There's no stopping her; Beck can only massage the budget to make it fit.

When they arrive home, Riley darts to her room to work on homework. Beck gathers up the opened but unpaid bills on their dining table, stealing them away to the laundry room. She loads the washing machine and lets it run and her body is on autopilot. She pays the phone bill and the sewer bill. She'll need Ellery to collect another check from somewhere before she can pay the power bill. She can ask for more hours at the gas station, but more hours means less time at home. It means more time with Ellery unsupervised.

She considers texting her father for a loan, but she doesn't.

The front door opens and shuts.

"Hey, Mom," Riley's voice calls, muffled through the walls.

There's only silence.

Beck pulls an armful of laundry from the dryer and begins folding. The warm scent of cheese and pepperoni begins wafting from the kitchen and Beck sighs because at least she's got food on the table. At least she's got clothes ready to go. This won't last forever, but at least it will last for now. Beck is tired. She leans her elbows down to the washing machine, presses her face into her hands, and she breathes through the space between her fingers, slow and even.

She opens her eyes when the door behind her creaks open.

"Hey," she says. "There's pizza in the oven if you want some in a second."

Nothing.

Beck turns to face the doorway. Just visible in the lighted space between the door and the frame, Ellery Birsching stands as stiff and still as a statue. Her eyes are wide and fearful, her grip on the doorknob so tight her knuckles are pale. The bags under her eyes are worse than they were in the morning. She looks like a ghost in the shallow hallway light, the sickly green of her eyes shining like dull metal in the thick shadows.

"Mom?"

Ellery's grip on the door tightens. A single, thudding heartbeat pulses in Beck's chest and she understands.

She's looking at Beck, but she sees a stranger.

"Mom? Are you okay?"

Her mother breathes sharply through her nose, and then her grip slackens. She blinks until her eyes are glassy like still water in the dark. Softly, she says, "Where are we?"

Beck takes her mother's hands and she pulls her into the laundry room, shutting the door behind them. Because Riley can't hear this conversation, can't know how bad it's gotten. She presses a palm to her mother's forehead and it feels normal. Not a fever, not any kind of illness their medicine cabinet will solve. Week by week, Ellery Birsching has been getting more scattered, more forgetful, but she's never been lost like this before.

"We're home," Beck says. "We're here at the house."

"Home," Ellery repeats. "Are you sure?"

"I'm sure."

"I could've sworn I was in Arizona." Her mother laughs. "Should've known by the cold. It sounds weird, but for a second, I thought you were Delia's girl."

"I'm Beck," Beck says, voice quivering. "I'm—"

"I know, I know . . ."

Ellery shakes her head and laughs, and Beck sighs. There's something that clicks for her now, and it changes everything. Not only is it getting worse, it's getting *faster*. Whatever is snatching away her mother's memories is getting stronger each day, taking more of her and leaving less behind. She pulls Beck into a hug and Beck closes her eyes, breathes in the scent of linen candles and laundry detergent. That night, Beck lies in her bed staring at her phone screen, thumb hovering over the phone number for their family doctor. That night, she calls and tells them that her mother is losing her mind. In two months, she won't have a mother anymore and her world will be different. In two months, she'll pull Backravel from her mother's walls and she'll think of that glassy stare through the door. In two months, everything will change, but tonight, Beck closes her eyes and she prays.

That night, the end begins.

6

Beck has a slipping problem.

That's what Ellery used to call them, anyway. *Slips*. Moments that sit right behind you. Moments you already lived but find yourself living all over again. Beck used to think it was a problem specific to her mother, this confusion between the past and the present. She would stand in their house and swear she was just traipsing through the desert, and Beck mistakenly believed that it was just a symptom of the growth in her skull that would eventually kill her. But here she is in a trailer in the middle of the desert, slipping all the way back to Washington. The velvety cool of the Everett air in early fall sits like oil on her skin.

The slipping didn't start in Backravel. It didn't start when her mother died, either. It would be easier if she could pinpoint the beginning of it. If there was a single switch that turned it on like the post that triggered Ellery's obsession with Backravel, maybe she could turn it off again. But as far back as she can remember, this is how it's been. The past sits behind her, invisible, but it always felt like a stranger breathing down her neck.

Even now, as Riley guides her into the trailer and the sound of the wind outside hushes to a quiet, Beck starts to slip. She's in the trailer—she feels the floor tilt slightly under her weight, feels Riley's palms against her shoulder blades—but it's like she's being touched through a thousand layers of skin, distant and clammy and cold. Instead, she's standing in the basement of the house in Everett, folding laundry, inhaling the pungent, crisp scent of hot dryer sheets. She's turning and looking into her mother's face, into the green eyes that stare back at her like she's a stranger.

That's the face Mr. Sterling made outside.

She's plummeting again.

"Okay," Riley says, so soft Beck almost doesn't hear her. "Okay. *Breathe.*"

They stare at each other—this is Riley she's looking at, not Ellery—and Beck clenches her fists just to feel the half-moon prick of her fingernails in the skin of her palm. It's just the two of them now. But Beck can't stop seeing the round eyes, furrowed brow, frightened pupils of Mr. Sterling's face. It was an Ellery Birsching staple once, a dizzying cocktail of fear, confusion, and anger.

"Before you say anything," Riley warns, "I want to make sure you're—"

"How did he forget?" Beck cuts in.

"I don't know."

"He *forgot* us."

Riley nods. "Yes. But . . ."

"It's just like—"

"—Mom." Riley deftly finishes the thought and her expression sours. "I know. I thought so, too. Can we talk about it? Without freaking out?"

Beck chews the inside of her cheek. She tries not to chase the thought that surfaces now, because if she says it out loud, Riley will want to leave Backravel. Instead, she inhales deep and closes her eyes. "Okay. Let's talk about it."

"Thank you." Riley steps into the kitchenette booth and makes a point of exhaling loudly like she's encouraging Beck to do the same. She pats the seat next to her. "That was weird, but there are lots of reasons people forget things."

"Within twenty-four hours?"

"Maybe."

Beck frowns. "I didn't mean to freak out. It's just . . . it was just like Mom."

Riley is quiet, watching Beck with wide eyes. There's a built-in caution to the way Riley talks to her these last few months. A product of Riley's weekly meetings with the school grief counselor, Beck thinks. It's a delicate balancing act she's adopted, giving comfort without enabling delusion. She might be the younger sister, but since their mother's death, it's like she's afraid to handle Beck without kid gloves.

"Do you want to hear what I did today?" Riley offers.

Beck nods.

"Okay. So don't be mad," Riley says, pulling a pack of peanuts from her bag. "But I kind of . . . got the tour."

For a moment, Beck's panic subsides, which she guesses was Riley's goal. A sharp sting of irritation takes its place.

"Without me?"

Guilt flashes in Riley's eyes. "I told her you were coming back, but she didn't want to wait."

"Who?"

"Avery." Riley clicks the underside of the trailer table and folds it down, converting the booth into a bed. She sighs and says, "The one the other kids were talking about. Avery apparently gives everyone a tour."

"Oh," Beck says. She bites the inside of her cheek hard enough to taste iron. After a moment, she shoves Riley playfully in the arm and musters a smile. She's not going to be hurt about this. She's *not*. "Some sister you are. What did she show you?"

"Not a lot," Riley says. "A café. Town hall. Mostly town history. I promise, she said she'll come do your tour tomorrow."

"I shouldn't have left." Beck sinks to the trailer sofa. The Sterling house is quiet now, blinds drawn and windows dark. "I should've just stayed and done the tour like Daniel said. I really wanted to go."

"No," Riley says. "I should've gone with you. I'm sorry."

"I guess we both suck, then."

There's a restlessness to the quiet after that, something unresolved, pulled taut like wire. Riley finishes making her bed and stifles a yawn. They get ready for sleep in silence, but Beck isn't tired. Thoughts stew in the air, hot and murky. She crawls into her suffocating bunk and turns to face the metal wall. Below her, at the kitchen table, Riley slides under her blankets and turns off the lights, leaving them in the swallowing quiet. If Riley's still awake, she doesn't say anything else. In the quiet, Beck makes a plan. Tomorrow, she'll get this town tour. She'll meet the mysterious Avery, keeper of forbidden knowledge. She'll get one step closer.

She won't think about what Mr. Sterling's episode means. She's here for one reason. Tomorrow, she'll be done living in the dark.

7

That night, Beck doesn't sleep.

She stares at the ceiling of the trailer, counting the bolts that connect metal panels one after the other. She lies awake until the sky turns black and the wind howls over the round shell of the trailer, until the little window beside her mattress begins to glow again under a slow sunrise. She's still awake when Riley stirs, silences her phone alarm, and starts getting ready for the day. Beck keeps her eyes closed and breathes slow, feels the faint heat of morning on her shins where her blanket doesn't quite reach, but she doesn't sleep. Stripes of sunlight pattern her face while she waits.

Riley finishes getting ready and Beck hears her pause. She lingers in the center of the trailer and Beck is sure her sister is watching her. After a moment of quiet shuffling, Riley makes her way out of the trailer, softly closing the screen door behind her. Beck listens to the clanking of silverware and dishes outside, but she can't quite make out the faint conversation. The Sterlings' promised breakfast, she guesses. Riley's laugh is soft and easy, like always. If she's still unsettled by Mr. Sterling's behavior last night, she's hiding it well.

Beck shifts to her side and unearths her notebook from under her pillow, scrawling out a handful of notes:

> *mr. sterling forgot us*
> *the woman in the desert*
> *who's ricky??? And avery???*
> *delia horton is in the guest log 23 times*
> *no cars, no churches, no cemeteries*

None of it is particularly coherent, some of it is repetitive, and other than Backravel potentially having a vendetta against the letter *C*, Beck can't find a pattern in any of it. She stashes the journal back under her pillow and shimmies out of bed. She throws on her windbreaker and wriggles the trailer door open, flooding the little space with surprisingly cool morning air. It pricks goose bumps on her forearms until she rubs at her skin for warmth. Thin white light washes everything away for a moment, and then she sees the yard. A wrought-iron table has been hauled to the center of the patio. Riley is planted in the chair closest to the trailer, blond hair neatly straightened to her shoulders, feet kicked up on a spare chair. The Sterlings sit opposite her, laughing at something she's just said, swirling identical wineglasses of something murky and pink. They look like a matching set, dressed in loose-fitting pastel crewnecks and exercise pants. Their laughter is loud but inoffensive, like a TV audience.

As if on cue, all three of them turn to face Beck.

"You're up," Mrs. Sterling says. She stands, but she doesn't move from the table. "There's breakfast. If you're hungry."

"It's *so* good," Riley says through a mouthful.

Beck cautiously makes her way to the table, eyes trained on Mr.

Sterling. Whatever happened last night, he seems to have bounced back. He takes a long drink from his glass, thick-faced watch glinting in the sunlight. Between him and Riley, there's an empty plate and chair. A peace offering. The table is covered in bowls of black beans, pico de gallo, and fresh tortillas. Curls of steam coil from a pot of black coffee. Mrs. Sterling pours orange juice into a pressed copper mug and slides it to Beck's empty seat.

"It's just so nice out this morning," Mrs. Sterling says. "We couldn't resist eating outside."

"Yeah," Beck says. "It seems pretty nice all the time out here."

The Sterlings nod but say nothing, their expressions uniformly happy in an eerie, unreal kind of way. The same way the weather is perpetually nice but relentless. The same way every new building in Backravel looks like it was made by the same hands, pristinely maintained and undisturbed by the world around it.

"Sit," Riley says, eyes wide in that way that tells Beck she's acting weird.

Wordlessly, Beck moves. She slides into the empty seat, feels the cold cross-hatched metal against her spine, cups her orange juice between both palms and tastes the tang of her own pulse on the back of her tongue. Without looking at Mr. Sterling, she asks, "Are you feeling better today?"

A pause.

"I thought we might eat breakfast before getting into all that," Mr. Sterling says, but he isn't angry. Beck can't figure out *what* he is. There's something antique to the way he speaks, a vintage curl to his vowels. "I'm sorry if I scared you, Rebecca. I'm not . . . *well*, sometimes. It's been quite some time since I've had a slip like that. I'm very sorry you saw it."

Beck closes her eyes. *A slip*, he says, and the word is too specific to be a coincidence. It was her mother's word, and it was the word Beck adopted in her absence. Maybe it's a word Ellery Birsching picked up from Backravel, or maybe it happened the other way around.

Under the table, Riley squeezes Beck's knee.

"It's okay," Beck says. Her pulse hiccups a little because things don't feel *right* here. Too much of this place is familiar, even if she's never been to Backravel before. She's never felt the crunch of red sand under her boots in the morning, but sitting across from the Sterlings, it's like she knows them. "You called it slipping?"

The Sterlings look at each other, then Mr. Sterling clears his throat. "I don't know if I can really explain it. I wouldn't worry about it."

"It can happen after a treatment sometimes," Mrs. Sterling cuts in. She places her hand tenderly over her husband's. "You've probably already heard all about the treatment center. Most people who visit do. I know you girls are probably here for the festival, but if you get a chance to check it out, you can't miss it."

"Maybe," Riley says.

But Beck's eyes turn to Mrs. Sterling and she focuses in like a laser. "What kinds of things do they do at the treatment center? If you don't mind my asking."

"They—" Mrs. Sterling begins.

Mr. Sterling pulls his hand away from his wife. "It's really not for us to say. Ricky takes his work very seriously. I don't think we should risk misrepresenting it."

Ricky. The name appears again, and Beck is hungry for more. Ricky and Avery, Avery and Ricky. There's a vital cast of characters in this town she still needs to meet.

"Who's Ricky?" she asks.

"He's . . ." Mr. Sterling starts, but he trails off, his gaze sliding to the side of the house.

Beck waits for him to finish his sentence, and for a moment, she's sure he's *slipping* again. From somewhere behind her, red rock crunches under sneakers. Beck turns and spots their visitor leaning against the trim of the house with her arms folded over her chest. She's a girl no older than Beck, watching them eat in impatient silence. Her face is half-drenched in the morning light. She squints through the glare, eyes trained on Beck with a vengeance. In an instant, Beck feels exposed. She didn't even realize they had an intruder.

"Morning, Avery," Mr. Sterling says. "What're you up to?"

Avery. It's the other name that's popped up over and over, though Beck doesn't recall seeing it in Ellery's notes. The tour-giver. Whoever Avery is, she's an unknown entity; a girl who apparently knows everything about Backravel, but not enough to become a main player in Ellery's picture of this town. Avery's brown hair is short and unkempt, chaotically bobby-pinned with a single-minded determination to keep it out of her face. She wears a baggy gray T-shirt and jeans that are too loose, belted at her slender waist and frayed at the hems. She pushes herself off the wall and approaches the breakfast table.

"Tour time," Avery says. She gently kicks the leg of Riley's chair. "I already gave this one a tour yesterday, but the other one slithered away, apparently."

"Beck," Mr. Sterling says, eyeing Beck with an unnerving smile. "If you've got questions about Ricky, this is the girl to ask. Isn't that right, Avery?"

"I'd hope so." Avery offers a winning smile. She grips the back of Beck's chair, and Beck isn't sure if this is meant to be intimidating or friendly. Avery looks at her and shakes her head. "He *is* my dad, so I hope I'd be the expert. Were you asking questions?"

Beck swallows. She stares at Avery, maybe for too long. She can't think of the right words to say or even where to start. She gets the creeping sense that she's shown too much of her hand already. She's been angling to learn more about both Avery and Ricky, and now, before she's even had a chance to be sly about it, Mr. Sterling has exposed her. Avery looks at Beck, dark eyes lingering on her face, and Beck is sure she sees a flash of confusion in Avery's eyes. Recognition, maybe. Just like Floyd at the Quick Stop. Recognition she can't quite place, like she's seen a ghost.

"Does she speak?" Avery asks, smiling a little to break up the quiet.

Riley nudges Beck's ankle.

"*Yes,* I speak," Beck finally sputters. She adjusts her glasses and pointedly avoids looking into Avery's eyes. "I'll save my questions, though. I'd rather do the tour first."

"Fine by me. Sounds like you're *really* excited." Avery brushes a bit of red dirt from Beck's shoulder. "Let's get moving, then."

Beck abandons her plate and dashes into the trailer to grab her backpack. Riley follows her inside without a word. She starts clearing space in her backpack, too, and Beck pauses.

"What are you doing?"

"I'll go, too," Riley says. "I can go on the tour again. I don't mind. I feel really bad about leaving you yesterday."

"No." Beck's tone is sharper than she means it to be. She takes a beat, softens. This is for the best, actually. She can't have Riley with her because Riley can't hear the kinds of questions Beck means to ask. If there's a chance Avery can answer some of her big questions,

Beck has to take it. Which means no Riley. "Technically *I* left *you*. And it's okay. I can go alone."

Riley arches a brow. "Oh, really?"

"Believe it or not, I can manage an hour without you," Beck muses.

"What changed?" Riley asks. She adopts a sly grin. "You want alone time with Avery?"

It takes Beck too long to pick up on what Riley's saying. She scoffs and shoulders her backpack. "You're an idiot. I'm not out here in the desert trying to find a weird desert girlfriend. I'm just trying to enjoy my vacation."

"Okay, okay . . ." Riley can't quite stamp out her smile. "Go enjoy your vacation."

A not-small piece of Beck wants to take it back and invite Riley along, even if it would make things more difficult. She doesn't like the thought of leaving Riley alone for another whole day.

Beck tosses a couple things in her backpack—phone, car keys, a crunched-up water bottle from the day before, her wallet—and she steps back out of the trailer. Avery has slipped into one of the chairs at the breakfast table, scooping a spoonful of black beans onto a tortilla. She turns when she hears Beck, and her expression is difficult to parse.

"Okay," Avery says. She takes a vicious bite of breakfast, then discards the rest on Beck's untouched plate. "Let's go."

• • •

Just like the day before, they make their way into Backravel on bikes. As far as morning routines go, Beck doesn't mind this one. The desert air is flat but it runs through Beck on the ride into town, sharp and sweet all at once. What Daniel lacked in conversational skills, Avery more than makes up for, doing her best to fill up every second of dead air. She points out the names of jagged mountains on the horizon and the meanings behind them. She talks at length about the development of houses around Sycamore Lane, hastily built to satisfy the quickly expanding population. She pedals and she talks, and even though Beck listens, she can't quite get a read on her tour guide. She's like a moving object, impossible to see clearly from a single angle. When she speaks, Beck hears the faintest trace of an accent, but not one she can place. They pass the end of Sycamore Lane and Avery motions to the open desert.

"Your sister said you're from Washington," Avery says. "Pretty different from here, right?"

"Yeah," Beck says.

"I've never been to Washington before," Avery says. "It seems like it would be really wet, though. Does it rain a lot there?"

"It does."

Beck doesn't care about the desert or how different it is from Everett. She's not interested in small talk. She's got a burning list of questions and, finally, she's potentially got someone to answer them. They pedal farther along the highway and Beck watches the wastes for any sign of the campsite she saw the day before. For any signs of the mysterious object her mother sought out here in the empty land that stretches on forever.

"Is there anything to do out here?" Beck asks, coyly trying to dance around her real question. "Any attractions?"

"In the desert?" Avery asks.

"Yeah."

"Does it look like there's any attractions?" Avery laughs. "No. All the stuff to *do* is in town. Out here is just . . . nothing."

"No one lives out here?"

Avery pedals along in silence for a moment. She glances over her shoulder with a brow raised. "Is there something specific you're looking for?"

"I saw someone out here yesterday," Beck says. "That's all."

"Huh," Avery says. She watches the desert, palm cupped at her brow to block out the sun. "That's weird."

After that, she falls quiet. Every few minutes, Avery turns like she's scanning the desert for strangers, but the wastes are empty. Whether or not she knows what Beck is talking about, the thought of someone existing out here in the scorching void seems to put an end to Avery's talkative mood. Craggy red rocks pile up as far as the eye can see, punctuated with scratches of desert brush and cacti. The sky is stale blue with heat. Even in the morning, the sun beats down on this stretch of desert and it seems impossible that someone could survive out here on their own.

When they reach the first buildings of Backravel proper, the tour begins. To Beck's surprise, it's an actual *tour* tour. Once they pass the Backravel welcome sign, Avery straightens like she's doing her best impression of a college campus guide. They bike along the main strip of town, just like the day before, and Avery points to each identical building, explaining its purpose. Here, a bank. There, a café. The park sits between two buildings, perfectly groomed and entirely empty, and Avery explains that it was created when the first family with children moved to Backravel. On every block, a rusting hub of military infrastructure lies untouched, and Avery says nothing about it. She has a paragraph prepared for every other object in town, but it's like she has a blind spot for the ruins. Like she doesn't see them at all.

"Do you know anything about all this military stuff?" Beck tries.

Avery shrugs. "It was here when we got here."

Beck stiffens, locking in on *we*.

"You make it sound like you were here when the town was founded," she says. Silently, she tries to crunch the numbers. Even if Backravel was founded just before Ellery began visiting, Avery couldn't have been more than a small child. It's not impossible, but it feels like it is.

"I was," Avery says. Her voice is a little different now. Hesitant, like she's been caught in a lie. Beck watches the careful furrowing of her brow. "I don't remember a lot about it, but I do remember all this junk being here when we arrived. We built the rest ourselves."

She says *we* again. Questions run a mile a minute in Beck's head. She needs to know more about Backravel's origins, who was here at the start, how they built this all from nothing. She's sure they're all questions Ellery already asked. But she has other questions, too. Delia Horton, the object in the desert, the *slipping*. Beck opens her mouth, but Avery holds up a hand to quiet her.

"I see that look," Avery says with a cruel half-smile. "And questions come at the end of the tour."

She says it like she's joking, but Beck knows she isn't. Every second she spends with Avery is odder than the last, and even though *all* of Backravel has been odd, Avery is her own brand. She doesn't like questions, but she likes talking. She's thorny, but she's not completely closed off. She doesn't dress like she's particularly concerned with how she looks, but she wants to control everybody's perception of this town. Maybe Beck started this tour primed to find a conspiracy.

Or maybe, whatever her deal is, Avery is covering something up.

They continue the tour, circling the rest of Backravel's main roads until they wind their way to the center of town. They stop in front of a squat building that looks like a fancy gym she might see back home. A wood sign reads BACKRAVEL MUNICIPAL HALL in thin black letters. Avery stops in front of it, gesturing broadly to the building.

"As you can see, this is the municipal hall," Avery says. "Backravel doesn't really have a *government* government, but this is where people meet and talk about what's going on."

"What do you mean?"

Avery arches a brow. "I don't know. People meet here to talk about laws. Event planning. I don't know."

Beck nods. "Do they meet a lot?"

"Not really," Avery says. "Honestly, it's pretty quiet here. The main reason they've been meeting recently is to talk about Backravel Days. Nothing that exciting."

Backravel Days. A flyer for the festival was included in the envelope from her mother. When convincing Riley to come on this trip, Beck mentioned the festival, attempting to spin it into a fun feature of their vacation. The flyer boasted a thriving farmer's market and a spectacle. It burns in her backpack, reminding her of how many lies this trip is built on. The festival has to be more than it seems, though, just like everything else in Backravel. There has to be a reason Ellery's letter included it. Beck clears her throat and tries not to sound too desperate when she says, "What happens at Backravel Days?"

"It's this annual festival we do. We shut down Main Street and everyone brings food and crafts. It's like a big party." Avery wipes away a streak of sweat from the back of her neck and rustles her unruly mop of hair. "Were you and your sister planning to go, or are you gonna be in Texas by then?"

Beck narrows her eyes. She doesn't know why it stings that

Avery knows where they're going next. There's technically nothing wrong with Riley telling people their plans, but there's a part of Beck that wants to decide what parts of her Avery and the rest of Backravel get to see. She wants to pick which parts of her are in the light. She swallows and looks away, out at the hazy horizon. "Yeah. We're going."

If this bothers Avery, she doesn't show it. She pushes her bike upright and pops her neck. "Honestly, I like the festival. It's something different. Days here can kind of run together after a while."

Something about this sounds off to Beck, though she can't put a finger on why.

"We can keep going," Avery says. "The only things in there are the conference rooms and the library."

"There's a library?" Beck asks.

Avery nods. "No detours, though. You can check it out later if you really want. I don't think *I* would go to the library on vacation, but it's up to you."

Beck laughs, surprising herself. Even as they pull away, her gaze is fixed on the municipal building. Avery might've brushed it off, but a room of books on town history is *exactly* where she needs to spend this vacation if she plans to fill in any blanks. She's sure it's where her mother started when she first arrived in Backravel. She wonders if Ellery Birsching took this same tour once, before she became a living collection of Backravel's secrets.

The rest of Backravel is unremarkable. It's even smaller than Beck realized the day before, only a few blocks and then a smattering of houses as it peters out into residential roads. When they circle back to the park in the center of town, Avery stops her bike and gestures to the steepest of the rugged plateaus. It's the same as yesterday, shrub-freckled and bald, flat in the shallow, hot light. A copper haze sits low on the horizon, obscuring most of the rugged cliffs and hills in the distance. Spiderlike plants with leaves like rubber tilt quietly in the breeze. The street is empty now—even emptier than it was yesterday. A chill skitters over Beck's arms, even though she's wearing long sleeves, even in the heat. She takes in the glittering windows and bright red rocks that line the street. That feeling blossoms again in the pit of her stomach. There's something wrong here; it's too empty, too clean, too alive and dead all at once.

"That's about it," Avery says, and Beck doesn't miss the relief in her voice. "Welcome back to Backravel Access Road. You have accessed Backravel. Any questions?"

"Millions." Beck laughs. She unearths her notebook from her backpack and flips it open to her bulleted list of questions, but they don't even scratch the surface. Now, on top of everything else she planned to ask, she wants to know about treatments, about the town's foundation, about the festival. She scratches her forehead. "I don't even know where to start."

Avery's eyes narrow. "Did you bring . . . notes?"

"Why wouldn't I?"

"Because that's weird."

"I have been told numerous times to save questions for this tour," Beck muses. "I've been saving them."

Avery scoffs. "Lucky me."

Beck shakes her head. "Okay, let me start with something basic. The treatment center. What are the treatments, and who gets them?"

"Why are you wearing a jacket?"

"What?" Beck blinks. If the comment is an attempt to derail the conversation, it's a jarring one. Slowly, Beck strips away her jacket and ties it around her waist, letting the desert breeze cool the sweat on her bare arms.

Apparently satisfied, Avery clears her throat.

"That's not basic," Avery says. "It's really hard to explain."

"Can you try?"

"It's a special kind of trauma-focused healing treatment, I guess. For people who are looking to recover from something bad that happened to them."

Beck arches a brow. It's the vaguest answer possible, but it's something. It means that Mr. Sterling is in recovery from something. She thinks back to yesterday at the Quick Stop, to Floyd behind the counter, beads of sweat collected at his brow. He said *everyone* gets treatment. Beck chews the inside of her cheek.

"Do you mean like physical trauma?" Beck asks. "Or like . . . emotional."

Avery shrugs. "Depends."

"Is the treatment center . . . part of the tour?"

"No. The tour is over."

This catches Beck off guard. She blinks and says, "Wait, really?"

"Really." Avery points to her notebook and says, "What are the other questions?"

For a moment, Beck is quiet. She considers pushing back, but she has a million more questions and it's clear Avery's willingness to answer is already wearing thin. Panic swells in her chest. She can't be running out of time already. Beck scans the page of her notebook and taps her pencil next to *Ricky*.

"You said Ricky is your dad," Beck says, mustering up her best journalistic voice. "Can you tell me about him?"

"Different question."

Beck waits for a *just kidding*, but it doesn't come. Avery's curls of deep brown hair flit at her ears in the light wind. She motions to the notebook again, impatient, and Beck realizes she isn't joking. She means to do this rapid fire. Beck pulls her notebook to her chest and stares into Avery's face for a long time before she finds her words. "You're just not going to answer?"

"You're not having any treatments done, so I don't see why you'd need to know anything about the center or my dad."

"How do you know I'm not here for treatment?" Beck asks.

Avery laughs.

"I'm serious."

"Because I was told you were here on vacation." Avery folds her arms over her chest. "Are you here for treatment, or are you here to get a tan, go to a festival, and leave?"

Beck tightens her grip on the handlebars of her bike. Her heart thuds, heavy with embarrassment. The rest of her questions burn, but it's useless to ask now. Avery already knows something's off about this, the same way Beck knows there's something off about Avery. They stand opposite each other in the quiet, waiting for someone to give.

"I don't know you," Avery says finally, looking up at the treatment center instead of Beck. "And I'm sorry if I seem harsh. But if you really did come to Backravel for a nice vacation, I suggest you cross the investigation stuff off your list. Find something else to explore for two weeks."

"Do you just give these tours so you can shut down questions?" Beck snaps.

"No." Avery smiles, a little crooked. "I give tours because I love my town."

Beck grimaces and Avery stares at her, stance casual like she could do this all day. Back home, Beck did whatever she needed to avoid conflict. She didn't talk back in class, didn't start fights online, hardly even pushed back when Riley shouted at her over rides home

from school. But this is her only shot to put the missing pieces together, and for once, she can't back off. She's too desperate and she's
running out of time.

"I don't want to be annoying, there's just so many things I
wanted to learn about Backravel. If I could just talk to your dad for
an hour, I'd—"

"So that's the end of the tour, then," Avery cuts in. She makes a
sweeping gesture to all of the restaurants and business along Main
Street. "I hope you enjoy your vacation."

"Avery."

Avery doesn't move. She's stubborn in a way Beck hasn't seen
in a long time, worse than Riley by miles. Stubborn in a way that
has Beck's eyes twitching in irritation. Beck looks up at the treatment center and sighs. She might be able to get somewhere later,
but she's not learning anything else today. It's clear now that Avery
never meant to answer her questions. This tour is meant to placate,
nothing more.

"I'm sorry," Beck says. "I won't ask about your dad anymore."

"Thank you," Avery says. "Did you want to grab something to
eat? The sandwich place on First is really good."

"I'm okay."

"You didn't eat breakfast, though."

There's something slightly disarming about Avery ignoring
Beck's questions in favor of noticing little things about *her*; unnec-
essary jackets in the heat and skipped breakfasts. She's watching
Beck as intently as Beck watches her, and it makes Beck's skin crawl.
She glances down the empty highway, toward Riley and Sycamore
Lane, then back at Avery. She didn't recount her leftover cash this
morning, but she doesn't have the money to be spending on lunches

out with strangers. And she doesn't have the patience to spend more time with Avery.

"I'm really okay."

"Was I *that* mean?" Avery muses.

"I need to get back to Riley," Beck says, though by now, Riley is probably curled up on the Sterlings' couch watching TV with them like she's part of the family. Beck runs a hand through her hair, pulling apart the matted tangles from days on the road. "She's too young to be left alone all day."

"You left her alone yesterday."

Beck chews the inside of her cheek. The heat is flat, hotter every minute they stay outside.

"I'm gonna go," Beck says, this time more resolute. "Thanks for the tour."

Avery's smile fades. She's disappointed, but she swings her leg back over her bike in silence. "Anytime. Tell your sister I said hi."

Without another word, Avery kicks off and pedals farther into the heart of Backravel before rounding a corner and vanishing from sight. Beck is left in the quiet, stomach growling and chest tight with a mix of hunger and frustration because everything she's looking for is *here*, but it's just out of reach. She tries to picture Ellery Birsching walking these streets, buying a pack of cigarettes and a sandwich down the road, sketching military ruins and planning her greatest story of all time.

Beck mounts her bike and rides back toward Sycamore Lane. One way or another—probably without Avery's help—she'll find the answers, too.

8

When Beck makes it back to the trailer, the sun is flat overhead, shearing the shadows of the houses on Sycamore Lane stubby and short. She leans her bike against the trailer, head watery like she's just stepped out of a dream. She lingers a little too long in the doorway, one foot in the trailer and one on the stairs. There's something about Backravel that makes even the people feel impermanent. A pinprick of fear takes root in Beck, makes her wonder if letting Avery go was a bad idea, makes her wonder if she'll get a chance to ask her questions again. Not that she would answer them.

Beck licks the dust from her lips and tries to swallow her nausea.

Inside the trailer, Riley is lying on the floor. Her hip is flat against a tiny vent, tank top hiked up over the bottom of her rib cage. A gush of cool air bounces Riley's hair against her cheek. She stares at the ceiling, but her eyes are miles away, dreamily fixed on something Beck can't see.

"What're you doing?" Beck asks.

Riley closes her eyes. "I just FaceTime'd Gabby."

"Oh, so you're not being a *total* loner."

"Nope," Riley says, and there's a pinch of mischief to her smile. "I'm not you."

"Extremely rude."

Beck closes the trailer door behind her and tosses her backpack on the floor. She rummages through the kitchen cabinets for a water glass. Outside, the Sterlings' back door opens and shuts. The trailer hums and the breeze hisses and, beyond that, the world is unsettlingly quiet.

"I can't even do a real impression of you," Riley whines. "I don't have anything to smoke."

Beck scoffs and strides swiftly to kick Riley in the armpit. Riley scrambles from the floor and pushes herself to her feet, backing into the bathroom door to avoid another attack. The trailer rocks a little with the momentum and Beck stiffens. Wisps of hair frizz at Riley's ears, just like Ellery's used to. She's opted out of wearing makeup today, and her bare face looks like their mother's, just fuller and with a more youthful glow. Beck touches her own cheek, tries not to think about how absolutely ragged she looks in the mirror every morning, with or without makeup. Always clammy, always tired, always near-skeletal. If Riley looks like Ellery in the golden, summery photos of her youth, Beck looks like her at the end of her life, pale and lifeless.

"Did you have fun today?" Riley asks finally, brushing crumbs from the backs of her legs. "While you were ditching me?"

"Do you think I had fun?"

"I don't know," Riley says coyly. "Maybe you're a good match."

"I had *so* much fun," Beck says. "Avery is the nicest person I've ever met. In fact, we're best friends now. We actually ended the tour early so we could start working on our friendship bracelets."

"Stop."

"I decided I'm going to finish the trip to Texas with Avery, instead. Anything to spend more time together. Do you think she'll get along with Dad?" Despite her best efforts, Beck smiles a little at the idea that she'd do anything willingly with her prickly, elusive tour guide. "Since she's coming with me, you'll have to stay behind and be the new tour guide."

"Okay, but joke's on them, I'm just gonna spend all my time eating Froyo," Riley says. "Tours are gonna be, like, three minutes."

Beck laughs at that, and Riley laughs, too. For a second, it's like the last few months crumble away and they can laugh like they did before their world turned upside down. Beck missed the sound of Riley's laugh, light and airy. She makes her way to the fridge and shuffles through the scraps of cooler food they hauled from Washington. Two more Lunchables, a couple boxes of frozen macaroni and cheese, a box of frozen corn dogs that won't fit in the trailer freezer, so they've been doomed to slowly thaw in the fridge. Three red Gatorades, which is Riley's favorite. A pack of jerky sits on the kitchen counter, unopened. Beck tears away the top with her teeth and extracts a particularly tough piece of meat.

"We should talk, though," Riley says. She waits for Beck to slide into the seat across from her and snags a piece of jerky for herself. "If I say something, do you promise not to get mad?"

"Depends on what you say," Beck says with a mouthful of jerky.

"I *hate* it here."

Beck stops chewing. "What?"

"I hate it so much." Riley's leg vibrates under the table. "It's so creepy. I don't know if I can do two whole weeks."

"Really?" Beck asks. It's not that she disagrees, but hearing it so plainly catches her off guard. In the last two days, she's thought a thousand things about Backravel. It's confusing, unconventional, unsettling, both too cheery and too dead all at once. It's full to the brim with secrets that keep Beck up at night, staring at the trailer ceiling, wishing she could see the whole picture. But she doesn't *hate* it. In fact, every moment she spends here feels more magnetic than the last, fills her with a hunger like she's never known. She scratches the back of her head. "What's creepy about it?"

"You don't think it's weird?" Riley asks.

"I mean, a little," Beck admits. "But why do *you* think it's weird?"

Riley puts her palms flat on the table like she's about to deliver a speech. "Think about it. It's super quiet everywhere. Like, there are a ton of houses, but I never see any people. And we're hours from any other towns. Everyone acts like a robot. I don't know. It's weird."

She's not wrong; it *is* weird, but not in a way Beck is afraid of. Maybe it's because she's spent more time in Ellery's notes than Riley has, but Beck expected this flavor of strangeness. She cleans her glasses with the hem of her shirt again, mulling it over. "Yeah, I can see that. But it's two weeks, the festival, and then we can go. Do you think you can hold on that long?"

Riley considers. "Are other people going to this festival? I haven't seen a single tourist except us."

"I haven't, either."

"I just get bad vibes," Riley says. She sighs and dons a tired smile. "But if you're sure you wanna go, I can stick it out."

Beck isn't sure what *vibes* she gets from Backravel. Mostly, she feels the wordless tug of the unexplored. When she first arrived in Backravel, there was a piece of her that thought Ellery's story would unfurl for her the moment she parked the car. She hoped Backravel would welcome her with open arms, let her pick up where her mother left off. But what she got is the opposite, and somehow, it's even more compelling. She wants to dig deeper, to know more, to see the world Ellery saw after her fifth, tenth, twentieth visit.

"Two more weeks," Beck says. "I'd say we could leave sooner, but if we show up in Texas early, Dad will—"

"I know." Riley sighs. "He'd know we lied."

Riley idly chews on another piece of jerky and stares out the trailer window at the horizon. Beck settles on the kitchen floor, back against the cabinets, and lets out a long exhale. She shuffles through the back pocket of her worn jeans and digs out her phone. Sunlight catches in the screen, flashing a light in Riley's face. She shields her eyes and makes an exaggerated hissing sound.

"Bad news," Beck says. "We need to call Dad."

Riley lobs a sharp glare at Beck. "Now?"

"While we remember."

Riley scowls. Though Riley's relationship with Ellery was rocky growing up, her relationship with their father wasn't great after the divorce, either. After the divorce, they only saw him in spurts. In visitations to his house in Idaho, then in Massachusetts, and now in Texas. Beck remembers the whispered fights at the end of each visit. Riley begging him to let her stay and him staunchly refusing. *Your mother needs you,* he'd say each time, no matter how desperately Riley pleaded. And on the plane ride home, Riley would throw a tantrum about how unfair it was that he'd make her raise her own parent. That he wouldn't *rescue* her.

Beck stands and takes a seat at the table again. The fact is that, as much as she doesn't want to keep lying to their father, they have to keep him updated or he'll get suspicious. And if he gets suspicious, he'll call Gabby's family. And once he calls Gabby's family, it's over.

It can't be over. Not yet.

"Fine, if you do all the talking."

"Why?"

"Because I hate lying."

"Then don't lie." Beck traces the outline of a coffee stain on the kitchen table. "Just tell half the truth. Tell him it's hot out and you found a cute Froyo place. Keep it simple."

"That's still lying," Riley says flatly.

Beck dials their father's number but pauses before calling. Quietly, she says, "We just went to the pool. We can only talk for a minute because we need to dry off before dinner. Gabby's grandma is making, uh . . . Italian. Okay?"

Riley shakes her head. "You're evil."

Beck smiles. With that, she calls. This time, the phone rings for almost a full minute before the line clicks. A pause, a breath, and then their father's voice booms on the other end of the line. *"Look who it is,"* he says. *"Having so much fun you almost forgot about Dad?"*

"No," Riley blurts out. "We were at the pool."

"Oh! Very cool," their father says. He's distracted, probably fixing dinner for him and Julie. Beck remembers the way the scent of his chicken noodle soup drenched the walls of the Everett house even now, years after he left. In the background, the TV drones on. Beck's never been to the house in Texas, but she can picture it perfectly: her father at a glossy kitchen island tossing fresh, hefty vegetables in a pot. Julie on their big leather sectional, knees to her chest, eyes glued to the TV screen. She imagines their two Yorkies nipping at each other all through the halls. It sounds wonderful for someone, but Beck can't picture it for herself.

She wonders briefly if Riley sees herself in that world.

"What're you guys watching?" Beck asks.

"Good question. Babe, which one is this?" A pause, then, *"Okay, this is the one where they get married without seeing each other."*

"Oh, we still need to watch that one," Beck says. "Gabby's TV has, like, five hundred channels. I'm sure we can find it."

"*Or,*" their father says. "*You can wait and Julie will rewatch with you. She watches all of them at least a dozen times. To be honest, I think the main reason she's looking forward to you girls moving in is so she has someone to watch* Love Island *with.*"

"It sounds great," Beck muses. "We can't wait."

"*Please. I need someone to distract her. At this point, I can quote the* Bachelorette *finale word for word.*"

"That's crazy," Beck says. "You should enter a talent show."

At that, their father chuckles. There's a thin scraping sound as he moves whatever he's cooking to a plate. He sniffs, then says, "*What do you think, babe? Should I do my Jessica impression for a talent show?*"

"*Oh, for sure.*" Julie's voice is far away, but the glimmer of laughter in her voice rings through the phone.

Beck looks up for a moment and catches the hint of a smile on Riley's lips. A strange expression for someone who adamantly didn't want to call. For someone who groans with frustration at the mention of their father. She stifles it quickly and takes a breath.

"We gotta get back soon," Riley says, too stiff. "We're having, uh . . ."

"Lasagna," Beck cuts in. "Gabby's grandma's favorite."

"*Sounds great,*" their father says. "*Me and Julie are having chicken cordon bleu. Neither of you is vegetarian, right? I know they make fake chicken, but not in my house.*"

They say their goodbyes and end the call, but even after the phone goes black and the trailer settles into an aching quiet, there's a buzzing restlessness in Beck's bones. She hasn't figured out enough of this yet. Day three, and she doesn't know anything more than she did before.

She glances out the window at the flat stretch of desert and it's like there's something whispering to her, pulling her toward the band of red rock around the valley. *Don't sleep yet,* the night breathes to her. *Come outside. Come see.* She thinks of the figure in the desert, standing in a wind-worn campsite. Her pulse stutters a little. There's still so much that doesn't add up. She needs to move faster.

"Game plan for tomorrow," Beck says, pulling herself back to reality. "I kind of want to go see the library? Avery showed it to me and said there isn't much inside, but I'm curious."

"The library?" Riley asks, shocked.

"I know it's weird."

"Should we both go?"

Beck hesitates. "If you want. I feel like you could find something more fun, though."

"You know, I don't know if I *love* being an unsupervised minor," Riley says. "You're not a great babysitter."

"I know, I know . . ." Beck trails off.

Riley stares at her, a glint of skepticism dancing across her eyes. She doesn't buy it, and Beck can't blame her. In truth, Beck didn't plan for distracting Riley their whole vacation. She didn't account for all the days she'd need to hide the research from Riley's view. Now, it's their third day in Backravel and it's the third time she's suggesting they go separate ways. She won't be able to keep this up the whole two weeks.

"Is everything okay?" Riley asks. "You seem kind of off."

"I'm fine," Beck says, maybe too quickly. "I think I just find it very . . . *interesting* here. I want to know more."

For a long moment, Riley is silent. Then she whispers, "Like mom?"

"No. Not like that." Beck swallows hard. Her chest feels tight, making it hard to suck in a breath. "I'm just curious. That's all. I mean, aren't you?"

Riley considers. There's a sag to her expression now as sleep catches up with her. But she's worried, too, and Beck's face feels hot. She doesn't have time for Riley to worry about her, doesn't have time to stave off Riley's concerns.

"I'm not, really," Riley says. "But I get it. I don't see it like you. All I can think about is how it went for Mom. It just makes me sad."

"I know."

For a while, they say nothing, facing each other from opposite sides of the trailer. Finally, Riley sighs and moves from the booth with a yawn.

"I promise," Beck says, "just a little more poking around and then we'll focus on vacation. And the festival."

"And Texas, right?"

Beck nods solemnly. "And Texas."

They settle into bed for the night, Beck in the loft bed and Riley in the kitchen booth. Nights in Backravel feel just as lonely as nights back home. While Riley goes through her multistep night routine, Beck finds herself lingering in the empty, quiet spaces of the trailer. It's the same way she lingered back in Washington, stuck like a ghost in the stillness. Sometimes, she likes it here in the in-between, cool shadows netting the halls, drinking in the muted sounds of cars outside. Usually, though, this is when it gets bad. When she's left with only the swirling mess of her own thoughts. In the quiet hours, the only thing to do is listen to the world outside and try to suffocate the thoughts of how much she's missed, how easy it would be to slide away completely.

Now, Beck listens to the sounds of the Sterlings' shoes chafing against the back patio, the screech of closing windows, the quiet murmur of the wind. But even if she focuses on the sounds, she can't quite snuff out the churning in her brain. It's like, in Backravel, there are two realities laid out before her: one where she continues to pull at this thread of oddness to find the truth, and another where she packs up like Riley says and leaves it all alone. She wonders if Ellery laid in this bed and thought the same thing. She doesn't need to wonder what her mother chose, though; Ellery Birsching wanted the truth, always and completely, no matter what it cost.

When the sun sinks low and shadows fill up the trailer, Beck rolls to her side and stares out the little round window at the stars like dewdrops, just within view, until she fades away.

9

The Backravel Municipal Building is less intimidating in the morning. In fact, the only frightening thing about the morning is the quiet. Even with the sun high overhead and various businesses peppered along Main Street opening their doors, Backravel's sidewalks are empty. Beck waits for someone, *anyone,* to acknowledge her perched on her bike by herself. But the handful of people meandering downtown pay her no mind. They idle like drones, determinedly minding their own business. An elderly couple walks into the diner hand in hand. A young woman walks quickly down the sidewalk with a pastel-pink sweatband and matching weights strapped to her ankles. Every other storefront is empty, and the only sound is the wind and that same mechanical hum Beck heard on her first day. She shakes it off and glides to the municipal hall's front doors.

Today isn't for people watching. It's for research.

Cool air rushes to meet Beck as she steps into the municipal hall, sending goose bumps up the length of her arms. There's a squat reception desk and three hallways ahead of her, each one clinical and indistinguishable from the others. Beck stares at the hallways for a long while before a small voice pipes up from the desk.

"Need some help?"

A woman sits at the desk, so petite she's almost invisible behind the countertop. Her dark hair is twisted into a delicate beehive, with horn-rimmed glasses sitting on the bridge of her nose. She smiles at Beck, motioning her over.

"I'm sorry," Beck stammers. "I've never been here before."

"I thought so," the woman muses. "You're new to town?"

"Yeah."

Beck glances at the nameplate on the desk. NANCY DEARBORN, RECEPTION. Nancy's eyes are pale green and flecked with brown, perfectly manicured brows arched in amused suspicion. No, not suspicion: *curiosity*. She smiles and her teeth are white as pearls. "Are you staying?"

Beck blinks. The question is odd, like a translation of a normal question with a word just slightly out of place. "Just a few weeks. For vacation."

"Oh. That's nice." Nancy's posture stiffens, but her smile is even broader than before. "I hope you enjoy your time here. Can I help you find something?"

"Right." Beck adjusts her glasses. "Avery . . . I don't actually know her last name. But Avery told me there was a library here?"

Nancy nods. Wordlessly, she rises from her desk and smiles. Beck's gaze catches on the surface of her desk, which is unnervingly clean. No stacks of paper, no loose paper clips, no stray sticky notes. No phone or computer, either. Her office supplies are all in their assigned places, though they look completely unused. It's just like the lawns and sidewalks throughout the rest of Backravel. Too neat to be real, like the whole thing is staged.

Beck follows Nancy down the rightmost hallway. The door to the library is only a few steps down the hall, though *library* is a generous word for the room they step into. It's a single room with five whole bookshelves pressed against the far wall. A table takes up the center of the room, and an old device rests in the corner collecting dust. It's the first imperfect thing Beck has seen since stepping inside.

Beck nods. She gestures to the device in the corner. "What's that for?"

"Oh, for the microfiche."

"The what?"

Nancy chuckles. "How old are you?"

Beck narrows her eyes. She adjusts her backpack straps. "Seventeen. Why?"

"Microfiche. That's how us senior citizens used to read the news. We have a couple older articles here, mostly from Ricky's collection. He's quite the history buff. But I doubt you'd find them very interesting."

Beck nods. "Would those articles say anything about Backravel's history specifically?"

"Maybe. Honestly, I don't touch them. I don't like to read much." Nancy swipes a stray bit of her hair behind her ear and something shifts in her expression. "You're sure you've never been here before?"

It's becoming a pattern, this moment of odd recognition. Something about it makes her skin crawl. It can't be a coincidence that so many people in Backravel are sure they've seen her before. Softly, Beck says, "I haven't."

"I'm having the strangest déjà vu." Nancy chuckles. "Like I've taken you to this room before, but a long time ago."

For the first time, it occurs to Beck that the people of Backravel might not be recognizing her, but her similarities to her mother. An ache pangs deep in Beck's chest, and she wants to press for more information, wants to ask if Nancy remembers what this echoed memory of her was like, what she looked for, but she can't speak. She bites the inside of her lip until she tastes the tang of iron on her tongue.

"I'll leave you to it," Nancy says. "I'll be out front if you need me. We just ask that you put anything you touch back where you found it."

"Of course."

With that, Nancy steps out of the library and closes the door. In the quiet, Beck gets to work. Most shelves are stocked with works of classic fiction: *The Catcher in the Rye, 1984, The Great Gatsby.* None of the fiction books were published later than the 1980s, if she's remembering her English classes right. Which is a gamble, since she's spent about 15 percent of her time in class these last few years actually listening. There are a few works of nonfiction, memoirs, and textbooks all gathered on a lonely corner shelf collecting dust. She scans through the spines, but there's nothing about Backravel itself. Nothing that can offer any new information on this town. There isn't a history book in sight.

Maybe it was optimistic to think she'd find useful information here. After all, Ellery was in Backravel dozens of times and probably combed each page in this library already. Anything useful is likely already buried in the chaos of her notes. Beck brushes the spine of a memoir and wonders if her mother ever did the same.

She pulls her hand away.

Next to the microfiche reader is a beige file cabinet with haphazard labels for each drawer. Some list a year, some a location, others just read things like SCIENCE. Beck tentatively approaches the cabinet and pulls open a drawer labeled 1955. Dozens of manila folders are crammed together with bits of paper peeking out from the tops. Beck runs a finger over the files and lands on one without a label. Inside, a roll of film is wrapped around a hunk of blue plastic.

Beck glances at the reader, then at the film again. No doubt one attaches to the other somehow, but that's easier said than done. She flips the roll in her hand and grimaces.

The door to the library opens suddenly and Beck tosses the film roll back into the file cabinet. It's Avery that steps into the room, looking around quickly like she expects to find it empty. Her eyes lock on Beck, though, and she flashes a knowing smile. A *menacing* smile. She closes the door behind her and folds her arms over her chest. Just like yesterday, she wears an overlarge T-shirt and jeans that she swims in. It's impossible to tell the shape of her.

"Hi," Beck says, though she's not sure if she should sound friendly or not. Something about the air in the room tells her she's in trouble. Avery's expression isn't happy or angry—it's just curious. Like a child who's just set a small fire, waiting to see if it'll burn.

"Finding anything interesting?" Avery asks.

Beck narrows her eyes. "Not particularly."

"Nancy called me. Said you might need some help," Avery clarifies.

Her smile broadens like she's just told a joke, but Beck's not sure what the punchline is. This means that Nancy snitched on her, then. Which either means that Beck looked more lost than she thought, or there's something here she isn't supposed to find. Beck shrugs off the small flutter of satisfaction she gets from the latter—she's on the right track.

"I've used libraries before," Beck muses. "I can probably figure this one out by myself."

Avery slides into one of the rigid chairs at the head of the library table and rests her elbows on the surface, chin smugly settled in her palms. There's a crookedness to her smile that looks almost cartoonish. She's the winner of a fight Beck wasn't aware she was part of. Avery blinks coyly, then says, "By all means, read away. I'm here if you need me."

"You don't have better things to do?"

"Not really."

"What were you doing before you got here?"

"Sitting in my room," Avery says. Then, with mischief in her eyes, she adds, "Thinking about how to make your day harder."

"Ha." Beck taps the corner of the microfiche reader. "Well, you keep brainstorming. I have reading to do."

"What are you trying to read? Maybe I can give you suggestions."

Beck shrugs. She's not giving Avery any more information than she needs to, especially when it's clear that Avery's sole purpose here is to watch her. "I don't know yet. We'll see."

Avery says nothing to that. Beck turns out of her line of sight. She digs back into the file cabinet full of film rolls, leafing through the manila folders she abandoned when Avery arrived. She wishes she looked like she knew what she was doing, but these labels mean nothing to her. Without even a draft of Ellery's story, it's impossible to say what exactly she found in this library, if anything. She's got Delia Horton, a woman who frequented Backravel for several years. She's got some mysterious object in the desert. She's got Ricky, the man behind the proverbial curtain making Backravel function. But she doesn't have anything connecting it all. There must be some kind of core to this mystery—a heart pumping blood to it all.

Beck lands on a file labeled INSTALLMENT BLUEPRINTS and

plucks the roll of film to freedom. Behind her, there's a slight squeak—Avery shifting in her chair to get a better look, probably.

She eyes the microfiche reader and tenses. It can't be *that* difficult to use. She pulls a bit of film from the roll and opens the lid of the reader, releasing a puff of dust in its wake. She expects the machine to operate something like the ancient overhead projectors from school back home, but she can't seem to make it click. Behind her, Avery laughs.

"What?"

"Nothing," Avery muses. "You keep doing what you're doing. I'm sure it'll work eventually."

Beck turns on Avery and narrows her eyes. Avery is leaned back so far in her chair it could topple to the floor any second. She has one brow curiously quirked, arms folded behind her head so that her T-shirt bunches up at her waist. Beck's eyes find the length of her neck, fix there a moment too long, and she looks away. A rush of embarrassment crashes through her and she rolls the film back up. Sputtering, she says, "Do *you* know how to use this thing?"

"You've never used one?" Avery asks.

"No."

"What kind of school did you go to?"

"A *nice* one," Beck scoffs. "Where we had stuff that wasn't a hundred years old."

"What's that supposed to mean?" Avery asks.

Beck shakes her head. Before she can say anything else, Avery's chair squeals again. She makes her way around the table and stands at the other side of the microfiche reader. She's shorter than Beck realized when she isn't on her bike. This close, Beck has to tilt her chin down just slightly to catch the dark weight of Avery's gaze. Avery holds out her hand.

"Watch me."

"I can do it," Beck says, and she's not sure why she feels so humiliated. Her grip on the film tightens. "Just show me how."

"Okay. Unroll it a little. You had that right."

Beck unrolls the film slightly. Scratches of what she's sure is a long article are just visible in the sheen of the film under the fluorescent lights. Avery pulls up a small compartment on the side of the machine, revealing a compact paper-reader underneath. Wordlessly, she reaches out and takes Beck's hand, guiding it to the reader.

Beck's breath catches, but she doesn't pull away.

"You push this through here, picture-side-up." Avery presses Beck's hand closer to the reader until the inner mechanics catch the film and hold it in place. "Push it a little farther. Just to give it some space."

Beck does.

Avery lets her go and Beck snatches her hand back, too quickly. It's not fear or irritation that hounds her now; she doesn't know *what* it is. Avery shoots her a confused glance, then focuses back on the reader. She presses a small red button at the back corner of the machine and it flickers to life. The screen in front of them lights up on a small corner of text. She motions to the knob on the side of the machine, twisting it once so that the text on the screen nudges slightly. "That's how you adjust it. Think you're good to use it yourself?"

"If you'll let me."

Avery scoffs and rolls her eyes.

Beck takes the knob, but Avery doesn't go back to her seat. She watches the screen, too. Beck swallows, tries to focus on the film and not on Avery's hovering, the warmth of another body only inches from her. She's not usually this irritable with people, but there's something about Avery that makes her want to fight back. This condescending sureness that she's always a step ahead. That she's successfully left Beck in the dark.

Beck twists until the words slide into place, tiny and impossible to read. A bit of text catches her eye immediately: . . . *land was developed for research purposes only.*

"This is what you were looking for?" Avery asks, confused.

"I don't know," Beck says. She adjusts her glasses and leans closer to the screen, away from Avery. She scrolls the reader down, skipping over blocks of murky text. Finally, a diagram comes into focus. Scratchy lines form a rough map and Beck can just make out a couple of the buildings: *Mess Hall, Excavation Site, Laboratory.* Beck glances away from the screen and closes her eyes, trying to picture the shape of Backravel. It *looks* like it might match the ruins interspersed around town, but without a side-by-side, there's no way to be sure.

"Do you know where I can find a full map of town?" Beck asks.

"Why?"

Beck shrugs. "Because I want to see it?"

Avery scratches her head. "I'm sure there is one somewhere in here. I don't know, though. There's a big one in my dad's office back home."

"The one I'm not allowed to see, right?"

"That's the one," Avery says slyly.

Beck shakes her head and focuses on the reader again. It's the way Avery says things like she *knows* she's the one barrier between Beck and the truth. Like she enjoys it. She wonders if Avery feels powerful when she sees Beck scrambling like this. There has to be a non-Avery way to get some information in this town, she thinks. There has to be someone else she can talk to that won't taunt her like this.

"If this treatment center is off-limits, who actually gets to go?" Beck asks, swallowing the defeat in her voice.

Avery sighs.

"Is it bad that I just wanna know more about Backravel? I drove, like, fifteen-hundred miles to get here. Is it that crazy that I want to know more?"

"But why?" Avery asks. "That's what I'm trying to figure out. Why drive fifteen-hundred miles to a place you don't know anything about?"

Beck focuses on the reader again, notes the tightness of her grip on the magnifying knob. She doesn't want to give Avery any more ground, doesn't want to answer her questions when Avery won't do the same. But she's getting nowhere with this, being monitored constantly and being placated when she tries to learn anything. She swallows hard and closes her eyes, feels the rake of Avery's eyes over her face. "This was my mom's favorite place in the world."

"Was?"

Beck nods.

For a long moment, Avery says nothing. When Beck opens her eyes, Avery's skepticism has softened. It's nice to see that there's a part of her, deep down, that has the capacity to care. The cruel, mocking arch of her brow is flattened. Maybe it's just the sharpness of the light and the closeness—the *quiet*—of the room, but for a moment, Beck imagines a trace of sympathy in the soft lines of Avery's face.

"Okay." Avery breathes. "Yeah. That makes sense."

"Does it?"

"I get it. It's not just me playing keep away, though. This stuff is . . . hard to explain. Most people who come here were invited. We don't get a lot of people just showing up. Most people kind of already know about the treatments because it's the reason they came here."

"You can't *try* to explain it?"

Avery presses her lips into a thin line, turns her eyes to the clock on the wall and then looks back at Beck. "I actually don't know the specifics. Only my dad does. And he's the one who decides which people receive treatment and which ones don't. If I thought you needed it, I would let you meet him. Does that make sense?"

"No." Beck presses her fingertips to her temples, massaging away the headache that begins to rear its head. "So you know for a fact that everyone in town *needs* treatment. And you know I don't just by looking at me?"

"It's different for everyone," Avery says cautiously, "but yes."

"Does it cost money? How often do people get treated? Does everyone getting treatment live here?"

"God." Avery laughs. "You ask a lot of questions."

"How could I not?" Beck asks. "Everything you say gives me more questions."

Avery watches her with a gaze too hard, too intentional. Beck swallows and looks away. She's usually better at keeping herself in check, but now it's like she's unraveling in real time, and Avery can see all the worn, tattered threads of her. Beck's cheeks flush.

"Some vacation you're having."

"Forget it."

The words spill out before Beck has a chance to soften them. She smiles to hide the way her voice cracks because she wishes she hadn't talked about her mother, she wishes she hadn't raised her voice, she wishes Avery would just disappear so she could skulk around in peace. Avery is silent, a twitch of concern plain on her face. Beck scrolls the film in the microfiche reader, though she isn't reading a word. She keeps scrolling, but after a vague set of blueprints and nearly illegible body of text, it ends abruptly. It's cut off deliberately, a major chunk of the article missing completely. When she scrolls back to the top, the article's title is missing, too. No author name, no title. Just a bulk of disembodied text and blueprints for what she can only assume *used* to be Backravel.

"What's the point of keeping an article here when half of it is missing?" Beck huffs.

"I'm sorry our library isn't up to your standards," Avery says, laughter ripe in her voice. "I'll make sure it's addressed in the next budget meeting."

Beck straightens. She doesn't particularly want to ask Avery for anything else given her low success rate so far, but with one article a bust and a thousand more to go, she imagines herself here for the entire two weeks, holed up at the microfiche reader, hardly making a dent. She wonders how much of this her mother attempted to read before giving up and looking elsewhere. She pulls the film free from the reader and rolls it back up, digging through the folders for another one.

This time, the film roll she grabs is unlabeled. She slips it into the reader without Avery's help and an article flickers into focus.

"Maybe you can, I don't know . . . tell me some fun facts about Backravel? Not the treatment center. Just some general town history? From a purely tour-guide standpoint."

"Lucky you," Avery muses. "Remember, you're talking to a primary source."

"Right."

Beck peels her gaze away from the microfiche reader and rubs her eyes. When Avery comes into focus, she's watching Beck with half-amusement, half-caution. Her eyes are the color of pennies underwater, that bright kind of brown that seems a thousand miles deep. It takes Beck a moment too long to form her question.

"How many people live in Backravel?"

"About a thousand? I think."

Beck blinks. Somehow, a straightforward answer is the last thing she expected. She nods, satisfied until the truth of the answer sinks in. That's too many people for Backravel to feel as empty as it does. That's too many people for her to have only seen a dozen since arriving. She makes a mental note to come back to that, because if she gets caught on the details, she'll never get anywhere.

"How many people were here when it was founded?"

"Well . . ." Avery trails off. Her eyes dart left, only for a moment. She's nervous, even if she wants to seem at ease. "There were four of us at the *very* start. Me and my parents. And Harlow."

"Harlow?"

Avery's expression sobers even more, the smugness dead on her lips. "He was my brother."

"Oh."

Beck doesn't need to ask more. Avery answers the same way Beck's had to answer questions about her mother for months. It's the dull ache of a past tense when you're used to present. Beck's fingers twitch at her sides. She looks at her boots. There's something strangely familiar about the name, though she can't quite place it. She knows the shape of the letters too well for it to be a coincidence. Another thing to revisit in the notes.

"I'm sorry," Beck says quietly.

"Don't be."

Beck swallows so hard she's sure Avery hears it. "So then . . . more people moved here? Where did they come from?"

Avery purses her lips. "Yeah, we had other people here pretty much right after we got here. My dad realized there was something special about Backravel that was different from everywhere else in the world. He wanted to share it with other people he knew from back home, so then *they* started showing up. I don't remember the exact order, but yeah . . . pretty soon, we had a whole community."

"Where did you live before?" Beck asks.

Avery stares at her a moment too long and Beck wonders if she's said something wrong again. But after a long pause, Avery's daze breaks and she blinks, rubbing at her forehead like she's on the verge of falling asleep. "I was really little. I don't . . . really remember."

There's a twist to the way she says it. She's surprised.

"You don't remember anything about—?" Beck starts.

Avery holds up a hand, posture suddenly rigid. She takes a step back and it occurs to Beck suddenly how close together they were standing. "Actually, let's talk about it later. I have to get going."

"What?"

"I didn't know you were going to take hours to find something to read," Avery says, quickly switching back to her self-righteous tone from minutes ago. "Not everyone is on summer vacation. I have other stuff to do."

"So you're done supervising me?" Beck asks. "Because I asked a question?"

"I wasn't supervising you." Avery's eyes dart to the door. "Look, I was just checking on you. That's all."

"Thanks. I guess."

Avery gives a terse nod, then makes a hasty exit to the hallway. The room fills up with quiet in her absence, and beyond the door, Beck can hear the quick tapping of Avery's footsteps as she retreats. Too quick to be walking.

She's running away.

Beck looks at the microfiche reader, then back at the door. She was onto something with Avery. For just a moment, she could taste that strangeness, that compelling mystery, magnetic and alive and just out of reach. She feels a tingle in her fingertips, a need to write everything down. Maybe she got too close and Avery sensed it. Maybe Avery is hiding something. Whatever it is, it leaves Beck with a flutter of hope. She might not have gotten a whole answer out of Avery, but she got something.

When she looks back at the screen, Beck's stomach drops. An image, grainy and monochromatic. She recognizes the sharpness of the mountains and the blankness of the sky. It might not be a picture of Backravel exactly, but it's close. It's not the skyline that catches her attention, though. On the desert floor, dozens of lifeless bodies stretch out as far as the photo can capture. Sheep, heads lolled against the dirt with blood pooling from their open mouths. Beck covers her own mouth with her palm to keep from being sick. A small caption under the image reads *Aftermath of Skull Valley Sheep Kill, 1968*.

She swallows her nausea and scrolls down to the single paragraph under the image. A chemical weapons test gone wrong, resulting in toxic fluids being dropped onto a field of innocent sheep let out to graze. Within hours, the article explains, the toxins killed every sheep in the area. *Residual chemicals make the land uninhabitable*, Beck reads. *US military advises strongly against accessing the land*.

"What . . . ?" Beck exhales.

Just like before, the end of the article is missing. And just like before, when Beck scrolls to the top of the film roll, the author's name and the article title is gone, too. Either they've been purposefully hidden, or someone else got them first. Beck tries to think like Ellery might have, tries to put the pieces together the way her mother's brilliant mind did. She dashes to her notebook and scrawls out a handful of notes:

check blueprints against town map
population around 1k
avery family founded backravel, not sure when
chemical weapons testing???

She pauses, taps her pen against the library table. The last note she considers writing feels wrong—bordering on insensitive—but if her mother taught her anything, it's that it's better to write *everything* down. Finally, Beck writes:

find out how harlow died

10

BEFORE

The summer after Beck graduates eighth grade, Ellery Birsching comes up for air.

Beck doesn't know why she leaves Backravel behind. Her monthly flights to Arizona screech to a halt, and suddenly, Ellery Birsching wants to make a life that doesn't revolve around her stories. One morning, she wakes up with gift certificates to a specialty waffle restaurant halfway across Washington. Another morning, she's packed a picnic basket full of homemade treats, hauling Beck and Riley to the coast for an impromptu picnic. All summer, the Birschings travel through forests, watch TV together, cook meals all huddled together in their cramped kitchen. Ellery buckles down and writes like a machine, churning out story after story to pay the bills. She throws what she can in a savings account—one that Beck will continue to use for years to come. Beck doesn't know why, doesn't understand what's changed, but she doesn't question it. After a handful of years spent with her mother tethered to her office chair, this is all she wants. Riley's laughter, Ellery's wicked smile, the sun and the open road.

It's a hot morning in June when Ellery rouses Beck from her sleep, drags her out of bed and into the car. She drops Riley with a sitter for the day, declaring that this trip is for the two of them alone. They drive for hours, singing along to show tunes while Ellery insists on keeping their destination a surprise.

And Beck pretends to be upset, but she doesn't care where they're going. It's just her and Ellery and no Backravel, no forget-fulness, no Dad talk, nothing unhappy. That's enough.

When they arrive at the river, Ellery tells Beck that it was her favorite place growing up. Beck inhales the scent of fresh pines draped over whitewater rapids. She feels the warm brush of the sun and the breeze over her pale skin. She listens to the pucker of water tearing over stone.

They rent kayaks that day, and Beck soaks it in, not realizing this will be one of her last pleasant memories of her mother. This will be their last truly good day.

They buck over jagged stones, laugh when Beck's kayak capsizes, and they carry on like there's no time in the world. Ellery laughs at Beck again when the screw of her glasses pops out and she frantically searches the bottom of the kayak for it. The right lens of her glasses flops into her hand, blurring half the scene, scrambling her vision.

"What are you doing, Dork?" her mother asks, voice echoing from every stone, every tree on the shore.

"My glasses," Beck hisses. "I lost the screw."

"What would you do if you found it?" her mother asks. "Put it back in? Just relax. Let the river do its thing. I won't let you drown."

For years, when Ellery thinks of the glasses screw lost in the jagged current of the river, she bursts into laughter. It's a joke that's only funny to her, and over time, it's funny to Beck, too. Even when everything else begins to fade and Ellery Birsching loses herself in her own mind, she thinks of the glasses screw and laughs.

Years later, Beck tries to remember the Ellery Birsching that floated on the river with her. Not the one afraid of her own mind, not the one in the hospital. She tries to conjure up the trickling sound of her mother's laughter, the gleam in her green eyes under a canopy of mammoth trees and gold sunlight. She tries to hold onto that good day, tries to use it to smother away everything else. *What would you do if you found it?* she hears at night as she slips into sleep. *What would you do if you found it?*

It doesn't work.

11

Beck spends the next two days between the library and the bike loop that circles town. Her notebook, which began with only a page of questions, blossoms into a pseudo-scrapbook of disjointed facts about Backravel. Little things that might mean nothing, but they're the kinds of things she used to spot in Ellery Birsching's notes— seeds that might grow into something she can really use. Since arriving in Backravel, the list of things missing has grown. First there were no cemeteries or churches, now she realizes there are no pets. No animals at all, for that matter. She hasn't seen a single car on the road, only parked under vinyl covers in untouched driveways. Most articles in the library are, unsurprisingly, entirely unrelated to Backravel itself. Decades-old newspaper clippings sometimes detail nuclear tests in the wastes of Utah, sometimes talk about the dawn of trauma-based healthcare, sometimes talk about random political events from the seventies and eighties. At night, after Riley falls asleep, Beck lies awake in her bed and tries to connect the dots. Maybe Backravel was initially a military testing site? Maybe Ricky's treatment center practices the methods in the healthcare papers? But none of that has to do with the things Ellery sought. There's still something crucial she's missing.

When she falls asleep, the slipping gets worse. Every night, now, she finds herself in a memory so real she can't remember where she is when she wakes. She grips her mattress as the sun rises and waits for reality to settle over her like a veil. With every morning in Backravel, she understands Ellery's confusion a little more. She isn't sure if that's a good thing.

Since the first day in the library, Beck hasn't seen Avery anywhere.

Today, Beck steers clear of the library. Her eyes are swollen from days of reading, and when Riley invites her to join the other kids at LemonDrop, she reluctantly agrees. She's almost halfway through this trip and no closer to understanding Ellery's note. It's hard not to feel like the walls are closing in.

They meet Daniel's friends inside, who pleasantly chatter over their coffees and treats. The frozen yogurt shop is busier this morning than it was the first time Daniel brought them, crowded with clusters of kids at the sofas, leaning on counters, laughing from the patio tables. It's the most people she's *ever* seen in one place in Backravel, actually. Sunlight cuts through the massive windows while Daniel silently makes Beck and Riley their coffees. Katie and Andy argue about the wording of a joke. Megan and Jack sit on a pair of stools at the bar, knees tangled together, sipping their drinks without a word. Beck considers it a small victory she even remembers their names. Her mind couldn't be further away.

". . . but then you disappeared."

Beck is pulled out of her swirling thoughts when she feels the weight of Katie's gaze land on her. Katie has the kind of stare that triggers a person's fight or flight, sharp and unyielding. She stares like she knows she's entitled to answers no matter how little she knows you. Her black hair is in a sleek ponytail pulled so taut Beck can see every follicle in her pale scalp. She's the kind of girl Beck might've watched in the quiet moments back at school, wishing she had the confidence to speak to her. Every detail of her is tucked neatly in place in a way Beck can only dream of.

"I'm sorry?" Beck asks.

"She wasn't listening," Megan muses.

"It's okay," Katie says, and her lips soften into a slight smile. "I was just saying I feel like we haven't seen *you* at all. Like, you were around that one time a week ago and then you totally disappeared."

Next to her, Riley stiffens. She smiles uneasily and puts a hand tenderly on Beck's back. Beck wonders for a moment if it's embarrassment or protectiveness in her eyes now. It's always been this strange balancing act between them, Beck stumbling her way through, unmoored, while Riley apologizes for her. She wonders if Riley's spent the last few days defending her from these comments. She wonders if Riley's agreed with them.

"She's been at the library a bunch, actually," Riley says.

"The library?" Daniel asks. He finishes making an iced caramel macchiato for Beck and slides it down the counter to her. "Why?"

Beck shrugs. All four of them are staring at her now, waiting for an answer they can make sense of. Beck isn't sure she has one. "I just think this town is really interesting. I wanted to know more, I guess."

Katie looks at Riley and arches a brow in a silent question. Before anyone can speak, she shrugs and moves on, apparently uninterested. "Well, I was telling Riley I think we should have you both over for a movie. We do movie night every Friday, so I think it would be fun to have new people."

Riley turns in her stool and stares at Beck, pleading quietly for a yes. She already knew about this get-together, then. Beck sucks in a breath because, like always, Riley has found a place for herself here within a few days, a feat that would take Beck months if not years. She owes it to Riley to do something fun, something not related to the story. But the idea of huddling in someone else's living room to watch a movie she doesn't want to see while there are things in Backravel to explore makes her sweat.

Beck shrugs and takes a long sip of her coffee, which tastes like the burnt end of a cigarette.

"That sounds fun," Beck says. "I'll probably sit this one—"

"No, you should come, too." This comes from Jack, the boy on the other side of Katie that Beck has almost entirely forgotten about. He's so assertive about it, for a second, Beck is sure he's joking. He props an elbow on the counter, sipping on a bright green fizzy drink. "We wanted to hang with both of you."

"I'm okay," Beck says.

It would be easier to just agree, but even back home, this wasn't her thing. To Beck, fun was never lingering for hours in another person's house, miles from her own bed, muscling through conversations she has to force herself to be interested in. This is why, even in Everett, there wasn't a single person she could call a best friend. This is why she only vaguely talked to other kids at school under the bleachers by the track, in the parking lot after school while she waited for Riley. She could barely stand it back home, but it's worse here where everything is slippery and unstable. Where her fingers ache to dig.

"Don't be rude," Katie says to Jack, condescendingly optimistic. She turns to Beck with a sickeningly sweet smile. "Riley was telling me so much about you. I just think it would be fun if we all hung out. You don't have to, but I promise it'll be fun."

Beck looks to Riley, but Riley says nothing, staring at the countertop instead, inspecting her nailbeds. Before Beck has a chance to deflect again, a face across the room catches her eye. At the other end of the counter, swirling a murky brown drink in a plastic cup, Avery watches her. Her eyes are trained on Beck, but when Beck spots her, she quickly looks away. Beck's eyes widen. Avery looks different today. Less tired, maybe. She idly swirls her drink in her cup, but she doesn't move.

"Earth to Beck." Katie giggles, tilting her head so that she's in Beck's line of sight. "You don't have to come if you don't want to. I just think it would be more fun with everyone there."

Beck doesn't answer. She nudges Riley in the arm and gestures across the counter. "Does Avery look different today?"

Riley looks uneasily from Katie to Beck. She shrugs.

Daniel slides a drink down the counter to another teen, then makes his way back to Beck. He puts his hands palm-down on the counter and, in his usual monotone, says, "What else are you doing Friday night? Digging for buried treasure? You can't come out for *one* night?"

"Hey . . ." Riley warns.

Across the room, Avery is watching her again. She watches her like this is a test and Beck is failing. Beck steels herself, tries to shrug it off, but there's that choking feeling. That panic that always wells up in her when the world starts to move too fast. She needs to focus, needs to pay attention to one thing happening at a time so she doesn't freeze. By the time she realizes it's taking over, it's too late. Most of the people around them have paused their conversations, eyes anxiously turned to watch Beck implode.

"I should just go," Beck says, quickly standing.

"Wait," Katie says. Her smile is nervous now, like she's in damage control mode. "I'm sorry. We just want you to feel welcome, too."

"It's fine," Beck snaps. "I'm *fine*."

Her voice is too loud and the shop is too small. Anxiety bubbles up in Beck's chest so fast it threatens to choke her. This isn't *her*—pulling all the attention in a room, making a scene. She doesn't know what's gotten into her, why she can't just tamp all this down like she usually does. Something about Backravel musses all the worst parts to the surface. It's like all of it is sitting just at her skin, ready to drown her at the drop of a pin.

She doesn't look at Riley.

She doesn't look at Avery, either, but she feels the heat of her stare.

"Beck," Riley says quietly, in the voice she always uses when she's trying to guide Beck back to earth. Somehow, the tenderness in her voice makes Beck feel even worse. Shame sears under her skin, leaves the pit of her stomach cold.

"I didn't mean to—" Daniel starts.

"We just want you to be happy here," Jack cuts in, and the last thing Beck needs is another voice in the chorus of people trying to calm her down. She closes her eyes because she wants to disappear. This is why she stays in the library while Riley socializes. This is why she doesn't do crowded places.

"You wanna get some air?"

The voice comes from behind her. Beck turns and finds herself face-to-face with Avery. She blinks, looks at the stool across the room where Avery was still seated seconds ago. She must've moved quickly. It takes Beck a moment to realize she isn't just offering a helping hand—she's intervening. Mediating. The shame in Beck's cheeks deepens. Avery's hand rests on her slender hip, jaw tight. With her other arm, she grips the counter. She's made a wall between Beck and the others.

Beck wonders if it's her or the others Avery's protecting.

"I'm sorry," Beck says. "I'm okay. Really. I'll—"

"I think we should go outside."

Avery puts her hand on the small of Beck's back and the touch is unexpected, and for a moment, it renders Beck speechless. She sucks in a breath and they make their way to the front door. Beck looks back at Riley and shrugs. Riley watches her with wide eyes that look like she might cry.

Outside, the sunlight is nearly blinding and Beck's head throbs in the brightness. She makes her way to a bench on the sidewalk and plops down, taking slow, measured breaths. Quietly, cautiously, Avery slides onto the seat beside her, knees angled toward Beck's. She waits what feels like hours before speaking.

"Take a deep breath."

Beck does. It doesn't help.

"What was going on in there?" Avery asks, softer than Beck expects.

"I don't know," Beck says.

"Katie and her friends are annoying, but they aren't bad people," Avery says. "I don't think they were trying to get to you, or whatever."

Beck nods. Her cheeks flush as her racing heart finally begins to slow and the world slides back into focus. Back inside, they're probably already whispering about how she overreacted. And Riley is probably already trying to defuse the situation like she always has to. "I didn't mean for it to be so dramatic," Beck says finally. "I was just trying to, I don't know . . . I just needed some air."

"Okay, good. We're getting air now." Avery's hair shifts just slightly in the breeze. "I'm not trying to give you issues. But you seem really . . . serious for someone on vacation. What's going on with you?"

Beck looks down at her knuckles, the ridges dusted with red, bright and pale in the unrelenting sun. She should feel hot, but her body is cold all the way through. A shiver works its way through her, followed by another. She can't panic right now—not with Avery inches from her—but convenience has never stopped a panic attack before. She expels a long breath and closes her eyes, letting the residual waves of fear rack her fragile bones and quivering muscles.

"Beck."

"I'm okay," Beck says. "Give me a second."

Avery does, but Beck feels the concern in her stare as it bores into the side of her face. Through a breathy laugh, Beck says, "I used to be better at keeping it together. I promise."

This is the first time she's had a panic attack in front of anyone but Riley, and there's a special flavor of shame that comes with it. A single tear blossoms and rolls down the length of Beck's cheek.

To her surprise, she feels a touch at her shoulder. Light, unassuming, but unmoving. Beck opens her eyes and finds Avery only a few inches away, genuine fear heavy in her brow. "Sorry," Avery says. "Tell me what you need."

Beck shakes her head and carefully lifts her glasses to her hairline, swiping away the tear with the back of her hand. "Things have just been hard since . . ."

"Since your mom?"

Beck can't find the right words to say out loud—isn't even sure if she has the capacity to say it out loud—so she nods.

"I'm sorry," Avery says. "I'm sorry you're going through that. You're not the only person in Backravel who's lost someone. I think, especially here, you're going to find a lot of people that get it."

Beck arches a brow. "Especially here?"

Avery says nothing.

"I'm fine. Seriously. Sometimes, I just don't know what to do with all this . . ." Beck starts, but she doesn't know what she means to say.

"Feeling?"

"Yeah," Beck says. "That."

For a long while, Avery is quiet. She pulls her hand away from Beck, but she doesn't move away. Carefully, tentatively, she says, "I'm not a person who likes to say when they're wrong. And I'm not saying I'm wrong. But some of this is what my dad's treatments are for."

Beck goes still.

"I'm not saying you need treatment. But I do wonder if maybe there's a reason you ended up here." Avery runs a hand through her hair, her eyes trained on her sneakers. "It wouldn't be the first time someone who needed us just . . . *ended up* here."

Beck looks at Avery, waiting for the punchline. It's not much, but it's an offer. It's a crack in the door, a hand extended. Beck's heartbeat is a slog, slow and anxious all at once. "Okay," she says. "What does that mean?"

"It means I think you should . . ." Avery pauses, sighs. "I think you should meet my dad."

"I thought he—"

"When we talked before, I didn't know you. I still don't. I wasn't trying to say you didn't need treatment, I was just saying . . . I don't know why you came here, but people don't just *show up* in Backravel. I didn't understand why you were here."

"You understand now?" Beck asks.

"No." Avery presses fingertips to her temples. "But I feel like I'm starting to."

This time, when Beck looks at Avery, Avery looks back. It's tentative, but it's something. It's enough for Beck. It's a step closer to Ricky, which is a step closer to her mother. It's a step closer to some answers. She can't pretend to understand what's finally clicked for Avery, but she doesn't have to.

"How about you meet me at the park tomorrow morning?" Avery says. "We'll go up together."

"I . . . yeah. I can do that."

Avery nods, but she doesn't smile. She claps Beck once on the shoulder and stands, sun caught in her dark head of hair. She stretches her arms over her head and yawns without bothering to cover her mouth. It strikes Beck what a strange creature Avery is, sometimes so authoritative, and other times so childlike.

"Eight o'clock on the dot," Avery says. "And bring good shoes. It's a long way up."

They both turn to face the outline of the plateau on the horizon, dusty in the afternoon haze. The treatment center gleams like a black stone on the cliff face, shearing through the dirt. After days of seeing it from afar, tomorrow, she'll finally step inside.

"Thanks, by the way," Beck says, halfway managing a smile. "For checking on me."

"Yeah, yeah . . ." Avery waves dismissively. "Go home. Get some sleep."

Avery pops her knuckles and heads back toward LemonDrop. On her way inside, she holds the door open for someone on their way out. Riley ducks out into the sunshine quietly, nodding to Avery. She slides onto the bench next to Beck and says nothing, putting a hand delicately on Beck's shoulder before snatching it away again.

"Hey," Beck says. "I'm sorry about that."

"No. I'm sorry." Riley sighs. "I shouldn't have let anyone talk to you like that. Especially after we ditched you the first day. I feel like such a bad—"

"You're not a bad sister." Beck chuckles, riding out the last waves of panic that course through her. "Seriously."

"I hate this."

Beck laughs. "It's okay."

"What happened?" Riley asks. She's trying not to sound as concerned as she is, but Beck feels it in the rigid lean of her shoulders, the spike in her voice, the white of her knuckles where she grips the bench. She scoots closer and leans her head on Beck's shoulder.

"I don't know. I didn't mean to get all weird."

"Were you feeling kind of overwhelmed again?"

Beck chews the inside of her cheek. For a moment, she's glad Riley can't see her face. She doesn't know what her expression looks like now. Her eyes are trained out to the horizon, past the plateau and past the hazy sky. She looks at something further away, and she feels something vibrate under her feet. The whir of machinery hums in her bones. Something is happening to her here, and it's worse than it was back home. It's worse because it's more real. It's worse because she can't tell Riley things are getting bad without activating Riley's damage control mode. It's worse because she has to do it alone.

"Being here is just a lot, I think," Beck says. "But I feel better now. Seriously."

Riley is quiet for too long.

Finally, her posture slackens and Beck feels the shift of her laughing. Riley leans away from Beck and smiles at her. "Now that Nurse Avery helped?"

"Stop," Beck says, shoving Riley lightly on the shoulder. "She *did* offer to help a little, though. Don't freak out, okay?"

Riley's expression sobers. "What do you mean?"

"She's gonna take me to the treatment center tomorrow," Beck says. For a long moment Riley says nothing. The quiet between them shifts into something apprehensive. Something fearful. Beck clears her throat and smiles. "I'm gonna meet her dad."

12

It's the little things that unmake Beck.

In the hours after Beck and Riley's return from town, the Sterlings decide to have a barbecue. It's a sweet summer night, just like every other night so far in Backravel, airy and light and tinged with the type of slight breeze that feels like a whisper across the back of your neck. But tonight, Beck isn't in the mood for a barbecue. She isn't in the mood for laughter and stargazing. She lies in the trailer bed, instead, waiting for it all to feel real. After looking for a way into the treatment center, she's finally found one. She's finally going to meet Ricky, the man this whole town apparently orbits. She isn't in the mood for a barbecue because she needs to pore over Ellery's notes and write out her questions. She needs to ask about the chemical testing she read about, the military ruins, Delia Horton, the desert. She wants to know *everything*.

She pinches Ellery's letter between her fingers, and she feels sick.

Come and find me.

The nausea is more persistent today than it was yesterday. There's an ache in her bones and a sag in her energy, though she credits that mostly to her days spent in the library. Beck massages her sore shoulder and wonders if the long drive and sleepless nights have finally caught up with her.

Beck presses Ellery's letter back into its envelope and she sees it. In the small corner of the envelope where one side folds over the other, stuck just out of plain sight, a small glint of metal. Beck narrows her eyes and presses her fingertip to the metal, drawing it into the light.

She's opened and closed this letter a thousand times, but she didn't notice the glasses screw until now. For a moment, she can't breathe. Something is happening to her, and it's not just her imagination. The little nub of metal isn't a figment of her imagination. She holds it up to the light and her breath catches. It's not the trauma making the memories sit at the nape of her neck like this because it wasn't like this back in Washington.

She's lying in bed, Ellery's notes scratching the skin of her forearms, but she feels the mist of bucking water on her face. She breathes it in deep and, for a moment, she loses herself in the memory.

The trailer door opens and Riley pops her head into the kitchen. "Everything's ready. Are you still coming out, or . . ."

"Yep. Coming."

Beck shoves the notes out of sight and scrambles to sit upright. She pushes herself to her feet and stumbles out of the trailer into the arid night. The Sterlings have rearranged their back patio, dragging their yard loungers and iron chairs around the squat black fire pit in the center of the yard. The iron table has been loaded with plates of hot dogs, condiments, and s'mores supplies. On a hot summer night in Everett, Beck might've heard crickets in the distance, but in Backravel, she's come to expect the silence. The crackling of the fire is the only noise for miles.

Mr. and Mrs. Sterling sit side by side on the far side of the fire pit, each roasting a hot dog on the open fire. They watch Beck with the sort of half-sympathetic, half-wary gaze that says they already know about her meltdown earlier. They've already dissected it with Daniel, and now they have to tiptoe.

Daniel stands alone at the table fixing himself a hot dog bun overloaded with ketchup and nothing else. He intentionally looks away from Beck as she approaches, and guilt knots her stomach. She makes her way to the table and tentatively takes a paper plate, mulling over what she means to say.

"Hey," she manages.

Daniel is quiet for a moment, then he looks at her. "Hey. How are you feeling?"

"I'm okay," Beck says. She slides a hot dog onto her skewer. "I'm sorry about earlier. I didn't mean to freak anyone out."

"Oh."

"You didn't say anything wrong. I was just . . . it's been a rough trip, I guess."

"It's okay." For a second, Beck thinks he might not say anything else. He looks at his mother, who makes a motion with her hand, egging him on. He clears his throat and continues. "I didn't mean to hurt your feelings. I just thought it'd be good for you to see a movie with us. But you don't have to."

"No, it's okay." Beck smiles. "I . . . I'll go."

"Cool," Daniel says, and his usual monotone cracks just a little. "It'll be fun."

Beck makes her way back to the fire pit and plops into the camping chair beside Riley, who's already worked her way through two hot dogs and has moved on to s'mores. There's an awkward quiet between them all tonight, like everyone expects her to fall apart again. Beck turns her skewer over in her hands, doing her best to ignore the familiar anxiety in her chest.

"It's a nice night," Riley says, breaking up the quiet.

"It really is," Mr. Sterling says. "I love it here in the summer. Nothing beats it."

"How long have you guys lived in Backravel?" Beck asks.

Mr. and Mrs. Sterling look at each other. Next to them, Daniel pokes at the fire with an empty skewer, turning a charred lump of wood onto its back. Mrs. Sterling bundles her arms into her sweater and says, "Oh, probably three or so years now. Since Daniel was twelve."

Beck blinks. She looks at Riley to see if she caught the oddness of the answer, too, but Riley is fixated on the fire. Licks of it flicker in her eyes, glassy and distant. Beck chews the inside of her cheek and looks at the trailer. No, if they only came here a handful of years ago, the dates in the guest log wouldn't make sense. "Did you rent out the trailer before you moved here, too?"

"What?" Mr. Sterling asks.

"There's a . . . uh . . ." Beck looks at the trailer door, then back at the fire. "Never mind. I must be confused."

She doesn't mention the guest book entries dating back a decade. She promised Riley this was a normal vacation and, while she's sitting next to Riley here at the fire, she won't go into interrogation mode. She's already ruined their afternoon—she doesn't need to ruin the evening, too. But she slips the thought into her ever-growing log of inconsistencies, holds onto it for later. Because something here isn't adding up.

"I was trying to learn more about Backravel the other day, actually. Do you know much about when it was founded?"

"Oh, that's tough," Mr. Sterling says. "Whenever Ricky got here, I guess. He's the one who found it and put everything together. We didn't get here long after he arrived, but everything was pretty much how it is now."

Beck nods. She makes another mental note, this time because either Mr. Sterling doesn't know when Backravel began or he's hiding it. It's the same way Avery can't place where she lived before Backravel. Beck's asked for specific dates a dozen times since arriving in Backravel, and no one seems to have a clear answer for any of it. There's a haziness like the red dust on the plateau that sets in every time the people of Backravel talk about the past.

"Can I ask how Ricky found Backravel?" Beck asks. "If you know."

"It's a fairly long answer," Mr. Sterling chuckles. He looks around and smiles. "We *are* around a campfire, though. If you two girls are up for it, I can give it a shot."

Beck nudges Riley, who startles out of her daze. It's strange; Riley's more distant today than Beck's seen her in a long time. It's one thing for Beck to space out, but Riley's always had the precise attention span of a hawk, focusing in on conversation effortlessly. Maybe it's the stress of the trip, but something is off with her, too.

"Sorry," Riley says with a nervous laugh. "What was . . . ?"

"Mr. Sterling is gonna tell us about how they found Backravel." Beck places a hand on Riley's shoulder. "Are you feeling okay?"

"Yeah, I'm fine. Just tired, I think." Riley scrapes a hardened bit of chocolate from her skewer and pops it into her mouth. "I might be getting sick?"

Mr. and Mrs. Sterling exchange a quick glance and then focus back on the fire. It was quick, but Beck notices it. Her heart skips a beat.

"Let me go get some juice and cough syrup," Mrs. Sterling says. "Arizona's a pretty different world from Washington. I wouldn't be surprised if you caught a little cold in the weather change."

"That's probably exactly it," Mr. Sterling agrees.

While Mrs. Sterling heads into the house, Mr. Sterling nestles deeper into his chair, leaning forward. "So, Backravel's history? Well, when *we* first landed here, we had lots of questions, too. There are little towns all over America, but none are quite like this. Completely isolated, totally self-sufficient, a place where you don't have to get into the weeds of small-town politics and all that. Ricky was more public back then, not so hidden up in his tower. He told me that he and his family had been living in a big city somewhere up north for years."

"You know Ricky pretty well?" Beck asks.

"I do," says Mr. Sterling. "We'd have to by this point. We meet up every week or so for treatment. Anyway, he tells me that, back home, he started having these dreams about the desert. He'd see this shimmering red valley, he tells me, all alone and untouched. And each time he sees it, he gets this feeling that he's supposed to be there. He tries to ignore it, but it starts taking over until finally he quits his job, sells his house, loads his family into a truck, and makes for the desert."

"How did he know where it was?" Beck asks.

"I don't know. It must've been some sort of beacon calling him here," Mr. Sterling says, wistful. "Ricky and his family were driving through the desert in circles for days, looking for the valley in his dreams. They drove until their truck broke down, then they walked. They were miles and miles from civilization, completely alone."

"Woah . . ." Riley breathes.

"When Ricky and his family were almost out of food and water, completely lost, they stumbled into the ruins. Ricky says all they saw was a rusty old sign calling this place Backravel. It was a miracle. He'd thought he and his wife and kids would starve in the desert, but they found food and water in the old mess hall, scrap material for shelter, a whole paradise left behind for them. He realized they weren't just going to survive out here, they were going to make a new life. It's like Backravel was waiting just for someone to come bring it to life. And out of the goodness of his heart, Ricky decided to share it with all of us."

As if on cue, Mrs. Sterling reemerges from the house with a bottle of cough syrup, a damp washcloth, and a glass of orange juice. She crouches in front of Riley and presses the back of her hand to Riley's forehead. It's excessive for what's probably a minor cold, but Riley takes the cough syrup and juice with a smile. "Thank you."

Mrs. Sterling turns to Beck. "You're feeling okay? No tiredness? Soreness?"

Beck shakes her head.

"You girls are here for two weeks total, right?" Mr. Sterling asks.

Beck flashes a quick look at Riley, who side-eyes her around the rim of her juice glass. Carefully, she says, "Yeah. Just through the festival."

"Maybe they should see Ricky before then?" Mr. Sterling says, this time to his wife. "Just to be safe."

Mrs. Sterling presses the washcloth firmly to Riley's forehead, but Beck just catches the tremor of concern in her face. Without looking at her husband, she says, "Oh, I don't know . . ."

"I'm actually meeting him tomorrow," Beck says. "Avery said I should."

"Oh," Mrs. Sterling says, almost too quiet to hear. "That's interesting."

Mr. Sterling seems less concerned. "It can feel intimidating, but I think that's because we all admire him so much. I mean, look what he's done with this place. There aren't many people in this world with such giving hearts. I think you'll find the visit refreshing."

"I hope so," Beck says.

Across the fire, Daniel is completely spaced out, just like Riley was moments ago. If the Sterlings notice, they don't acknowledge it. They just let him leave his skewer in the fire, flames eating away at an ashen bit of marshmallow still clinging to the metal. The fire putters to embers, leaving the charred logs like black-shelled beetles in the ashes, reflecting the thin moonlight overhead. Beck stares up into the sky and the width of the stars sucks the air from her lungs. It's so clear out here, untouched by city lights. It's like looking at a sky from centuries ago, suspended perfectly in time.

"Do you think he'll do . . ." Beck starts. "I'm not getting a treatment tomorrow, am I?"

"Oh, I doubt it," Mr. Sterling says. He pulls his skewer from the fire, patting away the ashes on the patio stones. "Ricky doesn't usually start treatment unless you've got a plan in place. And a plan usually means you're here longer than two weeks."

"Can you tell me what they are?" Beck tries. "The treatments?"

Next to her, Riley yawns. A fat moth flickers at her face and she doesn't even flinch. Either the situation at LemonDrop exhausted her more than Beck thought, or someone's drugged the marshmallows.

Mr. Sterling straightens. "I can tell you a little. It's different for everyone, though. The treatments—we call them *unspooling*—are natural and meditative. Unlike medical doctors who wait until you're already injured to treat, Ricky finds the source of the pain. Once you find the *source*, you treat that."

Source. Riley might be tired, but Beck isn't missing a thing.

"How does that . . . ?" Beck starts, though she's not sure what she means to ask. It's all so vague. "What do you mean by *source*?"

"It's very difficult for me to describe, Beck," Mr. Sterling says through a laugh. He wears a smile, but he's irritated. Just like everyone else in Backravel, he doesn't enjoy these questions. Beck can't imagine he enjoyed hosting her mother. "That's why the unspooling is Ricky's job. Heaven forbid any of us try to do it. I wouldn't even know where to start."

"It does work, though," Mrs. Sterling chimes in. "The treatment center is actually the reason we came to Backravel. Daniel had such severe asthma attacks all throughout his childhood. A few years ago, he had one that nearly killed him. We tried doctor after doctor, but nothing seemed to work permanently. A family friend told us about Backravel. She said this treatment center in Arizona was finding permanent cures for people who were otherwise incurable. If there was a chance we could keep Daniel happy and healthy, we were going to take it."

Beck glances quickly at Daniel. Even with his name said, even with his parents discussing his near-death experience, his stare is miles away. He's not listening at all. Beck fidgets in her seat. Even though heat settles low to the valley floor at night, Beck's blood runs cold. She's sure she's not making it up; something is wrong with Daniel. Something is wrong with Riley. She focuses back on Mr. Sterling.

"We stayed here for a week at first while Ricky did daily treatments. A week turned into a month and there were no asthma attacks. As long as we stayed here in town, Daniel's asthma attacks were gone completely. Ricky told us we could come back every few months for recurring treatment or we could stay permanently, but it was an easy choice." Mr. Sterling claps Daniel on the back, which finally rouses him from his stupor. "We decided to stay."

Daniel offers a sheepish smile and it's clear he hasn't heard a word.

"It was the right choice," Mrs. Sterling says. "Not just because of the treatments. This community is so giving. We all love and respect each other so deeply. Everyone does their part to make this little machine work. It's the total opposite of our world back home."

Back home. Beck purses her lips. "Where did you say you lived before?"

Mr. Sterling narrows his eyes. For a moment, Beck sees the same cloud pass over his face she saw in the library with Avery. The same momentary confusion. He stares at his wife and his lips part around a word he doesn't say. Mrs. Sterling nudges him once, gently. He rights himself and eases back into a smile.

"Minneapolis. Honestly, I wish I could say I missed it, but I don't. Not even a little."

"We don't need to go on for hours about ourselves, though," Mrs. Sterling says before Mr. Sterling can continue. "You're heading up tomorrow? Are you both going?"

"Just me, I think," Beck says.

Riley nods, half-present. "I don't think I was invited."

"You'll have to tell me what you think," Mrs. Sterling beams. "I wish I could go with you. I love to see people's faces when they see it for the first time."

Next to Beck, Riley's head dips. She catches herself mid-doze and sits up straight. Her eyes are wide, like she's surprised she nodded off so easily. Beck reaches across the space between them and touches Riley's wrist. Riley flashes the Sterlings a quick smile and quickly stands. "I think I need to get some sleep."

"Looks like it." Mr. Sterling chuckles.

Riley feebly rubs at her eyes. "I'm sorry. I don't know why I'm so tired."

"Thank you so much again for dinner," Beck says. "We'll see you guys tomorrow."

"Of course," Mrs. Sterling says. "Have a good night, girls."

• • •

In the trailer, Beck finally breathes.

Riley ambles to the kitchen booth and collapses onto the vinyl. She throws her arm over her face to block out the light and heaves a sigh. "Why am I so *tired*?"

"I don't know," Beck says. "Do you feel sick?"

"Just tired, I think," Riley says. "I'll just go to sleep early, I guess."

Beck nods. She grabs a plastic cup from the trailer cupboard and fills it with tap water, handing it to Riley. Her face *does* look paler than usual, more sallow, eyes more sunken. It's hard to say if it's just the harsh light or if she's getting sick. Beck sinks into the kitchen booth and slides to Riley's side, scooping her into a half hug.

"You sure you're up for tomorrow?" Riley asks.

"Ready as I can be," Beck says. "I think I'm just meeting him."

"And you're sure Avery asked *you* to go?" Riley clarifies sleepily. "You didn't ask to meet him?"

"What's that supposed to mean?"

"I don't know." Riley pulls away from Beck. She taps her fingers on the kitchen table, lips drawn to one side as she thinks. "Just . . . the questions you were asking out there, and meeting Ricky. It feels like maybe you're getting kind of sucked in?"

"Oh."

Beck tries not to look hurt, tries to swallow down the shame that rushes up like bile. But she's never been good at hiding from Riley. Immediately, her sister sees through her. She takes Beck's arm and pulls her back into a hug.

"I just think maybe coming here wasn't a good idea."

"I'm not . . ." Beck starts. "I'm not allowed to ask questions about things that are weird? I mean, don't *you* want to know more when you hear stuff like everyone in town going to the same treatment center?"

"I do, but not by *going* there," Riley says. "Isn't that the way Mom's stories always started? Her poking stuff she thought seemed weird?"

"It's not like Mom," Beck cuts in, maybe too sharp. In a rush, she sees herself standing in the laundry room back home, eyes wide, lost in her own mind. A shiver runs down her spine. "It's not."

"I just feel like maybe we should go."

"I thought you were making friends here?"

"I'm not making friends," Riley says. "I'm just killing time. I'd rather make friends in Texas. Where we're actually staying."

Beck nods. She gracelessly pries herself out of the booth and stumbles toward the bathroom, kicking off her boots in the process. Riley quietly begins assembling her bed, but there's something electric to the quiet. More questions she's trying to find a way to ask. More fear she's too nervous to express.

In the narrow, spit-dotted mirror, Beck catches a harrowing glimpse of a girl on the brink. Maybe Riley isn't the only one who desperately needs a full night's sleep. Deep shadows circle her eyes, blond frizz crinkling at her temples, her clothes frumpy and discolored from a week of constant wear. She hasn't had to impress anyone in a long time, but at the thought of meeting Ricky tomorrow, she pauses.

She uncaps her toothpaste. "Anyway, the meeting tomorrow will be fine. Avery will be there, too."

"That doesn't make you *more* nervous?" Riley asks from the trailer sofa.

Beck blinks. It's an odd question, and it strikes her in the space between her ribs. The gaping, dark center of her. Maybe it should make her nervous that Avery will be there, but for whatever reason, the idea of Avery guiding her up the plateau, leading her into the treatment center is a comfort. There's something familiar about Avery that she knows already. A certain sharpness to her that Beck's already endured. Beck already understands the rhythm of her and it's easy to fall in line.

She dips out of the bathroom and catches Riley as she nestles under her blankets.

"It'll all be fine," Beck says. "You sleep, and tomorrow we'll see if we want to stay. Is that okay?"

Riley nods. She reaches over and flips off the light over her head. In the quiet, Beck changes into a T-shirt and boxers and climbs into bed, but her heart still thumps too quick. She told Riley they could discuss leaving tomorrow, but it was a lie. Because she's not leaving this place without understanding the way it works, the way it consumes, the way it buries you. They just need to push a little longer. They just need to survive until then.

13

By the time Beck wheels into town, Avery is already waiting for her. She sits on a park bench with her feet kicked up on the seat of her bike. Her gaze is locked on an elderly couple leaving the diner, arms linked, but her expression is unreadable, head cocked just slightly, brow furrowed in thought. Beck approaches her cautiously, careful not to break her focus. She's forced her way back to a tentative calm today, but the anticipation still racks her.

She makes it almost to Avery's side before Avery blinks back to life. She runs a hand through her hair, pushing the curls away from her brow. The glassy daze in her eyes fades and she's alive again.

Beck isn't sure if that's a good thing. She cups her hand over her eyes and looks up at the plateau that takes up half the horizon. "I could've met you at the top. You didn't have to come all the way down just to walk me back up again."

"I didn't," Avery agrees. "But you're welcome."

Avery gracefully kicks her legs from their resting place and mounts her bike. Without another word, she motions for Beck to follow her. She's less comforting today than she was yesterday, maybe because Beck isn't currently in a state of panic, or maybe because something has changed. They glide through Backravel's pristine city blocks before breaking onto the black asphalt of the road that climbs the plateau. From the base, the treatment center seems miles away. With sudden clarity, Beck regrets skipping so many PE classes back home.

Avery must notice her expression. She pauses and eyes Beck with a smug grin. "You sure you're gonna make it?"

"Yeah. Absolutely sure." Beck narrows her eyes at the sun-rimmed plateau. "I guess I'm wondering . . . does *everyone* bike up?"

"Some people walk."

"So no cars?"

Avery nods. Her smile doesn't fade, and it starts to make Beck's skin crawl. "It's not that bad. I promise. We have some genuinely ancient people in town and they still make it up every few weeks. I think you can make it once."

Beck scoffs. Without another word, she kicks off and pedals toward the incline. The sun beats down, but it's not as hot as Beck expected. The heat lifts the higher they climb, soft on the breeze. The real frustration comes when Beck watches Avery soar up the incline with ease, tilting from side to side like the rise doesn't faze her. Beck notices the shape of her for the first time. She's not as lithe and willowy as Beck first thought. With each pump of her bike pedals, Beck watches the muscles of her calves flex, a faint glimmer of sweat at her exposed collarbone, the slight twinge of determination at her brow. She's not just gliding up the hill; she's showing off.

Halfway up the plateau, Beck runs out of steam.

"Stop, stop," Beck croaks. She squeezes the brakes and slides off the bike, clinging to the handlebars to keep from collapsing.

Avery skids back to Beck's side and hops off her bike.

"I need to walk the rest, I think." Beck wheezes. "Or you're gonna have to drag my corpse the rest of the way."

"You're not dying," Avery says. She pops her neck and starts walking, motioning for Beck to follow. "Most tourists struggle with the climb. Don't feel bad."

"Only tourists struggle?" Beck asks.

"Everyone else is used to it."

Beck nods. She wouldn't have an issue with the way up if she was allowed to drive a car. They climb the rest of the way up and finally round the massive side of the plateau, coming face-to-face with the treatment center. What looked like a sparkling black gem yesterday is much bigger up close. A modern, hospital-sized building, flat gray stone and sprawling black glass windows taking up the entirety of the plateau's scraggly surface. The road turns into a thin black driveway that leads all the way to the treatment center's massive front doors. A perfectly groomed lawn takes up whatever space is left, too green to be real. Beck spots the first uncovered car she's seen since parking the Honda outside the Sterlings'. A creamsicle-colored Cadillac is parked in the coiling driveway, too bright and too clean in the harsh light.

Avery doesn't slow at the sight. She wheels her way to the doors without even a pause. Over the hush of the wind, she yells, "Welcome to my home."

Beck screeches to a halt. "You *live* here?"

Avery glances over her shoulder. "Yeah. You like it?"

"It's huge."

"It's a treatment center. It has to be."

They make their way to the front doors. A small bike rack is nailed down on the front porch. Avery secures her bike and claps her hands together, expelling a cloud of red dust. Beck wheels up behind her and leaves her bike next to Avery's. She forces in one breath, then another. She will *not* panic today.

Avery gestures for her to follow. She elbows open the front doors.

The main room of the treatment center is nothing like Beck expected. It's wide and open and bright, an open floor plan with white walls and windows that stretch from the floor to the ceiling. In one area, there's a sleek black sectional and a glass coffee table. In another corner, a kitchen made entirely of brand-new appliances and concrete countertops that match simple concrete floors. Next to the front doors, a record player warbles idly, churning out an old tune she's sure her mother used to listen to at one point or another.

Avery motions to the sectional. "You can wait there. I don't know when he'll be done with his session."

Maybe it's the awe, or maybe she's just exhausted, but Beck does exactly as she's told. She makes her way to the sectional and sinks into the cool leather, lets it stick to the sweat at the back of her neck. Sunlight tilts through the windows, cutting bladelike sections of light on the floor. From here, the only thing visible outside is green grass and sky.

Whatever kind of treatment Ricky performs here—whatever *unspooling* is—Beck feels a seed of peace take root in her. It's probably placebo, probably nothing real, but she lets it sink in all the same.

Beck crosses and uncrosses her legs. Even though the sun bakes the craggy rocks outside, it's freezing in here. It's not just her nerves; a silent air conditioner somewhere above her pumps the wide-open room full of ice-cold air.

Avery makes her way to the kitchen and rinses out a glass. Without looking at Beck, she asks, "You want water?"

"Uh, yes. Absolutely."

Avery fills two glasses with water and places them on a clean, expensive-looking tray. It's odd to see her here, walking the floors of a room that looks like it belongs in a magazine for billionaires. Her hair is unbrushed, shirt ragged and ill-fitting, sneakers worn to their soles. Everything about this place is at odds with her. Beck wonders what Ricky will look like—if he'll match his daughter or the grandeur of this place.

She slides into the armchair opposite the sectional and hands Beck a glass of water. If she were less exhausted, she might try to hide how fast she gulps it down. But her throat feels like sandpaper and her vision is blurry and the minute she presses the glass to her lips, the water is gone. Through the base of the glass, she catches Avery watching her. The record player keeps singing and the air conditioner keeps churning, but other than that, the treatment center is silent.

"How do you guys afford all this?" Beck asks.

Avery shrugs. "I don't know. I'm not an accountant."

"You're everything else in town," Beck muses. "Tour guide, bodyguard. Not an accountant though, I guess."

"Sorry to disappoint."

Finally, a door at the far end of the room opens.

Two men step into the room laughing. Beck sits up straight, trying to make sense of them. The man on the right is almost identical to Mr. Sterling in the way he dresses, the way he stands, the pristine tuck of his button-up. But he's not the one that catches Beck's eye.

The man on the left is squat, broad-shouldered, and stocky. He wears a cowboy hat square on his round head, a patterned shirt tucked into worn ranching pants, and an elaborate pair of cowboy boots. His laugh is the one she hears, thundering and velvety in the wide-open space. At first, the men don't see Beck on the sectional.

They clasp hands and the shorter man claps the other one hard on the back.

"If you have any issues," the shorter, flashier man says, "just stop back in."

"Will do," the taller man says. He turns to look at Beck and Avery and he smiles. "Don't want to keep the ladies waiting."

Avery leans forward and picks a pebble from the bottom of her shoe. Without looking up, she says, "Bye, Teddy."

Beck sits entirely still. It's finally happening. It's *happening*.

The taller man—Teddy, apparently—makes his way out of the treatment center into the bright light, and then there are three of them left. The shorter man makes his way to the record player, picks up its arm, and slides it to a new track, dreamy and crooning. He puts a hand on his hip and turns to face Beck. He fixes his gaze on her with such weight Beck momentarily feels like she's being crushed.

"Rebecca?" the man asks. "I'm assuming?"

Beck gives a terse nod. "Beck. Yeah."

"*Beck,*" the man says, clapping his hands. "Avery told me that, too. Forgive me, my memory is not what it used to be. My name is Ricky Carnes, as I'm sure you already know."

Beck laughs a little, breathy and unsure. This is Ricky, then. But he's nowhere near what she pictured. She's not sure what exactly she imagined, but Ricky is the opposite. He's unassuming, rough around the edges. Other than the elaborate beading on his boots, he looks like any rancher she might see back in Washington. He grabs an orange from the kitchen counter and makes his way over.

"I hear you've been having a hard time lately, Beck," Ricky says. He slides his thumbnail under the rind of his orange and sucks the juice from his finger. "Before we start, do you want it to be just us? Or would you feel more comfortable if Miss Avery stuck around?"

Beck eyes Avery, who doesn't meet her gaze. She's not sure how she's supposed to answer this question. She clears her throat and wishes she'd said yes to that second glass of water. "Uh. I'm fine either way."

"Amazing." Ricky plops into the last open armchair. "Well, let's play it by ear, then."

Beck nods.

"I want to start by establishing a few things with you, Beck. Is that okay?" Ricky asks. "This is not a treatment session. You're not being charged. We don't need to hash out a full contract, but any-time someone comes to me for help, I like to lay a few ground rules. A baseline for us both to operate from. I think it tends to sort out problems before they even pop up."

"Oh," Beck says. She looks at Avery, who is thoroughly fixated on a loose string at the hem of her shirt. She looks back at Ricky, though it's hard to maintain eye contact with him. His eyes are the same color as Avery's, vibrant brown and clear as river stones. He looks at her with an intensity that makes Beck squirm. She sucks in a breath and nods. "Yeah. That's fine."

"Great. So, like I said, this is not a treatment session. I think of it more like an informational interview," Ricky says. "Avery says you've been wanting some answers about our town, how it got started, and what we're doing out here. I don't speak for everyone in Backravel, but I've been here a long time. I'll tell you what I can and we'll see if it helps you feel better. If you end up thinking treatment might be a good idea for you—"

From the armchair, Avery goes still. She eyes her father but says nothing.

"—we can discuss that later," Ricky finishes. "First and foremost, I'd prefer you not post the things you learn all over the internet. The people who come here for treatment value the sense of . . . *privacy* that Backravel offers. I'm an open book, but I do worry about our services getting overwhelmed. Does that make sense?"

"I think so," Beck says. Her fingers curl around the edge of the sectional cushion. If Ricky doesn't want any of Backravel's secrets finding their way into the world, what was her mother doing here? Why did he let a journalist visit over a dozen times? Beck wonders if the allure of a forbidden story was part of what sucked Ellery in. She wonders if Ricky knew Ellery was digging around in the first place.

"Perfect. I'm glad." Ricky sighs and leans back into his chair. "Well, let's start by answering some of *your* questions."

"Now?"

"Hit me."

Beck clears her throat. Shakily, she digs into her backpack and pulls her notebook to freedom. "So, my first question. When was Backravel founded?"

"An easy one!" Ricky declares, and his voice is so loud Beck flinches. "Officially, Backravel became its own unincorporated community in 2010."

"What about unofficially?"

"Unofficially?" Ricky strokes his jaw. "I found this spot in . . . 2007, I think. My wife and I left Texas with our children and drove west until we ended up here. Those years were mainly us deciding if we really wanted to start here from scratch. It's difficult to make a life in the middle of nowhere, especially when you've got mouths to feed."

Beck scrawls the years in her notebook, but she can hardly keep up. "Why did you leave Texas?"

Ricky's laugh is short. "My wife was a scientist. I was trying to break into the industry, too. We were trying to do something *notable,* but Texas was all dead ends. We couldn't afford housing, we couldn't find work. We could keep grinding for the machine and get nowhere, or we could set out on our own. We chose to make a path for ourselves."

"Mr. Sterling says you felt . . . *called* here?"

"Ah, that." Ricky laughs. "Do you need more water, by the way? A snack?"

Beck inhales. "Sure."

Ricky nudges Avery with the side of his boot. Avery reluctantly pulls herself up from the armchair and pours more water. She's different around Ricky. Quieter. She doesn't talk back when he speaks to her. Like a worker bee, she just moves without complaint. When Avery returns, she has three glasses of water and she says nothing, sinking back to her seat. She looks vaguely irritated, and Beck forces herself not to shrink down in guilt.

Water in hand, Ricky continues. "We were driving to California originally. I thought maybe that's where the desert would be. Death Valley or somewhere like that. I would have these dreams of a big, wide-open desert, but I didn't know where it was. We only ended up here when my car broke down on the highway and we were stranded. The minute I hit Backravel soil, I could just tell this place was different. It's not just the ruins. You feel it, don't you? There's something alive in the air. It's . . . *incredible.*"

Beck nods, but she says nothing. Of course she feels it, but *incredible* isn't the first word that comes to mind. *Jarring, unnerving, disorienting.* Something is off here, in a way she can't quite place yet. It's a secret everyone knows, but no one will tell. It's something they might not even be able to name. Ricky's story matches Mr. Sterling's retelling almost *too* well. Like he's reading from a script.

"How did that turn into the, uh . . . the treatments?"

Ricky smiles at that. "It's all connected, actually. Something about the earth here that makes my treatments possible. Though I'd hardly call them *mine*. My wife was the one who felt the unique energy here first. I was just the one who learned what it was capable of. She ran tests on the rocks for years but could never quite whittle out the reason it could do what it did."

"Which is . . . ?"

Ricky ponders that. "Magic."

"Okay." Beck chews the inside of her cheek, choosing not to dissect that particular word choice. She casts a sidelong glance at Avery, a quiet apology before her next question. "Your wife . . . is she here, too?"

Ricky's smile dims. Beck can't bring herself to look at Avery. This wasn't a question she had prepared, but she can't leave it unasked. The record player lets out a wobbly whine and, finally, Ricky sighs.

"She isn't."

"I'm sorry."

"Don't be." Ricky sits back. "It's natural to ask. And I try to be an open book. My wife and I split up several years ago. I wanted to use this place to help people, which she found morally reprehensible."

"Why?"

"I think some people are afraid of miracles, Beck," Ricky offers. "They always believe there has to be a catch. I'm an optimist, though. How about you? Do you believe in miracles?"

"I don't know if I've ever seen one."

Avery says nothing, but Beck only needs to glance at her once to see she's gone totally stiff at the mention of her mother. It's not a foreign feeling to Beck. She remembers the stomach-clenching conversations back home, Ellery going on for hours about all of their father's faults. The piece of her that loved her mother at war with the piece of her that dared to love her father, too. Even if she agreed, it was like betraying herself.

"Beck, I don't want to overstep, here . . ." Ricky begins. "But Avery told me you've been struggling with a recent loss. Many people in Backravel are in a similar boat, trying to find their footing after their world has changed."

"Oh."

Beck flushes. Her face is hot. She knew this would come up, knew this was the reason Avery brought her here, but listening to Ricky talk about it, it's like he's holding the blade already lodged in her chest and slightly—*just* slightly—twisting it.

"Grief is such a hard thing, and it gets so much harder when we swallow it all ourselves. When we hide it. Can you tell me about your mother?"

Beck pauses. She can't say too much, but she has to say something. "My mom actually used to come here a lot. That's why I knew about Backravel. She always told me and my sister what a special place this was. I guess I just thought, if I came here, I could sort of—"

"—connect with her," Ricky finishes. "It's normal to slip into the things your loved ones held dearly before they passed. It can help you see them again, even if it's just for a second. Do you feel like, coming here, you've . . . seen her?"

"I . . ." Beck swallows. "A little bit."

"What was she like?"

The answer spills quicker than Beck means it to. "She was a really stubborn person. She liked to know things about everything. She loved things that didn't make sense. She was, uh . . . she wasn't very organized. But she was so smart. She knew what I was thinking before I even did."

Ricky nods solemnly. "Okay, okay."

Avery watches Beck carefully now, and Beck can't tell if she's angry or if she's just listening. It feels hot in the room. Beck's pulse thunders and her head spins.

"Beck, you said she came here often." Ricky sits forward in his chair. "This is going to sound odd, but . . . was your mother a writer?"

Beck's eyes widen. "Yes."

Ricky claps so loud even Avery flinches. "I should've put two and two together. What's your last name, Beck?"

"Birsching?"

"*Not* a common name. Your mother . . . Ellery Birsching, right?"

It's like the floor slips out from under her. Beck's smile evaporates and she's left staggering, fingernails pressed hard to the inside of her palm. She'd expected it to hurt, hearing her name out loud like this, but she hadn't expected to feel so unmoored. Her mother's name on a stranger's lips.

"You knew her?" Beck manages.

"Of course I did." Ricky beams. He taps Avery on the shin. "You knew her, too. You used to help Miss Ellery up the driveway all the time. You don't remember?"

Beck turns on Avery, but Avery's eyes are trained on her father, wide and confused. She shakes her head. "I don't."

Ricky clicks his tongue, then pats Avery on the shin again. It's oddly formal for a parent. His smile is lopsided, almost apologetic. Finally, he quietly says, "Avery, do you think me and Beck could talk alone for a bit?"

Avery glances up. Her eyes track from her father's face to Beck's then she shrugs. She stands, grabs her water glass, and stalks into the halls of the treatment center without a word. It's silent for too long in her wake. Beck is left staring at the empty spot she occupied.

Ricky smiles. "I don't want to make it awkward. But if you're really Ellery's daughter . . . I know I said I believe in miracles, but this is incredible."

"What?"

"Your mother and I were friends, Beck." Ricky shakes his head. "I can't believe no one else has spoken to you about her. Ellery was here so many times. More than most who visit. I was so sorry to hear she passed. She had nothing but wonderful things to say about you girls."

Against her will, Beck's brow furrows and her nose crinkles up. She has to suck in a quick breath to keep from crying. She imagines Ellery sitting on this couch, opposite Ricky. She imagines a notebook sprawled like a baby over Ellery's lap as she picked Ricky's brain. It occurs to her, suddenly, that maybe it was never an exposé on Backravel she was writing. If they were such good friends, maybe it was Ricky's story, too.

"Um . . ." Beck starts. She has to steel herself to find what she was trying to ask in the first place. "I'm sorry. What was she doing here? If you remember."

"Oh, at first it was that story," Ricky says. "I remember the first time she barreled in here with her tape recorder and notebooks, demanding we answer for some man who said he'd been robbed. She had an idea that she'd write a story about a band of grifters in the middle of the desert like we were modern highwaymen."

Beck laughs a little at that. She can almost picture it, Ellery with wisps of blond hair falling from her recklessly tied-up bun. She had a nasty set to her jaw when she was on a mission. Usually, she didn't leave without a story. But Backravel was different.

"I told her everything I knew. I think, even from the first visit, she realized there was no story."

Beck's stomach clenches. "No story?"

Ricky shrugs.

"If there was no story, why did she come back?"

"Because the longer she spent here, the more she wanted to know. She wanted to understand how our community was created, how it worked. She asked a lot of the same questions you're asking now, actually."

"So she was still writing a story?"

"She never finished it, as far as I know." Ricky scratches at his jaw, uneasy. "A couple years in, I did consider us friends. I thought she was coming to the treatment center for another interview, but she actually came to tell me about the tumor."

Beck goes still. The diagnosis was only a few months ago. They only caught it weeks before she died. The doctor said that Ellery's brain tumor had come on suddenly, that he'd rarely ever seen it happen so fast. Her other scans had been clear, and then suddenly they weren't. It's impossible that she was aware of it years ago. It's impossible that she'd know she was dying and wouldn't say a thing.

"A few years in?" Beck asks. "What year?"

"Oh, it's hard to say. 2015?"

Beck shakes her head. "No. I'm sorry. We *just* found out."

"Right," Ricky says. His expression is somber now. "I know this might be hard to swallow. I never really approved of her hiding all of this from you. At the time, your mom and I worked out an arrangement. She'd only ever been an observer of my treatments until then, but it was clear that she would need to become a patient. I wanted her to stay here so I could take care of her, but she didn't want to relocate you girls. So we decided to see each other once every few months. Just enough to keep her healthy."

The cool push from the air conditioner sends a shiver down Beck's spine. She bites the inside of her cheek until she tastes iron on her tongue. Treatment for asthma is one thing, but treatment for a terminal brain tumor is something else. It's impossible. Beck says nothing because there aren't words big enough to capture the impossibility of it.

"You don't believe me," Ricky says.

"I just . . . *how?*"

"My wife was the scientist, not me," Ricky says. "I can't explain how it works. But something about Backravel allows us to help people in ways that seem impossible. I'm able to look into a person and see the root of what's hurting them."

"How?" Beck asks again.

"I wish I could be more specific." Ricky takes a long drink of water. "But I'll tell you what. Your mom didn't believe it, either. Until she was treated and realized she was living a lot longer than she thought she would. When she first told me about the growth, the doctor wasn't sure how much longer she'd live. And look at how far she made it."

He talks about her death like it was a victory. But Ellery Birsching's death was not a testament to her strength. If he'd seen her in that hospital bed, eyes glazed over and skin sallow, he wouldn't call it a victory for his treatment.

"I'm sorry," Beck says. "I'm just having a hard time with . . . I don't understand *how* she was treated."

"What do you mean?"

"Everyone keeps talking about these treatments. But what are they? How does it just . . . fix someone?"

"I would love to explain it to you Beck, but I'm being completely honest with you. I can only explain it by showing you. And I don't think it's a good idea, yet."

"How did she afford it?" Beck asks. She'd spent too many nights budgeting out just enough money for groceries to think treatment like this was in the Birschings' price range. The treatment center is too grand, too secret, too perfect for Ellery to have afforded even a single session.

Ricky laughs. "She told me once you were her little mathematician, always balancing her books for her."

"I was," Beck admits. "So I know she couldn't—"

"We worked out a deal. Like I said, I considered Ellery a friend. So I asked her for a favor. I needed her help finding something I lost years ago. I figured . . . I have the treatment she needed, and she had the investigative skill *I* needed."

Beck swallows. "What were you looking for?"

"Something that would help my treatments be . . . more effective." Ricky shakes his head. "As you can see, there was a military base here, once. A research station, I think. And I believe they found something that would make my treatments look like child's play. But there are so many years of documents and films and transcripts. I don't have time to look through all of it. Which is why I enlisted your mom."

"The source . . ." Beck trails.

She doesn't realize she's said it out loud until it's too late.

Ricky's smile is too wide, too eager. "Exactly. She told you about it?"

"No." Beck sighs. "She didn't tell us anything."

"I see." Ricky is quiet for a moment. Contemplative. The record player near the door skips, hiccupping onto a new, more upbeat track. Ricky pulls his hat up to dab away the sweat at his brow. "Beck, do you mind if I ask *you* a few questions?"

Beck nods.

"Your mom didn't tell you anything about Backravel?"

Beck blinks. "No. All I have are her notes, but she never told us much directly. She always kept her investigations really private. Even before she came to Backravel."

"Huh." Ricky huffs. "That's strange."

Beck arches a brow.

"Do you still have her notes?"

Beck is tempted to tell the truth, but something small clenches in her chest. She wants to trust Ricky, but it's all too perfect. The notes are the only thing she has left of Ellery. She can't give them up quite yet. Without pausing, she says, "I don't. I think she threw them all away."

Ricky frowns. "That's such a shame. I know she'd done so much work. I wish I could've seen what she had, even if it was just notes."

"So you could finish the search?"

"Yes, that," Ricky says. He looks out the window and the sun washes the harsh lines of his face in gold. After a moment, he says, "And for more selfish reasons, too. I thought, in her notes, she might say if I'd done something wrong."

"What do you mean?"

Ricky turns and the sun slides like a sheet over his face. There's a genuine pain in his eyes, something Beck didn't expect. For a moment, she sees him the way the Sterlings see him. A kind man with an apparent ability no one else in the world can match. A man holding up a whole world on his shoulders.

"I was hoping the notes could explain why she disappeared on us. I told you before that treatment is only truly effective if you live here in town. But still, we'd worked out a schedule. A session every few months to make sure she stayed healthy. But one day, she just canceled the rest of her sessions and disappeared," Ricky says, leveling his gaze at Beck. Before he says it, Beck understands. "I thought the notes might explain why your mother chose to die instead of coming back."

14

The way down from the treatment center is much easier than the way up. Beck pulls away from the lush green lawns and turns onto the asphalt driveway back to town, wind cooler than it was an hour earlier. She lifts her feet from the pedals and lets the bike glide toward the base of the plateau, wind streaming through her messy, unbrushed hair. She should have a million thoughts racing through her head, and she's sure they're coming, but right now her skull feels empty. Just wind, sun, road, and nothing.

She should tell Riley what she learned.

She can't tell Riley what she learned.

"Okay," Beck whispers to herself, careening her bike around another curve in the road. "Deep breaths. It's okay."

It's beautiful here. For a long time, Beck didn't understand why her mother called it such a beautiful place. A desert is a desert, she'd thought, but this isn't just a desert. The mountains are massive and unnamed, silently imposing on the horizon. The sky is clear blue and the earth is the color of crushed brick and Beck gets it. The military ruins and blistering heat are punctuated with cacti and sweet, dry winds. Soaring down the plateau toward town proper, Beck understands. She's just as amazed as she is afraid. In a way, the feelings merge into one.

Once, back in Everett, Ellery Birsching burst into the house at five in the morning. She'd been on a trip to Backravel again, sunburnt and hair unkempt, hollower in the cheeks than she was when she left. Beck was awake like she was always awake while Ellery was gone. If anyone asked why, she'd say she had a lunch to pack for Riley, an essay due in English on a book she hadn't read, and not enough time to do it all. But really, she was awake because she was waiting. She didn't want to miss the Ellery Birsching who came home. The days when Ellery returned to Washington were, oddly, when she was at her clearest. Now she understands why.

Because the Ellery that crashed into their home was freshly *unspooled*. She was recharged, even if it was just for a little bit.

But that morning, Ellery crashed into the main room of the Everett house and stumbled to the kitchen island. She pulled a notepad from her backpack and flung it onto the countertop, sketching a misshapen hunk of rock with scrub and cacti bordering its base. She drew with her brow furrowed, nose crinkled up in frustration. She drew like she thought if she didn't sketch fast enough she'd lose it.

Then, when she was done, she smiled at Beck and said, "I had a dream on the plane. I swear, this is where I'm going to die."

Beck pulls herself out of the memory just in time to veer off the black driveway at the base of the plateau and coast into Backravel's dusty downtown. She stops and looks up at the plateau, then closes her eyes. The plateau—the treatment center—is what her mother drew. And she was wrong.

Ellery Birsching didn't die at the treatment center. She didn't even die in Backravel. There's a faint flutter in Beck's chest, because maybe this is all for nothing. Maybe her mother never found any answers here. And maybe she's dooming herself and Riley to spiral into that same madness. Ellery Birsching was an incredible journalist, but she wasn't a psychic. There were things she didn't know.

Beck shakes her head and continues riding toward Sycamore Lane.

Her head is a thousand miles away when she almost collides with the animal lying dead in the road. Beck veers to the left, spinning her bike into the rut of red dirt at the road's shoulder. She skids off the seat and tumbles to her knees and her mouth fills with dirt. Scratches of red blossom at the numb skin of her knees. She hauls herself to her feet and makes a poor attempt at brushing off, then she eyes the creature in the road.

Not a creature. A *person*.

"Oh no," she mutters. She clambers back to the road and kneels at the person's side. A woman, dark hair matted with dirt and debris. Dust coats the sun-leathered skin of her face. For a moment, Beck is sure the woman isn't breathing. "No, no, *no*."

And then the woman sputters to life.

Beck jolts back, trips over her toppled bike and lands squarely in the dirt. The woman on the road stands, eyes wild like an animal. She searches the road for a moment, and then her eyes finally land on Beck. Slowly, she relaxes. Beck recognizes her as the woman in the desert from her first trip into town. The same stiff hair, ill-fitting clothes, and sun-worn expression. She rubs the dirt from her eyes.

"Wrong," the Desert Woman says. She coughs once, phlegmy and harsh, into the crook of her elbow. "Wrong, wrong. Too far. God, what have I done now?"

Beck blinks. "Are you okay?"

The woman stares.

"You were in the road. Did you . . . are you hurt?"

"No." The woman stares at the road like she's not sure how she got there, either. "How long have I been here?"

"I don't know," Beck admits. "I just found you."

The woman looks her over. Her eyes are steely and gray, too light for the cloudy whites of her eyes. She's been out here in the hot, dry desert for too long. Beck doesn't have to know where she came from or how she got here to know *that* much. People are only meant to be in the sun for so long.

"You shouldn't be here," the woman says. "Not yet."

"Not yet?"

"Or maybe . . . have we already met?"

Beck swallows and feels the scratch of dirt in her throat. She chokes on it, and when she looks up, the woman is sitting in the road with her legs crossed. She maintains a strange distance from Beck, like she's afraid to get too close.

"We haven't," Beck says. "You should get out of the road."

"Why? No cars."

It's a fair point, and strange to hear stated so plainly.

"Why were you lying in the road?"

"I was going somewhere." The woman stretches her arm across her chest and winces in pain. "I had work to do."

Beck cups a hand at her brow and looks behind her. The campsite stands all alone just like it was on that first ride back to Sycamore Lane. A red tent, a truck in disrepair, a cooler, a pile of small stones. It all ripples in the heat, a strange and disheveled oasis. Beck licks the dust from her lips and turns back to the Desert Woman.

"Is this your campsite?"

The woman eyes the campsite, but her expression is only disgust. She shakes her head. "That's *not* where I was going."

"Where were you—"

The woman looks at Beck again and her face changes. She lunges forward and takes Beck's leg in her shaking hands. Beck tries to kick free, but the woman peels up the dirty, scraped leg of her pants and eyes her shin. The cut is deeper than Beck realized. Her skin is torn and a glistening, dirt-smeared layer of blood coats the cut.

"You're hurt," the Desert Woman says. "You should've said so."

"Oh," Beck says. She pushes her pant leg back down and inches away. "I'm sorry."

She's not sure why she apologizes.

"I can help," the woman says. "Come with me."

The woman gracelessly hauls herself to her feet, and a puff of dirt falls from her. She moves swiftly toward the campsite. Something about the woman makes Beck's skin crawl, but she can't ignore the spark of curiosity that urges her to follow.

Up close, the campsite is even more elaborate. The red tent is smeared with dirt, but the inside is lined with worn, hand-stitched afghans and misshapen pillows. A stack of books rest against the tent wall, each one a tome on astrophysics, chemical experimentation, and other scientific things Beck's sure she should know about from school. Empty water bottles litter the floor of the tent and the ground of the campsite. The old truck kneels on its front fender, and the inside is covered in more pillows and blankets.

The woman dips into her tent and crawls out with a battered first-aid kit. She directs Beck to a busted camping chair and goes to work, gently cleaning and bandaging the wound on her shin. She bites her lower lip in determination and, without looking up, she asks, "Did you hurt anywhere else?"

"Uh, no," Beck says. She looks around the campsite, trying to commit as much of it to memory as she can. "I'm fine. Do you sleep out here?"

The woman rolls her eyes. She delicately wraps a bandage around Beck's calf, then takes a moment to check her work. The first-aid kit is ugly on the outside, but the contents look new. The woman looks into Beck's face and narrows her eyes. "I'm sure I've seen you."

"I don't think so," Beck says. "I just got here."

"I think you've been here," the woman says. "You were visiting. From Washington. I remember."

Beck freezes.

"But not yet."

The Desert Woman stands and surveys her campsite. She moves like a character in a broken video game, fractured and stilted, like she's pulled in a thousand different directions. Her dark hair is bunched into a low ponytail that gathers in a tangle between her shoulder blades. The creases of her knuckles are caked with red dirt that, at first glance, looks like blood.

Beck's mother looked like this toward the end. Not dirty, but lost. Splintered in a million pieces, every look a question. She would sit up in the living room and stare, brow tilted like she'd just re- membered she was afraid. *What is it?* Beck would ask, laying out a notebook, the TV remote, her mother's laptop like anything so simple could tug Ellery Birsching back to earth. It didn't matter what she suggested. Her mother needed something Beck couldn't give. She needed Backravel. Toward the end, her mother's mind was like dandelion seeds blown scattershot into the breeze. Asking what she needed was like trying to catch all the pieces of her in one hand.

"When did we meet?"

"It was before, um . . . after I lost my spot." The woman begins drawing a diagram in the air with her dirt-stained fingers. "After that, but before you got here."

Beck sucks in a breath. Pity like sour milk curdles on her tongue. "What did you lose?"

The woman presses her hands to her forehead. "I'm not as good at it. Ricky goes back and forth like he's born to do it. It's not as easy for me, okay?"

Ricky. There's something.

"What is he better at?" Beck asks, trying to mask the plea in her voice. "Where does he go?"

"I already told you once," the woman says as though that even remotely answers the question. "Look, I've been working on it. But it takes time and I keep getting confused."

This isn't working.

Beck takes a breath, stands, and crouches at the woman's side. The cooler is mostly empty. There are only two cans of Diet Pepsi, another half-gone bottle of water, and a plastic-wrapped grocery store sandwich submerged in an inch of melted ice. The woman plunges her hands into the cooler, searching for something. A couple of dead gnats float in the water and Beck tries not to show her disgust on her face.

"Can I help you get something out of there?" Beck asks quietly. "What are you looking for?"

The woman closes her eyes and slowly extracts the water bottle. "I just needed to focus. That's all."

The woman drinks her water and the campsite is quiet. Beck takes a deep breath and her panic flattens to a calm. The road back to Sycamore Lane stretches one way and the road into Backravel stretches the other way. This spot, halfway between, feels both dangerous and serene all at once. Beck focuses on the warmth of the sun on the back of her neck and she doesn't slip. She doesn't let herself. In this conversation, for once, she needs to be the grounded one.

The quiet seems to calm the woman, too. She puts her now almost-empty water bottle back in the dingy cooler and closes it. After a moment, her eyes widen. "You're *different*."

Beck arches a brow.

A thought takes root in her now, unlikely and wild. The woman in her mother's notes was lost and confused, too.

"Does the name Delia Horton mean anything to you?" Beck asks.

The Desert Woman blinks.

Beck feels her throat tighten. She shakes her head and it's like the whole world shakes with her. She unearths her phone from her back pocket and opens her photo album. One quick scroll, and she finds a cluster of pictures saved from her mother's Facebook page. *Remembering Ellery Birsching* it says now. She taps open a photo of her mother in her office back home, tapping away at her keyboard, pointedly flipping off the camera. It's a picture from a good day. Beck's revisited it more times than she can count.

"Have you seen this woman before?" Beck asks, holding the picture in front of the Desert Woman's face.

The Desert Woman shields her eyes from the glare. After a moment, she leans in, transfixed by the picture. She looks at Beck, and then looks at the picture again. After a moment, she laughs.

"I'm such an idiot," she cries. "Of course you're not her. You're Rebecca. Or . . . are you Riley?"

Beck's eyes widen.

"Yes, she said she had girls. Oh, you look so much like her."
The woman stands and her face is too close to Beck's. Up close, the
deep wrinkles of her face are even more visible. "You have glasses.
Rebecca, then. You look so tired."

"How . . ." Beck croaks. She clears her throat. "How did you
know her?"

"We're friends," the Desert Woman says. Her voice is dreamlike
now, lost in another time. "We *are* friends. Did she come with you?
She promised me she wouldn't bring you girls out here."

"What do you mean?"

The woman blinks. "Oh. Never mind. I don't know. You're here
now."

Beck looks into the woman's gray eyes and she's sure she's seen
them before. Not in a memory. On another face. This is the happiest
the woman has looked since they met. It's the most *here* she's looked.
Her small, round lips are curved in a near-smile. She doesn't know
what happened to Ellery, then. She doesn't know anything. Beck feels
sick.

"My mom." Beck breathes. "She, uh . . . she died."

The woman's expression darkens. She goes entirely still, then
paces to the camping chair and sinks into it. She puts her face in her
hands. "Oh. Oh no. No, that wasn't supposed to happen."

"What?"

"Here?" she snaps. "Did she die *here*?"

"No."

"What am I supposed to do now?" the woman asks, more to herself than anyone else. "She was supposed to help me. Now what do
I do?"

Beck winces. "What was she helping you with?"

"Remembering."

"Remembering what?" Beck can't completely hide the ire in her voice. Her heart races so fast she thinks she might black out.

"It's not a good day," the woman says, frantic now. "I can't . . . it's all mixed up. But maybe another day."

"Please," Beck says. "What do you remember about her? What was she helping with?"

"She was helping me . . ." the woman says again. She presses a shaking fist to her temple, and a rivulet of water from the cooler runs down her cheek. "I can't remember. She was helping me. I don't know."

She looks at Beck, and Beck recognizes her expression. She saw it on Mr. Sterling, and on her mother. Things that should be obvious slipping away. But the Desert Woman seems far worse than Mr. Sterling. Worse than Ellery, even. She's so lost in her own mind she can't find the surface, no matter how hard she swims.

"What's your name?" Beck tries.

The woman's face is an apology. "It's a bad day."

"It's okay," Beck says, even though it's not. She stands and brushes off her dirty pants. "If I go, will you still be here tomorrow? Can I come back and talk to you?"

A breeze floats under the tangle of the woman's hair, but it doesn't budge. She doesn't look at Beck. She stares at her own palms. "I would like that. I can try."

It's not an answer, but it will do. Beck swallows hard.

"You'll be safe out here?"

"No," the woman mumbles. "But don't worry about me."

Beck hesitates, then she turns away. Realistically, it's the best she can do. She can't leave Riley all night by herself, and she certainly can't bring a stranger back to the trailer. Before she heads back toward the bike and the road and Sycamore Lane, she pauses. "Thank you. For patching me up. I'll see you soon, okay?"

"Your mom patched me up a thousand times," the woman says. "It's the least I could do."

And Beck wants to stay. She wants to press for more. Instead, she nods and offers a curt smile. "I'll see you tomorrow."

The woman doesn't answer. Because she doesn't know if she will.

15

"This is it," Riley says.

They bike up to a house on Cedar Drive, a road nearly identical to Sycamore Lane in the labyrinth of Backravel's suburbs. Katie's house looks strikingly similar to the Sterlings' house; white siding, speckles of bright-colored flowers peppered along a cobblestone walkway. It's a standard two-story with a fenced backyard and a cluster of bikes tilted against the front porch. When Beck looks down Cedar Drive, she sees a dozen more houses that look exactly the same. The only difference between this road and Sycamore Lane is a curb at the far end of the street separating Backravel from the sprawling desert. Like the end of a video game map, the road cuts off, leaving Beck with a sinking feeling in the pit of her stomach.

She swallows and nods.

"It's gonna be fine," Riley says, though even she sounds unconvinced. She twists a lock of her hair around her pointer finger. "If it gets bad, we can leave. I'll leave with you. I promise."

Beck looks at the toes of her sneakers. Riley has been more intentional with these check-ins since they got here. Beck knows she should be grateful—she should feel loved—but the only thing it makes her feel is shame. She can keep it together. She can stay above water long enough to enjoy a movie night. After days of ducking and dodging around Backravel, keeping secrets close to her chest, she owes Riley this much.

When she looks at the desert beyond the curb, she thinks of the Desert Woman. Even in the heat of sunset, her skin feels cold.

Riley knocks on the front door and it opens almost immediately. Katie smiles at them, black hair released from its usual ponytail tonight. She wears an oversized jean jacket and a pair of black denim shorts. She hesitates for a moment, then pulls both Birschings into a hug.

"I'm surprised you actually came," Katie says.

"I had to drag her out of the trailer," Riley says, motioning to Beck.

"Thanks for hosting," Beck says, and her throat feels tight. "She didn't have to *drag* me, I'm just a little out of it lately."

"I get it," Katie says. She motions them into the house. "Shoes off, please. And yeah, I mean, you're the one who had to do all the driving. It's totally your right to be tired."

"Whatever," Riley muses.

Beck smiles a little, tentatively. Maybe this won't be horrible. She hasn't gone to a "movie night" since middle school because it's been impossible to leave the house for a full night between chores, bills, and her necessary, regularly programmed hours of emotional spiraling. But there's no dinner to worry about tonight, no overdue bills. She can, theoretically, relax.

She's not optimistic.

"Okay, one other thing," Katie says, stopping them before they reach the basement stairs. "I was talking to the others and it sounds like you've been hanging out with Avery a lot. Which is totally cool. In fact, I was like, we *never* see Avery outside the treatment center, so I asked her if she wanted to come, too."

"Avery's here?" Beck asks.

Her tone must come off more interested than she means. Katie and Riley share a knowing look. Beck flushes and fixes her eyes on the basement stairs. If Avery's here, she has to recalibrate. She can't relax, because now the treatment center and the Carnes family are back on the table.

"Yeah," Katie says finally. "She's downstairs."

"Are you cool with that?" Riley asks Beck. "I know you were—"

"Absolutely cool," Beck says, too quick. "I was just surprised."

Katie smiles and nods. She leads them into the basement, where a couch and a couple of mismatched armchairs face an outdated TV. It's the usual gang—Daniel in a slouchy sweatshirt and beanie, Jack in jeans and a T-shirt, and Megan in a floral-patterned summer dress. The group of them might look disparate, but to Beck, they're interchangeable. She skims over them to the girl all by herself in an armchair. Distant from the others, Avery sits and inspects her nailbeds. Her lips are curved in a bored frown, hair halfway pinned back, but not enough to keep the loose bits out of her face. She has her legs pulled up into the chair and she doesn't look up, even when the staircase groans under the weight of the three of them descending. But Beck feels her attention turn. Sharpen.

"Finally," Daniel says. He has a massive bowl of popcorn in his lap, which he quickly casts aside to shove a VHS tape in the TV.

Beck takes a long look at Katie's basement. Something about it unsettles her, though she can't put her finger on what. There's the squat TV that looks like an antique with a glass screen and dials Beck assumes are for changing the channel. There's a desk on the far side of the basement with a brand-new laptop and exercise ball replacing a standard desk chair. Every item in the basement feels like it's been plucked from a different year—from a different *decade*.

Before Beck can make sense of the basement, Riley gallops down the stairs and nestles herself comfortably between Daniel and Megan. She buries her hand in the popcorn bowl and shoves a fistful into her mouth. Katie collapses onto a beanbag facing the TV, leaving Beck with the last empty spot next to Jack on the love seat. Not ideal, but Beck swallows her anxiety and takes the spot. She's going to keep it together tonight. She's not going to worry Riley. She's not going to look like a wreck in front of Avery. Not again.

Avery's eyes are on her already, watchful and intense. Beck forces herself not to look back. She feels the burn of Avery's eyes on her skin. Avery, who doesn't belong in this room, mixed with this group of people.

"Now that everyone's here," Katie chirps, "we can—"

There's a croak from the top of the stairs. A woman's voice calls down from the main floor of the house, warm and sweet, just like Katie's. "You have everything you need down there?"

"We do," Katie calls back, clearly irritated. "Thanks, Mom."

"Thanks, Mrs. Horton," Megan calls, and the rest of the kids repeat after her.

But Beck doesn't thank Mrs. Horton. In an instant, it's like the room sinks. She looks at Riley, but Riley's eyes are trained on the TV as the previews for a handful of other outdated slashers start to play.

"Katie," Beck says carefully. "What's your mom's first name?"

Katie blinks, eyes Riley, then looks at Beck with a quirked brow. "Why?"

"I don't know. I thought I recognized her."

"Delia."

Delia Horton. Beck tries to keep her breathing even, tries not to show the twitch in her fingers. Delia Horton from her mother's notes. Delia Horton from the guest log. The woman who returned to Backravel over and over, just like Ellery. Beck's blood goes ice cold. She waits for Riley to react, but Riley just eyes Beck with confusion.

"How long have you guys lived in Backravel?" Beck asks because she can't stop herself. This time, she feels everyone in the room turn their eyes on her. But she can't leave it alone. "Sorry, just curious."

"It's okay," Katie says thinly, clearly annoyed. "Uh, we moved here a few years ago, I think."

"You don't remember what year?"

A pause. Katie pauses the movie. "I don't."

Beck nods. She wants to keep pushing, but she drops it. She can't take any more of Riley's glare and the silence settling into the basement. She chances a glance at Avery, who's still watching her like a hawk, and she can't tell if it's curiosity or concern thick in her brow.

Beck doesn't have time to worry about Avery. She's trying not to slip. Katie starts the movie again and the trailers fade into the real movie, and Beck doesn't watch because she has to focus. She measures her breathing, focuses on the feeling of the fake leather under her fingertips.

The movie drones on. The TV screen is a smattering of color and light, noise garbled like someone holds a pillow over the speakers. Before she can fully comprehend it, she's slipping. She expects it to scare her, but in the dark and the quiet, it's comforting. There's safety in slipping away. Just like always, she's unfastened from *here* and sent drifting quietly into somewhere else. Beck closes her eyes and leans into the numb rush. She finds herself back in the hospital room, counting the checkered turquoise floor tiles on the way to room 607. It's white walls, a round reception desk packed with exhausted nurses, pale sunlight sliding in through overlarge windows. Usually it smells sterile, but on Sunday mornings the hospital carries the scent of black coffee that the nurses bring to most patients' rooms. *It's one of the perks of being terminal,* Ellery Birsching says on her first and only Sunday morning in the hospital. *Free coffee.*

In Katie's family room, on her ratty basement sofa, wedged next to a stranger, Beck smells the fresh brew.

She blinks awake.

The room is quieter now. The movie ambles on and Beck wonders how much of it she's missed. She wonders how long she was spaced out. She's lost chunks of time before, but like most things, it feels different in Backravel. Through the blinds, she eyes the murky black night. Riley is asleep on the couch, head tilted against her own shoulder. The other kids watch the TV screen intently, but their eyes are glassy. Distant.

Beck imagines she looked the same a moment ago. Something seizes up in her, because it's almost like the others are slipping, too. In this quiet moment, they've all slipped into their own world. Together.

She swallows and straightens, closing her eyes.

A hand touches her shoulder.

"Hey." It's Avery stooped in front of her, unkempt hair nothing but a silhouette in the light of the TV. "Hey. Breathe."

Beck does.

"Nice," Avery whispers. "Are you okay?"

Beck takes another breath, settles back into the living room. The walls still tilt a little, leaning in like they mean to collapse, but at least she knows where she is. At least she knows *when* she is. This isn't like the slips she used to get back home. This is worse, more visceral, more consuming. Sweat beads at the nape of her neck. Beck realizes she's gasping for air. The others don't seem to notice, caught in their own orbit. Riley is still fast asleep, deep breaths wheezing through her slightly parted lips.

Beck dabs away a tear at the corner of her eye with her sleeve. "I'm good. Thanks. Uh, sorry."

"Fresh air," Avery says. A statement, not an offer. She holds out a hand and waits for Beck to take it.

Shakily, Beck rises from the sofa and stumbles out of the TV room, up the narrow stairs, weaves past the Hortons' vintage dining table and piles of clutter. Instead of slipping back into the hospital room, instead of hyperfocusing on Katie's mother and how she connects to Ellery's story, Beck focuses on the hand in hers, bony and calloused. Avery presses her way past a squeaky screen door at the back of the house and leads Beck quietly into the night. The sun has long since set and even the wispy dregs of red at the horizon have burnt away, leaving the black sky sprawling from one end of the earth to the other. Beck blinks away the fear that clouds her head.

"Where are we going?" Beck asks.

"You'll see."

Avery shoves her hands in her pockets and keeps walking. Beck follows softly at her heels, and the farther they walk from Katie's house, the clearer her head feels. There's a softness to the night wind as they reach the end of Cedar Drive. The houses are silent, blinds drawn, faint lights glowing from unseen living rooms. There's something about it that makes Beck's skin crawl. If someone told her that there was no one living in a single one of these houses, she might believe it.

At the end of the road, Avery steps over the curb and plants her feet squarely in the red dirt on the other side. She pivots and faces Beck, motioning for her to follow.

"I shouldn't leave Riley back there," Beck says. "I thought we were just taking a breather."

"We're finding a quiet place for you to relax."

"It's not quiet enough out here?"

Avery looks out at the stretch of desert ahead of them. "Quieter. And farther away."

Beck shifts from one foot to the other, still squarely on the road-side of the curb. Still on solid ground, in town, safely oriented in what's real. It's not just that this is a waste of time. There's something frightening about the idea of stepping outside the bounds of Cedar Drive into the dark, desert night.

"Why don't you like when I try to help you?" Avery asks. She turns to Beck with her hands shoved in her pockets, but the dark masks the details of her face.

Beck narrows her eyes. "What does that mean?"

"Do you like when I help you?"

"I can't tell if you're joking."

They stare at each other too long and Beck thinks, for a moment, that Avery might just give up on the whole venture. Then Avery bursts into laughter. The lingering hold of Beck's panic begins to dissolve and she laughs, too. She's not sure why. Maybe it's the absurdity of it all. Between her fear in the basement and the delirium of standing here with Avery, she can't help it.

"I'm just trying to understand you," Avery says. "I feel like you're having a really bad time here. But you don't want to leave, either."

Avery is right. There is something about Backravel that's eating away at her, but there's also something in her that lets it. It burrows under her skin, makes her feel helpless. Beck looks at her feet. "I don't know what it is. I don't . . . I mean, you saw everyone back there. It's not just me. There's something weird going on here."

"Yeah," Avery says, too plainly. "How about you follow me and we can talk about it?"

This time, Beck does.

She steps over the curb and follows Avery into the dark. Behind her, the lights of Cedar Drive streak until they're only pinpricks of white on a black horizon. The red dirt under their feet crunches and scrapes with each step. Beck takes one deep breath, then another. Avery wasn't wrong—there's something looser about the open space out here. Something almost healing. She feels better already.

Ten minutes into their walk, Avery stops without warning. She surveys the ground, then turns to Beck, hardly visible in the dark. "Here's good."

She sits abruptly, grabbing Beck's hand to yank her down, too. Avery is different tonight. She's not quite the same girl that gave Beck a tour of town a few days ago. She's less guarded, less apprehensive. Less cruel, in a way. For the first time since they met, Beck doesn't feel like they're on opposite sides.

Once they're both on the ground, Avery sighs and lies back, facing the sky. "This is way better than a movie night."

Beck watches Avery for a moment, wonders what she's doing out here. But she lies down, too. When she looks up, the sky is so much wider than she realized. Without the lights from town, the sky is crowded with stars. There isn't an inch of it left dark. It's overwhelming, almost. Infinite and unmoored.

"What was going on back there?" Avery asks.

"I was about to ask the same thing."

"You mean everyone being zoned out?" Avery is quiet for a moment. "It's hard to describe, but—"

"Please."

"—*but*," Avery cuts in, "I will try. It just comes with the territory out here. I don't know why, but the same thing that lets my dad unspool people also does this thing to you every once in a while. It's like you sort of . . . slide away from yourself."

"Like you're slipping." Beck breathes.

"Exactly." Avery clears her throat. Her eyes are still trained on the sky. "It kind of feels like déjà vu. It's not a bad thing, it just happens sometimes. I don't really like to watch movies because the minute I stop paying attention, it happens."

"Then why'd you come to movie night?"

After a quiet moment, Avery says, "Because Katie said you were coming."

"Oh."

Beck nods, but she doesn't look at Avery. She feels the heat of Avery's stare again, expectant and patient all at once. She knows she should answer the question now, explain what's been happening to her, but she hardly knows where to start. *I have a hard time telling the past from the present, not because of your town, because of my brain.* There isn't a clean way to make Avery understand.

"Since I got here, I think I've been having that, too," Beck says quietly. "But I was . . . in a way, I was already having it back home. Usually I just get it while I'm dreaming. Like I'm stuck in this loop of how things used to be. But in Backravel, sometimes it's happening while I'm awake. And sometimes it feels so real, it's like I forget where I am."

"It got worse since your mom?"

Beck nods. "Yes and no."

"What happened to *your* mom?" Beck asks.

Avery scoffs. "You're just going for it, then."

Beck's cheeks burn. Maybe it was an abrasive question, but it's plagued Beck since meeting Ricky. It plagues her when she looks at Avery. She wonders how Avery came to exist out here in the scorching heat, in a modern palace all alone, under a father her whole town thinks of as a god, the ghost of her mother lingering in her father's anger.

"I guess I am."

"Then I get to ask you something out of left field, too."

A strange warmth comes over Beck, a magnetism to the idea of lying out here and asking questions, speaking until her voice is hoarse, until the sun crawls over the horizon. Biting back a smile, she says, "We can take turns."

Avery flips back over to face the sky.

"Fine. I haven't talked to my mom in . . . I don't even know how long," Avery says, matter-of-fact. She massages the flat inside of her wrist, slowly thumbing each tendon. "It's like I remember her, but I also don't. She was really cut-and-dry. Like things were either good or bad objectively. We didn't get along that well—I remember *that*. She and my dad fought, but I don't even remember what they fought about. I just knew the whole time that, at some point, I'd wake up and I'd only have one of them."

"I'm sorry."

"I'm glad my dad stayed," Avery says, quieter than before. She's whispering now. "But I didn't think I'd never talk to my mom again. I didn't really think she'd just . . . disappear."

"You haven't spoken to her at *all* since she left?" Beck asks. She thinks about the months in the wake of her parents' divorce, the awkward forced phone calls, the promises that nothing would change. She imagines a world where there was none of it. Where her father disappeared completely.

"Not once."

"Did it have to do with your brother?"

"It's *my* turn," Avery says. "I've told you about my mom. Now I want to know about yours."

Beck rubs a bit of red rock between her fingers and it keeps her tethered, even if it's just for a second. Things feel less slippery out here in general, though, lying in the dirt next to Avery. Maybe that was the point. She should feel more afraid than she does. "My mom tried really hard after my dad left. I think. She was really scatter-brained, though. She had a hard time keeping track of stuff. Even before things got bad medically, she wasn't good at remembering stuff. But she wanted to know everything. Every single thing about every single person she met, no matter how small."

Avery says nothing, but Beck hears the slight scratch of her head adjusting against the earth. She doesn't need to look over to know that Avery is watching her again. This time, it doesn't feel like a burn. Beck is almost tempted to meet her gaze, but she doesn't. After months of avoiding questions about her mother, it feels nice to actually talk about Ellery Birsching. No sugarcoating, no prefaces, no bias. Just a portrait of who she was.

"She'd get so mad if she couldn't figure out how pieces fit to-gether in a story. She'd have these meltdowns. For days. She'd lock herself in her office and just stare at her laptop until she came up with something. She didn't write stories halfway."

"That sounds exhausting."

"That was before she started to . . ." Beck expels a long breath and closes her eyes. "She would go out and talk to sources for her stories, but by the time she got back to her office, she couldn't re-member what the story was about. She'd have all the info for the story, but she couldn't remember her own angle."

"You don't have to talk about it," Avery says. "If it's hard."

Beck swallows. She wonders if her voice is quivering, if her shoulders look tense. Does the hurt show? She touches her throat and she doesn't look at Avery because she can't stand it. She can't look at the pity in her face.

"It's okay. I . . . I can talk about it," Beck says. Under her breath, she laughs. "Then, she started forgetting non-story stuff. I had to tell her I'm a lesbian six times. It's like it wouldn't stick."

This time, Avery's silence is different. Beck swallows her next words. Maybe she shouldn't have mentioned it. She only meant to lighten the mood, but she can't remember the last time she came out to someone other than her mother. No one has cared since then. She hasn't kept it hidden, at least not on purpose. But with Beck, it's easier to bury everything, big or small.

She waits for Avery to speak and it feels like years.

Finally, Avery rolls onto her back, hands above her head. Beck steals a glance at her and sees the slight upturn of her smile. Despite the crispness of the night air, her chest is warm.

"Your mom was okay with that?" Avery asks.

"Which time?"

Avery laughs at that, breathy. Nervous, maybe. It's the opposite of what Beck expects from her. There's something different in the space between them now, a change in the magnetic field. Every breath a question, every look an answer.

She doesn't need to ask Avery to know that, in this, they're the same.

"She was never weird about it in like . . . a *moral* way," Beck says finally. "But I'd tell her, and then a couple months later I'd be talking about a girl at school and she'd make this face. Like I just dropped it on her out of thin air. Eventually, she stopped asking when someone said something she didn't understand. She started just assuming it was something she forgot, so she'd just leave it."

Avery says nothing again. When Beck eyes her, she's staring at the sky, but her expression is difficult. Her brow is furrowed, lips pursed in thought. Beck's gaze snags a little on a lock of Avery's hair that flutters against her ear. She knows nothing about the world Avery comes from, the things she's seen, the person she is under all this. But she *knows* her.

"What are you thinking about?" Beck asks.

"Your mom used to come here a lot?" Avery asks. "And she saw my dad a lot, too?"

"I guess so," Beck says. "I didn't know she was being treated until your dad told me, though."

"Huh." Avery doesn't move her gaze from the sky. When she speaks, she says each word deliberately like stone laid carefully in a row. "I'm sorry. If I seemed harsh at first. Sometimes, I wake up and it feels like I'm a different person every day. Like, sometimes I just think about my brother all day and I'm so sad I can't even get out of bed. Other days, I barely remember what he was like. I just get stuck in these cycles where it feels like I'm doing the same thing over and over again."

It's softer than Beck expects.

"That's part of why I like it here," Beck says. "Back home, I just wanted everything to slow down. People wanted me to move so fast. I would just lie in bed and try not to fall asleep so I could have a few hours where the world slowed down. Backravel feels slow like those hours in the middle of the night."

"Weird. I feel the opposite."

Beck rises to her elbows and raises a brow.

"Sometimes it feels like I've been doing the same thing for years.

Like I'm just waiting for something to *happen*. I've given hundreds of tours, been to a million movie nights, had dinner with my dad for decades."

Another breeze skirts between them and, silently, Beck is disarmed. She isn't usually a girl who wants big things because there's no point. Wanting is too hard, hurts too much when it never amounts to anything. But every once in a while, someone breaks through and Beck lets herself want something small and unattainable. A girl from English class with soft hands who shares her book, another from PE who wordlessly joins her under the bleachers for a cigarette, a girl with sleek black hair who jogs past the Birsching house every morning and smiles at her like clockwork. It's always girls perfectly out of reach.

Tonight, Beck notices Avery the way she notices those girls. In detail.

A delicate jaw, freckled and tan from the relentless desert sun. Dark, glassy eyes that hint at a joke only she knows. A single strand of dark hair that rests against the bridge of her nose. There's a little patch of discolored skin—a sunburn, Beck thinks—at Avery's hairline, only noticeable when you're this close. She is close, isn't she? Beck realizes it now, the way they're lying so close together their breath mingles in the dark. Maybe she didn't want Avery's help before because they're the same; machines built to perform the same function over and over, inching closer and closer to some impending end.

Beck sucks in a breath and stamps down that little flare as soon as it sparks. Avery Carnes has an expiration date. Beck will be here for another week, and then they'll never see each other again.

Avery hums a little, even quieter than the breeze. When she closes her eyes, Beck watches her. She softens a little, like she's listening to a song playing far away. Her brow is quirked just slightly, lips a flat line. Her lashes are dark and downy. Beck imagines them brushing, soft as insect wings, against her cheek.

"I can see this from my room, too," Avery says. "But I like it better out here. It feels more real."

"I see that."

"Stop me if this is too weird," Avery says, "But sometimes I come out here because I can hear the desert talking to me. It feels so familiar."

Beck swallows. "Like speaking in words?"

"Kind of."

"What kinds of stuff does it say?"

Beck pictures the mechanical whir she's heard these past few days. The subtle vibration of the earth under her feet. She feels it now, too, the almost imperceptible shift of the dirt against the skin of her arms. Maybe that's what Avery hears, too.

Avery shakes her head. "It's like a voice I've heard before, but I can't remember where. And I don't understand the words, but I know it's talking." Avery turns onto her side to face Beck. Specks of moonlight shine faintly in the dark of her eyes. "My dad doesn't like it when I come out here."

"But you do, anyway?" Beck asks.

"It's the same reason I keep bothering you," Avery muses. "Because it's something different. And it feels like I shouldn't."

They're quiet for a long time, Avery watching Beck and Beck trying desperately not to return the look. She didn't expect this tonight. She didn't expect to feel undone, to let someone see her this plainly. Just like that, she can't remember why she was hiding. Against the massive sky and the wide-open valley, they're laughably small, but they aren't alone.

And then Avery touches her.

Only a little—just her fingers shifting gently over Beck's, tentative and curious at once. Beck looks at her, and this time Avery looks away. Beck has to blink to convince herself she isn't making it up. But there's a crack in Avery here, a glimmer of vulnerability that wasn't there an hour ago. Maybe Avery's been waiting for someone to see her, too. Something is electric in the night air and it begins to unravel Beck at the seams, opens her wide, and she's a mix of fear and longing for it. Only an inch of skin against hers, but it's a live wire.

"Thanks for coming out here with me," Avery says. "I needed this."

With that, Avery sits up and it's like the ground slips away under Beck. She exhales and the world spins. She should be grateful Avery isn't looking at her, but instead, she feels cold. She swallows and rolls onto her side before sitting up, too. Avery clambers to her feet and helps Beck up. They stand facing each other just like they were when they left Cedar Drive. But everything feels different, now. Everything feels new.

Avery leads the way back to Cedar Drive and then, quietly, back to Katie's house. They pry open the front door without a sound and gently sneak to the basement stairs. If Ellery Birsching were here, she'd stay upstairs and look around the house, dragging out the connection between Delia Horton and the rest of this.

But all Beck can think about is the stars and the place Avery's skin met hers.

Back in the basement, everyone else is asleep. Riley lies on the couch, tucked under a mountain of blankets. There's a foot of empty surface area next to her, clearly left for Beck. The recliner across the room has been dressed with blankets, too. Avery takes a step toward it, but she pauses. She turns to Beck and, in the dark, she's hardly visible.

"Good night," she whispers.

Beck's chest tightens. "Good night."

They climb into their respective sleeping arrangements and say nothing else. But as Beck drifts away, she feels it—the sear of Avery's eyes on her from across the room. Beck nestles into the blankets, holds Riley close, and in the dark, she smiles.

16

Beck blinks awake in the low light, body sore and head full of dream and exhaustion. The morning is a blur of white and gray until Beck rubs the sleep from her eyes and reaches for her glasses, still half-folded on the carpet where she left them. Even blind, she can tell there's something off in the room. She shifts and her muscles ache for more. The couch is itchy and coarse and the room is silent. When she puts on her glasses, everything is the same as it was when she fell asleep. Except one thing.

Across the room, Avery is gone.

Beck sits up. The shawl of mismatched quilts and blankets gathered at her shoulders falls away, but she isn't cold. She waits for the room to come into focus, but it's not a trick of light. The recliner where Avery slept directly across from her is empty. Without her, the air slackens.

Beck gently nudges Riley's shoulder. "Hey, wake up."

"*Mmm,*" Riley groans.

"Did you see where Avery went?"

"Who?"

Beck frowns. Careful not to jostle Riley too much, she peels herself from the sofa and replaces the blankets, tucking Riley back in. Katie, Daniel, and the others are still asleep, too, arms and legs tangled together on the floor over a scattering of sleeping bags and pillows. It's the kind of thing Beck's always felt a twitch of jealousy for. She slips into her boots and wordlessly makes her way upstairs.

Katie's mom stands in the kitchen whisking in a bowl. Red gingham half-curtains hang over the windows, glass freckled with red dirt. Mrs. Horton smiles at Beck, but before she can say a word, Beck blurts out a question.

"Did you see where Avery went?"

"She's not downstairs?"

"No."

"Maybe she's getting ready in the bathroom," Mrs. Horton says, unworried. She motions for Beck to sit with a warm smile.

Beck slides into one of the velvet barstools against the kitchen counter. Half of her is excited to finally be sitting here with the woman from her mother's notes, but the other half is still stuck on Avery. She fell asleep looking at Avery's eyes and woke up alone.

"How did you sleep?" Mrs. Horton asks.

"I slept great," Beck says. "Thank you for letting us stay here, by the way."

"Of course. I love when Katie has friends over, but this is the most people I've ever had in the house." Mrs. Horton keeps whisking what appears to be pancake batter. The frying pan on the stove begins to smoke and Beck's stomach growls. Mrs. Horton continues, "And you girls drove so far. Are you liking Backravel?"

"I think so," Beck says. "It's definitely unique. How long ago did your family move in?"

"Oh . . ." Mrs. Horton trails off. "Only a couple years ago, I think."

Another vague answer.

"Why here?"

"Same as everyone else. We came here for Ricky." Mrs. Horton ladles a dollop of batter onto her frying pan. The air is sweet and thick with the scent of it. "Katie's dad . . . we had so many complications with his health. We tried dozens of doctors, but no one seemed to know what would make his lungs work right for longer than a year or two."

Beck nods, thinks of Daniel and his asthma. Another miracle, she guesses. Another case modern medicine couldn't crack.

"And then along came Ricky. I don't even remember how we got in contact with him. But right away, I knew this would be different. I visited a few times to see if it was the real deal, but . . . you girls have probably heard the same story a thousand times by now."

"Right," Beck says. "Have you met a lot of other tourists?"

"Hmm?"

"Other visitors?" Beck asks again. "All the time you spent visiting before you moved here. Did you meet anyone named Ellery Birsching?"

Mrs. Horton flips a pancake and purses her lips in thought. "It doesn't sound familiar to me. I'm sorry. Though I'll tell you what, people come and go all the time and I can hardly remember any of them. I only really remember the folks who stay."

"Before you moved," Beck starts carefully, "where did your family live?"

Mrs. Horton doesn't look at Beck, but her posture stiffens. After a long pause, she speaks, and her voice is tinged with nervous amusement. "You know, I barely remember."

Just like everyone else, Mrs. Horton's memory is blurry. Just like everyone else, she can only remember her time in Backravel. She was a visitor, too, once, just like Ellery, but unlike Ellery, she decided to stay. The reality of it sinks in. She moved her family into this strange pocket of the desert and now she's just like everyone else in town: contently confused.

"Do you feel like there's *anything* you remember from before you came here?" Beck tries. She's pushing further than usual, but she's desperate for something that'll make sense. "Like, from your life before—"

Outside, someone shouts.

"What was that?" Beck asks.

Mrs. Horton glances out the kitchen window and shrugs. "I'm sure it's fine, whatever it is. No need to . . ."

Beck slides out of her seat at the kitchen counter and slips out the front door. If Mrs. Horton notices, she says nothing, too focused on breakfast to care.

Cedar Drive is empty. Like every other road in Backravel, in the daylight it's clear that there are no cars parked at the road shoulder, only bikes scattered in people's yards, dirt-speckled from frequent use. Beck rubs at her eyes and the skin is more tender than it was last night. There's a slight tug in her lungs, making it hard to take a full breath. She shouldn't have stayed out so late—apparently, it's already wearing on her.

Down the road, a crowd gathers. Beck narrows her eyes. The crowd is huddled around something. She glances at the Hortons' front door, then makes her way toward the crowd. She pushes her way past a handful of whispering people and finds herself in the center of the crowd looking at the last person she expected to see.

Ricky Carnes stands with another man, hand on his hip, clearly dispensing directions. Just like at the treatment center, he's wearing an outfit she's never seen a real-life person wear. This time, his cowboy hat and boots are a matching shade of vibrant turquoise. His denim jacket is too pristine to have ever been worn outside the treatment center. Beck glances back to the road where the creamsicle Cadillac is now parked along the curb.

Ricky *drove* here.

"I don't know what needs to happen," Ricky says to the other man. "But this can't keep up. I feel like I'm running out of options."

"What should we do with her for now?" the other man asks.

Ricky mulls it over. "I just want her to be *better*. Take her back to the treatment center for now, I guess. I'll decide what to do from there."

For a moment, Beck is sure they're talking about Avery. But when the man turns away from Ricky, he kneels to help a woman to her feet. Not just any woman—the Desert Woman. Her eyes flutter open and shut again, and her head lolls to the side, but she's unmistakable. Beck watches as she's led away and her stomach twists. Until now, Beck was half convinced the woman was a figment of her imagination. But now, the rest of Backravel is interacting with her.

A few feet away, Beck spots Avery.

She sits in the dirt with her legs crossed, staring out at the empty desert. Beck rushes to her and crouches, waiting for Avery to look at her. But Avery doesn't move. She doesn't seem to notice Beck at all. Her eyes water in the bright light, but she doesn't blink. When she finally closes her eyes, a tear rolls down her cheek.

"Hey," Beck says softly. "Are you okay?"

Avery opens her eyes again. When her eyes find Beck's, she stiffens.

"What happened?" Beck asks.

Avery's nose crinkles, brow knit in childlike confusion. She presses her fingertips to her temples, massaging gently. The cool light from over the plateaus turns Avery's eyes to amber. Her haphazard bobby pins have failed her, leaving her hair messy and unkempt. She's still in her pajama shorts and T-shirt. Her knees are scraped and caked with red dirt.

"Have you been out here all night?"

Avery shakes her head, but she doesn't manage to speak. Behind them, the gathered crowd continues to whisper, but Beck tunes them out. The sunlight is thin this morning, warm without scorching, and it illuminates the fear in Avery's watery eyes.

"How long have you been out here?" Beck tries again.

Avery's lips quiver. When she speaks, her voice is hoarse. "Why are you . . . what do you want from me?"

"What?"

"Why are you here?" Avery asks.

"I . . ." Beck lowers her voice. "I was worried about you. I woke up and you were gone. I thought maybe you were upset about last night, or—"

"Last night?" Avery blinks and more tears dot her lashes.

Beck narrows her eyes. "Last night. You brought me out in the middle of nowhere, remember?"

Avery shakes her head.

Beck's chest tightens. This isn't right. It's not like how Ellery Birsching used to forget things, slow and fleeting, half remembered. Avery's memory is gone. Everything they talked about, everything they shared. It's all gone.

She wants to be sick.

"Alright everyone," Ricky bellows from behind her. "Show's over. Let's go home and give Avery some space."

Beck doesn't budge. She can't leave Avery like this, crying and alone. And she can't leave until she finds out what's going on. As the crowd clears, Ricky makes his way to them and squats at Beck's side. He looks strange this close, too human. It's the first time Beck notices the wrinkle lines in his golden skin. The spots of age at his brow. She'd originally thought he was in his early forties, but up close, he looks older.

"Better?" he asks Avery. "How do we feel?"

Avery nods at him. "Better."

"Good, good . . ." Ricky stands and brushes the dirt from his jeans. After a moment, he looks at Beck like he's just noticed her. She half expects him to shoo her away like everyone else, but instead, he pats her on the shoulder. "Pretty confusing morning, huh?"

"What happened?" Beck asks.

"It's a long story." Ricky motions for Beck to stand. "I appreciate you checking in. Unspooling is a delicate process, though. We don't want to disturb her."

Unspooling. Beck's eyes widen. "Is she . . . right now?"

Ricky nods.

"Oh."

Beck looks at Avery again, watching the way she gently rocks back and forth. She shakes her head. "Why?"

At first, Ricky doesn't answer. He looks out at the sun and tilts his hat lower to block the glare. Beck almost pushes further, but the longer she looks at Ricky, she realizes he isn't ignoring her. He moves into Avery's line of sight and says, "If I go talk to Beck for a few minutes, will you be alright?"

Avery nods.

Ricky tilts his head toward the road. "Come with me."

Beck is more compelled to listen than she'd like. She moves

quietly behind him, eyeing the stitching on the backs of his boots. Four snakes, pocked with gold thread, embroidered on the worn leather at Ricky's ankles. Together, the snakes form a knot.

Ricky leads them to a pair of squat gray rocks and motions for Beck to sit. Beck stares at the rocks, but she stays standing. The adrenaline coursing through her is too quick and too fiery to sit down.

"It's not a nice thing to see," Ricky says. "I don't like unspooling in public. It makes it look so painful, but it really isn't."

"It's not hurting her?" Beck asks.

"No," Ricky says. "It's changing her. But in a good way."

"How?"

"It's like a reset, in a way."

Beck chews the inside of her cheek until she tastes iron. Until now, everyone spoke of unspooling like it was an injury treatment. Asthma, brain tumors, lung complications. Beck spent hours with Avery last night, and Avery didn't mention any sicknesses. She seemed fine.

"Why does she need it?" Beck asks. "I didn't think she . . . she seemed fine last night. I don't understand."

"I know it's confusing," Ricky says gently. "I haven't made it very clear. But I don't want you to worry about Avery. She's got me for that. She wound up in a tough situation this morning and unspooling was our best option."

"What situation?" Beck asks. "Is she hurt?"

Ricky takes a seat on one of the rocks, patting the dust from his jeans. "Yes. Sort of."

"Was it the Desert Woman that hurt her?"

Ricky sighs. "Is that what you're calling her?"

"Uh . . ." Beck trails. "I don't know her name."

"Well, it's a very complex situation. But yes, that woman hurt her. She's been out here a long time, now. And I don't believe she *means* to hurt anyone, but being alone that long makes you desperate. It can really warp a person. Usually, she's just confused. Sometimes she lashes out. She isn't well."

"You can't unspool her, too?" Beck asks.

"It doesn't seem to work for her the way it does for everyone else." Ricky sighs. "If I knew how to help her, I would, Beck. Trust me. I've tried everything."

Beck nods, but she isn't convinced. Something still isn't adding up.

"Who is she?"

Ricky doesn't answer. He looks to Avery and his expression is a mix of fear and wariness. There's another layer to what's happened here, one Beck can't quite decipher. Avery sits with her knees tucked to her chest, looking into the white sunlight. She looks so small now, and something squeezes tight in Beck's chest.

"She um . . ." Beck clears her throat. "How long will it take her to be okay again?"

"Oh, not long." Ricky turns away from Avery and looks Beck over from head to toe. "We can check on her in just a little bit. For now, I want to see how you're feeling."

"Me?"

"Yes. You."

"Okay, I guess," Beck manages. "Mostly confused."

"No headaches? Nausea?"

"Oh." Beck blinks. She scratches the back of her neck and considers. "I think I'm fine?"

"And your sister?"

"She's fine, too."

"I'm glad to hear that," Ricky says, and the relief is plain in his voice. He laughs nervously. "When we first spoke, I admit I was a little worried about you. Backravel doesn't really . . . *agree* with everyone. I hoped it would be kind to you, but you never know."

"What do you mean?"

"Close your eyes," Ricky says. "You hear that, don't you?"

Beck doesn't close her eyes. She doesn't need to listen to understand. She's felt it a thousand times already since arriving in Backravel: the hum of machinery, the quiet vibration under her feet, the way her memories slide up behind her, threatening to swallow her whole. She feels it like a sound beneath the trickling of voices and the hushed wind. She shifts a little, digging her sneakers into the earth.

"You know what?" Ricky starts. "I think it might be easier if I showed you. Backravel will mean more to you than most tourists. In your mom's honor, do you want to see how this all works?"

A gentle breeze blows the stray wisps of Ricky's dark hair against his neck. Beck breathes and it's the first full breath she's taken since arriving in Backravel. Because yes, *this* is what she's been waiting for. Someone who knows what's going on and is willing to give her more than scraps.

"You want to show me now?" Beck asks.

"Is that a problem?"

"No," Beck says quickly. "I just need to get Riley. She's probably still asleep."

"She's fine with the Hortons," Ricky says, nonplussed. "It'll be half an hour at the most. She won't even know you're gone."

"Why can't Riley come?" Beck asks.

"It's not that she can't come. But I'm taking a chance on you, Beck Birsching. One I don't take on most visitors." Ricky flashes her an easy smile. "I think you'll understand. I haven't met Riley, so I don't know her like I know you. And I don't get the feeling she's here looking for the things you're looking for."

Beck glances down Cedar Drive at the Hortons' house. Riley is probably still curled under the blankets on the couch, arm sprawled over the empty space where Beck slept beside her. She shouldn't leave Riley behind, but she doesn't know if she'll get another chance like this. Ellery Birsching never wasted an opportunity to find the truth, even if it meant leaving someone behind.

Beck steels herself. She's waited this long for answers; she won't wait any longer.

17

The trip back to the treatment center is quiet. Beck sits in the passenger seat of Ricky's Cadillac, pinching the leather between her fingers to stay calm. They glide down Cedar Drive, slide through Backravel's streets like a whisper, and wind their way onto the driveway that twists up the plateau. There's something about soaring through Backravel by car that makes it seem so much smaller. It unnerves her, the wrongness of it; sweat beads at Beck's brow.

"How're we holding up in the back?" Ricky asks, too casual for the tension in the air. He glances up from the road, looking through the rearview mirror expectantly.

Beck twists in her seat to eye Avery. She's calmed down since the desert, but only a little. She takes slow, measured breaths and eyes the passing shrubs and rocks, but Beck doesn't miss the twitch at her brow. She's scrambling for traction in her own head, trying to hide the claw marks. Beck certainly recognizes the feeling.

"I'm okay," Avery manages.

Ricky casts a quick look at Beck. He swallows and dons a

winning smile. "Would it be helpful to do a little more? When we get home?"

Avery closes her eyes.

"Maybe not," Ricky concedes.

Everyone in Backravel practically evangelizes about unspooling as a practice, but this is a darker side to it. Messy and painful and disorienting. Beck wonders if she's been looking at this setup wrong the whole time. She'd thought Avery was in on it, working in tandem with her father to keep Backravel in perfect alignment. But whatever strange science is used on the people in town, it's being used on Avery, too. It's changing her, too.

"Are you sure this is a good time?" Beck asks. "I can come back later."

Ricky turns onto the last stretch of the driveway up the plateau. Without looking at Beck, he says, "I think now is a good time. I think now is the *perfect* time."

Beck swallows hard. She feels Avery's eyes on the back of her neck. The car takes the plateau much easier than a bike, and within minutes, they're parked in the driveway, sun blazing down on the pristine metal corners of the treatment center, bouncing from the oversized window like the whole house is made of mirrors.

Ricky eases out of the driver's seat and strides quickly to Avery's door. He opens it and guides her out of the car into the blinding light, but he doesn't lead her to the house. Instead, he watches her for a long moment while she finds her footing. Avery presses her palm to her eyes and sucks in a ragged breath, but she says nothing. Eventually, Ricky's expression cools. He looks at Avery like a disappointed dog owner who's found a mess on his floor. It's only for a moment, but it's impossible to miss. Not disappointment: disgust.

Beck's stomach drops.

"I'm fine," Avery says, steadier than she managed in the car. "I'm just gonna lie down. I'm sorry."

"We'll talk more later," Ricky says. The words are gentle, but his voice is sharp. He touches Avery's elbow and gestures to the house. "I think sleeping here is your best bet from now on. Like I told you before."

"I'm sorry," Avery says again.

Ricky looks up and catches Beck's eyes on him. Quickly he softens and places a hand on Avery's shoulder. "It's alright. Go get some rest."

Avery stares at him and doesn't move. She stares until it looks like she might cry. Then she sucks in another breath and shakily makes her way to the house. She doesn't look back, doesn't acknowledge Beck at all. The moment she disappears, there's a dip in the air. The minute she leaves, it's like Beck's alone. The air is colder without her.

Ricky turns to Beck and he's back to the happy, unbothered, charismatic Ricky she met the first time she visited the treatment center. The quickness of the change doesn't sit well with Beck. It's like a light switch—ominous and cold then suddenly warm and welcoming. She fights the urge to back away.

"First off, let me say how sorry I am for all this confusion," Ricky says. "I never meant for you to get all mixed up in my dysfunctional family drama. I know you have enough of your own."

Beck frowns. "Is she gonna be okay?"

"She will be. I hope you'll give me a chance to explain."

Beck nods.

Ricky motions for her to follow him into the treatment center, but this time, it feels even more foreboding. Beck expects there to be a sense of familiarity when they push through the massive front doors into the main lobby of the treatment center, but it seems just as foreign as the first time. It's a cold and minimal lobby, not the kind of place a person lives. Beck tries to imagine Avery—the Avery she spoke to for hours under the stars—living in this place and it doesn't click.

"Your mother told me you were quick," Ricky says, motioning for Beck to follow him down a long hallway. "Some of this might not be news to you. I'm not an inherently secretive person, but I do think that, if the whole world knew what kinds of things we're capable of here in Backravel, we'd be overwhelmed. Immediately. I'm all about sharing, but I'm one person. I can only do so much."

Beck nods.

"What's your impression so far, Beck?"

"About what?" Beck asks.

"About everything."

Beck puzzles over where to start. How much of her hand to play. She wants to trust that Ricky is honest with her, that he was honest with her mother. They make their way farther down the hallway. Just as expected, the deeper part of the treatment center looks just as cool and indifferent as the lobby. Floor-to-ceiling windows dump sharp light across a concrete floor. Black industrial beams hold the ceiling aloft. Numbered metal doors punctuate the length of the hallway, most likely leading to treatment rooms, but without windows it's impossible to see inside. The doors are unnervingly blank.

"I think it's a weird place," Beck says. "I think whatever those scientists left here, it's . . . doing something to people. But I don't really *get* it."

"That's a good place to start," Ricky says. His smile is proud. Beck looks at her feet. "I'll be the first to admit that I don't know *much* about the science behind unspooling. I mean, how could anyone? What we can do here in Backravel would be impossible anywhere else in the world. There were military scientists here at some point, and I believe they were mainly concerned with chemical weapons testing. I don't know if they abandoned the site when they were done, or if they realized what those weapons left behind and stayed longer. I wish I could tell you what they learned, but the only thing left of them are the ruins."

"The military buildings?"

"They're an eyesore," Ricky says, "but if there's a chance those original scientists left something behind we can use, I can't get rid of them. So I leave everything just as I found it."

It makes sense in the way everything Ricky says makes sense. Almost too neatly. Beck follows Ricky farther down the hall, pausing when he stops in front of a door numbered *3*. He watches Beck, then he pulls the doorknob, motioning for her to step inside.

On the surface, the room is uninteresting. The walls are tall and white and blank, no windows breaking up the expansive space. There's a sleek metal table in the center of the room with a chair on either side. The longer she looks, the more it reminds Beck of an interrogation room, cold and impersonal and sterile. A chill runs up Beck's spine. She hugs her arms to her sides to fight the sudden wave of cold. There's something else about the room, Beck realizes. Something unsettling in a way she can't name. Her legs feel restless, head light, jaw clenched. Her vision blurs just slightly, even with her glasses on. She looks at Ricky, and he nods knowingly.

"You feel it?" Ricky asks.

Wordlessly, Beck nods.

"This is where I work. Well, most of the time," Ricky says. He shuts the door behind them and the cold deepens. Ricky seems to notice the chill. He offers Beck a small smile. "It's okay. It's completely safe. Feel free to explore."

"There's not much to explore," Beck says. She takes another step into the room. "Pretty empty."

Ricky puts his hands in his pockets. "I just want you to really *feel* it. Once you do, it's easier to understand. Under normal circumstances, this is where Avery and I would've gone for her unspooling. It's safest here. A nice, neutral place. That way, even though the world is changing around you, your immediate environment stays the same. There's less . . . confusion."

"What does that mean?" Beck asks. She moves to the nearest wall and runs her fingers over the white plaster. It's like browsing the grocery store as a child, scuffing her sneakers along the tile floor and then touching a metal shelf. The staticky buzz of electricity dances at her fingertips. Beck's heart patters an unusual rhythm; she yanks her hand away. "The world changes?"

"Take a seat, Beck."

Not a request: a command. Beck's eyes widen, but she does as she's told, sliding into the nearest of the metal chairs. Her hands shake and she's not entirely sure why. Ricky sits in the chair opposite her and props his elbows on the table. That rushing, quivering feeling only grows stronger in Beck's bones. She grits her teeth to keep her jaw from chattering.

"These rooms are special, Beck," Ricky says. "I designed them myself. There's something about the earth in Backravel that does the impossible. If I tell you what I understand . . ."

"I won't tell anyone else," Beck promises, maybe too quick.

". . . do you promise to believe me?"

Beck blinks.

"Right." Ricky motions to the wall nearest to them. The cold deepens until Beck can't feel her fingers. "Whatever happened to the soil here in Backravel, for some reason or another, it can break down the matter of time itself."

He pauses, either for dramatic effect or because he genuinely wants her input. But Beck has nothing to say. She waits for the other shoe to drop, but there isn't one. *Time itself.* Her breath is short, heart racing. Finally, she manages, "T-time?"

"When I first arrived in Backravel, I didn't know what was causing it," Ricky says quickly now, like he means to squeeze in the rest of his explanation before Beck has a chance to doubt. "But my world didn't move forward like it was supposed to. At the drop of a hat, I found myself lost in moments I'd lived years ago like they *just* happened. Everything was so fresh. It was all so *clear.* All those little moments I believed were gone in the recesses of my mind were within reach again."

"I don't understand."

"I know. That's okay." Ricky smiles, but Beck doesn't feel the calm. "I don't fully understand it, either. But the miracle . . . it's impossible to ignore. As my family spent time in this valley, we tried to unearth more of what those first scientists discovered, but I don't think they were able to make sense of it, either. All I knew is that, the more I let Backravel change me, the more I could control it. I spent years honing my ability to *use* this place."

"So unspooling is . . ." Beck starts, but she can hardly find the words to describe what she imagines.

"There are some forms of hypnosis that believe, if you look back at your life with enough precision, you can find moments in the past you're missing. Or moments you want to access again. In the world outside, it's only a thought. In Backravel you can find those memories and you can step into them."

"I don't—"

Beck puts her head in her hands, but it doesn't stop the spinning. They've stepped out of the realm of reality into something more frightening. More impossible. What Ricky's talking about now isn't a medical treatment, it's—

"Time travel?" Beck blurts out.

"Not quite, I don't think," Ricky says. "It's more individual than that. Unspooling, the way I use it, is about locating a moment in your life before the pain began. Together, when we find that moment, we step into it both emotionally and physically. In a sense, they become the person they were in that moment."

"I'm still . . ." Beck trails off. "What do you mean by *the pain*?"

"Have you noticed something about the people who live here in Backravel?" Ricky asks. "Something we all have in common?"

The idea of trying to pick one thing that unites everyone in Backravel is absurd. The confusion, maybe, but most of the people in Backravel don't seem to fit together at all. It's like they're from different worlds, all dumped into a scorching melting pot. Beck taps her fingers against the metal table, chewing on what she means to say. It's all too bizarre.

"What I'll say is this," Ricky says. "The people here are different in many ways, but we all have something important in common. We all know what it feels like to lose. Even me. For some people, it's their health. For others, it's their happiness. For many, it's someone they loved. Everyone who comes to Backravel has lost something that they missed dearly. They come here hoping to find it again."

Beck arches a brow. "Even you?"

Ricky leans back in his chair, tilting the front legs off the floor. The brim of his hat casts a sharp shadow over his eyes, but his mouth is visible in the harsh light, tilted into an uneasy frown. Finally, he says, "More than I can name."

Another chill runs over Beck. His words are sharp in a way that Beck understands too well. She closes her eyes and lets it wash over her this time. There's comfort in the familiarity of it. Maybe Beck doesn't fully understand the unspooling, and maybe she hasn't lost as much as Ricky, but she's lost enough. The longer her eyes are closed, the more the world tilts away. She understands suddenly why Ricky wanted to explain this in the treatment rooms. She feels how easy it might be to slip back right now. To be the person she was before her world fell apart.

When Beck opens her eyes, Ricky is watching her.

"There's a reason you feel at ease here, Beck," Ricky says coolly. "Because I believe you're suffering from the same wounds as the rest of us. People outside this town will tell you it's unhealthy to miss the world the way it used to be. They told me the same thing when I lost my son. When you're in pain, they tell you to hurry up. The faster you 'get over it,' the sooner you can fit back into their world. You lose the thing you love most and they want you to reconfigure your world to move on without it. Patch up your severed limb and keep walking. It's complete insanity."

Beck sucks in a breath. How many times did grown-ups back home ask her what she needed to heal? How many times did they ply her with food and gifts and hugs, always hoping that it would sew up the hole in her chest? Her hurt is too much for people to look at, so they either try to plug it up or they look away. She's never felt so alone in her life as she feels now. The cold is unbearable in the treatment room. When Beck looks down, her knuckles are white.

"So the people who come here," Beck starts, "are trying to go back in time?"

"In a sense, yes." Ricky's smile is wider than Beck's ever seen. "I'm so glad you understand. I knew you would."

"I don't really. But I understand *wanting* to, I guess."

"Of course you do," Ricky says. "I knew from the moment I met you that you were the exact kind of person that would do well here. Do you mind if I make an observation?"

Beck shakes her head. She studies Ricky's hand, curled into a fist against the metal table. He isn't cold in this room like she is—at least, not visibly. His jaw doesn't chatter when he speaks. Whatever is happening to her, Ricky either doesn't feel it or he's accustomed to it. He leans forward and his metal chair groans under him. The way he sees her is unflinching and unrelenting. For a moment, Beck is sure there's nowhere in all of Backravel she could go where Ricky Carnes couldn't see her.

"Your mother spoke about you often," Ricky says. "I was so moved by her stories about both of you girls, but I was especially moved when she spoke about you. I was so taken by the idea of this young girl with the weight of the world on her shoulders. I thought to myself, *That's someone I could help.* You never got to be a child, Beck. All the adults in your life left you with their messes to clean up. Death, divorce, illness . . . you must be so tired."

Beck stares at Ricky because she doesn't know what else to do. She doesn't know what to say. She sucks in another breath and realizes that her fingernails are pressed hard to the skin of her palm. No one—not the counselors at school, the neighbors, her father or Julie, not even Riley—has talked about it like this. Shame flares in Beck's cheeks. Has her exhaustion been that plain on her face? Or does Ricky just *see* people in a way others can't?

"Why . . . ?" Beck takes a moment to gather herself. "Why did Avery have to be unspooled?"

"Because unspooling isn't just for physical injuries. Avery has a somewhat unhealthy relationship with the desert." Ricky looks down. "As does the woman you call the Desert Woman."

There's something in the desert that knows me. Beck recalls the quiet night settling in above her and Avery in the open desert. The way the dark closed around them as they spoke. The shaking in Avery's voice. *When it's quiet, I can hear it calling me.*

"Why did she hurt her?"

Ricky pinches the bridge of his nose. "I don't know what she's trying to accomplish out there, or what hurt she's hiding that makes her lash out, but when Avery wandered into the desert last night, I can only assume the Desert Woman saw her as a target."

"Why?"

"If I knew, it wouldn't have happened. If I knew what was wrong with that woman, I would help her. You would do the same, right? If you knew how to fix someone's hurting, you would do it?"

"Of course," Beck says.

"Tell me if you don't want to hear this," Ricky says, "but I believe your mother wanted to help that woman, too. She spent so many days out in the desert trying to understand what was wrong with her, but as far as I know, it never amounted to anything. And, eventually, she needed to focus on herself."

"Right," Beck whispers. "You unspooled my mom, too."

"When she found out she was . . . dying, she realized she didn't have enough time to do everything she wanted to do. She wanted to see you girls grow up, find love, make lives for yourselves. She had a whole life planned for your family, and suddenly, she wasn't going to be around for it. Every time she visited us, we were able to turn back her clock a little and stave off the inevitable."

"It wasn't affecting her in other ways?" Beck asks.

For a moment, Beck thinks Ricky will reach for her hand. But instead, he lays his palm flat to the table. Quieter, he says, "I begged her to stay here. If she stayed in Backravel, none of those hardships would've come up. *Death* wouldn't have come up. I'm sure you've noticed we don't have cemeteries here. We don't need them. When you turn back the clock, you can push off death forever."

"Not *forever*." Beck breathes. "That's impossible."

"There are so many things I didn't think were possible before," Ricky says. "It's incredible, the things that are possible here and nowhere else."

Beck nods, but it's like Ricky's voice is underwater. Maybe it's the fact that Ellery Birsching could have lived, or maybe it's the cold that's sinking deeper and deeper under her skin. Whatever it is, her mind is drifting far away from this room. She's miles from Backravel and Ricky and unspooling. She's treading water, just trying to breathe.

"I told you when you first came here," Ricky says, "that your mother was helping me with something."

"Finding the source," Beck says.

"You have such a great memory, Beck," Ricky says. "A journalist's mind, just like your mom. The little details don't escape you."

Beck tries not to feel insulted at the comparison considering, when she died, Ellery Birsching couldn't remember her own middle name. Ricky rights himself and takes a deep breath.

"Like I said, I found this place without really knowing what it was. I dove into unspooling and treatments before I fully understood how the soil here worked. And before I knew it was finite."

"Finite," Beck repeats.

"I don't know why exactly," Ricky starts. "Maybe the properties in the soil are wearing out. Or maybe I am. Maybe it's because this town continues to expand. But I'm having trouble . . . *maintaining* Backravel."

Beck thinks of Mr. Sterling that night at the trailer, confused about who she was. *It hasn't been a problem in a long time,* he'd said.

"More and more, people here are slipping through the cracks," Ricky says. "I've only ever been able to unspool people by a month or so at a time, just baby steps into the past. But now, even that seems too difficult. People need treatment more often, find themselves back in their dark thoughts earlier than they should. I don't know why, but I'm worried that our time in Backravel is running out."

"What happens when you can't do it anymore?" Beck asks.

"It doesn't matter," Ricky says. "I will never let that happen. I have reason to believe that there is a more powerful mineral source under the earth. A lab, of sorts. It's out in the desert somewhere. Your mother and I found mentions of this lab in some of the documents left here."

"More powerful?" Beck asks. "In what way?"

"With whatever kind of concentrate is in that lab, I could help people in a permanent way. I could help *more* people. No more of these little unspooling sessions that only last a few months. With more power, we could go back further, and we could make it stick. I could use these treatments to really change lives."

Ricky stands up now. He paces to the wall, runs his fingers over the surface, and he sighs. In the harsh light, Beck sees the slump of his shoulders, the way his head dips low in grief. He's being crushed under the weight of this place. He's trying to hold it up all alone, but it isn't enough. Beck knows the feeling too well.

"When I heard what happened to your mother, I wasn't just devastated because I'd lost a friend." Ricky turns to face Beck and his eyes are glossy with unspent tears. "I knew Backravel was doomed without her."

Beck blinks.

"But when you told me who you were, I thought it must be a sign. And then you told me you came here because your mother sent you a letter . . ." Ricky shakes his head. "I believe she must have sent you here for a reason. She must have wanted you to finish what she started."

"How?" Beck asks. Desperation drips from her voice no matter how hard she tries to mask it. "I didn't even know what unspooling was. How could I—?"

"You said your mother had notes, right?"

Beck says nothing.

"You've read all of her notes? Did she ever mention some kind of map?"

"I don't think so."

"Or maybe she mentioned a particular location she was drawn to?"

"I mean, she mentions tons of places she's drawn to." Beck pulls off her glasses to clean them with the hem of her shirt. Mostly, she pulls them off to break free of Ricky's eye contact for a moment. She needs to breathe. "I don't know if she ever mentioned a place like that."

"I see."

"But . . ." Beck says, "I can try to look, too?"

They sit there in silence a moment, Beck still in her metal chair, quivering in the cold while Ricky stands with his hands on his hips. It occurs to Beck that he stands between her and the way out of the treatment room. It feels like they've struck a deal now, but Ricky still watches her. Without windows or clocks, Beck realizes she has no idea how long she's been at the treatment center. The conversation feels like it's taken place over only a few minutes, but this town has tricked her before. It might've been hours.

Riley.

"I should really get back to my sister," Beck says. "She's—"

"Of course," Ricky cuts in. "But remember what I told you earlier. I'm trusting you with information I don't usually share with others. I know you and your sister are close, but I would prefer you kept this conversation to yourself."

Surely Riley's awake by now, and she's probably confused. They're supposed to stick together through all of this. Guilt knots in Beck's stomach. She's learned so much today, and Riley's still alone in the dark. But Ricky's right; she can't tell Riley about this, not when she's already worried about the slipping and the eerie atmosphere in Backravel. Not when she's already apprehensive of Ricky. Not when she watches Beck's every move for signs of weakness. If she tells Riley about everything she's learned, that'll be the end of their trip. Beck has to carry it alone.

Finally, Ricky moves. He opens the treatment room door and blood rushes to Beck's cheeks. Her vision spots for a moment. She braces herself against the cool metal of the table. Ricky leads her out of the treatment room, down the hallway, and to the treatment center's massive front door. Beck steps into the sun and the dry heat washes over her. She feels alive again, even if just a little.

"Thank you for your help with this," Ricky says, lingering in the doorway. "For what it's worth, Beck, I think you would do really well in Backravel."

And then Ricky closes the front door and Beck is on her own. The words echo, and she lets them soak in. The thing about Backravel is that it's impossible to tell if she should feel held or afraid. She's suspended somewhere in between, hanging onto the one thing that keeps her grounded.

After days of searching, she knows how Backravel was changing her mother. How it was healing her and how it was warping her. Pieces are clicking tenderly into place, painting a picture bigger than Beck ever imagined in the days she spent planning this trip. She has a handful of answers, but one question remains, bigger than all the rest.

If Backravel was saving her mother's life, why did she ever leave?

18

That night, when Beck sleeps, she dreams of the desert.

She stands at the base of the plateau. The sky is murky red, storm churning behind cloud cover, the low groan of thunder murmuring a threat. The sky isn't usually crowded like this, bruised with rain. The air is shallow, synthetic, and devoid of temperature. Beck doesn't feel anything. She doesn't remember how she got here or where she came from. She faces the highway but it's empty. She looks at her palms. She's rootless, stuck in place but unstuck in time. Ahead of her, seemingly miles away, she sees a pinprick of red on the horizon.

The campsite.

The desert between her and the campsite is flat. It stretches all the way to the ridges on the horizon, taut like latex. The landscape she knows is gone. Backravel, its outskirts, the rugged hills have all been stripped bare and there is nothing between Beck and the red tent. The earth under her feet hums, radiating strange heat that seeps through the soles of her sneakers. The humming is louder now, impossible to ignore. The sky is storm-gray with punches of red, electric with ozone, *alive*. It presses down and it's like she's in a tunnel with only one way out—forward.

She walks, pulse in her throat, tongue coated with tang. The sky pulses with her, veins of white lightning flashing like she's watching the backs of her eyelids. This is a dream—she *knows* this is a dream—but in Backravel, the line between real and imaginary is already hazy. Maybe dreams spill into reality. She's never been particularly good at telling the difference. Awake or not, she knows she needs to make it to the campsite. Everything else falls away until the red tent is all she sees.

Halfway there, the ground under Beck changes. It sinks with each step, sloshing under her sneakers. Beck glances down and the sides of her shoes are coated in something black and congealed. It makes a puckered sound when she lifts her foot. It takes a moment for Beck's eyes to focus, and she immediately wishes she never looked. Hot bile climbs up her throat.

Blood.

Next to her, a sheep lies on its side. Its black eyes are glassy, facing the red sky. It breathes faintly, lungs sputtering, hooves twitching. When Beck looks up, she realizes it isn't alone. There are hundreds of sheep just like it in every direction. The sheep bleat but they don't stand. They lie on their sides, keeled over and dying. Beck wades through the viscera toward the coiling smoke of the Desert Woman's campfire because she can't stop to make sense of this. Bits of wool and blood mat the skin of her ankles. She claps her hand over her nose and mouth to keep from vomiting.

It may be a dream, but the blood feels real.

When she finally makes it to the campsite, it's empty. The open door of the tent flaps like a flag in the storm wind. Something is brewing in the sky; the litter on the floor of the campsite twirls in the breeze, the air is so thick it feels damp, the hair on her arms stands on end. The cooler has been toppled and a thread of black water twists through the dirt. Bits of charred firewood are littered around the spent campfire. The light is strange here, stale like she's inside a room, not standing in the middle of the desert. All of that pales when she looks beyond the campsite. The earth shifts, the sea of sheep carcasses sliding along the desert floor toward a single point in the distance. One by one, they buckle over a lip in the earth and then disappear. Like the ground is swallowing them whole.

Beck takes a step toward the point when she hears the tent shift behind her. The Desert Woman looks different under the dim sky. Her denim coat is no longer stained with dirt, her hair is brushed, her face is hard to see. The longer Beck looks at her, the more she changes. Her hair isn't black, but the warm color of honey and lemon. Her eyes are green like summer leaves, like shallow creek water, like her mother's eyes. A rush of familiarity hits Beck like a fist.

"*Mom . . .*" she says.

Ellery Birsching smiles. When she speaks, her voice rattles with static. "*. . . the large test site at the Backravel Testing Ground, Arizona. Here, the chemical core holds field trials to determine the effectiveness of newly developed munitions.*"

"What?"

"*The trial runs conducted at Backravel simulate conditions ideal for exploring both matter and chemical makeup. Sampling devices positioned throughout the test area yield valuable information to chemical core researchers. Results from Backravel Testing Ground will reveal much we do not understand about the minerals here, their chemical properties, and ultimately their uses. Though we do not understand it yet, minerals extracted from the earth here at the testing grounds may help our research team comprehend the passage of time. It is crucial we understand the passage of time. We will uncover the mechanics of the passage of time.*"

Beck stares and she doesn't move. It isn't her mother speaking—she's only mouthing the words like a radio broadcast. It's a man's voice, taped and warped with time. Static crackles in her throat, stuck now, repeating a single phrase over and over: *"we must understand the passage of time."* The voice is so garbled it echoes. Beck claps hands over her ears and closes her eyes, waiting for it to stop.

It does.

"Beck."

The voice is loud now. Close to her. It's flat, urgent, *immediate*. Not her mother's voice. "Beck, *wake up*."

• • •

When Beck wakes, she knows she's going to be sick.

She lurches up in bed, striking her head against the ceiling of the trailer so hard the room spins. Cold sweat dampens the back of her neck and a fever blazes behind her eyes. She clutches the quilt wrapped around her legs and clumsily dumps herself from the bed.

She hits the floor and collapses to her knees, too weak to stay upright.

"Riley . . ." Beck chokes.

Stomach acid burns her throat. Her hands tremble, but she manages to grip the kitchen counter with sweaty fingers and pull herself to her feet. The appliances groan and the blue light from the TV sears brighter than it should, though that's probably because Beck's skull throbs so much it feels like it might cave in. The kitchen table bed is empty, sheets mussed into a mound of blue-and-black fabric. Riley's gone.

Beck can't remember the space of time between leaving the

treatment center and falling asleep. She tries to dredge up a memory of explaining her afternoon to Riley, but all she finds is a blank space where the memory should be. Her head spins, her body shakes, her throat burns.

"Riley," Beck calls again, voice coarse as sandpaper. It's enough to trigger the nausea she's been fighting back. Beck grabs the bathroom door and throws it open, but before she can make it to the toilet, her knees collide with something soft. She looks down and Riley is draped over the toilet, pale in the shallow bathroom light. Her blond hair is damp and plastered to her cheeks. She looks up, but her eyes are half-lidded and dull as a drowsy dog. Before she can say a word, Riley turns back to the toilet and vomits.

"What's happening . . . ?" Beck trails off.

She ambles toward the trailer door and everything tilts around her. One step, then another and she's outside. She tumbles down the trailer steps and lands on her knees in the dirt. Her fingers curl around the pipe railing and the world curves, fast and relentless around her. Beck throws her head back and looks hard into the tar pit sky. She hardly feels her back meet the earth. There are no stars, no clouds, just the black stifling void. She needs to stand up, needs to get back to Riley, needs to—

Beck rolls over and pukes into the flower bed.

Somewhere behind her, a door screeches open. Beck's fingers curl in the dirt and she tries not to pass out. Her throat burns like it does when she drinks too much from Ellery's liquor shelf, but this is a thousand times worse. A moment ago she thought she could stand. Now she just wants to die.

Footsteps crunch beside her. "Rebecca?"

Beck retches again, but nothing comes up. Next to her, she can make out the clean white toes of Mrs. Sterling's house sneakers. A hand gently touches her back and massages down her spine. Everything in Beck hurts, but when Mrs. Sterling takes Beck's hair and pulls it back, an entirely new ache blossoms. She slips back to a night over a decade ago after a stomach flu ravaged her kindergarten class. She remembers the cool of the mint-colored toilet seat against her sweaty arms, the flickering of the bathroom light. She remembers her mother's fingers against her neck, brushing her hair out of her face. She remembers Ellery Birsching sitting on the floor beside her whispering *oh baby* until the sickness subsided.

"Greg?" Mrs. Sterling calls across the yard. "Get me a glass of water. And a cold washcloth. And crackers. *Now.*"

Beck looks up, but Mrs. Sterling's face is a blur. Her glasses are gone, then. She hardly noticed. She takes Mrs. Sterling's shoulder and grips hard, biting back tears. She manages to croak, "Riley . . ."

"She's asleep?" Mrs. Sterling asks.

"No . . . inside. She's sick."

Mrs. Sterling's expression changes. She eyes the trailer door and grimaces. Beck was right—something *is* happening. It's happening to both of them, and Mrs. Sterling knows it. The night wind is sickly warm, but the sweat on Beck's face makes her shiver. She leans into Mrs. Sterling's chest and the world begins to sear out of focus.

"What's happening to us?" Beck asks.

Mrs. Sterling gathers Beck against her and rocks her carefully back and forth. Beck tries to pull herself from Mrs. Sterling's arms, but her exhaustion finally catches up with her. She tumbles away from the light, the gentle thud of Mrs. Sterling's racing heart the last thing in her ear.

19

"I wasn't sure who to call."

It's a whisper, just close enough to hear. Beck comes to life in a dizzying rush, but she doesn't open her eyes. She feels the scratchy, pilled fabric of the trailer sofa under her arms. The faint hum of the coffee machine is to her left. She's back in the trailer, though she can't remember how she got here. Her eyes are crusted shut. Last night's memory is hazy, but she's sure the last time she was awake she was doubled over in the yard. She swallows and feels the burn of her raw throat.

"It's okay. I'm glad you called."

Beck goes stiff.

This is Avery's voice, deep like she's trying to sound serious. The sound of it grabs Beck by the throat. She lies completely still and the trailer groans as Avery shifts from one foot to the other. "This is . . . I didn't think it was this bad?"

Beck doesn't move. She ignores the little clench in her chest at the concept of Avery seeing her like this, the mess and disarray, the loneliest parts of Beck laid bare.

"I thought two weeks would be fine," Mrs. Sterling says. "Greg hasn't seen them yet. I've kept him out."

"Why?"

"Because I don't know what to do with them. We can't just kick them out, but if this keeps up . . ." A long moment passes, then Mrs. Sterling shifts. "Greg would say we have two options. You probably agree."

Avery is quiet. "I think we have three."

There's something sinister to the quiet way Avery speaks. Danger has been apparent since the day they got here, but Beck's never tasted it thick in the air like she does now. Morning pours into the trailer through the half-open blinds—Beck feels it warm against her eyelids. Her skull throbs, her muscles ache, neck stiff, eyes watery. Whatever came over her last night isn't gone yet. In fact, it's worse today. Staying quiet is harder the longer she's awake. The weight of her nightmare sits heavy on her—the dead sheep, the radio transmission, the hole in the desert floor. She can't begin to make sense of it.

"Don't feel bad," Avery says, softer. Beck wonders what Mrs. Sterling's face looks like now to warrant the tenderness. Avery continues, "I don't want to do anything, either. It's just a bad situation. For everyone."

"You're going to tell Ricky?"

Quiet again. Avery shuffles and Beck can hear the cool rhythm of her breath as she approaches the sofa. When she speaks, it's more hesitant. She's a girl again, young and unsure. "Should I?"

"What do you think he'll do?"

"Hmm." Avery's weight presses into the corner of the trailer bed and Beck does her best to stay still. Fingertips ghost over the round of her kneecap, sending a spark all the way to her spinning head. "Can I talk to them first?"

"Sure," Mrs. Sterling says. "I'll give you space."

She leaves the trailer and it's just the quiet again. Just quiet and morning and the palpable heat from where Avery sits. She feels Avery's eyes rake over her and she fights the urge to squirm away.

"Hey," Avery whispers, shaking Beck's knee gently. "Wake up."

Swallowing her fear, Beck slowly opens her eyes. Sunlight is caught in the tangles of Avery's hair. She wears a slight smile, but it does nothing to mask the concern in her eyes. Whatever she and Mrs. Sterling were talking about—whatever Mrs. Sterling was afraid of—Avery is scared of it, too. Not scared in the way she was while she was unspooling; scared in a knowing way. She glances briefly at Riley, then her stare settles on Beck again. Something is coming.

"I heard you're sick," Avery says.

"Are you gonna be my nurse?" Beck muses as casually as she can muster. She shifts slightly and almost yelps at the pain.

"That depends," Avery says, quiet like it's a secret, "on how bad you feel."

Beck swallows the lump that forms in her throat. "Last time I saw you, *I* was the one worried about *you*."

A shadow crosses Avery's expression almost imperceptibly, like a cloud over the sun. Beck wonders suddenly if Avery remembers the desert at all, or if the unspooling took that, too. She wonders if Avery remembers the unspooling at all. There's something different in the air between them now, different enough that she's sure Avery remembers *something*. A push and pull, churning like water at the precipice of a dam. The drop is coming, Beck thinks. She just can't see it yet.

Avery shrugs. "That's how it goes. Up one day, down the next."

Beck rolls up onto her elbow, squinting away the strained light.

The inside of her mouth is gummy and swollen, eyes too big for their sockets. She wipes at her nose and her muscles ache. There's a not-small piece of her that wants to keep joking like this, keep the conversation a game, steer it away from the terrifying topic of what's *happening* to her. But she can't.

Something's wrong and Avery knows what it is.

"What's happening to us?" Beck croaks.

Avery's expression sobers. "You're sick. Both of you."

Beck thumps back on the pillow and the trailer spins. Across the trailer, Riley stirs but she doesn't wake up.

"*Why* are we sick?" Beck asks.

Avery stands and moves to the kitchen sink, filling a glass of water and Beck immediately aches for her to come back. She feels the cold in the place Avery sat. It's just the fever, she thinks, that makes her crave closeness. Avery doesn't look at her when she continues. "I'm not an encyclopedia. I don't know everything. But . . . I *have* seen people get sick like you before."

Beck narrows her eyes. Avery doesn't look at her, but Beck pictures her face. There's a way that Avery talks about Backravel sometimes, as though she isn't sure what side she means to fall on. Maybe it's the unspooling, but it's like she's being purposefully elusive to cover up something more terrifying: confusion. Avery's shoulders slouch and she turns to face Beck again.

"What did my dad say to you yesterday?"

"He just told me about unspooling," Beck says. "And . . . about my mom."

"Why?"

"I don't know."

Avery's gaze is unflinching. Beck should be surprised that Avery isn't privy to all of Ricky's movements, but she isn't. After their strange dynamic yesterday—the coolness between them, the disgust on Ricky's face—she's surprised Avery knows as much as she does.

"I don't understand why he'd tell you," Avery says. "You don't even . . . it just doesn't make sense to me."

Beck sits upright. "Do you even remember yesterday?"

"I remember enough."

"I was really worried something happened to you," Beck says. "Your dad said you were hurt. And then he . . . What happened?"

Avery says nothing.

"It's all gone, isn't it?"

"That's my business," Avery says coolly. "You need to worry about yourself. And your sister."

"We talked for hours." Beck breathes. "Do you remember?"

For a long moment, Avery says nothing. She looks at the floor with a heavy frown, hands in her pockets, and Beck can't even hear the sound of her breathing. Finally, she says, "I think you and Riley should leave."

"What?"

"The stress is getting to you. To both of you." Avery itches behind her ear. "You've got a lot going on. I don't think staying here will help."

"But—"

"Backravel will still be here if you decide to come back."

After what Ricky told her, Beck isn't sure that's true. She tries to push herself to her elbows again, but the fatigue in her arms flares up and she doesn't move. She says nothing. The trailer is getting smaller by the second. She and Avery were supposed to have an understanding— two lost girls looking for some sense—but apparently that can only get you so far. Beck exhales, sharp and hurt like a wounded animal. She's on her own, like always.

"You saw the treatment center. You got to meet my dad, like you wanted. You've had coffees and dinners and movie nights. You've learned stuff about your mom," Avery says. She moves close to Back now, slides a chair up to the edge of Beck's bed and takes a seat. "Why are you still here? Don't try to tell me it's about the festival."

Beck blinks and Avery's expression shifts. Her eyes are too dark in the hot light. Beck swallows hard. She eyes the glass of water in Avery's grip and her throat is like sandpaper. She wants to sleep, she wants to keep exploring, she wants to take care of Riley, she wants someone to take care of her. A war rages in her chest and she can hardly breathe. Here, at the end of her already-frayed rope, Beck reaches out and gently clutches the sleeve of Avery's T-shirt.

"There's a reason she stayed here," Beck says quietly, careful not to wake Riley. "She was trying to *help* Backravel. I want to finish what she started."

Avery doesn't pull away.

Beck imagines what her mother would do in this situation, presented with the same question. Her chest squeezes. Ellery Birsching would do what she did in real life—she would keep drilling into the same soil, digging for the same mystery over and over again, as long as it took, until she got somewhere. For months, years, decades. Until the grave, even.

"If you stay," Avery begins, and there's something uneasy in her voice, "you'll need help. People don't . . . *stay* here without help."

"You mean I'd need to unspool?" Beck asks.

Avery eyes her.

Beck's head throbs, her stomach churns, it all *hurts*. But it isn't the sickness that picks her apart. Just like Ellery before her, she waded into this dark, knotted mystery thinking time would help put the pieces together and, just like Ellery, she's becoming a piece herself. She isn't a detective—she's seventeen and she's tired and she wants something easier than this. Maybe it would be easier to just float with the current and let this town eat her alive.

"I don't know why, but people who stay here too long without unspooling get sick sometimes. If you want to stay, you have to unspool."

"Then I will."

"No," Avery says, too quickly. "I mean, if you do, you'll be different. You'd be like everyone else here. Confused."

"Okay."

Avery's expression darkens. "I don't want you to be different."

Beck shifts and curls her fingers around Avery's. Her eyes find the glass of water in Avery's hand. Through cracked lips, she whispers, *"Please."*

Avery's expression is difficult. Pale light cuts through the trailer blinds, cleaving her delicate face in two. Light and dark. Here and gone. She extracts her hand from Beck's, moves to tenderly cup the back of Beck's head. Her fingertips press softly, cautiously through the sweat-damp knots of Beck's hair and a spark shudders its way up Beck's spine. Wordlessly, Avery tilts the glass of water to Beck's lips.

Beck closes her eyes and drinks.

Her heart races.

"I could help you," Avery says finally.

Riley stirs. Avery tenses for a moment, waits for her to go still again, and Beck understands that whatever Avery is offering, it has to be a secret. Not Mrs. Sterling, not Riley, not even Ricky can know that she's relenting. A curl of brown hair rests soft against her cheek, rich as the bark of the great trees on the California coast. She's miles away now, looking through the blinds, mouth a stern line.

"What kind of help?" Beck asks. "I thought Ricky was the only one who knew how to . . ."

Avery looks at her. The tender line of her jaw is clenched, dark eyes watery. After a moment, she sucks in a breath, seemingly coming back to herself. She reaches for the water again and quietly asks, "How much longer do you plan to stay?"

"I don't know," Beck says.

Avery says nothing.

"Do you want me to go?" Beck asks.

Avery sighs. "I'm gonna try something. I've never tried it before. I don't know if it'll work."

Beck nods. That fluttering in her chest rears its head again, too bold to quiet. She tells herself it's nerves at the idea of unspooling. But a part of it is the place where Avery's skin meets hers. She wonders, only for a second, how long it's been since she was touched. She's been a fragile thing: a thing to steer clear of. Another current runs through her from her fingertips to the tips of her toes.

"Close your eyes," Avery says, and Beck does. "Now I need you to, uh, focus. On a specific moment."

"What kind of moment?"

"How about the day I took you to meet my dad," Avery says. The verbiage is clumsy and Beck is sure she's attempting to recite Ricky's speech from memory. "That morning, when we met before riding up. What do you remember about it?"

Beck squints. "It was pretty early. Like, eight?"

"More. What was it like? What did you see?"

"You were sitting on the bench. You were watching an old couple at the diner." Beck tries to picture it. The spark that ran through her moments ago kicks up again. She starts to feel like a conduit, patches of goose bumps pricking up all over her arms. She sucks in a breath. "It was colder than I expected."

"How did you feel?"

"Scared."

"Scared of what?"

"You," Beck says, almost involuntarily. "And your dad. I thought this was all a trap. Or that it was nothing."

Avery's fingers curl tighter in Beck's hair but she doesn't speak. Finally, she says, "Do you see it?"

At first, Beck sees nothing but the spotty dark of closed eyes. But then it comes into view. She sees the morning as clear as it was that day. The park, Avery staring distantly at the diner doors, eyes glassy and miles away. She smells the dry air and the musk of red dirt. Her fingers twitch with that same fear.

"If you see it," Avery says, "you can step into it."

The trailer seems miles away now. Beck searches for the feeling of the pullout mattress under her arms, but it's gone. She's suspended somewhere between the park and the trailer. It would be easy, she thinks, to take a step and land there. Before she can do it, panic sets in. This is wrong. Every bone in her body cries in protest. She gasps, and it's like she slams back to the trailer in a flash of brilliant light. Everything around her spins, but she sits up and opens her eyes.

"No." Beck gasps. "No, I can't do it."

"Did you see it?" Avery asks. She looks at her palms with wide eyes. "You saw it, right?"

Beck isn't sure *what* she saw. She slips all the time, but this was different. It wasn't like a memory; it was a window. It was so real she could touch it. A moment from the past, open in front of her all over again. It's just like Ricky said. It's impossible, but in Backravel, impossible is just a word.

"Do you . . . feel better?" Avery asks.

Beck touches her collarbone and feels the rapid rise and fall of her chest. She swallows the panic and closes her eyes. She *does* feel better, though only slightly. There's still a soreness to her bones and a spinning in her skull, but she can move. She can breathe.

"I think so." Beck rubs the back of her neck. "A little bit."

"What went wrong?"

Beck shakes her head. Maybe this is how unspooling always is, but the fear that gripped her was blinding. "If I stepped into it, I would've been that person again, right? I would've forgotten everything that's happened since then?"

"Yes."

"I don't understand." Beck sucks in a long breath, catches up with her heartbeat. "Would I remember the things we've talked about since then? Would I remember anything?"

"No, but you'd get used to that. Like everyone else." Avery looks back at the trailer door, then at Beck. She leans in close until Beck can feel the heat of her breath. "You can't tell my dad I did that. You can't tell him."

Beck blinks. "He said he was the only one who could do it."

"I thought he was."

Beck's stomach twists, but she nods. For whatever reason, Avery trusts her. Even with their conversation gone in the recesses of Avery's memory, she trusts. She cares enough to throw the rules out the window, even for just a second. It's dangerous, this trust. Beck isn't sure what to do with it. She stares into Avery's wide eyes, and there's something electric and dangerous crackling like a live wire.

"I won't tell," Beck whispers. "I promise."

"And I won't tell him. About how bad it's getting."

Beck narrows her eyes. "What would he do if he found out?"

"I don't know."

"What happens now?"

"If this happens again," Avery says, so quiet Beck has to lean forward to hear her, "you and your sister have to leave. I don't care how. You have to go."

"I can't leave until—"

"I don't care."

Avery's voice is stern, and her eyes are afraid. Beck looks down and Avery's fingers are curled around hers. Beck runs a thumb across the back of Avery's hand. She doesn't know why. If it bothers Avery, she doesn't show it. She holds Beck's gaze for another moment, and then she pulls her hand away. She paces to the loft bed and touches Riley's forehead, gently brushing a strand of blond hair away from her brow.

Beck is left with her hand resting cold against the thin mattress. The space feels lonelier now. Quieter. She feels every inch of the empty space beside her. She feels the phantom pressure of fingers at her scalp.

"Thank you for coming," Beck says. "To check on us."

"Yeah," Avery says. "Drink more water and eat some toast. And . . . let me know if you feel sick again."

With that, Avery turns and makes her way out of the trailer. In the brief second she swings the trailer door open, Beck spots the Sterlings standing in the backyard, watching. Mrs. Sterling's fist is knotted in the collar of her sweater. Mr. Sterling's arm is wrapped around his wife's shoulders. They've been waiting for Avery to emerge. They've been waiting for a verdict. Avery meets them and the trailer door shuts.

The conversation is too quiet to hear. Beck doesn't need to hear to understand, though. Her stomach aches with hunger and fear.

Riley is quiet in her bed, only visible thanks to a tuft of blond hair jutting out from under her quilt. Beck sighs, closes her eyes, and it all sets in like the air itself is heavier. She was right; their sickness is tied to all the rest of it. It won't get better unless she leaves. And she can't leave—she *can't*—until she finds what Ellery found here in Backravel. She can't leave until she finishes what her mother started.

20

"Yeah, everything's going really well over here."

Beck is propped on her elbows. Her phone lies faceup on the table between her and Riley, their father silent on the other end of the line. Riley's face is sallow in the phone light, the skin under her eyes still gray from sickness. Even now, she hunches over like she might fall asleep. But Beck needs her awake for this conversation. The swampy haze of sleep still sits heavy in the air, but Beck needs to focus. If they want to get to the bottom of this, they need to stay in Backravel. And to stay in Backravel, they have to keep lying.

"What's left on the agenda?" their father asks on the other end of the line.

Riley sighs.

"I don't know," Beck says. "Gabby's grandma has the house all summer. She's excited about some stuff happening next week. She wants us to stay for the fireworks and farmer's market. It sounds really fun."

"It does," their father admits. *"What's it called?"*

Beck looks at Riley. Riley stares back.

"I don't remember," Beck says.

"Huh." She can't tell if it's skepticism in her father's voice. She swallows hard. After a moment, he continues. *"What's the refund policy on your tickets? It might be fun if me and Julie drove in and picked you girls up. Then we could do the farmer's market thing together."*

For a reason lost on Beck, Riley's eyes light up at the suggestion. Beck eyes her for a moment, then clears her throat. The late-afternoon light paints the table red. They need to wrap up this phone call soon. If they only have a week left in this place, she intends to make use of every second of it. She needs to get to the desert, needs to see if anything comes to her. She needs to review Ellery's notes. She has a million things to do and she's running out of time.

Beck clears her throat. "That's a long drive. You don't have to do that."

"We don't mind the drive. Honestly."

"It's okay, Dad," Beck says.

"Riley's going, too?"

He's noticed that Riley is silent. Riley's head is strained to look out the window, gaze glassy and unfocused. Beck nudges her knee and gestures to the phone.

Riley frowns. "Yeah. I'm going. I'm super excited."

"Gotcha." There's something expectant in their father's voice. He doesn't believe them and he's waiting for a real answer. But Beck keeps her lips sealed, and by some miracle, Riley does the same. After an excruciatingly long quiet, their father sighs. *"Well. Keep us posted. We don't mind doing the drive over, and it would be nice to see you girls sooner than later."*

"Sounds good," Beck says. She presses her fingertips to her temples and they feel swollen like her brain itself is too full of relief and panic and questions. She's only got a few more days to figure this out. She needs to get back to the library, dig into her mother's notes, bike out to the desert. If she doesn't hustle now, it'll all be for nothing. She taps the table and dons a fake smile, even if their father can't see it. "We'll text you about the festival. But I don't want you guys to have to spend so much on gas and tickets and a hotel. It would probably be better if we just met you in Texas."

"Trying to say we're not cool enough for farmer's markets?" their father muses.

"Absolutely."

Their father chuckles on the other end of the line. *"Okay. Well, it's getting late over here. Talk to you girls later."*

"Love you," Riley chimes in.

The line goes dead.

Beck sinks back into the booth and laughs. "I don't know if he believed any of that. God. What a mess."

"Well, it would probably be easier if we didn't *have* to lie," Riley says.

"I know." Beck reaches across the table and lays her hand over Riley's knuckles. Her skin is colder than it should be, even now. "How are you feeling?"

"I feel okay." Riley tilts her head and pops her neck. "Better than earlier. But I'm serious. I really, *really* want to leave soon."

"I know."

Riley is quiet. The tension is thick and hot in the trailer. She traces the lining of the table with her pointer finger, lips pursed in a pensive frown. She's looking healthier now than she did in the morning, but the sickness is still plain on her face. More prominent, though, is the discomfort. She's not happy they're still here. She's not happy that she doesn't understand why. And the thing that eats at Beck is that she can't explain yet, if ever.

"Are you mad?" Beck asks.

"No."

Riley is quiet. She inspects her knees, eyes glassy and distant.

"What's wrong?" Beck asks.

"I don't know." Riley doesn't look up. "Do we even want to go to this festival? Maybe we should take Dad up on the whole picking-us-up thing."

Beck narrows her eyes. "What? How would that even work? We'd have to—"

"We'd drive back to Palm Springs and meet him there."

"For a festival that I just made up," Beck clarifies. "In a town where we have nowhere to stay. Without the friend we told him we've been staying with."

"I'm sorry," Riley relents. "It was just a suggestion."

"Why, though?" Beck asks. "You want to see him even sooner?"

Riley shrugs. "I don't know. Kind of."

Beck waits for an explanation. Since the divorce, Riley has been firmly anti-Dad. But now, presented with another week without seeing him, she seems upset. The refrigerator crackles in the quiet, and the creaky metal of the trailer groans as Riley shifts out of the booth. She paces to the window and looks outside, her back reduced to just the shadowed outline of her.

"I've just been thinking about how it'll be when we get to Texas." Riley runs her fingers through her hair. "I don't know how it'll be living with Dad. But I *do* want to go back to school. And meet people. And, I don't know . . . I'm kind of excited? Like, Dad pays his bills and buys groceries and will drive us to school. He'll probably help us save for college. He'll be like a real—"

"—adult," Beck finishes.

Riley turns to face her. "A parent."

Beck grimaces. She itches at her nose, avoids eye contact. A thought creeps up, snaking its way past any semblance of rationality. She knows that Riley means he'll be a parent in comparison to their mother. But after everything, it feels like a slap in the face. After the scraping and saving and long nights keeping them afloat, she still wasn't good enough for Riley. Within a few months, none of it will have mattered. They'll be with a *real* parent.

She swallows that thought.

"A few more days," Beck says. "Then we'll leave. And you can do all of that stuff."

"*We* can," Riley corrects. "It's gonna be better for you, too."

Beck says nothing because there's nothing to say. *Better* seems so far away she can't picture it. Maybe Riley can see herself settling into her new life and finding a way to make it real. But for Beck, it feels miles out of reach. Only one week, but it feels like she won't make it that far.

Texas is the next step for Riley. For Beck, all she can see is the end of the road.

With the call out of the way, Beck focuses on the task at hand. She extracts Ellery's notes from her backpack like they're radioactive, careful not to tear or fold any of the loose corners. She's spent hours staring into these pages, but not with the knowledge she has now. Riley bundles up in the lofted bed, face turned to the TV, and sleeps. Beck does not sleep—she reads.

Like a language half-learned, there's something easier about reading Ellery's notes now. When she sketches the Quick Stop, Beck can feel the gush of air-conditioning inside. When she mentions the long road into Backravel from Sycamore Lane, Beck feels the wind in her hair. And when she describes a treatment center planted on a great, red plateau, Beck's stomach clenches like it did the first day she saw it. In a way, reading these notes now is the closest she's come to hearing her mother's voice in the last three months. It's like Ellery is here, in the trailer, working the story out the way she always used to. Beck fights the urge to turn into her old self, too, sitting on the carpet picking at staples.

Eventually, Beck opens a note that makes her pause.

It's a drawing—a desert landscape with a rigid horizon and an empty highway running along it. It's indistinct in the way most of the desert views in Backravel are, but there's something strange about this drawing in particular. Along the desert floor, Ellery has drawn dozens of black stones all converging on a single point. A scribbled hole in the earth. At least, that's what the crude drawing evokes, though Beck's not sure if that's because it actually looks like a hole or if it's because of her dream. Along the top of the paper, in Ellery's handwriting, it reads: *Like flat stones in the desert. Over and over and over. Like flat stones.*

None of this is what grabs Beck's eyes, though. There are a few harsh lines sketched on the far right of the page. She wouldn't have recognized it the last time she looked at these notes because she hadn't seen it in real life yet. But on the right side of the page, Beck recognizes the tattered outline of a tent and a cooler and a kneeling pickup truck. She recognizes the shape of a woman in the desert staring back at her. There's only two people that connect the unspooling and the sickness and Avery and her mother. She's already talked to Ricky Carnes.

Good day or not, she needs to talk to the Desert Woman.

Quietly, Beck places Ellery's notes back in their piles and throws on her green windbreaker. She shoves her notebook into her backpack and shoulders it, making silently for the trailer door.

From the lofted bed, Riley stirs. The brightness of the TV is a dim reflection in her glassy eyes. Riley yawns, then manages, "Are you leaving?"

"Uh, yeah," Beck says. "Just for a second. I just want to check something out."

Riley turns over and looks out the circular window. "It's getting dark. You shouldn't—"

"I need to," Beck says, a little too frantic.

"You can't wait for tomorrow?"

"I . . ." Beck trails off. "I don't have time."

"Okay." Riley rubs her eyes. She ponders a moment, lips quirked in a thoughtful half-frown. Then, she looks at Beck. "Can I come with?"

"I'll just be a little bit," Beck says.

"Please." Riley slides off the loft bed and looks Beck square in the face. "I don't know what you've been doing the last week, but I don't want to spend another night alone here. I'm not having fun. And I feel like you're . . . I don't know what you're doing."

Beck weighs her options. Riley at her side might make things harder, but it's not worth it to fight. Beck's fought enough and Riley's spent enough time alone. She doesn't have to tell Riley everything. Carefully, she says, "Do you promise not to be mad at me?"

Riley narrows her eyes.

Together, Beck and Riley layer up and grab the bikes leaning against the side of the Sterling house. They make their way from Sycamore Lane, down the highway, and toward the desert. Nausea bubbles like a boiling pot in Beck's stomach, though she's not sure if that's a symptom of being sick, or if it's because there's something to be afraid of. The last time she saw the Desert Woman, she was being hauled away. Last time she saw the Desert Woman, Avery was hurt.

To her relief, the campsite is still standing when they arrive.

It's empty, but still standing. Beck climbs off her bike next to the decrepit truck and stretches her arms. Riley parks the bike next to her, eyes wide like she didn't expect the campsite to be real. Her face is still pale, but she's more alert now.

"What is all this?" Riley asks. "Whose stuff is this?"

"There's a woman who lives out here."

"Are you sure we should be here?"

"No. But I just want to talk to her."

Beck eases her bike to the ground and steps carefully into the campsite, dodging the garbage and litter between the tent and the truck. There's more here than there was before—water bottles from town, deli sandwich wrappers, discarded Band-Aid boxes. Beck nudges an empty juice carton with the side of her boot and soaks in the disarray. The setting sun spreads like a blush over the red tent flap. The tent door is only half-zipped, giving away just a glimpse of the inside. A nest of sleeping bags is tangled into a makeshift bed. A cool breeze flutters the tent window against the plastic, too quiet.

"They just let someone live out here like this?" Riley asks, almost too quiet to hear. "They have enough money to help her, clearly. I can't believe they just leave her here."

Beck nods. It isn't sadness in Riley's voice, it's anger. The Desert Woman, as far as Beck can tell, is the only person in Backravel living like this. The only one wandering the wastes alone. And maybe everyone in Backravel is afraid of her, but after only a single conversation with the Desert Woman, Beck hasn't found anything to be afraid of. A lost woman looking for things she can't remember is something Beck knows well.

"I asked Ricky about it and he said she's dangerous," Beck says. "But I don't know. I've talked to her and I don't think she's violent. She's just . . . confused."

"You've been talking to Ricky?"

Beck swallows. "Not that much."

"This isn't the lady who hurt Avery, is it?"

"You heard about that?" Beck asks.

"From Daniel the other morning."

Beck grimaces. "I don't know. Ricky said she hurt Avery, but not physically. It all just feels really vague. I can't figure out what actually happened."

"Hmm." Riley paces to the abandoned truck and peers inside the window. It's quickly clear that the Desert Woman isn't home. After an uncomfortably long silence, Riley faces Beck and asks, "Where do you think she is?"

Beck shrugs. She makes her way closer to the tent while Riley peers inside the truck, hand cupped at her brow. Beyond the nested blankets and books, Beck spots something shiny. A makeshift lab is set up against the back wall of the tent. In one beaker, rust-colored powder is splattered against the glass, caked tight at the bottom of the container. In another test tube, a murky brown liquid quivers like the ground is shaking. Beck eyes the stack of books, some dedicated to organic chemistry, all tattered and beaten like they're decades old.

"It's like a lab in here," Beck says without looking at Riley. The scent in the tent is tangy and metallic, and it burns Beck's throat when she breathes. She ducks back out of the tent when her eyes start to water. "There's no way she sleeps in there."

When she turns, Beck spots Riley halfway inside the pickup truck, feet dangling out over the dirt. Eventually, Riley emerges. "There's so much stuff in here."

"Okay," Beck says. "I don't think we should mess with anything while she's not here, though."

Riley laughs. It occurs to Beck that it's been too long since she's heard the sound. She looks out at the expanse of desert between the campsite and the rugged cliffs on the horizon. There's a ringing in her ears, quiet at first, and then deafening. Her head is lighter the longer she stares, and by the time she looks away, she can hardly balance. The mechanical whir she's heard a thousand times since arriving in Backravel rears its head, but this time she's sure it has a source. It's coming from *somewhere*.

Beck wipes at her nose and turns back to face Riley. Riley's nose twitches a little as she mulls over whether or not to speak. She pats the dust and dirt from her pants and rights herself. Finally, she asks, "What's the deal with Avery, anyway?"

"Ha," Beck muses. "I don't know. I don't think there's a *deal*."

"When you said you were best friends I thought you were being sarcastic."

"I was."

"But then . . . ?"

Beck scoffs. "What do you mean?"

"I heard you guys on movie night. When you came back inside."

Beck shrugs. She walks farther into the desert, following the faint, metallic hum. It's almost alive now, changing pitch up and down just slightly. The wide expanse of red rock pulls at her, tugging her farther from the campsite. She tries to focus on Riley's questions, but the farther she walks, the harder it is to think of anything but the desert.

"She's not who I thought she was," Beck says. "I guess that's a good thing."

If Riley says something else, it's lost. Beck takes another step toward the jagged mountains and something crunches under her boot. When she looks down, she's sure she's dreaming again. Something brittle and sun-bleached crumbles to a fine powder in the dirt. Beck stoops down, but it only takes a moment to recognize it as a bone.

"Oh my god." She breathes, but she doesn't move away. Scattered for as far as she can see, more bones jut up from the red dirt. They're too thin to be human bones, but Beck already knows that. Because she's seen this span of desert before and she's waded through the carnage. It's just like she saw in the newspaper clipping back at the library, and just like she saw in her dream. There were hundreds of sheep here once. Hundreds of sheep died here, their bones left to bake in the unforgiving sun.

"Beck?" Riley calls, but Beck doesn't look at her.

Without warning, the sky goes dark. Beck staggers back, rubs at her own arms to make sure this is real. She can't see Riley in the sudden night. She can't hear her, either. The horizon looks the same, and in the distance, she can see just the faint outline of Backravel. The humming is louder now, grinding and clashing somewhere under her feet. Something is happening to her. Something is *changing* in her.

To her right, two pinpricks of red light sear through the dark. Taillights. She recognizes the shape of them as her mother's. They grow in the dark, like the car is getting closer.

Finally, the car reaches her, but it keeps going, reversing down the taut cord of black highway. It passes Beck, but she can't see the driver. The white headlights beam into Beck's face and she has to shield her eyes from the glare. The faster the car backs away, the more crooked the world feels. It's like everything around her is moving in reverse—the wind, the sound, the rotation of the earth. It's going the wrong way. Her heart beats inside out.

The earth fizzles and cracks. In flashes, the buildings of Backravel plink in and out of view like a bad bulb. The ruins, the new buildings, both, neither. It's all too large, expanding until it towers over her, punching hard into the thunder-bruised sky. Beck feels her breath shorten and stick in her chest. It can't be real, but she feels the rock under her feet and the bite of the wind over the ridge.

Beck shuts her eyes as tight as she can. She doesn't know what she sees, can't find the words to describe it.

Finally, when the blinking subsides and the lights in town go dead, Beck hears a faint groan from behind her. She turns just in time to see the earth buckle and dip like lungs filling with air only to sigh it all out. The dirt splits and, in the small void between, something dark descends into the ground.

"The source," Beck says.

She ambles toward the pit on shaky legs. The earth rumbles and Beck falls to her knees. Something in the pit ahead of her comes to life, making the atmosphere heavy and electric. The pressure builds until Beck can hardly think.

And then all she sees is light.

An explosion erupts from the hole in the earth, bright and blinding. It punches out in a shockwave of dust and fire, too fast to outrun. Beck doesn't get a chance to even try. The explosion catches her where she stands, hot and bright and—

•   •   •

When Beck opens her eyes, she's back at the campsite. It's quiet save for the sound of her own panicked breathing. She's crouched, fingers dug into the red rock, sweat beading at her brow. It still isn't night quite yet; it's dusk, just like it was when they got here. None of it—the sudden darkness, the disappearing town, the explosion—was real, but she can still feel the heat of it on her clammy skin.

"*Breathe*," Riley says, and it's clear she's been saying it over and over. She crouches next to Beck and runs a hand over her back. "Please. Just breathe."

Next to Riley, another face looks down at Beck. Slowly, the Desert Woman comes into focus, steely eyes searching Beck's face. There's something almost motherly about the rise in her brows. When Beck blinks, the Desert Woman squeezes her hand.

"What happened?" Beck asks.

"I don't know." Riley breathes. "You just fell down. Are you—"

"Did you see the explosion?" Beck cuts in.

Riley stares at her and says nothing.

The Desert Woman squeezes Beck's hand again. The loose ends of her hair brush the tip of Beck's nose. "It's okay if you saw something. It's harder not to the farther you go."

"What was it?"

"Things time already took," the Desert Woman says. "Maybe things it hasn't given yet."

Beck sits up straight, recoiling from the Desert Woman's touch. She clutches the collar of her shirt and catches her breath. Riley's hand finds her shoulder and Beck isn't sure if she means to protect Beck or hold her back.

"When did you get here?" Beck demands.

The Desert Woman stands up and pats the dirt from her already dirt-stained pants. She's smaller than Beck realized. "You came here looking for me, right?"

Beck and Riley lock eyes but say nothing. Beck *was* looking for the Desert Woman, but she's found something bigger. Ricky was right; there's something in the expanse beyond the campsite. Something powerful. Something dangerous.

Before Beck can speak, the Desert Woman's gaze shifts to

Riley. For a moment, her eyes narrow like she's scanning Riley for info. Then her expression softens into familiarity. She smiles.

"Riley Rose Birsching," the woman says, and there's a glow to her. She's proud of herself for remembering. "Swim lessons. You graduated level ten."

Riley's expression does something strange. Her brow quirks, eyes widening. She's disarmed, just like that. At some point, in all of their meetings, Ellery told this woman about Riley. About the things she was proudest of. She told this woman the kinds of things she couldn't manage to tell Riley to her face. A slow wind pushes Riley's hair across her face, but she doesn't budge.

"You both look so much like her," the woman says. "She said so, but seeing you in person . . ."

She doesn't finish her thought.

"What are you . . . ?" Riley starts.

"Miss . . ." Beck tries, but it's stilted and awkward. How do you address a person with no name? Beck purses her lips. "I wanted to ask you some questions. I know last time you said it wasn't a good day. Do you think . . . would it be okay if we talked right now?"

The Desert Woman nods.

"Okay." Beck swallows hard. "What happened the other day?"

"When?"

"I saw you . . . um . . . Some people had to take you away." Beck rubs the back of her neck. She can't look the Desert Woman in the eyes. "They said you maybe hurt someone? A friend of mine."

"Hurt someone?" the Desert Woman asks. "Who said that?"

"Ricky."

The Desert Woman bristles at that. "I didn't . . . No, I did not hurt anyone. I wouldn't. And this time, I would remember."

"What do you mean?"

The Desert Woman gestures to her tent. "I'm working on something new. I think it'll put me back in order. I want to be able to *think* again."

Beck turns and the glass inside the Desert Woman's tent catches a stray bit of setting sunlight. The experiments in her tent have a purpose, then. Riley seems to notice the glass, too. She fixes Beck with a curious look, but says nothing.

"You told me our mom was helping you with something," Beck says. "Do you remember what it was? Do you remember why she was here?"

"She . . ." The Desert Woman turns to survey her campsite. Her expression lights up. "Oh, I need to show you something."

"Please," Beck says, "We can look in a second. Why was she here, though?"

"She wanted to go back to stretch things out longer than she should," the Desert Woman says. "Then, when I told her how it really is, she changed her mind. That's why he wants me out here. So I can't tell anyone else."

"How it really is?"

The Desert Woman turns and looks into the sinking sun. Her dark eyes glow in the harsh warm light, almost red in the glow. In this light, Beck realizes it's impossible to tell how old she is. She looks the same as Ellery—just a little worse for wear—but her eyes look much older. The skin at her matted hairline is wrinkled and spotted with age. She takes a deep breath and closes her eyes.

"It'll kill you."

"What?"

"Backravel," the Desert Woman says. "It'll kill you if you don't go backward. It was killing her faster and faster."

"No," Beck says, too quick. "No, Ricky says Backravel was keeping her alive."

The Desert Woman blinks.

"You believe him?"

"I . . ." Beck swallows. "I don't know what to believe."

"He's a liar." The Desert Woman spits. "I would know."

"What do you mean?"

The Desert Woman sighs. "It kept her alive for a while. But Backravel doesn't *save* anyone. It just waits."

"I think we should go," Riley says.

"What?" Beck turns on Riley and she can't quite hide the irritation plain on her face. This is the most coherent conversation she's had with the Desert Woman. They can't go *now*.

"Please," Riley insists. "I don't feel good."

"Oh." This is the Desert Woman. She reaches for Riley, but Riley backs away. "You're sick already, aren't you? I wish I knew sooner. I would've kept you girls away. She never wanted you here. She never wanted you to see this."

Beck and Riley exchange a look. Beck fights the urge to tell the Desert Woman about the letter. She *did* want them here in Backravel. She wanted to be found, whatever that means. And she doesn't want to force Riley to stay here with her, but there's so much more she needs to decipher. She can't sleep without knowing what it all meant. What Ellery had to do with all this. What she was trying to accomplish.

"Why did you say I shouldn't trust Ricky?" Beck asks.

The Desert Woman blinks. "Did I?"

They're losing her now. Beck recognizes the glassy, exhausted look Ellery always got after a long conversation. She's burning down to the wick, running out of steam. Beck doesn't want to force her to dredge up old, painful memories that are clearly lost to her, but they're running out of time. "If we come back tomorrow," Beck asks, "will you still be here?"

"I can try," the Desert Woman says. "Wait. Oh, *wait*. I have something for you, remember?"

Riley gives Beck a small nod. They wait patiently while the Desert Woman ambles wordlessly to her truck and opens the driver's door. She pries open a compartment on the floor of the truck and fishes through it, finally pulling something free. When she turns, there's a rolled bundle of papers in her grip.

"What is that?" Riley asks, but Beck is almost certain she already knows.

"Your mom gave me this," the Desert Woman says. "Because we were friends. And because she said I would keep it safe. And I have been. But I don't know what it—"

Beck doesn't wait for the Desert Woman to say her usual *I don't remember what it says*. She scrambles to her feet and snatches the papers from the Desert Woman's grasp. She turns them over in her hands and the low light makes the words hard to read. But the most important parts—the parts that make Beck's blood run cold—are clear as day. THE CURIOUS CASE OF THE TOWN THAT TIME FORGOT the title reads. *How a small town in Arizona created a self-sustaining commune based on fear, lies, and crime.*

And under the title, a name in searing print. *Ellery Birsching.*

21

It's dead night when Riley and Beck make it back to the trailer. Slats
of lights from the Sterlings' house sear through the blinds, but the
sun has vanished, leaving them quiet in the dark. They don't speak
for a long time, moving like machines on a track with only a single
purpose: to sit and read the words their mother left behind. Beck
breathes, but she's far away from herself. The paper is starchy against
the skin of her palm, slick with sweat. The culmination of a decade
of Ellery's work is finally in her hands and she's never been so afraid
in her whole life.

Riley collapses into the booth. She lies back on the vinyl, hair
near-white against the red. They watch each other, they stare at the
mussed stack of papers on the table, and they don't speak. There was
an unspoken agreement on the walk that they wouldn't read until
they were alone. But now, it's fear that keeps them still.

"How did she get it?" Riley asks.

"I don't know."

"Should we read it?"

Beck nods. Shakily, she takes the papers and begins to read.

Jay, when you get this, buy yourself a drink.

No, call me. The drink's on me.

Anyone who's met me knows that I am a big believer in writing things down. I'm a notetaker through and through because memory can only do so much, but if you get it right, writing is forever. That's why I can track every one of my stories back to the moment it struck me. I've got all those original notes—all those sparks that caught fire—in a little box back in Everett. I can trace them all, optimistic start to exhausted finish, in aching detail. But this story is different. This story made me wonder if beginnings and endings mean anything, if a story really is a line, if a person is who they are or if we change each moment we're alive. I don't know if I'm the same woman I was when I got here.

This is the story of Backravel, AZ.

This story isn't finished, a fact that's plagued me for all the years I've been writing it, but I am finally facing the facts. Can a thing that loops itself endlessly through time ever truly be over? Where does it even begin?

I will tell you where Backravel begins from my point of view.

It starts on a sunny day in January 2012, on a thin black highway in Arizona, watching the strangest sunrise I've ever seen.

The story isn't a long one, clocking in at only twelve pages, but it's unmistakably Ellery Birsching's work. It has all her signature turns of phrase, her long-winded anecdotes that she seamlessly ties to her theme. It's a harrowing story of a small-town cover for a mountain of fraud and deceit. It tells the tale of a treatment center on a cruel plateau peddling a modern snake oil, sucking in unsuspecting, grieving Americans and then robbing them for all they're worth. She cites the curious case of the Hortons, a family that disappeared off the map only to reappear as loyal citizens in Backravel. She details the amount of money Ricky's treatment center has drained from the Hortons and speculates that he's extracted the same from every other family in town. She theorizes that Backravel does one of two things with its victims once it's sucked them dry, either turning them back into society with no memory of their time in Backravel or, if they're useful, keeping them in its grip forever. Drugs, she thinks. Or some other form of poison and mind games used to convince people their memories never happened. That they're going back in time. Even here in plain text, Ellery seems unsure. To her credit, the piece is well-researched and documented down to a T. Beck fights the urge to crumple the papers to her chest, to inhale the stale scent of old coffee and dusty mornings from the pages.

But the story isn't finished. It's missing the most important part—the part where unspooling can actually stave off death.

Riley tenderly takes the story for herself, reading in dead silence.

"Wow," she says when she finally finishes. *"Wow."*

Beck stands and grabs the backpack of notes. Maybe she can cross-reference some of the notes with the story. Maybe she can use that to find something deeper. Something *real*. Ellery must not have wanted to write down anything she wasn't sure of. That's why she didn't mention the things that actually matter. The unspooling, the forgetfulness, the forgotten lab somewhere in the desert. "I don't even remember notes about the fraud."

"I'm sure they're in there," Riley says, and Beck detects a slight edge to her voice. She stops digging and stares at her sister. "I think . . . we should take this to the police."

"What?"

"I mean, this is actual fraud. Honestly, it's super irresponsible she didn't take this to the police sooner," Riley continues, leafing through the story's pages without reading them. "I don't know how long she had all this evidence, but if she thought there was a crime, she should've reported it."

"I guess . . ." Beck trails. "You don't think it's weird, though? All the stuff Ricky and the Desert Woman told us isn't even in here."

"Told *you*," Riley corrects. "I don't know what you're talking about. Because you've been, what, looking into this the whole time we've been here? And just leaving me out of it?"

Beck opens her mouth to defend herself, but she can't find the words. Quietly, she says, "There's stuff missing. Stuff I know Mom knew about."

"I don't know what Mom knew and didn't know."

"She wouldn't have come back here a thousand times if that was the whole story," Beck says. Riley has never been as caught up in the mystery of Backravel, but after the illness and after the Desert Woman, she *must* know there's something bigger here. Beck's hands quiver at her sides. "There has to be more of her story somewhere. There's no way she . . ."

"She what?"

Beck stops herself before the words spill out: *there's no way she abandoned us for twelve pages.*

"This isn't what she was looking for," Beck says again. She shuffles the last page of the essay back into the stack. "We have to keep looking."

Riley is quiet for a long time. She works her thumb over a ring of coffee stain on the table, mouth a thin line. "It's enough, though."

Beck stares.

"Like, this is what she found out. That's why you came here, right? It wasn't just a vacation. You wanted to see what she wrote about." Riley taps the printed essay. "I'm tired. We're both sick. I don't want to stay here anymore. I want to leave."

"I know I haven't told you everything I've learned," Beck says.

"But haven't you noticed the way people forget things? The way we keep getting sick? Don't you feel the way your memories just, like, *sit* here?"

Riley grimaces. "I don't know. But there are people who can look into that. People who will actually know what they're doing."

"Like who?"

"Police? Detectives?" Riley shrugs. "Not us."

Beck plucks the first page of Ellery's essay from the stack again. She brushes her pointer finger over her mother's name and tries to swallow the anger boiling in her. Riley sits across from her and she doesn't even look devastated. She doesn't look like this essay has pulled the rug out from under her. She casually peels back the trailer blinds and looks into the dark like she's considering leaving before the sun rises.

"You heard that lady," Riley says. "Mom didn't want us to come here."

Beck puts her head in her hands. Finally, without looking at Riley, she says, "But she *did* want us to come here."

"What?"

"I . . ." Beck chews on how she wants to say it. Because there's no good way to tell your sister you're a liar. "Please try not to be mad at me."

Riley watches Beck as she leans down to her backpack. She pulls out the tattered envelope from Ellery, and it takes only a moment for Riley to register the handwriting. Her expression goes dark and her eyes flit to Beck. "What is that?"

"It's from Mom."

Riley takes the letter and gently removes it from the envelope. She reads it, then reads it again, turning it over in her shaking hands like more words will magically appear if she holds it at the right angle. Finally, she slaps the letter on the table and slides it back to Beck. Coolly, she asks, "How long have you had this?"

"Um. I got it about a week before we left."

"Right." Riley lets out a sharp exhale. "So right around when you told me you wanted to come here, right?"

"I—"

"Why didn't you show me?"

"Because I knew you wouldn't want to come," Beck says. "You wouldn't believe it was real."

"I mean, either this is from Mom, which means it doesn't mean anything," Riley snaps, "or it's from someone else who wanted us to come here."

"It's from her. Look at the writing."

Riley pinches the bridge of her nose. She's fighting back the anger now. Beck braces herself for the blow, but it never comes. Tenderly, Riley says, "I think we really should go. I don't like the way Backravel is making you act. And I think you'll feel better if we leave."

Maybe it's that she thought Riley would be angrier. Maybe it's that she knows she deserves real anger. But something in Beck switches.

"Why do you talk to me like that?"

"Like what?"

"Like you have to brace me for everything you say. Like you're my therapist or something."

Riley pauses, recalibrates, softens her voice. "I'm not trying to talk like that. I'm just saying that, whatever this note was about, we found Mom's story. It's all done now. So we should go."

"I'm sorry that you don't feel good," Beck says. "And I'm sorry I didn't tell you about the letter. But I am *so close* to figuring out this stuff with Mom and I don't want to leave yet. I want to stay."

"Why am I even here?" Riley asks.

"Stop."

"You brought me just to ignore me."

"No, I just . . ." Beck steels herself. "I have given up so many things I wanted for us. And the whole time, all I wanted was to understand what it was that was happening to Mom. I know you don't care about what she was doing here, but I do."

Riley's cheeks go red. "I don't *care*?"

"It doesn't seem like it." Beck's heart is racing now. She doesn't talk like this to Riley—in fact, she doesn't talk like this to *anyone*. But she can't take much more. She's scraped herself clean giving up what little life she had left in her. She's the shell of a girl, left with only want and loneliness. This is the only thing left that matters. "You never cared about Mom's story. You were always so *mad* at her."

Riley scoffs. "Yeah. I was mad at her. And I hated her story."

"Then why did you even agree to come here?"

"For *you*," Riley hisses. "Because I'm stupid and I thought it would help. I wanted you to go back to who you were before. I thought . . . I don't know, I thought if you saw it was just a regular town, you'd go back to being normal."

Beck stares. For the first time tonight, she's genuinely at a loss for words. She presses her fist slowly, softly into the table. She feels sick, and not in the regular Backravel way. "I'm sorry that I've been in a bad mood since our *mom died*. I'm sorry that I can't just get over it like you."

"It's not just since she died," Riley says. Her voice quivers a little, eyes glassy and aching. "You've been checked out for years, just doing whatever Mom said like you didn't even want to be your own person."

"I did what I had to do." Beck sucks in a breath. "I had to make sure we were okay. That *you* were okay."

"But I never asked you to do that."

"You didn't have to."

Riley is on the verge of tears now. "It wasn't just you taking care of me. I don't even think you understand how scary it was for me to lose both of you at the same time. The more we lost Mom, the more you shut down. Do you know how hard I worked to keep you moving?"

Beck stares at Riley a second too long, hurtling toward a thing she doesn't mean to say. *I think you might do well here,* Ricky told her. Riley's right in a way that hurts. There's an open wound in her, and it's been bleeding for everyone to see. She's broken just like everyone else in this town. Beck's heart races and any other night she might be able to stop herself. She might be able to dig her heels into the rock and keep from toppling over the ledge. But not with Ellery's story on the kitchen table. Not with her head throbbing to the point of wishing she was dead. She doesn't have time to stop herself.

"You don't have to stay."

"What?"

Riley's voice is quieter than Beck expects.

"If it's that bad, leave. Obviously being here is not interesting to you. If you want to just go to Texas and never know what happened to Mom, you're free to go."

"How would I go?" Riley asks, indignant.

"I'll drive you to the nearest bus stop," Beck says. "And then I would come right back here. Because I'm not leaving until I know."

"Oh my god." Riley's laugh is incredulous. "There's nothing to find. Mom didn't finish her story. She died and now we know what she found out. That's *it*."

Any other night, Beck would back off. But tonight, she doesn't slow down. Riley sinks into the kitchen booth and plants her face in her palms. Beck paces to the sofa, and then back to the center of the trailer. All the driving, all the hours in the library, all time spent weaseling her way into the treatment center, and she still doesn't have the answers. She's so close she can taste it, and Riley wants to throw it all away.

If she's going to get to the center of it all, she'll have to do it alone. Ellery Birsching was alone. After all this time, Beck supposes she'll be the same.

"I'm not going to—" Riley starts.

Outside, a door slams. Beck turns and pries open the kitchen blinds. The Sterlings spill into the shadows of their backyard. Draped across their arms, Daniel's head is lolled back and his chest convulses. He clutches at his throat while his parents drag him through the gravel toward the road.

"Daniel." Beck breathes.

She looks at Riley and something is different. They've had a million fights over the years, but this time, something's broken. Beck looks at her sister, but Riley looks back at her like she's a stranger.

After a long moment of quiet, the Sterlings clamor back into the yard with Daniel in tow. Riley shivers like she's stepping out of a dream. She runs out of the trailer into the night, and Beck chases after her. Even from several feet away, Daniel's gasps are loud and wet.

"What happened?" Riley asks.

"Asthma attack," Mrs. Sterling says, but she looks at Mr. Sterling like he might have a better explanation. "His treatment should've helped. It should've . . ."

"He thought treatment felt different this week, remember?" Mr. Sterling says. "What if—"

"It doesn't matter," Mrs. Sterling cuts in. "He needs to see Ricky. *Now*."

"Does Backravel have an ambulance?" Beck asks.

Mr. and Mrs. Sterling look at each other, which means no. Daniel continues to wheeze, breath whistling in his throat. Even in the dark, Beck can see the violent contraction of his ribs. It's just like the asthma attack the Sterlings described at the fire. The one that almost took Daniel's life. If no one helps him, he's going to die tonight. He's going to die within the hour.

"My car," Beck mutters. She digs through the pockets of her windbreaker until her fingers curl around the round fob of her keys. She hasn't touched them since arriving, but this is an emergency. While Riley crouches at Daniel's side, whispering calming affirmations, Beck stumbles through the dark, unlocks the car, and throws herself into the driver's seat.

Even with the door closed, even with the wind howling over the metal, she can hear Daniel's wheezing. She closes her eyes and takes a deep breath. She can't quite stave off the creeping feeling that something is wrong here. That this isn't a tragically ill-timed asthma attack. She clenches her fingers around the steering wheel, jams the keys in the ignition, and turns them.

Nothing happens.

"*No*," Beck pleads.

She tries again, and the engine gives her a dull cluck. Barely an attempt. She tries again, stamping on the gas this time, but it's the same. The car won't start. She drove it all the way from Everett without a hiccup, but after less than two weeks of neglect, it won't start.

She steps back out into the night. Daniel's wheezing continues, joined by his mother's cries. They're all huddled there in the red rock and scrub; Daniel on his back staring up at the night, Riley at his side, his parents clutching his hands like they might keep him tethered here. They're gathered around him like they're sure they'll lose him any second.

"Please," Mr. Sterling begs into the phone. "Please. He's not going to—"

She's sure it's Ricky he's talking to. All of Backravel is sure that Ricky Carnes is the only one who can reach into the very matter of Backravel and bend it to his will. But it's not true. She felt it in the trailer, head in Avery Carnes's palms. She saw the past in front of her so vividly she could live in it if she wanted to. It seemed impossible at first, but now she's not so sure.

Wordlessly, Beck moves into the huddle and crouches at Daniel's side. His ribs suck in with each wheeze, each convulsion harsher and deadlier than the last. He looks at Beck and all that teenage apathy and sour attitude is gone. In his eyes, she sees the same horror she saw in Mr. Sterling, in the Desert Woman, in Avery.

Beck plants her palm against the soil. Her voice shakes when she says, "Can you remember a few days ago?"

"What are you doing?" Riley asks.

Beck doesn't answer her. She focuses on Daniel's eyes and she keeps talking. "You know how this goes. Maybe you can help me? Think back to a few days ago when you could breathe. Can you picture it?"

Daniel closes his eyes. He keeps gasping against her, but he understands. Beck feels the heat of Mrs. Sterling's and Riley's glares. It'll be worth it if she can keep Daniel alive, though.

"Okay, now remember how the wind felt on your skin. Remember what the ground felt like under your feet. Do you see it?"

Daniel nods.

"Okay," Beck says. "Now step into it."

Daniel writhes hard against Beck's legs, and for a moment she's sure she's made it worse. He sucks in a breath and grabs Beck's hand, squeezes so tight she feels her knuckles crunch against each other. Something changes in his face—it takes Beck a moment to recognize it. A small cut above his right eyebrow fades, then vanishes. Finally, Daniel collapses into Beck's lap and his breathing steadies. He inhales then exhales, inhales then exhales, and Beck laughs.

Mrs. Sterling laughs, too, dabbing at a tear that rolls down her cheek. She leans down and scoops Daniel into her arms. "It's okay, baby. It's okay."

But Riley doesn't laugh. She looks at Beck with wide eyes, and even in the dark, it's clear she's horrified. "What . . . *was* that?"

"I—"

Beck doesn't get a chance to explain herself. A car door slams from the curb of Sycamore Lane. Beck turns and spots the unmistakable creamsicle color of Ricky Carnes's Cadillac. He steps out of the car, the embellishments on his hat gleaming under a particularly bright streetlight.

"Where is he?" Ricky asks.

"He's here," Mrs. Sterling calls out, cradling Daniel's head to her chest. "But he's okay. I don't know how, but . . ."

She hesitates. Avery didn't want Ricky to know she was able to unspool. Mrs. Sterling's silence tells Beck there might be a good reason for that.

Ricky steps into the backyard, and it occurs to Beck that this is the first time Riley's ever seen him. She stares with a mixture of awe and fear. Finally, Ricky's expression breaks into a smile. He crouches down between Beck and Riley, putting a hand on each of their shoulders.

"What did I tell you about miracles?"

Beck gives a small laugh. Riley is silent.

"How about we all go up to the treatment center?" Ricky says. "I want to make sure Daniel's feeling okay."

Mrs. Sterling nods and helps Daniel to his feet. Mr. Sterling steps into the backyard to help her, his hair disheveled from running his hands through it. Beck makes no move to join them. She stares at Riley, who stares at the ground.

"I want you two to come along," Ricky says.

"Why?" Beck asks.

"Because I want to make sure you're feeling okay." Ricky turns to Riley. "Do you think we can manage that?"

Riley seems to understand it as well as Beck does; this isn't an offer, it's a command. As warm and inviting as he may seem, they don't have the option of staying behind. Ricky helps Riley to her feet and they walk toward the Cadillac. Beck follows them like a shadow. She casts one glance back to the trailer with a frown. It's all falling apart.

It's all falling apart and it's her fault.

22

It's quiet in the hallway of the treatment center.

Somewhere far away, a vent crackles and a machine beeps, but the air around Beck is stale. They all arrive at the treatment center together, but in the blur of people rushing to help Daniel, Beck is scooted into a waiting room by herself. She waits for Riley to emerge, but she doesn't. The bald head of the moon peeks over the bluffs, only a sliver of silver crossing the toe of Beck's boot. When she's alone like this, she can hear the labored sound of her own breathing. She needs to focus on *solutions*. She needs to fix things with Riley, figure out who to trust, find the lab Ellery was looking for.

At the end of the hallway, a door opens. Beck can just hear the voices on the other side, but they hush before she can make them out. Beck half expects Riley to step into the hallway wearing the same expression she always wears after a fight. A frown that says *I'm sorry, but I won't back down*.

But it's not Riley who steps into the hallway. Avery closes the door cautiously, presses it shut behind her without a sound. In the dim moonlight, Avery is strikingly small, shoulders stooped, stance narrow, footsteps fleeting and delicate. Avery stands in the shadows a moment too long, hand still on the doorknob. When she turns, Beck can't make out the shape of her face.

"Is everything okay?" Beck asks.

Avery is still. When she finally moves, it's like the whole night moves with her. Beck can't look away. She wearily rubs at her eyes. "Yeah. He'll be fine. He's just resting now."

"Okay," Beck says.

Avery makes her way to the seat beside Beck. She slumps into the chair and leans back with a sigh. They haven't spoken since the trailer and the silence that settles in the space between them burns. Beck doesn't know what to say. She doesn't know what to do with her hands. She doesn't know what Avery remembers. She doesn't know who they are to each other, but there's something in her that aches to fill in the blanks.

"Was it you?" Avery asks.

"Was what me?"

"Daniel." Avery runs a hand through her mussed-up hair. "His mom says he was dying. Then suddenly he wasn't."

"How would it be me?" Beck asks. "Ricky's the only one who knows how to unspool."

Avery eyes her now. There's a small smile that plays at the corner of her mouth, and Beck stares at it a moment too long. They both turn to face forward and Beck catches her breath. With Avery, it's like she can pretend the whole world isn't crashing down around her.

"Where's Riley?" Beck asks. "I need to talk to her. I need to . . . we need to figure some stuff out."

"She's with my dad," Avery says. "He wants to make sure you guys aren't too sick to stay for the festival."

The festival. Beck nearly forgot about Backravel Days. It seems so miniscule now compared to everything else she's learned. She can't imagine enjoying a street fair knowing that this whole town is a scam. Knowing that there's something else at play here, worse than the fraud and the lies.

"What happens if we're not?"

Avery shrugs. "I guess you'll leave."

"That would probably make you happy."

Avery turns in her chair, shifting her feet up onto the cushion so she can face Beck fully. The suddenness of her stare is unnerving and Beck has to look down to hide the surprise on her face.

"It wouldn't make me happy if you left," Avery says, quieter than she was before. "But I'd be happy you weren't dying."

"What if I don't want to go yet?"

"Beck," Avery says.

Beck's not sure she's ever heard Avery say her name. There's a heat that blossoms in the pit of her stomach. Avery's face is half-shadow in the dim hallway, but her eyes sear with purpose. She waits for Beck to say something, but Beck can't find the right words. She wants to go to protect Riley. She wants to stay to uncover the rest of Ellery's story. She wants to go to regain some of the clarity she's lost.

She wants to stay for Avery.

The door at the end of the hallway opens and Mrs. Sterling steps into the light. She motions for Beck to join them. Hesitantly, Beck rises from her seat and fixes Avery with a long look.

"Be careful," Avery says.

Beck nods.

She makes her way down the hall and Mrs. Sterling ushers her into an unmarked room she can only assume is Ricky's office. The room is unsettlingly large. Beck wondered, when she first visited the treatment center, how it could possibly be so big for such a small town. Ricky's office answers that question. Just like the hallways, his office is floor-to-ceiling industrial windows and concrete floors. Ricky sits in the center of the room at a glass-top desk, scrawling something in his notebook. Mr. Sterling sits across from him with his hands in his lap like he's just been given detention.

When Beck enters, Ricky slaps his notebook shut.

"Where's Riley?" Beck asks Mrs. Sterling.

Mrs. Sterling's smile is pained. "Why don't you go take a seat. We'll explain."

Beck slides into the seat next to Mr. Sterling, and Mrs. Sterling takes a seat next to her so that they've got her sandwiched in. Ricky watches all three of them in silence for a moment, then he sighs. The air-conditioning vents above them click and shift in the quiet and Beck thinks she might scream.

"I don't know how you did it," Ricky says, "but I believe you saved Daniel's life back there."

Beck looks at Mrs. Sterling. One of the two of them told. Silently, Beck nods, but she doesn't offer any further explanation. She doesn't *have* any explanation. What she did should be impossible, according to Ricky.

"Daniel doesn't remember what happened. He'll likely be shaky for the next few days as he settles back into himself. I advise being gentle with him. I believe all of us are aware of how unsettling it can feel."

Beck stares. She expected anger or punishment, but Ricky isn't angry. In fact, he speaks so clinically about it, Beck's almost sure he's dealt with rogue unspoolings before. But this isn't what she cares about. She's happy Daniel is okay, happy he'll be back to normal, but there's a key person missing from this room and Beck isn't leaving until she finds her.

"Where's Riley?" Beck asks.

Mrs. Sterling slips her hand over Beck's. Both of the Sterlings look down and Beck knows something is wrong before Ricky even parts his lips to speak.

"Riley . . ." Ricky says, "has decided to leave."

Beck's breath stops short. Mrs. Sterling's grip on her hand tightens, both a comfort and a warning. It's like the room is darker and more vibrant all at once, walls sucking inward as Beck manages a breath.

"When?" Beck asks. "Just now?"

"Yes."

"Can I . . . talk to her?"

"No, unfortunately." Ricky presses his pen into a stray sticky note on his desk, leaving an ink blot in its wake. "I don't know if you realized how ill your sister is. If I'd seen her in person before tonight, I would've acted sooner. This is my own fault. I excluded her from activities in town and took your word that she was feeling alright. Honestly, she wouldn't have lasted much longer in Backravel without help."

"I don't understand," Beck says.

"She was putting on a brave face, Beck," Ricky says. "But she wasn't well. You aren't, either, though you seem to be adapting better than most."

"Does my dad know?" Beck asks.

"Not yet. I thought I'd let you break the news." Ricky shifts a little in his seat and Beck realizes this is not the end of the conversation. "Listen, because of how severe the situation is, I'm going to be taking care of Riley the next few days. I want to make sure she's had a full recovery before she leaves Arizona."

"So she's here?"

"Yes."

"You're not . . . unspooling her, right?"

Ricky frowns. "I'll do what I need to do to keep her safe. I know it's scary, but I need you to trust me."

"I need to see her." Beck leans forward. "Please let me see her."

"No."

"Why not?"

"Beck," Mr. Sterling warns, and the condescension in his voice makes Beck ill. "You've done a lot tonight. You didn't just save Daniel. You saved your sister, too."

"It'll all be okay in the end," Mrs. Sterling jumps in. "You can stay for the festival and then, when it's done, I'm sure Riley will be all better. After the festival, you two can go to Texas together if you want."

There's something too rehearsed about this. It's all too ideal for how miserable Beck feels. They're hiding Riley from her for a reason. If something's happened to her . . . Beck holds a hand to her stomach to keep from being sick. She shouldn't have fought with Riley like she did. She shouldn't have dragged Riley here in the first place. Her only job was to protect her sister and she's ruined it all.

Ricky eyes Beck, then turns to face Mr. Sterling.

"Could Beck and I have a moment?" Ricky asks. "Just the two of us?"

Mr. Sterling nods and stands. Mrs. Sterling lingers a moment, hand clasped around Beck's, and then she stands, too. Silently, the two of them leave the office and then it's only quiet, the ease vacuumed out of the room with them. Beck measures her breaths, forcing herself not to slip like she always does. Ricky's eyes are on her and she can't slip right now. She has to stay here, no matter how bad it hurts.

After a moment, Ricky sighs.

"I'm sorry about all of this," he relents. "I know this must feel terrible. You've been trying your hardest to keep it together, but I see you. I know this isn't easy."

Beck shakes her head. She doesn't want comfort from Ricky Carnes, the man at the center of this whole hurricane. But when he speaks, it's like he's the only one who's ever stood in her shoes. Beck puts her face in her hands.

"You don't have to hide it," Ricky says. "Beck? You don't have to hide."

"What?"

"You have a hard time staying present, don't you?" Ricky asks, and Beck feels the quiet deepen around her. "Don't be embarrassed. It means you're already fitting in here."

Beck swallows hard. She fixes her eyes on Ricky and her cheeks are on fire. It's always been easier to stand in the back of the room when it gets bad like this, unseen and unheard, letting the waves of it wash over her. Ricky Carnes sees her in a way that simultaneously makes her feel at home and makes her want to disappear.

"It wasn't this bad back home."

"It's like I told you. Backravel is different from the rest of the world. Everything that's ever happened to you is right here at the surface. The good and the bad. For some of us, it's a lot more bad than good. If you were to stay here, I could help you manage it."

"I just want everything to slow down," Beck manages.

"Listen, Beck," Ricky says, too soft. "I know you must feel so alone right now. I'm sorry that things have gone the way they have. If there's anyone else in the world who knows how you feel, it's me."

Beck looks up.

"I have been in your exact shoes. Losing the people I love the most on all sides. I know how desperate it feels." Ricky sits forward and the shadows that fill the office stretch long across his face. He pauses a moment, then says, "You aren't alone. As long as I'm here with you, you aren't alone. Since the very beginning, it's been my mission to keep the people in Backravel from ever feeling that kind of loneliness."

Beck sucks in a breath. She feels queasy, and she's not sure if it's the loneliness or the familiarity. Ricky is right; she's never felt more alone in her life. Ellery is gone, speaking to her in clues that don't make sense. Riley is gone and probably won't ever forgive her. Her father is hundreds of miles away, happily tucked into a life Beck can't imagine herself joining. Avery is here, but only barely. She's here, but trying to keep her is like holding a fistful of sand, watching bits slip between your fingers.

"I was looking for the, uh . . ." Beck wipes at her nose. "I was looking for the lab you were talking about. But I don't know where—"

"Don't worry about that right now, Beck."

Beck nods.

"Here's what I'd like to talk about. I'd like to talk about your future in Backravel. I wasn't kidding when I said I thought you would fit in here. I think you understand that now. And I'm sure there's a lovely life waiting for you in Texas with your sister and your father if that's what you want. But . . . does that life feel like it's yours?"

Beck considers. All this time, she's imagined Riley shifting easily into their father's world. She'll make new friends in Texas, she'll eat three meals a day, she'll get a car when she turns sixteen and their father will teach her how to drive it. But when Beck tries to picture herself there, it's empty. She's an ugly, misshapen piece that doesn't click anywhere comfortably. In Everett, she had a purpose. In Texas, she'll have nothing.

"Are you asking me to stay?"

"If that's what you want, Beck."

Beck looks out the dark window and something opens in her like a room she's never wandered into. She has a choice. She *can* slow the world down. And maybe her fear of Ricky was unfounded, because despite the crimes Ellery's story accused him of, right now it's like he's the only person in the world speaking her language. If she stays, she'll have time to get the full picture of Backravel. She can find out what he's hiding. If she stays, she'll have time to understand Ellery. She'll have time to do anything she wants.

If she stays, there's Avery.

"You don't have to make a decision tonight," Ricky offers. "Think it over. Enjoy the festival. We'll talk soon, whatever you decide."

"Okay."

Beck leaves Ricky's office and her head is spinning. The whole drive back to the Sterlings' house, she thinks. She imagines her mother sitting in the same chair, facing Ricky Carnes, offered the same choice. She chose not to stay. She chose not to bring them to Backravel. She chose to die instead of staying here.

It can't have been just the fraud and the cover-up. Her mother chose to die instead of living in Backravel. There has to be a reason why.

23

The twenty-four hours after Riley are silent.

Too silent, even for Beck. That night, after Daniel's asthma attack, the Sterlings take her home and slide silently into their normal nightly routine. And Beck gets ready for bed all alone, listening to the howling of the wind outside the trailer. She lies awake in her casket bed, waiting for the lumbered sound of Riley's snoring. The emptiness feels wrong. Nothing erases the fact that Riley is gone, that Beck misses her, that she's alone all over again. She can't feel the sadness without the guilt that comes with it because she told Riley to leave. This loneliness wasn't an accident; she made it for herself.

The next morning, Beck stays in bed for hours. She feels hopeless the way she used to back in Everett, too tired to even drag herself from her bed to the kitchen. Her phone rings again, followed by a text from her father, and she ignores it. If the wheels were spinning before, they're completely stuck in place now. No more lies: Beck Birsching is out of steam.

When she finally manages to get herself out of bed, it's already past noon. The town is quiet in that unnatural way it always is, like the people of Backravel simply power down when she isn't looking at them. Silently, Beck bikes out to the desert alone. If she's stuck here without Riley, she'll at least make the most of it.

When she gets to the red, barren stretch of land where the campsite should be, it's gone. Beck wanders out into the wastes and lets the sun bake her alive. She wanders and wanders with no end point in sight. She searches for the humming from underground that drew her in yesterday, but it's gone, too. A call comes in from Texas and Beck ignores it. She doesn't know what her goal is. She doesn't know what to do with herself. She has to keep looking, but no matter where she turns, it feels like this is where the road ends.

You stay in Backravel or you leave. Maybe there's nothing else to find.

Beck bikes back to the library, backpack stuffed with her mother's notes. She stands in the small room of files, digs through rolls of film and tattered old books, but the words swim on the pages. She stood in this same room with Avery only a week ago and her world was entirely different. She checks her mother's crude maps against the ones she finds in the film, but she can only think about Riley. And Avery. And her own rotting guilt. Nothing in the library pulls her. The only pull she feels is back to the treatment center.

Toward Riley.

Toward Avery.

Defeated, Beck bikes back into Backravel, sweaty and lethargic. The trek up the plateau was difficult the first time she came here, but with her mind a thousand miles away, the glide up the winding road is easy. By the time she arrives at the treatment center, the silence has gone from unnerving to disturbing. Afternoon careens into early evening, time sliding away like it always does here. It occurs to Beck that maybe Ricky was right last night; maybe she's becoming acclimated to this place. She looks down at Backravel and it's entirely motionless. A dead town in the dead wastes. Her heart thumps anxiously in her chest.

Up ahead, a door creaks.

Beck looks up and Avery is watching her, halfway inside the treatment center. She wears a ratty pair of running shorts and an overlarge T-shirt, her nest of dark curls sitting like a halo at her brow. She eyes Beck for a long while before she speaks.

"I didn't think you were coming over," Avery says. "Are you looking for my dad? He's out right now."

"Oh," Beck says. She wheels her bike to the entrance of the treatment center, slipping into the shade of the great metal awning. She wipes the sweat from her brow with her sleeve and catches her breath. "No, actually. I was looking for . . . I just wanted to come over. I feel a little—"

"—shaken up?" Avery asks.

"Yeah. That."

Avery motions Beck inside. She pours her a glass of water and they make their way down the long stone hallway toward the treatment rooms. There are no windows on the door, but Beck still fights the urge to peer around each one. Riley must be here somewhere.

"I'm sorry about your sister," Avery says.

"Is she in one of these?" Beck asks, motioning to the unlabeled doors.

Avery shrugs. "Believe it or not, my dad doesn't tell me everything. Especially not if he thinks I'll just tell you immediately."

"Would you?" Beck asks between sips of water. "If you knew, would you tell me?"

Avery says nothing to that, which tells Beck she said too much. They round one corner, then another and Beck finds herself in a hallway she hasn't walked before. Avery keeps shuffling along, bare feet brushing the concrete, until she pauses in front of another un-labeled metal door. She casts Beck a quick glance, then pushes her way inside.

The room on the other side of the door is not what Beck expects. It's a bedroom, massive windows facing the desert north of Back-ravel. It's the first view she's seen in the treatment center that isn't pointed at town. Against the wall is an unmade bed, white sheets and comforter. Other than the bed, a desk, and a square rug in the center of the room, it's entirely unfurnished. Beck spots a closet with the door ajar. The pile of T-shirts and jeans are unmistakably Avery's.

This is the opposite of what Beck expected from Avery's room.

"This is your room?"

"It is," Avery says. She makes her way into the room and plops down on the bed, arms spread wide, facing the ceiling. "Do you love it?"

"It's . . . very clean."

"No, it's not."

"Well, it's definitely not messy."

Avery laughs, but only slightly. She doesn't look at Beck, instead hugging her knees up to her chest so she can roll onto her side. "Did you actually just come here to look for your sister?"

"Kind of," Beck says. "Or to see you."

"Me?"

"I'm just . . . I can't think. I wandered around for hours this morning because I didn't know where to go. I just want something to fix all this, but I don't know what to do. The only thing I could think of was coming here."

Avery sits up and eyes Beck. "Why?"

"I don't know." Beck takes off her glasses and cleans them with the hem of her shirt. Something has shifted in the room and speaking feels dangerous. But she needs to be brave. She needs to put words to the fear that's been swelling in her chest. "I've just been really confused. And people keep telling me things are gonna work out, but I don't believe them. Things didn't work out for my mom. They say Riley will be fine and I'll get all the answers I need, but it just feels . . . like a lie?"

Avery's eyes narrow. "You mean my dad told you that?"

"Not just him. The Sterlings, too. Everyone."

"You think *everyone* is lying?"

"I think there's something wrong with Backravel." Beck clenches her hands into fists at her side to keep from fidgeting. "Things just don't add up. If it's so great here, why can't anyone remember anything? Why can't people move away? Why does everyone get sick when they stay?"

Avery stands. She makes her way to Beck and takes the glass of water from her hands, setting it gently on her small desk. She feels that same ache she feels whenever Avery stands close to her, both comfort and fear at once. Maybe she's said too much and she's shown too many of her cards, but there's nowhere else to turn. There's no one else who's seen her greatest fears like this, even if Avery can't remember.

"Why does *everyone* have to be unspooled?" Beck asks. "He said it's for people who are hurt. Every single person here is hurt?"

"I . . ." Avery trails off.

"You don't know, do you?"

"Beck," Avery says. It's the second time Avery has said her name out loud. It sounds strange. It sounds right. "I don't know if this is a good time to talk about this. You seem really upset."

"I am upset," Beck says.

"We all question it sometimes," Avery says. "Maybe I shouldn't have questioned it so much out loud. To you."

"What's that supposed to mean?"

Avery's quiet burns. Beck watches the feathery dark of her lashes and she steels herself. She wants to reach out. She wants to take Avery by the shoulders and make her understand that she's another piece in this game. She wants to figure it out together. She doesn't want to be alone anymore.

"When I was sick," Beck says, "you helped me. You know how to unspool because he does it to you all the time, right? You told me before that it would feel like your life never changes, and I think that's probably because your dad just resets everyone in town every few months."

"Beck—"

"But you don't even remember that conversation."

Avery looks at her and she doesn't need to say anything. Because Beck has seen this look before, every night before bed, facing the trailer mirror. The face of a girl reckoning with what's been done to her. What she's allowed. Beck has tasted this particular mix of fear, anger, and shame before. Her fingers curl into a fist and she sucks in a deep breath.

"I do remember," Avery murmurs.

For a moment, Beck pauses. "What?"

"Not all of it, but some. I remember walking with you." Avery's breath is a shudder. "And I remember waking up and feeling different than I did the night before. I couldn't remember what we talked about, but I remembered you."

"Does he know?"

Avery shakes her head.

"He's going to do that to my sister." Beck breathes. "I can't let him do that. Please. If you know how I can get to her, I promise, we'll leave. I got myself involved in this, but Riley doesn't want any of it."

"It's not like you think," Avery says. "It's a good thing. Sometimes it feels better to forget. People here are *happy*."

"My second night in Backravel, Mr. Sterling forgot who I was. He was confused and he was scared, because he knew he lost a memory he was supposed to have."

"He wouldn't forget you if you stayed here," Avery says. "That's how it goes with us. You remember the people that stay because eventually they're just . . . here. And you forget the ones that don't."

"Why do you barely remember your brother?" Beck asks. "Or your mom?"

Beck thinks of Avery forgetting her and it's more crushing than she expects. She thinks of herself in Texas, acclimating to a new life, mind snagged on the girl from the strange town in Arizona who will never recognize her again.

"Do you feel happy here?"

Avery blinks. Beck can't tell if she's angry, scared, or both. Her thick brow is flat, either with contempt or confusion. Her cheeks are red now, and Beck's sure she's almost gotten through to her.

"How does it keep going like this?" Beck asks. "Someone must've questioned it by now. There's no way everyone has gone along with this . . . *brainwashing* for so long."

"It's not brainwashing," Avery says, flat.

"He's taking your memories."

Avery's jaw is set, dark eyes blazing with the quiet, scorching type of anger. Beck shrinks away, and there's a tangy taste in her mouth. This isn't how she pictured the coin falling, but she should've expected that Avery would stay loyal. Beck's only known Ricky for a few days and it's hard to imagine turning on him. He's had control of Avery's brain for years. Even now, his claws are sunk deep into her, turning her head with a gentle kind of violence.

"I'm sorry," Beck relents. "I shouldn't have—"

"Why are you doing this?" Avery asks. "What if people like living like this? What if we like this . . . this haze?"

Beck stares at her. It feels too dangerous to just stand there, to let this fear and rage boil up in her until it bursts. She looks at Avery and she sees a twist of anger in her. For a long time, Avery is quiet. In the space of only a few seconds, she changes. Something in the air shifts, slackens like a cord. She tries to hide it, but her breath is fast. Beck feels it fan over her face and she's aware, too quickly, of how close they're standing. She hasn't backed away. Avery hasn't backed away. When Avery looks up, her eyes shine with fresh tears.

"What am I supposed to do about it?" she asks.

"You can get out," Beck says. "I don't know what's happening, but your dad told me people are starting to remember things, like the unspooling is getting weaker. How long until you're only going back a week? Or a few days? Wouldn't that make you miserable?"

"I don't know what'll happen."

"Then you have to find out."

Avery's jaw tightens. "Why do you care?"

"Because I do," Beck hisses. She's not sure where it comes from, this spitfire between her ribs. She's never fought with anyone like this in all her life, now she's fighting with everyone. She fights with Riley and with Avery and with herself, stabbing at anything that moves. It's like, for the first time, there's something to cling to. There's something to scrape toward. For the first time, she wants to see tomorrow, and she's stuck in a town where there's only a million todays. She sucks in a breath, but it doesn't quell the blaze. "Because I know if it was me, I wouldn't do anything. I'd just sit there and keep living the same day forever because I'd be too afraid to fight it. And I'd be so fucking miserable."

"It's not like I haven't thought about it," Avery says. "Most days I wake up and it's like I can't figure out where I am. Or who I am. I can't tell if I'm looking forward or backward. I don't know how long I've been here or how much longer it'll be like this. But I don't know what the world is like outside anymore, either."

"Doesn't that scare you?" Beck asks.

Avery's voice is hardly more than a whisper. "When I think about it for more than five seconds it makes me want to scream."

"You helped me," Beck says. "I want to help you, too."

The quiet morphs, hot and restless, and something in Avery changes, too. Before Beck can find her footing, Avery springs forward. Her hands find the curve of Beck's jaw and she pulls them together with enough force to send Beck teetering back into the bedroom door. She gasps a little, but it's cut short when Avery's mouth finds hers.

The kiss is too quick, and it eats away everything else in Beck's whirling brain. She fumbles for traction, sighs into Avery's mouth, knots her fingers in the unruly mop of her hair. It feels like she expected it would, soft against Beck's knuckles. Her mouth is soft, too. Her lips part, and for a moment Beck's world is only Avery. Only quick breaths and a pulse that races like a bullet train. She's wanted before, but this wanting is more. This is the kind of want that swallows everything else; all the fear and the hurt and the confusion melts away and she's left with only this. A fire where Avery's fingers press hard to her skin.

Avery pulls away and she's breathless.

"What are you . . . ?" Beck starts.

"I'm sorry," Avery whispers against her mouth, words fumbling, falling from her lips. "I don't know. I just don't want to think anymore."

Beck's breath is ragged. She pushes a curl of Avery's hair behind her ear. "What do you want? Really?"

"I want you to stay," she whispers. "I don't want you to go."

Beck's fingers skirt down the length of Avery's arm. "If I stay, I want you to remember. I want you to remember me."

Avery takes Beck by the waist and kisses her again. Beck's hands find Avery's neck and she cups her closer, kisses her deeper, lets the white-hot want fill her up. Avery guides her away from the door and eases her to her bed and Beck loses herself in the warmth of her mouth. She lets yesterday and tomorrow fall away from her, leaving only Avery. Only now. She kisses Avery until the sun dips under the horizon and the darkness eats them alive. Tonight, she's not alone. She's scared, heart racing, iron pooling on her tongue, but she's not alone.

Tonight, she's not lost.

Avery comes up for air and she eases away to look Beck in the eyes. The closeness of her is almost too much to take. She breathes. *"Please stay."*

Beck nods and takes Avery's face in her hands, kissing her because she doesn't know what will happen tomorrow or the next day. None of it matters now.

Now, she wants to be touched. To be felt down to her very fiber and to be real to someone else. She wants Avery's calloused palms to press her so deep into the mattress it leaves an impression. Even if they wake up tomorrow and this night is gone, lost in that corner of Avery's mind that's only a void, the outline will remain. Beck Birsching existed in Backravel and she chose to be wanted like this. She existed in Avery's bed, between her hands, and the imprint of them will be stamped into this place long after they're forgotten. A girl stuck in place and a girl lost in time, fingers intertwined for one night before they're swallowed whole.

24

When Beck wakes, the room is still murky with night. She wakes slowly for once, no nightmares or panic attacks to startle her to life. For a moment, she forgets where she is. The bed is too soft, the ceiling too high, the wind too quiet to be the trailer. This isn't the trailer, she remembers. The window of Avery's bedroom faces the bald cliff over Backravel. Pinpricks of white light gleam from the valley floor like starlight laid to earth. For a long, quiet moment, Beck just stares into the night and lets her mind sputter to a temporary calm.

Next to her, Avery shifts. She nuzzles into her pillow, the unruly mop of her hair caught in the fabric of the pillowcase. Memories blossom in Beck's fingertips first. They were tangled in Avery's hair only a few hours ago. The ghost of a kiss, lips quirked into a half-smile, still prickles on Beck's lips.

"Avery?" Beck whispers. Her voice echoes in the wide, empty space of Avery's bedroom, but Avery doesn't stir. Her nose twitches in her sleep and Beck's breath sticks in her throat. She wonders what this means, if Avery will remember it the way Beck does. Lying here against Avery's pillow, remembering the way she was touched, Beck is still hungry. She wants to lean across the distance and kiss Avery again, keep kissing her until the sun creeps over the toothy horizon. She wants to be remembered, to be touched again. It's a new feeling.

She doesn't know what forever means, especially here, but there's a little pool of forever between them right now. The kind that will only last a moment. The kind that will be gone when the sun comes up.

Outside Avery's room, the light clicks on.

Yellow spills from under Avery's bedroom door, a thin slot of light against the concrete. Beck stiffens and watches it carefully. After a moment, a silhouette crosses the light. The tapping of hefty footsteps is barely audible, but Beck hears it. She isn't the only person awake in the treatment center tonight.

She's not entirely sure where she is in the treatment center, but according to her memory of Ricky's office, the footsteps are coming from there.

Tenderly, Beck slips from under Avery's blankets and fishes through the dark for her shirt. She only has a brief window to look for Riley, and she's not wasting it. She presses her ear to the door and listens until the footsteps fade away and only the sound of the churning air conditioner is left.

She shouldn't leave this room. She should wait until daylight when Avery is awake. But she doesn't listen to the whisper of fear warning her to stay put.

Beck slips out of Avery's room into the narrow hallway of the treatment center. The light is brighter than she expects and Beck has to rub the sleep from her eyes. Maybe she shouldn't poke for answers. She's half-asleep, delirious from Avery, dizzy and fatigued by the sickness that's been dogging her. Riley's not here to bail her out of trouble this time. If she blows this, she's alone.

But if it's Ricky walking the halls, following him is worth the risk.

She follows the footsteps.

Beck's knuckles scrape along the walls as she goes, a little guarantee that she's still moving. Her head spins, tilting the concrete floor under her feet. She tries not to think about how the footsteps might be a janitor or some other staff on their way to something mundane.

She finds a door and tries the handle, but it's locked. Another door opens on a room of file cabinets identical to the ones in the library, complete with nonsense labels. She keeps staggering along, trying every door, trying not to collapse into the tall windows that peer over the valley. One door leads to what she can only imagine is a treatment room with two chairs and blank walls. Beck shakes her head and keeps moving. This isn't what she needs.

Finally, she reaches the end of the hallway and opens the final door. She gropes along the wall for a light. A steely breeze runs the length of her calves from somewhere in the dark. She sucks a breath through her teeth when her fingers finally catch on the light switch.

The room blinks to life.

The office, finally. She sees it more clearly tonight. The massive windows, just like the ones in the hallway, flat and black with night. Bookshelves line the other walls, full to the brink of collapse with a mix of new and seemingly ancient spines. In the center of the room, there's a sleek glass-top desk that glows from the humming fluorescents. Beck makes her way to it and she tastes the stale film of fear that coats her tongue. It's strange that the door is unlocked and open like this, but her head spins and the light is blinding.

She shouldn't be here. It's not too late to stumble her way back through the sterile halls and tuck herself into Avery's bed.

But it *is* too late. Because, in the center of the desk, Ricky's leather journal lies alone. Beck stares at it a long time before she approaches, breath heavy. There's no title, but she knows it's Ricky's. She pulls the massive desk chair back and slides into the seat, prying open the journal. The pages fall open, stiff with age, filled top to bottom with slanted handwriting. One page is bookmarked. Beck opens to it and the date reads *July 28, 2020*. Beck holds her breath:

Welcome back, Ricky.

Only a month this time. Only a month before things started leaking through. Until we started feeling sick again. We're coming back here more often than we wanted these days. The unspooling is a singularity growing ever nearer. Back to the start more often than we wanted, and more time spent unspooling the others, too. You spend all your time reading and writing, recording it all just to keep up. How much longer can this last before there aren't enough hours in the day to outrun the inevitable? What have we gotten done? Are we any closer? We cannot last when we're stretched this thin.

It may be time to extend an olive branch again. If she's still Wynnie, maybe she'll help.

All notes should be up to date, and anything missing will be easy enough to piece together. You're beginning to remember, though, even when you unspool. Do you think the others feel the same thing? They might sense it, too, the way these treatments are getting weaker. You're beginning to see all those times from before, even though they should be gone. What does it mean? Is it Backravel getting weaker, or is it you?

The surface won't do it anymore. We need to get to the real thing.

Beck swallows. Her hands tremble and her head swims. The words are in English, but they make no sense. It's one thing if Ricky's been unspooling everyone in this town to keep them in his orbit. But if she's reading this right, Ricky's been unspooling *himself*, too. It makes sense in a strange way; he would have to unspool to stave off the illness that creeps in over time. Beck looks at the walls, the desk, the tables that line the office and she realizes it. Notes and notes and notes, cabinets of them, neat stacks of paper bound with plastic-ringed spines. It's a less chaotic version of Ellery's office, but the essence is the same. Beck's heart races.

The notes are for Ricky. Clues, she realizes, to orient himself every time he unspools. He isn't above the consequences of going back in time. He forgets just like everyone else. But he has a road map back to the present, and the map is getting more complicated with every reset. He has to relearn this world every time.

Beck leans down and pulls open one of Ricky's drawers. It's full of sliding folders, just like every other cabinet in Backravel, but these have to be the important ones if they're in his desk. She scans for Ellery's name and her gaze snags on something unexpected: AVERY.

Beck opens the folder and finds a small stack of papers written by typewriter. Her fingers burn to pull the papers free and read them, but she stops herself. If Beck is right, so much of Avery's life has been dissected and exploited by the person meant to love her most. If there are secrets here about Avery's life in Backravel, she deserves to read them first. She deserves to hold her own secrets close.

She pulls the papers free and tucks them into the pocket of her jacket.

None of the other folders are familiar. Beck opens another drawer and she sees it. A dozen wadded-up balls of paper piled at the back of the drawer with achingly familiar handwriting. A little plastic bag gleams in the overhead light. Beck squints at it and makes out the distinct shape of small screws. *Glasses screws.* A notepad lies flat in the drawer with several pages ripped out. On one of the only remaining pages, there's a single sentence written over and over. Beck recognizes the loops of the handwriting, not quite right in some of the lines, but by the bottom of the page, it's perfect.

Come and find me.

A practice page. A rehearsal for the real thing. A letter that Ricky no doubt delicately folded, stuffed in an envelope, and mailed to Everett. The letter in Beck's backpack that she's clung to for weeks, that she's followed like a beacon. The whole reason she's here, and the whole reason she refused to leave when Riley begged her. Ricky's grand speeches about miracles were all fake. It was all a lie. The Desert Woman was right—she never should've believed there was good in Ricky Carnes.

It wasn't just a lie, it was a trap.

Another cool gust rushes the office and Beck realizes where it's been coming from. One of the windows on the back wall isn't a window at all. It's a door to a small patio, and right now, it's open. Ricky Carnes stands in the doorway with his arms folded over his chest.

"Seen enough?"

Beck turns so hard she hits her wrist against Ricky's desk. Pain sears up the length of her arm. Ricky's dressed in silk pajamas, slate gray and uncreased. He surveys the walls of his office with a proud smile like they're looking at a trophy room, not the web he's spun to keep this town in the dark.

"What is all this?" Beck asks. Her voice shakes, even as she tries to tamp it down. She grabs the notepad. "What is *this*?"

"I believe I should be asking the questions here," Ricky says. "Why are you going through my things?"

"Did you forge this letter?"

"Rebecca."

Beck's exhale is ragged. Her anger is a hot, boiling thing. It rises and sears behind her eyes. She ruined everything in her life because she believed this letter was a promise that there was something here beyond death and pain and grief.

"Are you happy?" Ricky asks without moving from the doorway. He's softer in the tender office light, stripped of his cowboy hat and eccentric mannerisms. It's like looking at him for the first time. He's just a man, dark circles under his eyes and back slightly slouched in exhaustion. But his shadow is long, reaching almost all the way to Beck's feet. There's still plenty of reason to be afraid. Her scratches his chin. "You found all my memos and zoning documents. Congratulations. It takes quite a bit of paperwork to keep a town alive. I don't advise going through all of it. It's quite boring."

"That's *not* what this is."

"You're referring to my notes to myself? I leave them all the time. I highly recommend it."

"Stop lying." Beck breathes. "Please."

Ricky's smile sobers. He hangs his head down like he's disappointed. "Fine. I told you I would be honest with you. So let me be honest with you."

Beck's grip on the notebook tightens.

"I respected your mom," Ricky says. "She was incredible, and at first, she understood my project in a way most people can't. Backravel exists because we're trying to find our way back to something. Your mom wanted that, too. And I needed her help, just like I told you. This town was never supposed to exist like this forever. I believed . . . I *believe* that there is a way we can all go back far enough to stay truly happy. I don't know why your mom gave up on us. I never will."

Beck's brow furrows. She wonders if Ellery Birsching sat in this office once, talking about Backravel's great purpose. She wonders what the final straw was that pushed Ellery away. What was the red flag that finally broke through to her?

Ricky finally moves. He steps into the room and shuts the balcony door, vacuuming the sound from the office. It strikes Beck, suddenly, that she's alone here with a man who has proved time and time again that he will do anything to keep his town and his secrets safe. Her eyes dart to the door and she wonders if she has time to make an escape.

But she stays frozen in place while Ricky paces the room, finally settling in front of her, tracing his finger along the desk's glass surface.

"I thought, because I trusted your mom, I could trust you, too. In fact, I thought I could trust you *more*."

"What?"

"You lived such a depressing life before you came here, Rebecca. Only ever half-alive, always trying to keep others afloat." Ricky shakes his head. "I really wanted this place to help you. All you mother's stories about you hurt my heart. I mean it. I felt so genuinely sad for this girl with the weight of a dying mother and a collapsing family on her shoulders. For years, I thought getting you here would make you happy."

"That's not—"

"No. It's my turn to speak." Ricky's expression isn't as soft as his words. He's already made a decision, and in this place, he's judge, jury, and executioner. Beck knows what's going to happen before he parts his lips to speak. "I don't know what I'm supposed to think of this, though. I keep offering you help, and it's like you only see something you can climb. I can't trust you here. I can't let you undo the things I've worked so hard to build. Our town . . . it's not like other towns. My people won't survive anywhere else. I can't let you kill them."

"Are you going to . . . ?" Beck can't finish the sentence.

Ricky's eyes widen, and then he laughs so loud Beck's blood runs cold. "I'm not going to kill you. I don't *kill* people. But I know how to purge a poison. I'm not going to hurt you. I'm asking you to leave."

It doesn't hit her at first. The terror of it comes slowly.

"No . . ." Beck starts.

Ricky's stance softens and he leans forward. "You've run your sister into the ground with illness and refused to help her. You've tried to use the secrets I shared with you against me. You're a danger to the people around you. For your sake and mine, I can't let you stay here."

"Please."

"You don't understand it yet, but I am offering you a kindness I wouldn't offer most people."

Ricky smiles finally and Beck thinks she might be sick.

"I'll even let you remember us. Someone should. Soon, the world will know about this little town. I just wanted Ellery Birsching's daughters to be a part of it."

Soon. Beck's blood runs cold. She doesn't know what Ricky's planning. She can't go yet. Not with Avery and the Desert Woman and the Sterlings still in danger. She wonders if this is why Ellery ran. Maybe Ricky turned her out, too, when she started pushing back. And now that he's realized Beck is useless to him, Ricky is going to destroy her.

"What are you going to do?"

Ricky straightens. The office door opens behind him and a broad-shouldered man enters the room. Ricky doesn't need to speak for it to be clear; she's being led from the treatment center now. Her head rushes with thoughts, but all of it comes back to Avery. What Avery will think when she finds out what happened, how betrayed she'll feel, how alone she'll be.

With that, he motions for the man in the doorway to escort Beck from the premises. Beck rises from the desk chair and leaves behind the scratch pad full of discarded notes, all in Ellery Birsching's handwriting. She follows the man out of the building and casts a single glance at Avery's closed bedroom door. Avery, who's still asleep, and who will have another few hours of dreams before she finds out.

They never got a goodbye.

25

BEFORE

It's been forty-eight days since Ellery Birsching died.

Beck doesn't sleep, she just stares. She doesn't live, she just drags herself from one part of the house to another. She spends an hour on the living room couch watching a show she can't retain. She moves to the kitchen island and she eats a bowl of cereal she doesn't taste. She takes a shower and stares at the wall, lost in swirling thoughts of days on the river and inside jokes she won't tell again, until the water goes cold. She drags herself to bed and does it all over again.

Riley is ready to reemerge first. She makes it back to school for their final week before summer vacation, and she comes home every day with flowers and sympathy cards that she carefully packs for their impending move. At night, she asks Beck how she can help her.

And Beck shrugs, because she doesn't know.

She coordinates movers over the phone with her father. She downloads homework that her teachers email to her and she doesn't touch it. She lies awake and she wonders how this happened. Why this happened. How her world could be so different so quickly.

On the day the letter arrives, Beck is a worn-down machine on a routine. She gathers up the mail and scatters it on the dining table with thousands of other letters. But out of the corner of her eye, a single word catches her off guard.

Backravel, AZ.

A return address.

And for the first time in forty-eight days, Beck Birsching comes alive. She tears open the letter and she reads the single sentence once, twice, a thousand times in a row. She traces each loop of her mother's handwriting until her eyes blur with tears. She unfolds the flyer about the Backravel Days festival, but that hardly interests her. The only thing that interests her is her mother's gentle command: *Come and find me.*

And even though Texas waits for her and the world is still spinning, for a moment, Beck's world slows to a halt. It reaches back, calls her to follow the letter to the place she was never allowed to go.

That night, Beck hatches her plan. Because there is nothing in the world she won't do for a slice of the Beck that used to stand in this kitchen. She will drive thousands of miles through the desert, barge into towns in states she's never visited, break backward through time itself if it means she can get her old life back. If she can get a little of herself back.

When she holds the letter tight to her chest, she feels Ellery's arms wrap around her, too. And even if everyone else says it's over, it's time to move on, Beck looks backward. It's been forty-eight days too long. Ellery Birsching never left her behind; she isn't gone yet.

26

At the Sterlings' house, the air smells like lavender. After weeks spent preparing, Mrs. Sterling's floral arrangements are plucked, sorted, and ready to display. Despite the vibrant colors in the Sterlings' backyard, Beck feels hollow. She doesn't rise when Mrs. Sterling offers her breakfast. She doesn't rise when Daniel accidentally runs his bike into the trailer. She doesn't rise when Mr. Sterling starts hauling the flowers to Backravel's main street.

Finally, there's a clicking sound at the trailer lock.

Mrs. Sterling's head pokes around the doorway and she meets Beck's stare with a sympathetic smile. "Hey you. How're you feeling?"

Beck turns over to face the wall.

She hardly knows where to begin. As if losing Riley weren't enough, she managed to lose Ricky and Avery, too. She managed to lose the only connections she had to Ellery Birsching in the first place. She wonders what Avery thinks of her now. When Beck closes her eyes, she feels Avery's fingertips on her skin, Avery's lips on her neck. The endless, world-stopping numbness she's felt for the last several years vanished for just a moment last night. She was alive, she was herself, and now it's all gone.

"Can I talk to you?" Mrs. Sterling asks.

"Sure."

"Okay." Mrs. Sterling maneuvers her way down the center of the trailer. Gently, she reaches into the loft bed and strokes a stray bit of Beck's hair. "I know it hurts. I know you're scared."

Beck's eyes are hot with tears. She leans into Mrs. Sterling's gentle hand and she's reminded of the way Ellery used to do her hair before school. The tender tugging at her scalp, one fold of hair laid over the other. She hurts more than she can describe. Finally, Beck croaks, "I don't know what to do."

Mrs. Sterling takes her shoulder and turns her over so that they're face-to-face. "I know. There's not much you can do. But I think we can make you feel a little better."

Beck follows Mrs. Sterling into her house, and it dawns on her that it's the first time she's been inside. It looks astoundingly similar to the house back in Everett, with mismatched wood floors and water-damaged ceilings. The furniture has been well-loved and, despite only being the three of them, it's like no one's done a deep clean in years.

Mrs. Sterling leads Beck to the first-floor bathroom and has her take a seat on the closed toilet lid. She shuts the door behind them, the space so tight Mrs. Sterling is practically standing in Beck's lap.

"I wanted to help you get ready," Mrs. Sterling says. "For tonight."

"Tonight?"

"The festival."

"Oh." Beck wipes at her eyes. "I don't think I'm invited to that anymore."

"Of course you are. We all are." Mrs. Sterling reaches into the medicine cabinet and pulls out a makeup bag. She carefully removes Beck's glasses and brushes her face over with powder. "Look at that. We're the same shade."

Beck tries to lean into the calming brush strokes across her face, but her mind races. She has to help Avery. She has to help Riley. She can't just sit here and go to a festival and try to pretend her world isn't over.

"I don't think I can do this," Beck whispers.

"It's not what you wanted it to be," Mrs. Sterling says, "but you're still here. Not everyone survives their worst day."

Beck nods, only half listening. She stares into the mirror and tries to see something worth fighting for. It's not the mistakes that haunt her—not the misspoken words or the wrong choices—it's the empty stare meeting her through the glass. Mrs. Sterling pulls out a small pot of gold glitter and presses it gently to the corners of Beck's eyes.

"You look just like a woman that used to stay with us," Mrs. Sterling says. "It must've been years ago. I hardly remember her."

Beck opens her eyes. Just when she thought she didn't have the willpower for hope, there's something else. "Ellery?"

"I think that was the name," Mrs. Sterling beams. "Did you know her?"

Beck nods and she's fighting tears again. "Yeah. She, uh . . . she was my mom."

"Ah." Mrs. Sterling stoops down and takes Beck's face in her hands. "You have her eyes. And her cheeks. If I didn't know you,

I'd think you were a younger version of that same person. Stranger things have happened."

"Yeah." Beck closes her eyes again. "How do you . . . why do you stay here?"

"Hmm?"

"I don't know how long your family has been here, but don't they ever want to see the world outside Backravel?"

"You know, I've thought about this before," Mrs. Sterling says. Her voice is as smooth as river stone, and Beck lets it wash over her. The makeup might not be calming, but Mrs. Sterling's gentle voice is. "Sometimes I get this urge to just run for the hills. I wake up some days and think, *I can't do this again. I can't do one more day like this.* I think everyone gets that way sometimes."

Beck nods, mostly so that Mrs. Sterling will keep talking. Because that pain isn't universal. It's just a part of living in Backravel, tethered to the same chunk of time forever with no escape. At one point, Beck thought it sounded perfect. Now, it sounds like a nightmare.

"But then I look at Daniel and I think about what could happen to him if we left. The world out there is so cruel and life is so short." Mrs. Sterling's fingers pause on Beck's face. "Here, Daniel will always be safe. He'll always be alive. I'll always have him."

"You don't wish you could see him grow up?"

Mrs. Sterling goes stiff. When Beck opens her eyes, Mrs. Sterling's gaze is glassy and distant. She hurts. She sucks in a small breath and smiles again. "I always wanted a daughter, too. Your mom is so lucky to have two of you."

Mrs. Sterling finishes Beck's makeup and hair, transforming her into a shinier, smoother version of the mess she's always been. Night begins to descend on Backravel and the Sterlings make their way downtown to enjoy the festivities. Even from Sycamore Lane, Beck can hear the dull roar of the festival downtown. Instead of making her way to the bikes, she staggers back to the trailer.

On the kitchen table, her phone rings.

Beck closes her eyes and answers the call.

"Hello? Beck? Hello?"

Her father's voice is frantic on the other end of the line. Beck cups her hand over her mouth because she doesn't know what to say. She doesn't know where to start.

"Hey, Dad."

"Oh my God." Her father's laugh is full of relief, which Beck doubts will last long. *"You've had me and Julie scared shitless over here. What's going on with you two? Neither of you will answer the phone?"*

"Um," Beck starts, but her throat is tight and hot. "I think I'm in trouble."

"What do you—"

Before he can finish his sentence, the weight of the last forty-eight hours catches up with Beck and lays her flat. She drops her phone on the kitchen table and she cries. She cries for Avery and for Riley and then she cries for the deeper wounds. She cries because her mother is gone and she can't reach her anymore. She cries because the life she'd settled into before has disappeared and she doesn't know who to be. She cries because all the years she fought and clawed to survive didn't mean anything. She's still useless and alone.

Outside the dusty window, specks of dirt freckle the sunlit horizon. All those untouched cliffs, sun-worn and empty, hold this town in place. There's a not-insignificant part of her that wants to stay here in this trailer until it rusts and melts into the earth like everything else in Backravel. She'll come apart, too, maybe. Decay like the rest of it—just ruins in the desert.

"I don't know what's going on," her father's voice mumbles through the phone.

After some shuffling, Julie's voice emerges. *"Hey, Sweetie, can you tell us what's going on?"*

Beck swallows her tears and she starts from the beginning. She tells them about the fake trip to Palm Springs, the trailer in Backravel, Riley's illness. She mutters *I'm sorry* over and over but it isn't enough. "I don't know what to do," Beck says. "I don't know what I'm supposed to do."

"You need to hold on tight," her father says. *"Julie and I are getting in the car right now and we're going to be there to get you. And Riley. And then we'll talk about this, but for right now, do not leave that trailer."*

"Okay." Beck breathes.

She spots a stack of papers jutting from the corner of her bed and narrows her eyes. Julie and her father continue to scrape and shuffle through the phone, but Beck reaches for the papers. The AVERY file, Beck remembers.

In her hand, her father speaks through the phone. *"We love you. We'll be right there."*

The line goes quiet.

For a long while, Beck doesn't move. Carefully, she pulls a loose page from the file and holds it in the light. Ricky's handwriting is more jagged than Ellery's, and once she reads the page, Beck wonders if it's panic that sharpened his words.

They're meeting more frequently every year. Either I'm losing my touch, or the unspooling doesn't work like it used to. I don't want to lock her in the house, but I'm running out of options. They're like magnets, and the minute I take my sight off Avery, she's back in the desert. I can't get rid of her. I can't get rid of Wynnie. And I can't stop them from meeting. Running out of time.

Beck thinks of the morning after movie night, of the crowd separating Avery and the Desert Woman by force. The facts click into place and suddenly Beck understands the thing that confused her most then. Because Ricky was never protecting Avery from the Desert Woman. He was fighting to keep them apart.

Beck pockets her phone, throws on her windbreaker and sneakers, and makes for the trailer door. She might've failed every other step of this trip, but she won't fail now. She won't let Avery stay stuck in this loop forever.

27

Downtown Backravel has transformed into a carnival of light and noise. Beck hardly recognizes it as her bike skids to a stop at the park. The street is lined with booths full of foods, crafts, and produce.

A rusty grate sits atop a chipped metal barrel. Rows of sizzling vegetables, burgers, and steaks smoke from the makeshift grill, and the scent makes Beck's stomach ache. Lights are strung all down Backravel's main road, outlining the playground equipment in the park, the fences of nearby houses, the awnings of every little shop. Orange, red, and purple streamers hang from the lampposts, rich and vibrant as the Backravel sunset itself. For the first time since she came here, the street is crowded with people, all of their faces shiny with glitter and stick-on gemstones.

Beck bites the inside of her cheek to keep from crying. She wants to love this, but she can't. No one here knows what's really going on in Backravel. They might be starting to remember things from their lives outside, but it isn't fast enough.

From the corner of her eye, Beck spots a familiar face.

Katie sits at a temporary tattoo booth looking bored, chewing incessantly on her gum. Her dark hair is in braided pigtails that rest neatly on the space between her shoulders and collarbone. She digs at a loose bit of her nail, oblivious to the festival roaring on all sides of her.

"Katie," Beck calls. "Where's Avery?"

Katie raises a brow at her. "I don't know. She's probably helping her dad get ready for his speech."

"Speech?"

"Yeah, apparently Ricky's giving some big speech tonight." Katie pushes herself up from her seat. "I thought you and Riley already left. I haven't seen you in days."

"Sorry," Beck says. "We've had a lot going on. Have you . . . heard from Riley?"

Katie fixes Beck with a strange stare.

"She's been really sick and I haven't been allowed to see her. I've just been really worried about her."

"I haven't seen her," Katie says. Her expression perks up just as quickly as it sobered. "But if Ricky's taking care of her I'm sure she'll be just fine. Don't worry about it. Enjoy the festival."

"Yeah."

Beck keeps wandering the walkways of the festival, dancing around gathered crowds and displays. In the center of the park, a makeshift stage has been set up with more streamers and lights. No doubt this is where Ricky is planning to give his speech. She tries not to panic over it, but Ricky's words from last night echo in the back of her brain. *Soon, the world will know all about this little town.*

She has to find Avery fast. Something tells her they don't have much time.

Finally, the crowd quiets and turns to face the stage. Carefully,

Ricky Carnes steps up onto the platform in a slightly more embellished version of his standard uniform. His jacket, pants, and hat are all the same creamsicle color as his Cadillac, the embedded gems glimmering in the soft streetlight that bathes the stage.

But Beck only watches him for a moment.

Behind him, Avery steps onto the stage. Dark circles ring her dark eyes and Beck wonders what she was told this morning. She wants to run up onto the stage and take Avery by the shoulders. She wants to tell her—to *promise* her—that she never meant to hurt her. She wants to drag her miles away from the father who's kept her trapped in this town, in this loop. Mostly, she wants to hold her again, and this time she wants to know she won't lose her. Avery Carnes, her girl lost in time.

Before Ricky begins to speak, Avery looks up and scans the crowd. Her eyes find Beck and she scowls. Beck feels her world go dimmer.

"Hello, everyone!" Ricky calls from the stage. "How are we feeling tonight?"

The crowd cheers back to him. Beck thinks she might be sick.

"Alright, I appreciate everyone coming out here for this year's festival. It's a beautiful night and I have some amazing things to share with you all. First of all, thank you for another wonderful year together. Our little town has been growing and growing, and you've all done an incredible job of making everyone feel welcome. You know it is my goal to have this town be accessible to anyone who needs it."

Beck looks around at the crowd and her stomach drops. They're listening to Ricky, but there's a glazed look in their eyes, a stillness as they watch like they're androids powered down until they're needed again.

When Beck looks back at the stage, Avery is gone.

"Speaking of growth," Ricky continues with a small laugh. "I have something exciting to share. Tonight, I'm going to attempt something I've never done before. We are all here because our lives have not been easy. We're all here because we don't want to be a part of a world that is obsessed with the next thing, the next thing, *the next thing*. We came out to this desert so that the world would move a little slower, and we've done it. Look at us. We've had no death, no loss, no sadness. When I founded this place, I couldn't have imagined how successful it would be.

"I want to give something back to you all. So tonight, I'll be taking us back further than we've ever gone before. All of us."

"What?" Beck breathes.

"For a long time, I've been trying to figure out how to keep up with you all as Backravel grows. Tonight, I have an answer. So go enjoy yourselves tonight, dance with someone you love, eat something delicious, and when it happens, you'll know. Tomorrow, we're waking up to a brand new Backravel. We—"

Someone grabs Beck by the wrist and pulls her out of the crowd. Beck stumbles backward as she's led out of the mass of people into a space between two festival stands. She's pushed up against the wall of the Quick Stop and finds herself inches from Avery's face. Anger racks her and her breaths are short and sharp. She presses her palms to Beck's shoulders to keep her in place, and for a moment, Beck is sure Avery means to kiss her again.

Instead, she says, "Start talking. Now."

"I'm so—" Beck starts.

"Where did you go?" Avery cuts in. "When I woke up, you were gone. After all the shit you said to me last night, you don't get to just leave."

"I know, but I didn't have a choice," Beck says quickly.

"Then why . . ."

Avery glances at the stage. Ricky finishes his speech and hops down into the crowd to mingle. At the end of the street, a radio plays old tunes and Mrs. Sterling dances with Daniel. Katie and her friends are lined up at a stand selling grilled corn. There's a peaceful happiness to the crowd that makes Beck sick, and she's sure Avery is wondering the same thing. How can everyone else in this town be so happy when they're all stuck in place?

"I know it doesn't make sense," Beck says, "but I need you to see something."

Avery shakes her head. "No. I need . . . I don't know. I'm just so confused. I don't understand what's happening."

Avery's hands quiver against Beck's shoulders. Beck sucks in a breath and carefully lays her hand over Avery's. She looks hard into Avery's face and her chest tightens. How many versions of Avery have been ripped up at the roots to keep her in the dark like this? How many lives could she have lived if she was allowed to blossom? Avery feels different from everyone else in Backravel because she never had a choice.

Beck wants to stay here with her. She wants to hold her close and let her cry through the hurt. But there's someone that Ricky has been hiding from her for years and tonight, she needs to find out why.

"Will you come with me?"

Avery nods.

• • •

The light and noise of Backravel falls away as Beck and Avery stumble toward the campsite. Avery's grip is tight around her wrist. Beck leads her across the scraggly dirt until Backravel itself dies away and only the desert is left. Beck glances over her shoulder at Backravel as it shrinks into the horizon.

"Avery," Beck says. "When you said you felt called into the desert sometimes . . ."

"Can you just tell me where we're going?" Avery asks.

"There's someone you need to meet," Beck says. "I don't know why."

Beck swallows. The pink sky darkens quickly to sunset. It always feels like sunset here, over and over. Time always slides toward an end but never actually does. It bleeds into the horizon, cruelly endless, and Beck finds it difficult to breathe.

The campsite emerges finally, and Beck isn't sure if she's relieved or afraid. The pieces are finally coming together but there's one key part missing. There has to be a reason Ricky would keep Avery and the Desert Woman apart. Ricky is the puppeteer behind it all, but there has to be a reason *why*.

When they reach the edge of the campsite, Avery lets go of Beck's wrist and stumbles to the center of the site. Her confusion fades, replaced by a glassy awe. She surveys the campsite and her face goes slack. She's been here before.

Avery spins slowly and soaks it all in. The truck, the tent, the cooler. Beck wonders what it looks like through her eyes. If she's right, Avery has stood in this exact spot a thousand times. Maybe she saw the truck when it was new. Maybe she saw the tent when it was first set up. And maybe, if Beck's lucky, she knows why the Desert Woman is out here like this. Maybe, with a helping hand, Avery will remember something that makes this all make sense.

But Avery's eyes well with tears, and Beck rushes to her side.

"Wait." She breathes. She turns and looks into Beck's eyes. Her lips quiver when she says, "I know where we are. I know who . . . where is she?"

Beck blinks, only inches from Avery's face. Avery's ragged breath fans over Beck's face, and then she looks back toward the road. Sunlight catches in the tangle of her hair. She stands and faces the road as footsteps crunch in the red rock.

The Desert Woman freezes in her tracks. Both Avery and the Desert Woman say nothing, staring at each other like wolves circling before the kill. Beck bites the inside of her cheek; maybe this was a bad idea.

"No way." Avery spits. "No fucking way."

"Avery," the Desert Woman pleads. Only one word, but Beck can tell she's herself again tonight. Her hands drop to her sides and she looks at Avery like she thinks Avery will vanish into thin air. Her brow softens and she takes a tentative step toward Avery. "You remember."

"Who is she?" Beck asks.

Avery turns on her, and her eyes are wet with tears. "Who is she? She's my *mother*."

28

Of *course*.

Beck's breath catches in her chest. The Desert Woman flinches away from Avery's voice. Seeing them together, it seems obvious. The shape of their cheekbones, the unruliness of their hair, the way their eyes are round as moons and watery as a shallow pool. All the times she saw the Desert Woman she should've put two and two together. All those nights Avery felt the tug of the void, it was another loop. The desert wasn't calling her into its grasp; it was calling her home.

Both of them have been trapped in this loop since it began, struggling against the tide as it endlessly washes them to shore.

"I thought you said your mom left?" Beck asks.

"Yeah. She did," Avery snaps. "But I guess she's just been, what . . . camping in the desert? Why?"

"Avery—" the Desert Woman starts.

"No." Avery presses her fingers to her eyes and, for a moment, Beck is sure she's crying. She looks at her mother again with fury burning in her eyes. "No, I'm asking the questions. Everyone keeps confusing me, but I'm done being confused. Where did you go?"

"I've been here," the Desert Woman croaks. "I was here the whole time."

"Why?"

"You," the Desert Woman says. "I was trying to come back to you. I've been trying to come back to you since . . . I always get so close, but then you're gone again. I don't always remember. You never do."

"Bullshit," Avery hisses.

Beck's gaze flits between Avery and her mother as they fight and she tries to remember to breathe. They can't get stuck arguing like this—something is happening *tonight*. Ricky's speech implied that, whatever grand plans he has to set Backravel back, it's happening now. They don't have time for this. She takes a step forward. "You know he makes you forget, right?"

"Please," the Desert Woman begs. She ambles forward and, for all the rage in Avery's face, she doesn't shy away. The Desert Woman collapses to her knees in the dirt at Avery's feet. She takes Avery's hand between hers and cradles it to her chest. "Avery, I don't know how long this time will last. Please don't be angry with me. Please let me explain."

"You left." Avery breathes. Beck can hardly hear her over the breeze. "You abandoned us."

"I wanted to stay," the Desert Woman says. Desperation seeps from her voice. She holds tighter to Avery's hand like she's afraid Avery might slip through her fingers. "You probably don't trust me. But I didn't want to leave. Me and your father, we couldn't agree what to do. He and I both knew what this place was capable of. I was worried about the sickness, he was only worried about time."

"I don't remember that," Avery says, but it's not angry like she was before. Her voice wavers.

"I told him I wouldn't let him go back anymore. I told him we had to leave Backravel." The Desert Woman is nearly out of breath as she explains. Beck understands it all too well—it's the same way Ellery Birsching used to rush through her stories, desperate to finish them before the thought was gone. As scattered as she is, the Desert Woman is trying to stay here, in the now. "You were getting so sick. The sickness had already taken your brother. I thought it would take you, too."

"What?"

"I wouldn't have let him unspool you." Tears dot the Desert Woman's eyes. "If I was there, I would've stopped him."

Now, Avery looks at Beck. There's another layer, Beck realizes, that makes the truth of it even worse. The Desert Woman was a scientist once, the Desert Woman came here with her family, the Desert Woman has been in this loop a long time. Beck looks at the woman, crumpled and desperate, and she shakes her head.

"When did you come here?" Beck asks.

The Desert Woman closes her eyes. "It's been so long."

"The military ruins," Beck says. "When you came here, were they ruins?"

After a moment that feels like a lifetime, the Desert Woman shakes her head. "They were ours. After the weapons tests, we got to examine the remains. We were so excited about what we might learn here, all alone. We'd never seen anything like it. A mineral that broke down time itself."

Avery says nothing.

She remembers.

"What happened?" Beck asks.

"A place like this is not a gift. Miracles aren't just given. They have to be made. And they have consequences," the woman says.

There's a sudden clarity to her, an intense sharpness Beck hasn't seen before. Her hands ball into fists. "It doesn't just change time. It's a poison. You've already seen it work. Dozens of the scientists here got so sick they couldn't move. Grown men and women. When it came for Harlow, he was too little to stand a chance."

"Harlow," Avery echoes. She stares into the red dirt, hands balled into fists. She pulls her fingers out of her mother's grip and blinks away a tear. She looks almost like she did on the day Beck saw her unspool, vulnerable and afraid and confused all at once.

"You were here at the very beginning," Beck says. "Ricky's story about finding the ruins was a lie. He's been here since the beginning."

The Desert Woman says nothing.

Beck looks at Avery. "All three of you have."

It finally sinks in and it's like the world is tilting under Beck's feet. Not only has Avery been stuck in this place, reliving the same loop while Ricky treats this town like his personal playground; she's been stuck in it for decades. Her brother didn't die a few years ago, he died *decades* ago. Avery has lived a whole life stuck at seventeen, strung like a puppet by a father who didn't know or didn't care how it hurt her.

Avery looks at Beck and it's clear she can't take much more of this. Beck feels a pang of guilt for bringing her here. Of course it would've been worse to leave her in the dark, but it doesn't feel like it now. This is why Ricky wanted them apart. Because no matter how many times he unspools Avery, she can't forget her mother's face.

"I wanted to get you away from here. I wanted all three of us to escape." The Desert Woman presses her fingertips to the dirt, but she doesn't push herself to her feet. She remains there, racked by the weight of whatever terrible truth she's forcing herself to remember.

"Your father thought, if we stayed, he could work this place to his will. He could keep us alive and healthy forever. He could pull Harlow back from the dead."

"Why did you leave, though?" Avery demands. "If you knew it was hurting me, why did you just . . . let it?"

"I didn't leave. I stayed." The Desert Woman closes her eyes. "Even when I didn't have food or water. Even when it was so hot I thought it would kill me. Even when I didn't remember why I was staying, I stayed. I learned how to unspool myself, too, but I wasn't very good at it. I lost track of things so many times. But I couldn't forget. I had to find my way back to you."

Avery's eyes widen. "I found you before."

"And then he made you forget."

"Why?"

"He tried to protect you from me. I never got to protect you from him."

Avery presses her fingertips to her temples. The Desert Woman stands and takes Avery's face in her trembling hands, a study in contrasts. Avery's skin is soft, sun-kissed, youthful. Despite the Desert Woman's relatively young face, her hands are calloused and spotted with age. In her glassy eyes, Beck sees a thousand memories scattered like desert starlight, disconnected and lonely. "I wanted to see Harlow grow up," she says. "I wanted to see him as a man one day. I've imagined his face a thousand times. But . . . I wanted to see you grow up, too."

Avery's gasp is small, covering up a sob. She pulls away from her mother's grasp, brow furrowed.

"I lost Harlow first," the Desert Woman continues. "And then I lost you, too."

Avery presses her face to her mother's chest and holds her tight.

Beck isn't sure if it's forgiveness or if it's just all the years of hurt built to a single moment. The Desert Woman's expression softens. She knits her fingers into Avery's hair, apprising the mop with a mix of admiration and concern. The expression is small, but it catches like a snag in Beck's chest. It's a mother's expression. It's been too long since Beck has seen it.

"Every time, I thought if you saw me, I could save you," the Desert Woman says, twirling a lock of Avery's hair between her fingers. "But as soon as you remembered, you'd forget again. Ricky couldn't bear losing Harlow. He didn't see how he was losing you."

"I missed you," Avery says.

Beck looks out at the flat desert that stretches to the toothy horizon and fear swells in her chest. They don't have much time left. "Ma'am . . ." Beck starts, but it feels unnatural.

"Wynona," the Desert Woman says. "That was my name. Wynona Carnes."

"Wynona," Beck repeats. "You said once that Ricky was planning something. I think he's going to do it tonight. We need your help to—"

"Tonight?"

Wynona goes stiff. She lets go of Avery and eyes Beck. The bleeding light of sundown is beginning to fade, and the harsh lines of Wynona's face soften in the dark. Her tears are gone and the only thing left in her eyes is fear. She looks at Avery, and Avery nods.

"What is he planning to do?" Beck asks. "Do you know?"

Wynona looks out at the desert, too, but her gaze is more specific. She's looking for something. "Does he already know how to find the entrance?"

"Entrance?" Beck asks. "To the lab?"

"He couldn't," Wynona starts. "The only person that knew was your mother."

Before Beck can ask more, Avery clears her throat.

"Then he might know."

Beck and Wynona turn on her at once. For a moment, the wind is the only sound between them. Avery's expression is difficult. It's not guilt exactly, but the anxious line of her mouth says she knows more than Beck thought.

"I don't know anything about a lab," Avery whispers. "But you left your backpack in my room last night."

Her mother's notes. Beck fights the urge to be sick. If Wynona is right and Ellery knew the lab's location, she probably recorded it in those notes. That's why Ricky sounded so confident in his speech. That's how he knows it will be tonight.

"This is my fault," Wynona says. "I should've destroyed that lab years ago. Once I understood what he wanted to use my work for, I knew I had to stop him. At first, I camped out here to make sure he didn't find the lab. But the more I unspooled . . . I lost it, too."

Beck and Avery shoot each other a glance. Beck doesn't have time to be shocked. An engine purrs in the dusky breeze. All three of them—Beck, Wynona, and Avery—turn to face the long stretch of highway leading back to town. A car glides down the road, headlights a smear in the dark. It strikes Beck how odd it is to see a moving vehicle in Backravel. The sight catches her off guard.

The car comes to a halt at the roadside and Beck recognizes it. Shiny, creamsicle orange, reflecting the thin moonlight as it sets into the valley. It's Ricky's Cadillac, parked at the highway shoulder. Beck tries to peer into the windows, but they're tinted black, and only her own warped reflection stares back.

After a quiet moment of shuffling, the driver's side door opens.

Ricky steps out of the car and dramatically throws the door closed behind him. He slides a quiet, coldly hateful look at Beck, and then he turns to Avery. "Get in the car."

Avery stares at him, then at Wynona, then at Beck. She wipes at her eyes and looks at the ground. "I don't understand."

"Avery—" Wynona starts.

"Get away from her," Ricky snaps. "Both of you. Haven't you hurt her enough?"

Beck's surprise dissipates and she's left with fear and anger. She turns on Ricky and it takes all of her willpower not to charge at him for everything he's done to Avery, to Wynona, to her mother. What he might've done to Riley. *Riley*. She can't leave here tonight without Riley.

"Where's my sister?" Beck demands.

Ricky arches a brow. He's still wearing his elaborate outfit from the festival, the intricate beads of his hat shining in the low light. He moves to the backseat of the Cadillac and throws the door open.

There, buckled in, is Riley.

Beck rushes to her and Ricky doesn't stop her. Riley's head is lolled back against the headrest, and her face is pale and hollow. Beck wraps her arms around Riley's slender shoulders and she can just feel the rise and fall of her chest, the gentle hush of her breathing. She's alive, at least, but she's so much worse than the last time Beck saw her. If she's been unspooled, it isn't helping.

"What's wrong with her?" Beck asks, voice shaking. She bites the inside of her cheek to keep from crying. "What did you do to her?"

"I have done nothing but let her rest. No unspooling," Ricky says. He doesn't look at Beck when he speaks; his eyes are trained only on Avery. "She's sick, though. I don't know how much longer she'll last."

"Why are you doing this?" Avery manages.

"Because it's what we've been working for since the beginning," Ricky says. Even now, there's an unbridled enthusiasm in his voice that makes Beck want to believe him. That's the problem with Ricky, and with Backravel in general—he believes all of it, so everyone else does, too. In Ricky's story, he's the hero.

"Ricky," Wynona warns.

It's the first time Wynona speaks directly to Ricky, and it seems to catch him off guard. He turns on his banished wife with a grimace, and for a long moment, he doesn't speak. "I know you don't believe me," he says, softer than Beck expects. "But I can fix all of this. I hope you're willing to try being a family again. It's . . . the only thing I've dreamed about. All these years."

"Even if I wanted to help you," Wynona says, "I don't know where it is."

"I don't, either," Ricky says, "but *she* does."

Beck looks up. Ricky is staring at her now with a smile that makes her sick to her stomach. Avery and Wynona stare at her, too, confused expressions nearly identical. She feels guilty all over again for not making the connection.

Gracelessly, Ricky tosses her backpack to her. It lands in the red dirt with a thud.

"I don't . . ." Beck trails off.

"I thought I hit a lucky break with these notes," Ricky says. "But I genuinely can't make heads or tails of them. I know she must've put the lab's location in there, Beck, so you're going to help me find it."

"Beck . . ." Avery warns.

"How would I know?" Beck's grip on Riley tightens. She just needs to get them out of here. The rest can come later.

"I know she found it. There's no way she spent the amount of time she did in this town without finding it," Ricky says. "So I need you to start reading and find me that lab."

Beck closes her eyes. She's combed over Ellery's notes a thousand times these last few months, but there's nothing as coherent as a guide to an abandoned lab. There's nothing to piece together. There's no knowledge to gain. "I don't know the way," Beck pleads. "I promise. But Riley—"

"—will be fine. If I can get into that lab." Ricky turns and crouches next to Beck and she fights the urge to bolt. Something flashes at Ricky's hip, metal caught in the moonlight. A gun. Beck swallows and holds completely still, even as Ricky puts a hand on her shoulder. "If I get access to it, I can zip her right back to the way she was when you two got here, like none of this ever happened. I can do that for both of you, if you want. But I can do more than that, too."

"Ricky," Wynona warns.

In a swift motion, Ricky unsheathes the gun from its holster and points it at the sky. He doesn't fire, but the sight of it is enough to stop Wynona in her tracks. Beck looks to Avery, but she's gone pale, eyes glassy and miles away.

Ricky turns back to Beck. "You've seen what I can do with the limited resources I have. I've kept this whole town alive and healthy and happy. If I had access to the concentrated, purest form of the soil in Backravel, I could do so much more. I could reach back further than you can imagine. With that kind of power, you could see your mom again. And I could see my son."

Tears well in Beck's eyes and she's not sure if it's hate or hope she feels more. She hates Ricky down to her core for what he's done, but there's still a piece of her clinging to the miracle of Backravel. The impossibility of a place that defies death. It's disgusting, how much she wants to believe what Ricky is selling her.

"I don't know where it is," Beck says again.

Ricky shakes his head, gliding his thumb gently over the metal of his gun. "I think you can figure it out. So how about we give it a try?"

Shakily, Beck begins rummaging through Ellery's notes, but it's impossible to see clearly as dark sets into the valley. Under her knees, she feels a tremor in the earth. That metallic humming is still alive, and it's louder in the desert. It must have something to do with the lab, she realizes now. She thinks of the sheep in her dream and the black stones in Ellery's notes. All converging on a single point far out in the desert valley. She thinks back to the first day in the library with Avery, the blueprint of town. It occurs to her now that there was a small square far from the rest of the camp marked LABORATORY.

"You don't have to do this," Wynona hisses at Beck. "It's okay if you don't know where it is."

Beck nods, but maybe Ricky is right. Maybe she *can* piece together where the lab is. Maybe it's been calling her, just like it called her mother. Beck looks at Riley, lifeless and limp in Ricky's car, and she understands why the Sterlings stayed here. She understands why all of the people in Backravel remain here even if it's killing them. Because sometimes helping the people you love and doing the right thing are two different paths.

Carefully, Beck wades into the desert. Ricky, Avery, and Wynona follow at her heels, a fractured family reunited at last. The farther they walk, the louder the humming grows. If the others hear it, they don't show it. No one says a word, but Beck's head feels lighter and her vision begins to fade. Just like the night she saw the visions of Backravel and the explosion, reality is beginning to feel thin.

"What are we thinking, Beck?" Ricky asks from behind her. "Are we getting close?"

Beck sucks in a breath to keep herself balanced. "I'm . . . do you not hear that sound?"

Behind her, Ricky shakes his head. Wynona and Avery share a glance but stay quiet. It occurs to Beck that they might not hear the sound because they're accustomed to it. Because all three of them have unspooled so many times the sound is a part of them.

Finally, Beck takes a step forward and she falls.

She tumbles down a small decline, and then the earth opens below her like a gaping mouth. For a split second, she's in freefall. And then she hits the ground with surprising force, knocking the back of her skull against concrete. The humming is so loud she can hardly hear her own thoughts. Above her, the purpling sky is only a circle. The three Carnes look down at her with three different expressions. Wynona, a tearful disappointment. Avery, worry and fear. But Ricky's is the one that scares her most. He grins wider than she's ever seen.

"You *did* it," Ricky calls down to her. "This is incredible, Beck."

Without hesitation, Ricky hops onto the ladder leading down to the floor where Beck lies. Once he reaches the concrete, he motions for Wynona and Avery to join him. After a moment of hesitation, Wynona helps Avery onto the ladder, and then descends herself.

Avery kneels next to Beck and, in the quickly deepening dark, Beck can still see the shine of her eyes. But maybe that's the dizziness talking. Her head spins and the edges of her vision go dark.

"You're bleeding," Avery whispers. She tenderly swipes her fingers across the back of Beck's skull and, when she pulls her hand back, her fingertips are red.

Avery helps Beck to her feet and the four of them stand together facing a long, black hallway that extends deeper into the earth. Before they keep walking, Ricky turns to face Beck. He can hardly mask his glee at their discovery.

"I hope you'll forgive me."

Beck can hardly hear him. The more her head spins, the more she cycles back to Riley in the car, hardly breathing. She cycles back to the hospital room where Ellery Birsching decided to die instead of revealing this place. Beck is going to die down here in this lab and it'll all have been for nothing. All of the Birsching girls dead trying to chase the same little sliver of impossible. What did she think was going to happen at the end of all this?

She can barely remember.

"I hope you'll forgive me, too," Ricky says, flicking his gun in Wynona and Avery's direction. "We were never supposed to be like this. All I've ever wanted was for all four of us to be a family again."

"I know you did." Wynona's voice is gentle, like a classroom teacher a moment from snapping. "I know you *do*. But don't you remember what Backravel was doing to people back then? If you expose people to this, everyone will die."

"They won't," Ricky insists. "I've kept them alive for God knows how long. And if I can go back even further . . ."

"We don't know what'll happen," Wynona says.

"We can't know until we try," Ricky says. "The fact that you would just give up on us because of what *might* happen."

"Ricky—"

"*Stop*," Ricky snaps. He closes his eyes and takes a deep breath. "You act like I haven't thought this through. Wynnie, I have thought about nothing else. Every day since he died, I have woken up and thought about the day I could finally get us back. I . . . have been waiting to see him again. For so long."

Beck's grip on Avery's arm tightens. Avery looks at her, eyes big and glassy and brown and full to the brim with fear. In her gaze, Beck watches the world shift. She sees what Avery sees—a mother she thought long gone coming back into view. A father she thought loved her shifting into a grief-racked monster. Decades of temporary lives, forgotten.

"Dad," Avery says, hardly more than a croak.

Ricky's expression is difficult. It cracks, just a little. Widens and makes room for her. He lowers the gun. "I'm so sorry for what this has done to you."

"How long have I been like this?"

"If I didn't keep you here," Ricky says, "then we could never go back to how we were. If you got older, you wouldn't be there when our family finally came back together. But having to unspool you over and over . . . I'm very sorry, Avery."

"Ricky," Wynona tries again.

"That's enough of that," Ricky cuts in. He motions to the hallway ahead of them. "Who would like to do the honors?"

Wynona looks at Beck and Avery, then she nods. She walks cautiously into the hallway, almost entirely veiled in the dark. After a few echoing steps, a light flashes on. The tunnel lights all blink to life, bulbs dim and flickering. Avery moves to follow her mother, and she holds Beck upright. They walk arm in arm down the hallway into the unknown.

"What's this?" she asks.

Wynona eyes the station with a frown. "A cure, I hoped. Something to undo the effects of the soil."

"Is that what you were working on up there, too?"

"I think so." Wynona touches one of the beakers wistfully. "It was working, to an extent. I'm clearer now than I have been in a

very long time. If we could release something like *this* to the people
in town, maybe we could get everyone out of here in one piece. We
could—"

"That's not what we're here for," Ricky says, finally stepping into
the lab. "What I'm here for is *this*."

He makes his way to a large glass chamber and places his hand
against it. Inside, a deep red smoke coils against the glass. After all
this time, it still looks volatile. Deadly.

"This is why you never told me where your lab was, then?" Ricky
asks Wynona. "I wish I knew what made you so afraid of me. With
your work, we're going to undo time itself. We're going back to the
beginning."

"Ricky—" Wynona tries.

Ricky turns on her. "With this, we're going to be a family again."

"You don't know what'll happen," Wynona says. "That kind of
power could kill everyone in town. You're willing to risk that?"

Ricky eyes the lever outside the chamber. In the faint mechanical lights, the gold embellishments on his shirt flash like sparks.

"I promise we'll all be happy when it's over. Things will go back
to the way they were before we lost the people we care about most.
It'll be like none of this ever happened."

Wynona holds Avery to her side now, eyes wild like an animal
out to protect her cub. Her gaze flickers from Ricky to Beck and back
again. She wants to leave, but she won't abandon them. She won't
abandon Backravel. Her expression softens. "It won't bring him back.
You already know it won't. Close it before you—"

"You never even tried." Ricky's voice is cold. It quivers, just a
little, but he betrays nothing. "You knew we could go back but you
never tried. I fought for so long to get here, and I had to do it alone
because you wouldn't help me."

"This isn't—"

Ricky pinches the bridge of his nose and then, in a sudden explosion of anger, he shouts, "No more. I don't want to hear any more."

"Rick—"

"Let me show you," Ricky says. He doesn't say it to Wynona this time, or even to Avery. This, he says to Beck. "Let me show you what I've been waiting for. It took a long time. I hope you'll find it's worth it."

Beck braces herself against the wall to stay upright. When she'd first arrived in Backravel, everyone had acted like Ricky Carnes was like the sun, giving light to all the people who live in Backravel, sustaining them all in his glow. But Ricky Carnes isn't a sun. He's a black hole, growing deeper and stronger every day in this cursed desert valley. He's a black hole, and he's trapped them all in his cruel orbit, waiting for the day he could suck them into the ether.

"The people up there don't deserve this," Beck says, and it's like the voice comes from outside of her. "They're all stuck here. It isn't fair."

"No, what the world does to them *outside* isn't fair," Ricky corrects her. In his sweaty palm, Beck catches the glint of his gun flashing in the machinery lights. His hand is shaking, either from the strain of keeping the gun pointed or from the fear. "What I'm giving them is a second chance at happiness. You think they don't deserve to go back to a time before they were hurting?"

Beck's fingernails dig into the skin of her palms. "There is no time before the hurting. We're all hurting all the time. And we . . ." She doesn't know what she means to say. Her whole body shakes with the weight of this thing crashing over her. ". . . We can only move on."

Ricky's brow arches.

"Ricky," Wynona pleads. "Please listen to her."

"I'm not throwing away the chance of a lifetime because a *child* thinks it's a bad idea," Ricky scoffs. "Wynnie, I don't even remember his face. You're not the ones who dedicated your whole lives to making this happen. You don't know if it'll work or if it won't. And none of you trust me, so I guess I'll have to do it myself. Like usual."

"Ricky."

Ricky points the gun at Wynona, and an electric silence strikes between them.

Fear bubbles up in the pit of Beck's stomach, not just of dying. Not just of Backravel falling to ruin. She fears what'll happen if this works. If they go back, what then? If it works and they really do go back like Ricky promised, what then? Future and past tangle together into one murky horizon, and Beck can't tell if she wants it or not.

"Stop," she says, quiet at first. Then, Beck lunges for Ricky's gun, breath short in her chest and head spinning.

Ricky turns in time to see her, and Beck finds herself looking hard into the black barrel of the gun. She imagines the spark before the end, but it doesn't come. Before Ricky fires the gun, he yanks down on the lever beside the chamber, and the lab is suspended in empty space.

The door of the chamber swings open and a pungent scent decks Beck in the throat. She crumples to her knees, and she hears Wynona do the same behind her. Her veins feel too tight for her limbs, her face swells, and her stomach twists in knots. She feels for the floor, but there's nothing there. Her fingers dip into something cool like water. The walls of the lab swim in front of her, rippling like heat waves on the flat black highway. She feels the strange sensation she felt back in the trailer, her head tilted into Avery's hand. There's another world rushing up to meet her, and it would be as easy as stepping into it.

Something moves in front of her.

Ricky drops to his knees, too. His expression twists, no longer desperate like it was moments earlier. Tears cloud his dark eyes. He reaches in front of him, and Beck catches the ghost of a name on his lips. *Harlow.*

In some capacity, he's done it. He's looking into the face he's longed for all these years. Beck searches the wavering space in front of her, but there's no one there. The lab unravels under her, crumbling away like sand through fingers. The air shifts, no longer alive with electricity and panic. Instead, Beck smells a sweet summer breeze laced with fresh water and pine needles. The wind rushes her, and she can see it. Sunlight that filters through a thick canopy of pines and freckles the dirt.

It worked. Against all the odds, Ricky's plan worked.

She shouldn't follow the light. Stepping into the memory means there's no coming back. It means leaving Riley and Avery and Wynona and Texas behind. It means stepping back into a world she hasn't lived in for years. But it also means she can erase the pain and the loneliness and the nights spent waiting for a mother that has long since disappeared.

Beck sucks in a breath. She closes her eyes.

She steps into the sunlight.

29

Beck is on the river.

Water gushes lazily at the shore, rhythmic as a heartbeat, tipping the kayak under her bare legs. Her paddle dips under the glassy surface, handle pressing gently at her blistered palms, but the kayak doesn't move. Wind breathes through the thick tunnel of pines, warm and dry and familiar. She's come here a thousand times, but it's been years since she smelled the wind, felt the flecks of cool water spraying her thighs, let the sun warm her eyelids.

Beck is on the river.

She's been on this river a long time.

She tightens her grip on the grain of her paddle. Another kayak sloshes casually through the frothy current at Beck's side. Her chest seizes up when she sees her; Ellery Birsching, paddle laid across her cargo shorts. Her hands float carelessly over her legs, palms facing skyward to soak up the sunlight. Frizzy bits of her blond hair sway at the nape of her neck.

Beck watches her mother breathe, the rise and fall of her chest, the slight twitch of her eyelids.

"Mom," she finally says.

Ellery's expression changes. Her eyes flicker open and she fixes Beck with a strange look. For a moment, Beck thinks her mother doesn't recognize her. But slowly, Ellery smiles. "You're here."

"Where are we?" Beck asks. Her voice echoes like she's in an auditorium, slapping back at her louder than the waves. The sound is wrong. It doesn't match the world she's in. "How did I . . . ?"

She grabs at her own shirt, feels the slick skin of her neck. She's a real human being and, as far as she can tell, this river is real, too. Panic sets in and, suddenly, it's hard to breathe.

Ellery doesn't seem to notice. Calmly, she says, "You're still moving, I think. You should be able to remember where you were. Or where you *are*, I guess."

Beck stares, but Ellery doesn't elaborate further. She closes her eyes and she feels it, the way the wind ripples just a little against her hair, how the kayak bucks up against her legs. It isn't suspended in the water or held in place like she first thought. No, it's swimming backward in the waves. Beck's eyes dart open.

"Am I unspooling?" Beck asks.

Ellery doesn't speak. It's her turn to close her eyes, tilting her face toward the sun. Beck studies her and her chest aches. It's the first time she's seen her mother *move* since the hospital, and it makes the hurt deepen. The pictures can't capture the way the shadows crawl over her brow or the slight twitch of a smile always waiting at the corners of her lips. There's so many little details of Ellery Birsching that Beck's somehow forgotten these last months. The stout upturn of her nose, the dark creases under her eyes, the way her blond hair always has a few more flyaways on her left. Beck is losing her so much faster than she thought.

But here, her mother is whole. This isn't just a memory; it's the past.

Beck smiles.

Isn't this what Ricky promised? Before the explosion, he promised the unspooling would be good for everyone. Even if he couldn't fully explain it, he knew deep down that it would work. Every person who'd ever been crushed under the weight of their own heartache could find the place they were happiest. Before the hurt began. If all of that was true, then maybe this is real. Maybe it *can* be forever. Centuries might slide away, but she'll always be here, on this river, warmed by the spotty sunlight and calmed by the pleasant quiet.

Beck reaches over the side of the kayak and slips her fingers into the water, letting it beat against her knuckles. Her fingers don't ache anymore from the bunker. Her tangle of nausea has subsided.

"Am I really here?" Beck asks.

She's struck again by the oddness of her own voice. The tinny echo of it. If it's not right, it doesn't seem to bother her mother. Ellery shifts a little in her kayak and a lock of her hair breaks free from her ponytail. Eventually, she sighs.

"*You* are."

"You're not," Beck says.

"To you, I'm here." Ellery smiles, bittersweet. "To me, I'm not really anywhere."

Beck looks down. Just like that, her cheeks burn and her eyes swell. Of course it's still a memory. She wonders if everyone has tumbled back into a memory just like this one. Maybe Riley is tucked into the passenger seat of Ricky's car, fondly remembering an outing with their mother. More likely she's in a happier memory, somewhere with her friends, lying in a field and naming stars and laughing about something senseless. Riley has countless happy memories to live in, and Beck can't imagine many of them feature their mother. She could be anywhere.

But Beck could only end up here. On this river in a time that feels like a hundred years ago, paddling beside a woman who made herself into a mystery Beck couldn't solve no matter how hard she tried.

"Why . . . ?" Beck starts, but fear catches in her. How can she even phrase it, this question that has been on the tip of her tongue for almost a decade? She gathers herself. "Why did you keep leaving? Why couldn't you just come home?"

Ellery looks at her like Beck is a strange specimen presented in a petri dish. "I was trying to."

"No," Beck says. "You were writing your story. I read it."

"It wasn't finished."

"You went to Backravel so many times." Beck bites the inside of her cheek. "You knew it was doing something to you and you kept going anyway."

Ellery makes a small sound like she's just realized the problem. Like she's just realized there *was* a problem. She dips her paddle in the water but it doesn't move her kayak. "When I unspooled the first time, I didn't really know what it was. I was just trying to . . . when I started, I just wanted a little more time. With you girls. Then, when it wasn't working, I just wanted to go back to the beginning, before it all started."

"The beginning?"

"Before I ever came here."

"Why?"

"I thought if I never found Backravel, I could go back to who I was before."

Beck blinks. *Who she was before.* She tries to imagine Ellery

Birsching before Backravel, but the idea of her that long ago is a blur. Backravel and Ellery, tangled together and inseparable, is the only thing Beck can get her head around. There is no Ellery Birsching without this little town that eats and eats and always hungers for more.

"I don't think it would've helped," Ellery says, tugging Beck from her daze. "Time in Backravel moves however it wants, but the rest of the world keeps going. The things I did . . . maybe I could undo time here, but it would never undo it for you and Riley."

"It could have," Beck says, and it comes out as a croak. It's so much weaker than she means. "If we came here with you. Why didn't you?"

Ellery cocks her head to the side, considering. "I did think about it. Wouldn't it have been nice? We could live here forever. Centuries. Like flat stones in the desert, watching echoes of the same sunset forever."

Beck closes her eyes.

"But that's what Backravel is," Ellery says finally. It's too tender. It threatens to pull Beck to pieces, the soft timbre of her mother's voice. "An echo. It's the same thing repeating over and over, but it's less each time. You stay here until all the little pieces of your life outside chip away. All the things that make you the person you are. The more time you spend in Backravel, the less of you there is. How long until you forgot about your homeroom teacher and the first flower we planted back in Everett? How long until you forgot about your dad?"

"Oh," Beck mutters. The air feels colder now. Her hands begin to quiver. "That's what happened to . . . that's why you chose—"

"I thought I could use Backravel to find my way back to when we were happy. And then I wouldn't have to lose you and you wouldn't have to lose me. But we all lose each other eventually. Living in an echo isn't enough."

"Mom—"

Ellery's grip on her paddle tightens. Beck can't remember the last time she saw her mother so serious. "The people in this town are scared. They've lost themselves and they're stumbling in the heat looking for something real. I'd rather be . . . I would rather be here, in this place. Where the echo dies. In the quiet."

"*Mom*," Beck croaks.

"I'm sorry," Ellery says. "I wish it was different."

Even though the kayak continues to bob in the water, Beck is sinking. It's a different kind of sinking than before, though. The sunlight slips through the trees and Ellery is smiling and Beck feels, for a moment, happy. Ricky controlled all of Backravel, but he didn't control Ellery Birsching. He didn't choose how she died, and he didn't choose how she lived.

Beck's kayak snags on a tall rock under the water. She braces herself against the boat's side and, when she looks up, her vision is out of focus. The trees on the shore are a smear of green and yellow, hazy in the midday light. She fumbles with her glasses, touches the thin metal rim that runs along her right cheek. The lens is gone.

But there, next to her boot, a glittering speck of silver. *Metal*. A little serrated stub partially wedged under her heel.

Beck leans down, careful not to tip her kayak, and presses the pad of her finger to the screw. She lifts it close to her nose and inspects it with her one good eye. A little grime caked into the grooves, a few spots of oxidization. It's just a screw like any other, just like the one she lost all those years ago. It's comically small, actually, now that she looks at it. A speck that's haunted her for a decade.

"What now?" Ellery asks, a little smile in her voice.

Beck's eyes flutter shut.

What would you do if you found it? Years rush back to Beck faster than the churning water, thick enough to make her dizzy. How many times has she dragged herself back to this river, curled up in the shell of this memory, let herself believe that the Ellery Birsching on this river still existed somewhere?

"You're gone," Beck says, and it's not a question. She knows it in the innate way she knows when Riley is sad or when it's going to rain.

Ellery nods.

Beck curls into herself, pressing her forehead against her knees. Ellery was right the way she always is—this isn't a real place. It's only an echo. And it feels incredibly, impossibly empty now. Beck's fought her way back to this river, and she's still alone. She weeps quietly, and then loudly. She threw away Riley and her father and a whole future just to float here, on this river, alone.

"Look," Ellery says, almost too soft to hear.

Beck raises her head and dabs the tears from her eyes. There's someone on the riverbank ahead of them. A person standing on her own, green shorts too wide for her slender legs, hair a mop of cedar-brown in the scattershot light. Avery is by herself and she doesn't move. She watches Beck, all the way at the water's edge with her toes submerged in the current.

"What's she . . ." Beck starts. "What's happening?"

When she turns to look at her mother, they aren't level anymore. She's ahead of Ellery's kayak by several feet. Panic surges in her chest and she shoves her paddle into the water, trying to stop the gap from widening. Ellery looks just as content as always, though, soaking up the thick sunlight spilling from a split in the trees. When she speaks, she's so far away.

"I think it's time to decide."

"Decide what?"

"What's next."

Beck shakes her head. It's not a surprise, but the pain still stabs at her. Ricky promised forever, but forever isn't real. There isn't a world where she and Ellery both live. If she survives this, if she climbs into the Honda and drives all the way to this river, it will be pale and tired, red as summer drifts to fall. It won't remember the girl and her mother who skipped along the current a decade ago. It will have moved on.

"It's not enough time," Beck says. Her voice is a whine, like she's actually eight again. "I waited so long for this."

"I know."

"I don't want to go yet."

"I know."

Beck stares at her mother, but Ellery's eyes are fixed on a point far away. Beck follows the line of sight and sees it. Avery isn't alone on the shore anymore. Riley stands next to her, blond hair pinned back so that her ponytail bristles like a paintbrush. They both watch Beck on the water, expressionless. They're waiting for her to come to shore. To come back.

"Riley . . ." Ellery says. Beck looks at her mother and, finally, her contented smile has dimmed. Tears bead in her eyes and she leans forward. "I wanted to see her one more time. Is she safe?"

All at once, reality crashes over Beck. No, Riley isn't safe. If she's alive, she's lost in a memory, too. She needs help. Beck's chest tightens and she grips her paddle. She can't stay here while Riley's in danger. She has to go.

"How do I get out of here?" Beck asks.

Ellery's gaze snaps to Beck. "You've decided?"

"Riley . . . she's—"

"Go to shore," Ellery says, brow furrowed. "I think they'll help you. Go."

Beck's mouth curls into an involuntary frown. "Mom. I'm so sorry. And . . . thank you."

Ellery nods.

Beck stops paddling against the current and the kayak finally drifts forward. She closes her eyes, leans back against the wood, and spreads her arms wide. The sun covers her, the water ripples across her knuckles that just skirt the surface. She doesn't fight it anymore. She floats with the flow, bobbing and dipping under the shade of a pine that covers her face in shadow.

When she opens her eyes, the shore is full.

Avery and Riley are joined by her father and Julie, the Sterlings, her homeroom teacher, their old babysitter. The kids she used to skip class with, her neighbors that used to bring cookies on Christmas. They all stand in a cluster and they watch.

Beck looks back and Ellery Birsching continues to float in place, but she's so far away Beck can hardly see her. She waves her paddle and gestures to the crowd. And Beck understands, but she's not ready to go. She's not ready to leave this river.

She wants to live, but living means never going back.

On the shore, Avery kneels in silence. She reaches out for Beck. She's only a few yards away now, and if Beck paddles right, she'll be within reach. The others begin kneeling, too, reaching for her hand.

Metal crashes like thunder from everywhere at once. Something is coming, and if she doesn't slip out of this memory now, it will catch her.

She paddles hard toward the shore and the crashing grows louder. Her heart races, and the sky begins to change color. Red seeps into the wide-open sunlight like blood. The crowd begins reaching for her more frantically, spilling into the water to catch her hand.

With one final push, Beck eases her kayak to shore.

She reaches out and grips Avery's hand. It's just how she remembers, calloused against the tender skin of Beck's wrist. Avery pulls her from the boat and the whole world shifts. The sky goes dark without starlight, the trees collapse inward, and in the middle of the river, Ellery Birsching's kayak continues to buck against the increasingly violent waves.

"Mom . . ." Beck whispers.

She doesn't need to see Ellery to know this is goodbye. No more clues, no more visions, no more promises of a reunion that doesn't exist. This is the end.

Avery pulls Beck out of her memory and back into real life, and Beck's eyes blur with an unspoken goodbye.

30

Beck feels her pulse in her eyelids.

The earth rumbles under her, hard and cold. She gasps and turns onto her stomach, gagging into the concrete floor of the lab. The warmth of the river still glows on the skin of her arms, but only for a moment.

She opens her eyes and it's gone.

Red lights flash from the machines surrounding her, strobing in time with the pounding in her skull. It smells like burnt plastic and smoke, the air tangy with electricity. She searches the lab for any signs of life, but she can't tell the debris from the bodies. She closes her eyes and adjusts her glasses. One lens missing, bent out of shape. A cut runs the length of her cheekbone, crusted with blood. It could be worse; she prays everyone else's injuries are just as minor.

On the far side of the lab, there's a flicker of movement.

Wynona hauls herself to her feet and braces herself against the wall. She groans and holds her side, but she stays upright. The stiff length of her hair is flat at her back, jacket disheveled, eyes wide with panic. "Avery?" she calls out. "Avery, wake up."

Beck scans the room and spots her, propped against a sparking piece of machinery. Avery's head is lolled against her shoulder, eyes closed. Beck starts to drag herself across the lab, but Wynona staggers in front of her and collapses to her knees at Avery's side. She takes her daughter's face in her hands, kisses her forehead, whispers something desperate into her ear. Avery's eyes twitch open for a fraction of a second, then slip shut again.

"Is she . . . ?" Beck starts.

"We need to get out of here," Wynona hisses. *"Now."*

Beck nods. She pushes herself onto her elbows and drags herself along the floor of the bunker, picking up bits of shrapnel and dust in the shredded hem of her shirt. With her glasses busted, it's difficult to see clearly, but she can just make out a mound of dark near the tank. Ricky, probably.

Metal groans against metal, and Beck wonders if the whole lab is coming down. The machinery that borders the tank is alive for the first time in decades, spitting sparks and flashing numbers that Beck can't read. She ducks her head under her sleeve when one of the machines catches fire. Whether it be collapse, fire, or explosion, this place is coming down.

Beck finally reaches Ricky, heart in her throat. She pulls herself onto her knees and Ricky's body rolls away, lighter than it should be. Completely limp. She tries to hold back the gag that works its way up her throat. When she presses her fingertips to the tender place beneath Ricky's jaw, she feels nothing.

Ricky Carnes is dead.

She swallows down her panic, tears streaming from the corners of her eyes. She needs to get out of this lab and back to solid ground. They can worry about all the rest of it—getting out of Backravel, apologies, goodbyes—after she gets out of this lab.

Beck turns back toward Wynona, who's slowly helping Avery to her feet. Avery's eyes are half-lidded, and when she goes to take a step, she collapses into her mother's side. Side by side, Beck sees it. They look so much alike, it's shocking she didn't realize it sooner.

Wynona looks to Beck and her frown deepens. "Can you stand?"

"I think so," Beck says.

"You have to."

Beck sucks in a ragged breath. If she can make it back to the surface, there's a life waiting for her. A new school. TV with Julie. Cooking with her father. Maybe she could never picture it for herself because she hadn't seen it yet. But even if it's terrible and different, she has to try. She cannot live in the past anymore. She has to keep going.

Footsteps clank against the bits of scrap metal littering the floor. Beck turns to see Wynona half dragging Avery across the lab toward the exit. There's only one exit, and they're running out of time. Beck glances at Ricky's body, facing the ceiling with eyes wide open. His son is the last face he saw before he was gone. She can't see him clearly, but there's a ghost of a smile on his lips.

They'll have to leave him here.

"I know you're tired," Wynona says to Avery. "It's okay . . . it's okay. Put your arms around me. It'll be okay."

Avery flops forward and links her arms around her mother's neck.

Beck pushes herself onto one leg, then forces herself to her feet. She takes one step, then another. Her heart barrels up her throat and her arms shake, but step by step, she forces her way to the exit.

A crash sounds from the lab. A tall computer explodes into flames, rocking the whole building under the impact.

Back at the ladder, Wynona waits. Dusky light pours into the opening, a promise that there's a world outside if they can move fast enough. More crashing sounds from behind them and Beck sucks in a ragged breath. They have to move *faster*.

"*Help*," Wynona calls up the ladder. She turns frantically to Beck. Avery is slouched against the ladder at her feet. "She can't climb out. We're trapped. We—"

"No." Beck breathes. "There has to be a way."

Wynona looks at Avery, then at Beck, and a tear glistens in the dark of her eyes. She looks up the ladder, and her skin is a spill of sunset. She sighs, then says, "You have to go, then."

"What?"

"You have to go get help."

"I can't." Beck's blood runs cold. "It'll . . . the lab won't last that long. You'll all—"

"—die," Wynona finishes. "If you don't run fast enough."

Beck strains her neck back to look at Avery's face. A smattering of dirt is smudged across her cheek, but otherwise, she's fine. Slowly, Beck nods. She makes her way to the ladder. Her muscles ache with strain, sweat damp at the back of her neck. The world spins around her and she can barely see the rungs right in front of her. But to get out of this place—to get out of this town—she has to push through. It's one ladder, a bike ride down the highway, and a knock on the Sterlings' front door.

If they're even home.

If they'd even help.

Beck rests her forehead against the ladder and tries to swallow her panic. She only makes it up one rung when a face appears in the circle of daylight overhead. Beck squints into the light trying to make out the stranger's face.

"They're in here," a woman's voice says. "Greg, quick."

Mrs. Sterling. Beck collapses to the base of the ladder. Another face appears overhead, and this one is Mr. Sterling. Without hesitating, he turns and begins climbing down.

"Is anyone hurt?" he calls before his feet touch the floor.

"I think so," Wynona says. She has her arms hooked under Avery's armpits, half hoisting her to her feet. "Avery. She can't climb."

Mr. Sterling nods and wraps his arm around Avery's waist, pulling her from her mother's grasp. Wynona stares for a moment like she's been robbed all over again. Like she's been left all alone. But then Mr. Sterling grips the ladder and begins dragging Avery toward the surface.

Mr. Sterling bites his lip to hide the strain of lifting himself and Avery to safety. He grunts, then calls, "Your other girl is down here."

When Mr. Sterling makes it up the ladder, a second pair of legs begins descending. When recognition sets in, Beck wonders if she's dreaming again. Her father lands squarely on his feet at the base of the ladder, eyes wide with panic.

"Where's Beck?" her father bellows.

"I'm here," Beck says, but her voice shakes.

Behind them, the lab bursts into flames. Beck's vision ripples at the corners, murky and red. She tries to push herself to her feet, but her muscles cramp with each movement. Her father turns, and his expression is a strange thing. Relief, horror, but no anger. He steps aside to let Wynona begin her climb to the surface, then he holds out a hand.

"We have to get out of here," he says. Sweat glistens at his pale brow. "Quickly."

Beck curls her fingers against the concrete and tries not to vomit. She reaches up, and for only a moment, she's back in the hospital room in Seattle. She's sitting at her mother's side, and she knows it's the end. Her mother turns and holds out a hand, knuckles bony and pale against the off-white hospital sheets. She took her mother's hand then, and held it as the end came rushing in like a tide.

Her father takes her hand, and the world goes black.

31

Beck is in a hospital room.

White walls, beeping machinery, starchy curtains covering the floor-to-ceiling windows. For a moment, she thinks she might be in a memory again. She waits for the smell of stale coffee and the scratch of branches against the window. The familiar rhythm of a waking dream. The watery edges of a memory not quite formed. When she turns her head, she expects to find Ellery Birsching's steely eyes staring back at her. But there's no one. Just an empty chair, plastic and layered with jackets and purses. The paper wrapper for a fast-food cookie lies crumpled on the bedside table. Beck curls her fingers against the hospital bed and closes her eyes. This isn't a dream.

Something is different.

If there's one thing she knows, it's that she's left Backravel. There's a weightlessness to her now—she feels it the way she can inhale a full breath. That creeping, clutching sense of dread coiled in her gut for the last month is mostly dissolved, replaced by a quiet sense of calm. The quiet is truly quiet, the throbbing hum of machinery finally silenced.

Wherever she is now, she's out.

Voices mumble from the other side of the hospital wall. Beck scoots onto her elbows to get a better look at the room. Her glasses are missing, blurring the details, but she can see the general shape of it. A vase of white flowers sits on the windowsill, petals scattered on the floor. She can see just a sliver of the world outside the window—a rusty-red sunrise creeps just below the horizon, no oak trees in sight. Instead, there are buildings outside. Big ones, sliced by the thin white glare from the sun. She's in a real city, not a fake little town.

Beck touches the hospital bed, touches her face, and slumps back against the pillow. She's alive, somehow. She doesn't know where or when she is, but she's alive. It doesn't feel good or bad; it feels impossible.

There's a small knock at the door.

"Good morning."

A man's voice. Her *dad's* voice. Beck turns over and sits up, and for the first time, she feels the ache in her neck where she hit the bunker wall. She tenderly touches the top of her spine and it throbs. All at once, her mind is a blur of questions—*who else made it? Is Backravel exposed? What happens to the people now?* She craves the answers like air, but instead of asking a single one, she croaks, "Dad?"

Two figures enter the hospital room and her father wraps her in a tight hug. The other visitor, Julie, leans close and presses an object to Beck's side. *Her glasses.* Beck slides them on and lets the world slip into focus. Deep, gray bags circle her father's eyes, and Julie's hair is flat like she hasn't given it a good Texas curl in weeks. They're miserable.

A sudden, icy fear takes hold.

"Riley . . ." Beck says.

Without letting her go, her father sighs. ". . . is fine. She's going to be okay."

Beck closes her eyes and relief washes over her. Her father's hug is warm, but she still shakes. It feels impossible that they're here. There was a moment Beck thought she might never see her father's face again. She clutches the fabric of her collar so tight the fabric juts between her fingers and she croaks, "I'm so sorry."

"Don't be sorry." Her father lets her go, takes her shoulders tenderly and looks hard into her eyes. "If you hadn't called us . . . just, don't be sorry."

"We're so happy you're safe," Julie chimes in. She leans on the hospital bed but keeps her distance like she's too afraid to touch Beck. Like she's not sure she's allowed. She looks at Beck, then at her father, and nods. "I'll give you two a minute."

When Julie leaves, the door closes behind her and the silence is suffocating.

"I'm so sorry, Dad," Beck croaks. "I'm so, so—"

"I wasn't there like I should've been," he says, and he doesn't look at her. He eyes his lap, lips curled in a thin frown. "I should've realized how . . . *hard* a change like this would be for you girls. For you especially."

Beck can't find the words to respond. The hospital walls beat in on her and she's dizzy and tired. She touches the back of her head and feels the rough crosshatch of stitches in her skin.

"What happened to me?" she asks.

"The doctor said you hit your head pretty hard. You've got a pretty gnarly concussion." He sits forward in his chair. "Beyond the physical injuries . . . that's what we're still figuring out."

She thinks of the red smoke in the chamber, of the amount of toxin she let into her body over the last few weeks. "Are Riley and me going to be okay?"

"I think so," her father says. "From what I understand, they've got some kind of agent that can help reverse the effects of . . . whatever it is that got into you girls. And everyone else in the town. I'm going to be honest with you—I don't really understand a lot of what we've been told so far."

Beck nods. The agent must be the cure Wynona was working on, she thinks. While Ricky was clawing for ways to go back, Wynona was focused on healing. She wanted to heal everyone. She wanted Backravel to survive.

"I don't think she's gonna talk to me again," Beck says. "After all of this . . . I don't know what to do."

"You and your sister will be fine," he says. "Because the people you love most can also be the ones that hurt you deepest. But I believe you can find a way to forgive each other easiest, too. I know it's going to be hard for both of you. There's so much change. But we're here to help."

"Can I see her?" Beck asks.

• • •

Riley's room is identical to Beck's, but in her room, the curtains are drawn and the first sheets of pink light leak in, faint on the tile floor. She lies back against her hospital bed, but her eyes are wide open, lips pursed, awake. Beck hesitates to enter; she wonders for a moment if she's allowed.

When Riley spots her in the doorway, she smiles.

Beck breathes.

"You're up," Riley says. There's a slight croak to her voice. "Did you see Dad already?"

"Yeah," Beck says. "I wanted to see you, though."

Riley nods and pats the space at the end of her bed. Up close, her eyes are bloodshot and her skin is paler than it should be, but otherwise she seems unharmed. Beck places a hand on her shin and tries not to cry. She should've known better than to trust Ricky. She should've protected her sister. The guilt makes her sick all over again.

"I—" she starts.

"Can I go first?" Riley asks. "I don't wanna interrupt. I've just been thinking about what to say."

"Oh. Okay."

"I'm sorry if you thought I didn't care about Mom," Riley says. "And I'm sorry you thought you couldn't tell me about her."

"*You're* sorry," Beck says. "I don't even know where to . . . I've been such a horrible sister. Everything that happened back there was because of me. I put you in so much danger. I'm just . . . I'm so sorry, Riley."

Riley reaches out and takes Beck's face in her hands, pulls her into an awkward embrace over the plastic guard rails of her hospital bed. "The whole time I was sick, I was just thinking about how much I wished you were there. I was so scared that town was gonna take you, too."

"It didn't take me. Or you. Or anyone else, I think."

"Dad said they got everyone out," Riley says. She shifts a little and Beck sits up straight. Outside, the shiny buildings of the city gleam through Riley's window, coating the whole hospital room in a faint white glow. Slowly, Riley says, "I know stuff with Mom was different for you. But I miss her, too. I'm gonna miss her every day. But we have to try Texas."

"I know," Beck says. She wipes at her eyes. "I know. And I will."

"I don't want you to be alone anymore," Riley says. "And I don't want you to leave me alone again, either."

"I won't."

Riley nods. She lets out a long breath. "Okay. That's what I had prepared."

Beck smiles at that. "It was very mature. Ten out of ten."

"Even though you *interrupted* me again."

"I'm sorry," Beck says sheepishly.

"Do you think they got Katie and Daniel out, too?" Riley asks. "What are they all gonna do now? Just . . . go back to the real world?"

"I guess they'll have to," Beck says. She imagines the Sterlings trying to reintegrate into normal society. It's bittersweet, thinking of the people in Backravel stepping out of its grasp for the first time. For some families, Backravel has only been a few months. For others, Beck imagines, it's been years. Decades even. The worlds they knew before will be long gone. They'll have to reenter the world brand-new and all alone.

"What about Avery?" Riley asks.

Beck closes her eyes. What about Avery? What about the girl lost in time? The girl with eyes like desert rock and hands that touch more tenderly than they should. Beck thinks of her and her chest feels tight.

"I don't know," Beck says.

"I saw her. Just a little bit ago."

Beck's eyes widen. "She's *here*?"

"Everyone is, I think." Riley thuds her head back against her pillow. "I saw Avery heading to the roof."

Beck peers out Riley's window and, at just the right angle, she can make out the corner of the roof. She can make out the silhouette of a girl standing against the railing awash in sunlight. She looks at Riley, and Riley nods.

"Go," she says.

Beck nods. She gathers up her hospital gown and slips out of Riley's room into the hallway. She follows the signs pointing to ROOF ACCESS and it strikes her how full this hospital is. The rooms are all crowded with nurses and families visiting loved ones. Not everyone in this hospital is an ailing citizen of Backravel, recovering from years in a churning loop. There are lives outside Backravel, people moving forward. Moving on.

She silently pushes her way into the stairwell and climbs toward the roof. When she reaches the top of the stairs, the door opens to a completely different world. It's quiet and cool like a balm to Beck's racing mind. In the gentle morning, Beck blinks through the sherbet light. It's a lonely rooftop terrace, colder than expected, peppered with untouched benches, groomed shrubs, impersonal walkways. The skyline blinks to life one building at a time. A girl stands alone at the railing overlooking the city, watching it wake. Beck's breath hitches a little at the sight of her. A girl, impossibly tethered to a single place, suddenly unbound. Seeing Avery at the hospital is like seeing a cell phone in an old picture. It's the wrong place, wrong time.

"Checking on me?" Avery asks without turning.

"Sort of." Beck kicks a pebble from the walkway with the side of her sock. "Though I'm guessing the update is 'bad.'"

Avery laughs, humorless.

Beck moves, pulled quietly to Avery's side. She sidles up to the railing and places her hands next to Avery's. The orange glow of the rising light drenches Avery's delicate face, but it's clear she's exhausted. It circles her eyes like bruises. Her stare is glassy, but it isn't distant like it was in Backravel. She's present now. Alive.

Beck slips her hand over Avery's and she doesn't pull away.

"I'm sorry," Beck says. "About . . . everything."

"When you lost your mom," Avery says, almost too quiet to hear, "what did you feel? The first thing."

Beck looks down at the place their hands meet. "I didn't feel anything. I think that was the problem. It's like the stone fell and it never quite—"

"—hit the bottom," Avery finishes. "I can't tell what I feel. I know he loved me. I think he was telling the truth about wanting our family back. But the things he did . . ."

"You can still love what you remember about him," Beck says. "And you can still be mad at him for the bad stuff, too. The world doesn't stop when you lose someone, I guess. You keep feeling."

Under her breath, Avery whispers, "How am I going to keep going?"

Beck squeezes Avery's hand tighter. She pulls Avery to her chest and they stand there, still, soaking in the rising sun in silence for a long time. Beck closes her eyes and she imagines all the directions Avery's life can go from here. All the new things she can try, all the new people she'll meet. When they laid together under the stars, Avery said she wanted to feel like her life was moving again. Now, for better or worse, it will.

Beck imagines her own life branching off, too.

She wonders if Avery will be in it.

"What can I do?" Beck asks.

"I don't know. I don't know what to do with myself now."

"Tomorrow, then," Beck says. "Tomorrow, what do you want to do?"

"I want . . ." Avery rubs at her nose. "I want to feel like I can keep going. Like I know how. I don't want to be afraid to look forward and lose everything behind me. Does that make sense?"

"I think so."

"I want to know there's an end. Somewhere. Eventually."

Beck squeezes her hand.

Avery turns, just a little, and Beck sees the whole horizon in her stare. Quietly, Avery says, "And I want to see you again."

"Really?" Beck muses. "After—"

"I want to see you again," Avery repeats. She touches Beck's face, brushes her thumb across Beck's lower lip. "I don't want to lose anyone else."

It's there again, that tightness in Beck's chest. That fist to her stomach. That flash of free fall, like missing the bottom step. But Beck isn't afraid. The forever Avery promises is different from Ricky's forever—from Ellery's forever. Avery's forever isn't endless. It's a promise that there's more tomorrow.

Beck smiles, moves her hand to cup Avery's jaw. She presses her lips to Avery's. The breeze over the railing is cold with morning when it sneaks between them. Avery takes Beck's face in her hands and kisses her deeper, smiling into her mouth.

Night blooms into day, quiet and without pause. They stand there a long time in the silence, watching the last freckles of starlight burn away. Beck feels it here, the way time is a moving thing. The way one breath folds into the next, the way the horizon is brighter each time she blinks. She feels the simple warmth of Avery's hand against her hip and knows she'll feel it there a hundred more times before she reaches the end.

Maybe Avery will change, and maybe Beck will change, too. Maybe, in a few years, the whole world will be different. Right now,

Beck only feels the heat of Avery's hand under hers. She isn't pulled forward or backward. There's only two timeless girls, unshackled, watching a sunrise that finally looks the way it should.

For once, there's only now.

Acknowledgments

You would think a second book would be easier. Like any skill, you would think that repetition would simplify the process. *You did it once before, just do the same thing again. Where Echoes Die* has taught me an incredibly valuable lesson about writing, though—no two books are the same, and trying to treat them the same will get you nowhere. Those who are close to me know the type of grief this book gave me from conception to final draft. To the community of writers, publishing staff, and friends who have kept me afloat throughout this process, there aren't enough thanks in the world. This book would not be here without you, and I might not be, either.

I first want to thank my incredible editor, Sarah Grill. Thank you so much for stepping in to guide this book to the finish line. Your thoughtful questions and patience made this finished product possible, and I look forward to all the creepy, funky books we'll get to make together moving forward. I also want to thank Jennie Conway, who took a chance on this book and who helped me foster the initial idea into a story I could love. Thank you to Kerri Resnick and Peter Strain, whose collaboration made this stunning cover. Thank you to Rivka Holler, Brant Janeway, Gail Friedman, Mary Moates, Carla Benton, NaNa Stoelzle, Michelle McMillian, Steve Wagner, and all the other folks at Wednesday Books who brought this book to life.

Thank you to Claire Friedman and Jess Mileo, my literary agents. You have both been my rock during these last two years. Thank you for fielding my midnight panic questions, for reassuring me through a thousand panic attacks, and for believing in my writing, even at times when I didn't. Thank you to the rest of the team at Inkwell Literary Management for all your work making author dreams come true.

Every time I do this part, it gets harder to thank all the friends who have come to my aid, and I'm sure I will forget someone. Thank you to Alex Clayton and Anna Loose, who stayed in the trenches with me over these last two years, watching *Love Island*, listening to my woes, and sending reels that pulled me back from the edge. Thank you to Lachelle Seville for your unwavering support and friendship, and for loving this book first. Thank you to Allison Saft, my author chaos twin who helped keep me on track all the way to the finish line. Thank you to Ava Reid and Rachel Morris for your friendship and writing commiseration, to Rebecca Mahoney, Tori Bovalino, Adrienne Tooley, Erica Waters, Cayla Fay, Alex Brown, and Jessica Lewis for encouraging me through the hard parts, and to Megan Lally and Bekah Corral for reminding me that, sometimes, I'm good at this. Thank you again to the Tea Timers: Rachel Diebel, Sylvie Creekmore, Maylen Anthony, Adrian Mayoral, and Ingrid Clarke.

Thank you to Davis for diving head first into the world of books. Thank you to Dad for your support and for always asking the most terrifying and encouraging question: *What's next?* Thank you to

Grandma for believing that writing makes me a celebrity even when I don't. Thank you to Mom for the kind of support I cannot name or put words to. And thank you to Carly for your inspiration, for the late-night brainstorming sessions, and for the ways you shaped this book from its very first scene.

And thank you to anyone reading this now, whether I know you or not. Thank you for trusting me to tell you a story about grief, and I hope it heals as much as it hurts. Goodbye is never easy, but it's only the beginning.